THE INFLUENCE

MATTHEW JOHN SLICK

StoneHouse Ink 2010
Boise ID 83713
www.StoneHouseInk.net
ISBN 978-0615525730

First Hardcover Edition: 2010
First Paperback Edition: 2010
First eBook Edition 2010
Second Paperback Edition 2011

The characters and events portrayed in this book are fictitious. Any similarity to a real person, living or dead is coincidental and not intended by the author.

The influence: a novel/ by Matt Slick. -1st ed. p.cm.

Cover art by StoneHouse Ink

Published in the United States of America

All the doctrine taught in this book by Sotare, the angel, is biblically accurate. This includes the teaching about God, sin, salvation, man's nature, the fall, truth, judgment, and the person and work of Jesus.

I took considerable license when talking about angels and demons fighting, their being injured, demonic forces "tweaking peoples' minds," and what happens after some characters die. The Bible says we continue on after death, but I took literary license to convey basic biblical themes of heaven and hell. I hope you enjoy this book.

May the Lord be glorified in these pages.

Matt Slick
http://www.carm.org

Chapter 1

NEAR THE CEILING OF an immense, dark cavern, a tear in the fabric of space wrenched open and was followed by a twisting metal sound that echoed among the craggy walls. Below, jagged rocks littered the ground, some jutting upwards, others forming scattered crevices.

Gray shadows shifted in distorted patterns, forced to flicker by the numerous fires that burned everywhere. A huge hole was in one end of "The Cavern." It revealed a deep tunnel that swallowed any light and sound falling into its darkness.

Between two large boulders heavy, green leathery creatures with twisted fangs and huge, bony heads huddled around a carcass. It had been gutted and dismembered and lay in disarray among the small fissures that scarred the floor. They snapped bones into shards and shoved them into their mouths and crunched them with their powerful jaws.

On the higher ledges, buried in permanent shadows, dark creatures sat motionless. Only their red eyes moved as they surveyed the landscape and watched the others. They had huge twisted fangs, massive shoulders, and immense hind legs poised to lunge at any beast that ventured too close. Their large scales reflected dim flickers of firelight. They watched in quiet stillness.

A shimmering whirlwind danced over a fire. It was a single entity comprised of thousands of insects. Only, they weren't insects. They were smaller elements of the whole, a horde of tiny, twisted creatures with wings and legs that hummed in frantic swirls, moving, flying, and churning in unison. The whole mass reflected the ever-present firelight as it glided slowly over the rocks, creeping along the crevices, avoiding the flames and moving with an unknown purpose.

Above the creatures flew the winged demons. They resembled human skeletons encased in tight leathery skin. They had long tails that cut through the air as they whipped back and forth. Deep black holes housed their yellow eyes. Their skin was dark brown, almost black in appearance, and they were flying towards the rip in space as they growled in mournful, threatening wails.

One of them clawed the face of another. It responded by slashing at the wing of the first, sending it down into the rocks below to be mauled by whatever demons were nearest its fall. In a moment a third rose to take its place and fought with the one remaining. It used its wings to beat the first, thudding against its chest, punching, and growling. From below, yet another grabbed and clawed at the two, then another joined in, and another. They fought, screeching and tearing with feet and gripping talons. Cries of agony fell downward as wounded creatures tumbled into the blackness below.

The battle raged until finally, two of them, one larger than the other, managed to thrust themselves into the rip, which instantly closed. The rest squawked angrily and began to glide back to the shadows below, snarling and spitting at each other on the way.

The two creatures traveled through a tunnel of heat and light, carried along by the rushing, thunderous wind. They passively moved through the portal, absorbing the images and instructions which filled their minds. Suddenly, space ripped open and they were thrust into bright, blue light. The smaller one growled in pain and both instinctively shielded their eyes. With wings held open to stop their fall, they hovered in the air and waited for their sight to adjust. After a few seconds, the larger beast lashed out at the smaller, which ducked, turned, and raced away. The remaining demon hovered, looking around and gathering its bearings. It gurgled with a low, faint rumble.

Below the creature, in a large garden sat a man in a gazebo. He stared into the distance, lost in thought, unaware that hell itself had opened behind him and spat out a black-winged assassin.

The creature hissed. Then, slowly, it glided earthward until it landed on the branch of one of two trees. It hissed again and leaned forward to examine the man as it let a low, rumbling growl fall earthward.

The demon examined him, cocking its head from side to side. It studied its prey, the human victim that would soon join it in The Cavern. It folded its wings behind its back, leaned forward, and slowly slithered downward, as it wove its way through the tree branches.

***

Kathy let her black hair blow gently in the air as she drove down the interstate. The rush of air felt good. With the window rolled down, the road noise was loud, but she didn't mind. It was soothing.

The wind threw a strand of hair between her lips. She pulled it away, then checked her lipstick in the mirror. Her green eyes were hidden by sunglasses, and her light complexion had only a few, small wrinkles creeping out from her eyes. She lowered her glasses for a moment and checked them.

Kathy was an attractive 40-year-old woman who was a regular at the gym. Her light frame was well proportioned. At five foot six, she was energetic, fit, and healthy.

She put her glasses back on and her thoughts turned to her father. He was a widower. A couple days ago he had to have emergency galbladder surgery and now it seemed there was a complication. She didn't understand exactly what it was, but the doctors said he'd probably need to be watched for a few days after he was released. That was the only reason she had dared to leave her husband, Mark, who had been showing serious signs of depression in the past few weeks. As she mechanically drove along the familiar interstate, she reviewed the series of events of the past few months.

It began right after they had visited their son's grave. Mark sat silently next to the headstone, fingering a blade of green grass he had casually ripped from the ground. He stared at the two dates engraved in the stone. "One year," he had said to Kathy. "He only lived one year."

She reached out and let her soft hands form around his tense, strong shoulders. He didn't respond. She knew this was a difficult time for him. So, she withdrew and slowly walked back to a cold cement bench at the edge of the grass. He needed to be alone for a while. She looked at her husband as she sat.

Mark wore his dark hair short. Though his belly could have been a little flatter, at 42 he had managed to retain his slim, muscular build. He was about six feet tall and had a strong chin and hazel eyes. He wasn't particularly handsome, but he was nice looking and had an attractive quality of self assurance that was gentle and consistent. It had made falling in love with him easy for Kathy.

The wind brushed through some trees and slowly bent their shadows across the grave and onto Mark. The gentle sound of rustling leaves was all she could hear in this perfectly manicured cemetery. Nothing was out of place, including their pain.

Though she still grieved over the loss of Jacob, she had somehow found a way to deal with it. She had managed to handle it, as much as any woman could who had endured the loss of a child. She still hurt, but she had learned to cope by talking to her close girlfriends and leaning on her loving husband. He had always been there for her. That is, until the past few weeks.

Mark, on the other hand, was a man who always tried to appear self-reliant. He was the kind of person who was tough and strong, measuring himself by his accomplishments and his ability to stand strong under pressure. That is why he had become a civil engineer. He liked to solve problems, difficult ones, and his skill at doing so helped him to earn a reputation for getting things done. Kathy admired his strength and intelligence, but she also pitied him for them. She learned long ago that a person could fall in his strengths as well as his weaknesses.

After a while, Kathy got up from the concrete bench and stepped onto the green softness and slowly walked back to him. Mark could hear her approach.

He stiffened slightly. She could see him lift a hand to his eyes and then lower it. Kathy knelt down.

"I miss him," he said, still staring at the headstone.

"I miss him, too," she responded softly. She rested her head on his shoulder.

Jacob had died unexpectedly in his crib seven years earlier, just before his first birthday. After tests and consultations, the doctors could offer no solid reason except to say that, unfortunately, this tragedy sometimes happens.

They dealt with it in their own way. They cried a great deal and talked with friends. They even went to counseling, which seemed to help Kathy, but not Mark. He resisted talking to the counselor and after a while stopped going.

Mark had been particularly bothered by not knowing why Jacob had died. He was a problem solver and not having a reason for Jacob's sudden death gnawed at him. It eventually became a haunting misery. The only way he could deal with it was to ignore it, occasionally drink a little too much, and bury himself in his work.

As time passed he would sometimes talk about Jacob's death and tell Kathy how much it still bothered him. On more than one instance he told her that if only he knew why Jacob had died, then he would finally be at peace—and he wanted peace. That is why they hadn't visited the grave in years; that is, until six months ago. He wanted to finally face his own pain and frustration. But their visit didn't help. It made things worse.

Kathy remembered how she and Mark were driving home from the gravesite. She saw his white knuckles as he gripped and repeatedly kneaded the steering wheel. He was flexing his jaw muscles constantly and occasionally he would exhale hard. She noticed he was driving too close to the car in front of him, but thought better of mentioning it.

She had stared out the car window, let her mind wander, and imagined what it would be like if Jacob were alive. She was hurting, too, but it seemed that Mark was having a rougher time.

After about twenty minutes, he broke the silence. "I really miss him," he muttered.

"I miss him, too," she said gently.

"If only I knew why he died. Maybe that would help me get over this." He paused and then blurted out, "It tears me apart not knowing." He gripped the steering wheel tightly and rolled his knuckles over the top again. "I thought this had passed. I mean, I thought I'd let it go enough to be able to deal with it."

Mark shook his head. "I never wanted to burden you with my problem."

"I know. But it's okay," she said tenderly.

She studied his eyes. They were wet with tears. Mark was a good man, and she hated to see him like this. He was hurting and she wanted to comfort him. But there was nothing she could do except to be there.

The visit had only served to rekindle Mark's frustration. Why had Jacob died? Did he and Kathy do something wrong? Was there some purpose behind Jacob's death? If so, what was it? Was some cosmic force at work? If there was a God, why did he let this happen? And the one thing that bothered him the most: why couldn't they have any more children? It had taken them years to have Jacob and then afterwards, nothing. The doctors didn't have any explanation since there wasn't anything wrong with either of them. Kathy just never got pregnant.

Mark was angry and the lack of answers made it worse. The wound of Jacob's loss would not heal.

Of course, Mark wasn't the only one struggling. By visiting the grave and reflecting on how they couldn't get pregnant, Kathy was once again reminded of the abortion she'd had while in college. The man who got her pregnant wanted nothing to do with her after he found out. He told her to get an abortion and turned a cold shoulder. So she turned to her girlfriends and they unanimously urged her to get rid of it. Her best friend at the time said it was an easy procedure that would solve her problem. She would only be aborting a "blob of cells, a fetus," as she put it. All Kathy would be doing was "terminating an unplanned pregnancy." After all, the fetus wasn't human and it was her right to choose to do with her body what she wanted. After all, she wasn't ready for children.

Her friends were gentle and persistent. They subtly bad-mouthed the guy who had abandoned her and repeatedly pointed out that with the pressures of school, and the financial pressures of having a child, that it would be impossible for her to have a child. So, in the end, Kathy went through with the abortion.

The doctor's office was a sterile, clinical-smelling place that was over- air conditioned, and was staffed with nurses in colorful scrubs. They were nice enough people who seemed to care about her, at least superficially. Their rehearsed smiles made it all seem so terribly shallow. After filling out some forms, she had to sit in a flimsy hospital gown alone in a small room while she waited to be summoned. Kathy could remember the sadness she felt. She wanted to be a mom, but, not right then. She rubbed her belly and stared at the fabric gown covering it. It was a small room with a picture of the ocean on a wall. The voices in the hall were muffled. She remembered staring at the floor, waiting.

No one told her about the aftereffects. Over the years she couldn't shake the feeling of guilt, and it slowly had gotten worse, especially since she couldn't get pregnant now. She felt as if she had betrayed herself as well as the life in her womb. A pang of guilt and shame stabbed at her heart again as she remembered Jacob and the abortion.

She shook the memory away and focused on some passing trees, then took a deep breath. She knew that the guilt she felt about her abortion never really got any better. It just became more distant.

Kathy remembered what it was like to hold Jacob in her arms, to smell him, feel his soft skin, nurse him, and watch him look deeply back into her eyes. She had loved him so completely, so thoroughly. She was so fulfilled with him.

Then he died. It was a horrible shock. Kathy found his lifeless body in the crib after his naptime was over. She had become hysterical and called Mark on the phone, screaming and sobbing. He rushed home.

The trauma for both was unbearable. For weeks she secretly blamed herself, as if the abortion had some karma attached to it: a "life-for-a-life" type of thing, she thought. She had mentally beaten herself up constantly, wondering why she didn't check on him one more time during his nap. Why hadn't she suspected something? What happened to her mothering instincts? Was she a failure as a mother? What could she have done differently? Did Mark *really*, somehow blame her even though he said he didn't? The questions had no satisfying answers.

She went to a counselor and talked to her friends. They wept with her and were always willing to listen. It took a while, but after several months she began to feel halfway normal.

She remembered how during her recovery process she had once again brought up the abortion to Mark. She needed to process it once and for all. He shrugged it off. Of course, she had told him about it before they got married, but Mark didn't want to talk about it. He got angry and yelled at her. He didn't want to hear about her pregnancy by another man. As a result, she felt a little abandoned in a time when she was deeply hurt. If she had ever needed his strength, that was it. But, she had to accept the fact that he had his weaknesses like everyone else.

Kathy shook her mind clear once again and focused on the road. She turned her thoughts to Mark's present condition. About a week after their graveside visit, he had gone to a local New Age bookstore hoping to find information on God, divine purpose, reincarnation—anything that might give him answers since there were no medical ones. He bought several hardbacks and read them quickly. Though there were occasional wise sayings, most of it was too subjective. Then he went on the Internet and studied whatever he could find about life after death, angels, and God. He devoured information on sudden infant death syndrome. He wanted answers and hoped he could stumble onto anything that would give him a clue. Nothing satisfied him.

Then someone told him about the Universalist Life Church in town and how people there knew about purpose and meaning. They were nice, but they didn't have any better answers. He quit going.

"Church is just a social club," he told Kathy. "I'm not interested in that crap. I need facts, not feelings."

Mark told her about two months ago that his drive to find answers was starting to become an obsession. He described it as a living thing, a parasite that was sapping the life out of him and that he couldn't control. She knew he was right. He was not only becoming more frustrated after their visit to the grave, but his temper was getting shorter and his sense of humor had seemed to vanish.

So, she very carefully suggested that he see a psychiatrist. Mark reacted in his predictable, negative way.

"I don't need to see a shrink," he pronounced as he turned his back on her and walked away. She dropped it. But after two weeks he surprised her and said he was ready to get some professional counseling. They both went.

The psychiatrist recommended that he take a vacation and prescribed some antidepressants to help him deal with things better. Mark scoffed at both ideas. Taking medicines to help him only made him feel weak. He was too much of a fighter, too much of a man to give in to this immature stupidity.

"No, I don't need a vacation," he told Kathy sternly. "What I need are answers. I just need more time. I can handle this."

She knew he was suffering. But she also knew it was getting in the way of their marriage. She was tired, too. She wanted all the despair and tumult to be gone so she could get back to loving Mark. After all, it was having an effect on her as well and she was beginning to put up a protective wall around herself. She didn't like it.

So here she was, driving down the long freeway, letting her eyes mindlessly focus on the grey lanes ahead of her, oblivious to the passing blur of green trees that marked an increasing distance between them. There was nothing she could do right now. Her father was in the hospital and needed her.

She hated leaving Mark alone when he was as depressed as he was. "I'll be fine," he had said in his usual confident voice. "Don't worry about me. I know I'm struggling, but, really, don't worry. I'll be okay. Besides, it will probably be good for me to be alone. Go help your dad. He needs you."

Mark's words didn't make her feel any better. The only thing that eased her conscience was to insist that he at least take a vacation while she was gone. It was the only way she could feel halfway decent about leaving. Mark again scoffed at the idea but Kathy was determined and after a few hours, he reluctantly agreed. Besides, he had vacation time coming and it was slow at work. So, after a quick call to the boss, Mark had two weeks off of work and she was on her way to see her father.

She looked in the rearview mirror. The traffic was sparse.

She drove on, oblivious to the invisible, winged creature sitting in the back seat.

***

Mark had been sitting quietly in the gazebo for two hours, staring blankly at nothing, listening to the wind move through the trees, and hearing the water trickling over the rocks in the small stream that flowed through his garden. This was his retreat, his place to relax. But he couldn't. His frustration and anger had robbed him of peace and left him feeling numb. *It's probably a reaction to the prolonged frustration and stress*, he thought. He didn't care. He liked not feeling anything.

Mark ran his fingers through his hair. His shirt tightened against his shoulders as he moved. He rubbed his face with his hands and heard the whiskers scrape against them. He let his hands fall onto his lap then he looked up and saw the sunlight filtering through a tree. He squinted before looking away.

There was a tangled mass of vines that snaked under some nearby bushes. He focused on the jumbled twisted trail of dirty grays and browns as it struggled in the shadowy underbrush. "That's my life," he said into the air.

Over the months his frustration had grown into anger. His

anger led to resentment and resentment to self-condemnation as he realized his failure to find the answers to the questions echoing in his heart and mind.

He clenched his fists and gently pounded on his thighs. A rose moved softly in the breeze, catching his attention. He noticed the sweet scent as it wafted through the air.

From the corner of his eye, a small butterfly glided by, turned, and landed on the flower. In the past, such a subtle event would have delighted him, but not now. His emotions were as empty as his stare. Then the butterfly flew off. Mark did not follow it. Instead, he continued with his same numb gaze as he looked at the bloom without really seeing it.

"Life is useless and meaningless," he said in a monotone.

He continued to stare. The rose was a brilliant red, perfectly formed. Mark got up and without taking his eyes off it he walked out of the gazebo, calmly reached down, and tore it from the stem. A thorn drew blood.

Once back in the gazebo he sat down, opened his hand, and let the rose fall into his palm as he coldly examined it. Then, unexpectedly, the same butterfly suddenly appeared and landed on a petal. It was a soft white creature, delicate and light.

Mark considered them both and discovered he wanted to crush the life from both the flower and insect, a hateful act, but one that might make him feel something. The white butterfly slowly opened and closed its wings, gracefully probing the flower, oblivious to the danger. Mark closed his hand. He felt the wings momentarily flutter against his fingers as he squeezed it into stillness. He turned his palm downward and let both fall to the ground.

He stared back at the bush, found another flower, and considered plucking it as well. Then he looked back to the ground. One of the butterfly's wings moved. Mark could also see a couple of legs stirring. That's when he felt a twinge of unexpected remorse. It caught him off guard. But at least it was something. He stared at the wing as it moved more and more slowly, until it finally ceased all movement. A soft breeze dragged the corpse a couple of inches.

He exhaled hard, gritted his teeth, and clenched his eyelids together. For hours he had been alone, thinking about his life, thinking about Jacob, Kathy, and all his unanswered questions. He realized that for weeks he had been trying to bury all the frustration somewhere deep inside. He thought he had it under control and neatly tucked away. But he knew he had only been fooling himself and it was time to face the inevitable collapse of his willpower. There was too much frustration, anger, and remorse to keep buried indefinitely.

He opened his eyes. They were filling with tears. He blinked them away.

"No," he muttered in defiance.

He clenched his fists. "No."

He dropped his face into his hands and after a pause softly said, "No."

He slid off his seat and onto his knees for a full minute, waiting.

"I'm so tired," he finally said quietly.

He *was* tired, very tired. His prideful stubbornness was worn out and he knew it. So he did the only thing left to do. He gave up and let everything cave in on him.

It began with a single, long groan. He slammed his fists into the wood slats again and choked out wails. His sobbing filled the garden. Saliva ran from his lips and mingled with the mucus that dripped from his nose.

He hated what was happening. He despised the fact that he had grown weak and vulnerable through the prolonged suffering of unanswered questions. The struggle was too much, too exhausting. He pounded on the wood flooring again and again and forced out one word over and over, "Why? Why? *Why?*"

He dropped his face downward until his head rested on the wood. He cried loudly and welcomed the hard, gut-wrenching convulsions of release. The tears dropped from his face and the moaning cries he hurled into the garden were muffled by the breeze moving through the leaves that only seemed to applaud his pain. He wept. He sobbed and he pounded the flooring with his fists and spat the snot from his mouth.

His wailing went on for several minutes before it finally began to subside, surrendering reluctantly. Mark fought to regain his composure by clenching his teeth.

His back hurt from the strain. His open mouth was dripping saliva and when he tried to look through his wet eyes he saw only defused and blurry forms. He tried to blink them clear and waited until he felt stronger so he could force his crying to stop. He did. Then after another minute, he managed to sit up on his knees and wipe his eyes. A remnant of exhaustion forced his breath to shudder as he inhaled. He knelt there on the ground and waited until it finally seemed to be over.

He thought about Kathy. He was glad she was not there to see him like this. Then he looked down to the tear and snot-stained wood. Both the butterfly and the flower were gone. He closed his eyes once more.

A few feet away stood the dark monster, silently and imperceptibly studying Mark. Its black eyes locked menacingly on him as it took a single step closer.

Mark, oblivious to the creature, battled his own fatigue and let himself collapse onto the floor of the gazebo, rolling onto his back. "I do not want to go through this anymore. I have to have answers." The leftover tears rolled down over his ears.

The monster unfolded its wings, raised them above its head, and spread them wide. A dark shadow, undetectable to Mark, covered most of the gazebo as well as him. The beast leaned forward and gurgled out four, intense words. "I will kill you." It lowered its wings and took another step.

Mark stared out at the trees and momentarily enjoyed a soft breeze that touched his face. Exhausted, he whispered into the air, "I hate this. I don't care what it takes. I want out of this pain."

The creature listened.

Mark lay there for a few minutes recovering.

It studied the man. Countless centuries of dealing with humans had taught it to pay attention to tears, the tone of voice, breathing, heartbeat, position of the body, and most importantly, the words. The creature calculated as it examined its prey.

Finally, Mark sat up and forced himself into a seat. He

exhaled hard and wiped his eyes again. He felt better after the release of the emotional outburst.

The creature brought its wings closer to its leathery body and took several short steps forward. It began to crouch down as it approached, stopping a few feet away. It reached out its clawed skeletal hand and placed it over Mark's chest, careful not to touch him. The creature waited. After a few seconds, its mouth formed a contorted grin and it stepped even closer. It extended its left hand towards Mark's head and raised a single finger that bore a two-inch long talon. The creature repositioned itself and then slowly extended the talon into Mark's right temple.

He felt nothing.

The demon reached further in, very carefully searching.

Mark sat motionless in the seat, resenting how he had lost control. He was disgusted with himself and the situation.

"I can't take this anymore," he said.

The demon twisted its claw and suddenly a wave of peace brushed through Mark's mind. It caught him off guard.

The creature moved the claw a little more.

The feeling of great peace spread throughout his mind as Mark exhaled slowly. It felt good. He savored it. Mark thought that this was probably the physiological result of an emotional release. Nonetheless, he enjoyed it.

The demon tweaked Mark's mind a little more and the peaceful sensation grew stronger. He let himself feel it as he relaxed his body and closed his eyes for a few seconds.

The demon carefully reached with its other skeletal hand and extended a second claw into Mark's mind. It searched carefully for a moment before it found what it was looking for.

Mark began to lose focus. He exhaled slowly and his breathing grew shallow. He was puzzled by the feeling but he didn't care. *Yes,* thought Mark. *Yes.*

The creature knelt down next to him, careful not to displace the claws. It came closer, drawing its mouth nearer to Mark's. Then it synchronized its breath with his. As he exhaled, it inhaled. As he inhaled, it exhaled.

Mark felt the peace deepen. He welcomed it. His muscles

involuntarily relaxed. He let his hands drop to his sides. His head wavered slightly. There were no more tears, just restful peace.

The creature moved its claw a little further and Mark's mind fell deeper and deeper into the comfort.

Then it moved, brought its lips to Mark's ear, and spoke into his mind, "Rest, rest." Mark had a sensation of words, but there were no words. He could not focus on them, but he felt them.

The creature whispered into his ear again and Mark heard his own thoughts. "You are a good person. You don't need to suffer like this. It isn't your fault."

The sensation of language seemed to echo within him as the creature continued to speak. Mark, exhausted and weak, let himself listen. He wanted to.

"You have been robbed of the goodness you deserve."

The creature gently and purposefully moved one of its clawed hands, searching for the place in Mark's brain that released endorphins. This was an old trick that required a subtle movement.

It spoke again, slowly. "What do you think will happen if your pain continues? What will your wife think as you become less and less of a man?"

With that, the demon skillfully tweaked Mark's mind with a talon from its other appendage. Mark felt shame. The creature moved deeper into Mark's mind and manipulated it again. Mark felt indignity flush through him. He moved uncomfortably, recoiling from the feeling. Mark loathed the idea that Kathy would surely grow to despise him in his weakness. His body tensed and his breathing quickened.

The creature let Mark feel it for a few seconds and then manipulated his mind again. "You don't deserve the hell you have been going through. You are a good man."

Mark began to relax as the peace slowly returned at the manipulative hand of the demon. *I am good*, Mark thought to himself.

"You have a good heart." The words continued in his mind. "You are a *good* man. You are a *great* man who deserves to have his best life now."

Mark felt himself agreeing. The creature smiled in mockery.

"You need to help yourself. There is a way. There is an answer."

The false peace that Mark felt was growing with every manipulation and word that entered his mind. He had never felt anything like it before. It was wonderful, blissful. He wanted more of it, so he let his mind fall further into its comfort, hypnotized by the creature's masterful skills.

"You deserve peace and rest." The creature knew Mark wanted to hear the words. "You need rest. You must free yourself. You need peace. You need rest." The demon tweaked the pleasure center of Mark's mind and he felt a wave of pleasure, but this time it was mixed with a sensation of security and safety. Mark wanted it. He savored the sensation.

"Do you want peace?" asked the creature.

"Yes," spoke Mark softly from his altered state of consciousness.

"Release yourself. Release yourself to me."

Mark relaxed. He closed his eyes.

"Good," whispered the creature into Mark's mind. It studied him. Mark was now in a trancelike state, open to suggestion, easily controlled. Mark heard more words.

"It is not wrong to want peace. It is good. You have been through enough misery."

The creature looked around. There was a small storage shed at the edge of the garden. The door was open and in it a rope hung on a hook. It devised a quick plan and looked back at Mark. The demon moved its claw within Mark's brain and searched for that place where despair and misery reside. He wanted to know what was in Mark, but it was careful not to hurry. It leaned down towards him and gently moved a claw. Mark felt despair. Then it whispered a single word into Mark's mind. "Suicide." With that, it delicately caressed pleasure into Mark's mind as it repeatedly whispered, "Suicide. Suicide. Suicide."

Mark felt pleasure with every word. The creature moved its other clawed hand further into Mark's mind.

"Suicide," whispered Mark to himself.

"Find the rest you seek. Find the peace. Get the rope from the shed."

Somehow suicide made sense. He opened his eyes and looked towards the storage shed.

"No fear." Mark listened. The monster moved its claw and said, "Feel the truth in your heart. Do what is right for yourself. Visualize the victory of choice. Don't worry. It will be okay. Free yourself. Listen to your heart."

Mark was weak and vulnerable. There was no alarm, no anxiety. The creature was dampening his instinct for self-preservation, an easy accomplishment after Mark's emotional breakdown.

Suicide, he thought, as the demon caressed his mind so he would feel good each time he thought of it.

Mark closed his eyes and relished the idea, half awake, half unaware. He looked down the path in the garden that came to a fork. To the right was the house; to the left, the shed.

The creature caressed his mind and whispered, "Get up."

Mark stood up.

"Get the rope." The words were so much a part of Mark now that he didn't question them. He began to walk towards the shed. The creature moved with him.

"Good," came the words deep within him. "Good."

As Mark moved toward the shed, there were no thoughts about the purpose of life, Jacob, Kathy, or self-preservation. They had been pushed away by the calm and peaceful manipulation of the demon. Nothing mattered now. He felt only the need to commit suicide. It seemed so right. The creature continued to caress Mark's mind. It felt good.

With a slow and determined walk, Mark headed out of the garden. He passed the small stream and approached the shed. Just inside, hanging on a hook, was the rope. He carefully lifted it, turned, and began his short journey back.

The creature walked carefully beside him, still caressing his mind.

There were two large trees in the garden. Mark headed for one on the left.

The creature started to speak again. Mark heard the words in his mind as if they were his own. "I need peace and rest. It will be so easy. I will use the rope and my problems will end." With every word came peace, blessed peace. It was all so clear to him now.

He looked up to find a limb. He felt the rope in his fingertips and looked down at it to get the feel of its weight. He held one coil of rope in one hand and with the other launched it into the air and over the limb. It tumbled down on the other side and dangled in front of his face. He needed to secure the other end to something solid.

"The gazebo," came the words.

Mark found a supporting post and tied the loose end to it. Near the tree was a small boulder.

"Stand on it."

Mark moved towards it.

"Peace is coming."

The demon subtly moved its hand deeper into Mark's mind and whispered, "Good. This is what must be done. This is good."

***

The demon watched Kathy from the back seat of her car. It was a dark green form of bones and loose skin that appeared wet, but it wasn't, and when it moved it creaked like wet leather. There were occasional open wounds with small crawling infestations that glistened in the sunlight. Jagged bones protruded here and there in a disjointed pattern and occasionally broke through the skin. Its eyes were black and two long, sharp ears jutted backwards. It examined her.

Kathy nervously glanced in the rearview mirror and back to the road. She took a long breath.

The creature leaned forward slowly. It opened its mouth and extended its tongue. Saliva dripped and fell to the floorboard. In its mouth were rows of jagged and rotting fangs. It hissed.

It leaned forward some more and drew close to the back of Kathy's skull. Wider and wider it gaped until its jaw dislodged with a pop, just large enough to engulf her entire head. But the creature stopped, closed its eyes, and shuddered in a perverse pleasure. Then it withdrew. It was not able to kill her that way. So, it closed its mouth as it sat back in the seat and hissed again.

Kathy did not know why, but she felt uneasy and glanced to the rearview mirror several times as she looked around to see where other cars were. Everything was fine, but she could not shake the sudden uneasiness.

She figured that she was more worried about Mark than she realized. It prompted her to call him so she reached into her purse to get her cell phone. It took only a moment to find it and flip it open with one hand. She glanced down at the numbers and hit the speed dial for home. Within seconds, the phone was ringing.

The creature studied her and then looked around. Two lanes to Kathy's right was a car. The creature sprang through the door, opened its wings, and quickly matched the other car's speed. Flapping rhythmically, it moved down and entered the vehicle.

The phone was ringing. She tapped her left foot on the floorboard. "Please pick up the phone."

In the other car a man was driving. Upon entering, the demon sat in the back seat. It glared at the driver, examining him, and then it raised its left clawed hand flat, pushing it through the seat and around in front, onto the man's chest. The monster held its hand and waited. After a second, it smiled. The man was exceptionally vulnerable.

There was no answer on the phone.

The demon reached into the brain of the man and extended a single clawed finger as it searched. It glanced back over at Kathy, two lanes away, and then back at the man. There! The beast found what it was looking for and began to quickly tweak his mind. The creature leaned close and shouted into the man's ear, "Danger! Danger!"

Sudden fear raked through the driver. His heart began to race as adrenaline dumped into his system. He knuckled the steering wheel and glanced at the mirrors. The creature tweaked him some more as it looked for the place of panic; when it found it, it grasped it and simultaneously screamed, "Watch out! You're going to die!"

The man clutched the steering wheel harder and frantically glanced at the rearview mirrors again. He didn't have time to think, only to react as the manipulation of the demon began to overpower him, forcing him to respond. He quickly turned his head, looking for danger. The demon tweaked his mind with stronger jerks of fright as it took its other clawed hand and placed it over the driver's own hand on the steering wheel. It strained to turn the wheel towards Kathy as it screamed into the man's mind. "Watch out! Turn!" The man panicked and jerked the wheel towards Kathy's car.

At that moment, she glanced down to the cell phone in her right hand. Out of the corner of her eye, she saw the car heading directly for her. Instinctively, she slammed on the brakes and swerved to the left. The careening car was heading for her, but she reacted just in time. It barely missed her.

The demon opened its wings and, with a screech, rose through the car into the air. Meanwhile, the man swerved in order to miss the center guardrail and somehow managed to avoid crashing into it. He straightened out the car.

Kathy took her foot off the brake pedal and regained control. She was okay; shaken, but okay. The man was, too. The demon descended into her car again and howled into her mind, "Die!" Suddenly, it jerked its head upward.

"No!" it shouted.

Then it jumped through the roof of the car and flew quickly off. Three hundred miles away, Kathy's father, lying in his bed at the hospital, opened his eyes.

***

"Yes, the rope," came the words into Mark's mind.

Use the rope to free myself.

The monster was getting bolder. Still in a state akin to a hypnotic trance, Mark grabbed it and formed a makeshift noose.

Kathy's father, John, closed his eyes again.

***

Far away, an angel turned his head and listened. He was bathed in a gentle white light that emanated from his body. Huge and powerful wings thrust out from his back as he glided in the blue sky. He had no claws, no fangs, and no leathery skin. He wore a long white robe that flowed like water as he flew. The angel's hair was long and white; it, too, flowed in the wind. His face was human in appearance. Although he was not armed with talons and fangs, he was muscular and formidable in stature.

The angel listened, hovered, and then, with a sudden jerk, tucked his wings and dove through the sky at great speed.

***

The beast continued to speak into Mark's mind as though its words were his. "I will have the peace I deserve. I need to do this."

Mark looked at the end of the rope and adjusted the noose. But he hesitated. His natural instinct of self-preservation was surfacing. The demon whispered, "This is right and good." The creature tweaked Mark's mind, releasing endorphins. Mark's resistance weakened.

"Get on the rock." Mark looked at it.

"Get on the rock." He walked towards it and lifted his leg. With a single thrust, he boosted himself two feet up off the ground.

"Put the noose around your neck."

The balance between self-preservation and suicide moved one way and then another as the battle raged between Mark's will and that of the demon. Mark hesitated. The monster moved its claws deeper into his mind and tried to weaken his resistance.

Mark focused on the rope. He pulled it towards him. The creature tried to forcefully increase the sensation of tranquility within Mark's mind, but it could see that he was still resisting its manipulations.

The demon was able to do no more. The outcome was not guaranteed, but its victory seemed near.

Mark looked at the rope, wavering between decision and

diluted fear.

"Peace and rest." He felt the words again. He brought the rope closer. But Mark's self-preservation instinct was not entirely gone. He held the rope still. He was deciding, struggling. The creature held on to Mark's mind.

"Peace, I need the rest and peace," said the demon softly. Mark leaned towards the rope.

"Peace" said Mark, faintly. "I need peace." Mark opened the noose.

A flash of white streaked across the garden and slammed into the demon, ripping its claws from Mark's mind. Mark winced slightly. The impact sent the demon tumbling, wings flailing. It growled horribly as it clawed into the air, not knowing what had happened. The angel grabbed one of the demon's wings and tore at it, ripping the leathery skin and snapping a bone underneath. The creature cried out in agony and tried to lock its jaws on the neck of the angel, but the angel was too fast. The monster jerked violently and struck its enemy in the face. The angel continued to hold the wing. *Snap!* Another bone broke. The demon growled and punched the angel in the face, but the angel held on stubbornly and locked his arms around the creature's chest. The evil being bent its head down, dislocating its neck, and buried its teeth into the angel's arm causing him to recoil in pain and loosen his grip. The demon twisted violently and forced its neck bones back in place with cracking and grinding noises. It saw its enemy and, for a split second, was blinded by the light so close to its dark eyes. It spat into the angel's face, and lunged at him with its fanged mouth wide open. Its attack was met with a crushing fist that slammed into the side of its head. A single fang flew out of its mouth, along with a splatter of green. The demon kicked at the angel again and managed to free itself; in an instant, it flew down into the ground, disappearing into the dark earth, screaming and cursing. The sound quickly faded. The battle was over.

The angel quickly looked back at Mark, who was still standing on the rock, rope in hand. He flapped his wings once and in an instant was beside him. He leaned towards Mark and whispered in his ear, "No, this is not the way."

Mark's head swayed a bit and he blinked.

"Suicide is not the answer."

Mark looked at the rope. His mind began to clear.

"Suicide is not the answer," repeated the angel. "This is wrong. Do not do this."

The fog clouding his mind faded; in a flash, he pushed the rope away and stepped back in horror. Falling from the rock, he tumbled into a bush, flailing his hands about as he tried to gain his bearings.

The angel looked around to make sure the demon was not returning.

The noose swayed. Mark could scarcely believe what he had almost done. He got up and moved away from the rope, staring at it in horrified disbelief. It was still swinging back and forth, twisting slowly in the air. He took another step back, almost tumbling again. After a few seconds, he went into the gazebo. He stood there in shock, staring into the garden, recovering, waiting. Then after a minute he sat down and buried his head in his hands, pulling his hair in his fists.

From behind the shed, a flash of dark streaked towards him. The hideous creature was back. Its wing was damaged, but not enough to overcome its blinding rage. In that same instant, the angel stepped in front of Mark and took the full force of the impact of the charging monster. They rolled on the ground, but the evil creature was no match for the angel.

Mark was oblivious to the battle. He was recovering from the shock of what he had almost done, exhausted and ashamed. He looked out at the rope and a wave of gloom flushed through him. It was followed by a surge of nausea that crawled up his throat. He swallowed hard as he fought to hold back the horrible mix of confusion, fear, and dread.

Off to the side, near the edge of the garden, the demon kicked and clawed with all of its strength, driven by insane anger at having lost the battle over Mark. Its vengeance had overpowered its will and the demon retaliated against the angelic warrior with all of its strength, but the angel was too strong. They wrestled, intertwined, fighting with kicks and punches until they broke apart.

Just for a moment, the two of them faded, becoming semi-transparent. The angel's light dimmed ever so slightly and the monster lunged again, but missed. Wings flapped furiously as each tried to gain position, until finally the angel grabbed the beast by the throat and squeezed. The demon flapped violently, and its whole body shuddered. It clawed in vain at the hand that held it at bay. The angel squeezed even harder. The creature gasped for breath and kicked hard. But the angel repeatedly deflected the enemy's blows by shielding himself with his wings.

The monster's eyes flared as it sensed its imminent loss. It grasped the angel's arms and tried to pull them from its throat, but it could not. The angel held firm, squeezing tighter and tighter, driving his fingers into the leathery flesh, puncturing its skin. The demon continued frantically to beat its wings, causing small gusts of wind to briskly whip the angels robe to and fro. It gurgled a weak growl as it tried to claw itself free from the angel's grip. But it was no use.

Soon the creature's eyes began to fade, becoming pale. Its wings beat more and more slowly, until finally, they stopped. Its arms fell limp at its side as it lay suspended in the powerful grip of its victor.

The angel held the demon for a while minute making sure it was utterly defeated. Then, he turned it over and with great effort, ripped its wings from its back. The flesh tore and bones broke, sending a cracking noise into the air. Then the angel let the creature and the wings drop and watched them disappear into the ground. He turned his attention to Mark.

Above the garden, a twist in the fabric of space ripped open. The angel looked up and immediately stretched it wings to full width.

***

John opened his eyes. His ribs hurt, but he didn't mind. It was nothing compared to the pain he was in when his infected gallbladder threatened to rupture and kill him, an excruciating experience. At first he had thought his pain was due to gas so he postponed going to the doctor. But after a day of unrelenting and increasing discomfort, he finally realized that something was seriously wrong. By the time he called for the paramedics, he was doubled over, barely able to stand. They rushed him to the hospital where he had emergency surgery. Everything went well and the doctor said that he was healing fine.

John felt good, considering the situation. Besides, he would be out of the hospital in a day or two and Kathy would be there to help him. John looked forward to seeing her again. He closed his eyes once more.

"Lord," he said quietly, "I thank you that you are sending Kathy to help me. And I thank you that you have heard my prayers for her and Mark. Once again, I thank you for your provision and I ask that you heal me quickly so that I might once again be used in your service. Thank you for giving me more time in this world to honor you. Amen."

***

Above the garden, a distortion in the air produced a faint darkness that cloaked part of the garden. The angel looked up. A black slash had opened and a flicker of flames and wisps of smoke flowed out from the rent, ascending and dissipating as they cast a faint and fleeting shadow on the garden below.

A small, dark black winged creature slipped through the opening and hovered in the air as it slowly beat its wings. It turned and bowed its head low and backed away. The angel kept watching. "No," he said aloud.

From within the rip, a second figure emerged. It was more than three times the size of the first. Its huge wings spanned thirty feet and they billowed back and forth slowly, keeping the creature aloft. A single, large, and twisted horn protruded backward and upward from the giant creature's reptilian head. Its chest was massive, lined with ribs that were occasionally exposed by open sores. It had a raised vertical ridge from its neck to its leathery abdomen and a long, thin tail that whipped the air.

With two large red eyes, it stared down into the garden. It slowly opened its jaws, inhaled, and howled an unearthly roar audible throughout the spirit world, its echoes reverberating even after the creature fell silent.

The angel kept its wings spread as he focused on the evil forms above him.

The gash in space closed.

Staring down at the angel were a demon and a prince. The demon was the same kind as the one that the angel had just vanquished. It was formidable, but not nearly as much as the prince. That one was massive and strong. Its feet were hooves and its huge skeletal hands ended in long, razor-sharp talons. Fangs jutted from its mouth. It looked down at the angel and flapped twice as it moved to a treetop and rested. The demon followed and landed on a lower limb, near its master.

The angel opened his right hand, raised it to the heavens, knelt down, and whispered, "Oh Mighty One, I need help against a prince."

Chapter 2

MARK SAT IN THE gazebo, head in hands, eyes staring blankly at the dirty wood flooring. The sun was setting and long gray shadows had begun their slow crawl across the garden. The birds chirped at the setting sun and the water from the small stream meandered over rocks, softly trickling.

Would he tell Kathy what happened? He didn't know. All he could do was try and get through the next few hours without falling into another deep depression.

What was I thinking? He shook his head. *Idiot. What an idiot!*

Everything was all wrong: the aggravation of unanswered questions, the disturbing memories of Jacob's death, Kathy's absence, his father-in-law's surgery, and most of all, that he had almost killed himself. Nausea rumbled lightly in his gut. He sat back in fearful disgust.

The angel watched him. He approached and whispered into his ear. "The voice you heard was not your own. It lied to you."

Mark raised his head as he remembered the thoughts that seemed to flow through his mind. They seemed focused. Then he remembered the peace, the soothing and seductive peace. He leaned forward and dropped his face into his hands again and exhaled hard.

The angel watched and glanced regularly up to the treetops. The prince glared down, silencing the birds with a reptilian hiss from an open mouth full of rotting fangs.

Mark sat there running everything over in his mind. It didn't make any sense. His thoughts had somehow seemed foreign to him but, at the same time, they were his. It was strange. He didn't understand.

He shook his head as he remembered the desire to put the noose around his neck. He looked up at the rope and watched as it swayed gently in the breeze.

More nausea poked at his stomach. He rubbed his belly in an attempt to combat it. He convulsed once and, to his surprise, his stomach ejected its contents with a forceful spasm. Leaning over the rail of the gazebo, he vomited into the dirt, groaning with each heave.

A flash of light moved across the sky. The angel looked up, as did the prince. Above the garden, another angel hovered momentarily, surveyed the garden and the demons, and slowly descended, giving wide birth to the prince before gently landing next to the angel.

"I came as quickly as I could," he said. "I am Nomos."

"Welcome, Nomos. I am Sotare. I remember you."

Nomos nodded humbly. Like Sotare, he also glowed with a soft light, had equally broad shoulders, and was cloaked in a white robe. But in contrast to Sotare's white hair, Nomos' was black.

Sotare continued. "I sent a demon back to the pit, but now a prince and its slave are here."

They looked up into the trees. The prince and demon were staring back, studying them.

"You have encountered a prince before, is that not true?" asked Sotare.

"Yes, the same one that is above us." Nomos touched his left side, where the light was slightly dimmer. He was still looking up. "Its name is Nabal."

"I have heard of it," said Sotare. "Do you know why this creature is here?"

"I do not. I only know that a prayer came and I was sent with great haste."

Sotare looked at the man. "He is not one of ours. Today he was almost seduced into suicide by a demon."

Nomos responded. "If a prince is here, then this man holds great importance."

"Yes, and it means that a battle is coming."

The angels looked up at Nabal. Its huge breadth cast a shadow over the gazebo. The light of the sun passed through the spirit-demon, and its intensity lessened in the process. Around the prince, an aura of light shimmered slightly as the sunlight glinted off the edges of its tight leathery skin.

The slave demon flapped its wings. One of them sliced through Nabal's shadow, sending darker slivers earthward.

"Nabal has many slaves," said Nomos. "I see only one."

"It would seem that the others are doing its bidding elsewhere."

Sotare glanced around uneasily while Nomos studied Mark.

***

Mark was very tired and utterly downcast. He slumped in the seat. A subtle urge to cry returned, but he forced it away with a groan and a flex of his fists. He let his body collapse further in the bench. Despair coursed through him. He stiffened in defiance and hit his thighs. "Crap!" he muttered.

Completely dejected, he sat alone in the garden's shadows. He thought about the inner voice that now seemed somehow not his own. He frowned and gritted his teeth. It didn't make any sense. But he couldn't shake the idea, the feeling that there was something else involved. That's when he thought that maybe there was a spiritual force influencing him.

"I'm losing it," he said aloud. "I must be going crazy." The two angels listened carefully, as did the evil creatures above.

Mark shook his head. "It doesn't make any *sense*." His own

words were somehow soothing. "I've never seriously thought of suicide before. What's happening to me?"

He paused momentarily to look about the garden and listen to the trickling of the stream. A bird warbled in the distance. This was a serene and peaceful place but it failed to uplift his spirits. He let his head fall back as he stared at the underside of the roof. He could almost taste the despair. He sighed heavily and shook his head. "Stupid!"

The angels kept their gaze on him, but occasionally glanced back at Nabal.

"I wish I had answers." He continued to stare blankly at the roof. "I don't know what to do. I don't know what to *do*." Mucus trickled down the back of his throat and he instinctively spat it out as he turned his head to the side.

Mark turned his attention to the sky and he could see the early arrival of a bright star that had poked through the dusk. "God, I don't know if you are there, but if you are, I need help. I need help. Please, I need help."

The evil creatures in the tree shuddered and the prince opened its mouth silently, displaying its fangs. It hissed in anger and warning.

Both angels glanced up at them, still listening to Mark. He continued.

"There is nothing left. I almost killed myself. I don't know what to do anymore. I don't even know if you exist. But if you are there, then I ask you to help me. I give up. I give up."

With that, Nabal howled. It was a terrible and hideous cry of anger. The slave demon trembled and cowered. Nabal struck it hard across the face with its fist and sent it plummeting down from the tree. The slave protested with a groan as it fell, but it quickly regained its composure and returned to where it sat before, bracing against the threat of another strike. Nabal's attention, however, was now directed elsewhere; its steely-eyed expression was menacing as it focused intently on both the angels and the man.

Sotare and Nomos had instinctively crouched. They flexed their wings to their full width as they waited for an attack.

But none came. The prince stayed where it was, while the slave trembled at its side.

The angels relaxed and turned their attention back to Mark. They were not sure why a prince would be involved, but they had learned long ago there are movements in the spirit world far beyond their comprehension and that archangels of God and principalities of darkness were somehow able to sense what was and was not significant. The prince was there because it had been sent by a principality, which meant that Mark had attracted the attention of an incredibly evil power. Neither angel knew the significance of Nabal's presence, but both feared finding out.

"Have you ever encountered a principality?" asked Nomos.

"No," replied Sotare. "But I have seen the damage one of them can cause to our ranks. I hope that the Sovereign will spare us both such an encounter. But if it should occur, we will both fight to the end."

Nomos nodded slowly in agreement. Above them, Prince Nabal was looking down, red eyes shining. Its mouth formed a grotesque mockery of a smile. Did it know something the angels did not?

"What are we called to do?" asked Nomos. "You were the first here. Have you received your instructions yet?"

"I have not. They will come soon."

Nomos looked up at the prince and the demon. "Why have they not attacked? A prince can defeat us both. Why do they wait?"

Sotare did not answer.

A soft breeze crept through the garden, soothing Mark. The angels were watching him.

"Do you still wonder?" asked Nomos.

"Yes."

They knew that humans were complicated emotional creatures, weak and irrational. They were capable of both good and evil, and they seemed to be easily influenced by the spiritual realm. They could not fly. They had to eat and dispose of waste. They possessed little strength. They got sick and grew feeble. They lived and died. Yet the Sovereign was interested in them and loved them greatly.

"The Sovereign has his reasons," said Sotare after a pause.

The Almighty communicated his instructions through the angelic realm and the angels moved accordingly. So many times and in so many ways they were enigmatic instructions. But the angels knew that when God commanded, they obeyed. Even the demonic forces had restrictions and could only operate as was permitted by the Almighty. It was all beyond them.

Of course, this greatly perplexed the angels, who did not know why God permitted the existence of evil. But they were not to ask. Their job was to carry out instructions in an inexpressibly complex and infinitely old plan in which they had long ago been created as participants. At the center of God's ultimate propose was fragile humanity. They knew that God saw everything and was infinitely wise. They trusted His divine judgment even if they did not understand it.

Sotare looked at Mark and wondered why this mere human, this weak and vulnerable biological creature was so important. Nomos stepped closer, moving next to Sotare. He, too, examined the man.

Suddenly, Sotare dropped to his knees and gathered his wings around him. He pressed his chin to his chest. Nomos stepped back and also knelt down. Though they were vulnerable to attack, the evil ones did not move. They knew better. No evil one, however strong, had ever survived when attacking an angel while he was receiving instructions from the Almighty. Stories flourished about principalities and princes who had attacked the weakest of angels when they were receiving instructions, only to vanish into thin air, never to be seen again.

Nomos took this time to study the man while he waited for Sotare to rise. Sotare continued kneeling, motionless, with his head down for two, three, four minutes. At long last, Sotare folded his wings back behind him, raised his head slowly, and stood up. Nomos stood up, too, saying nothing.

"I have my instructions," said Sotare. "I am to appear to the man and speak to him."

Nomos stared at Sotare in amazement before he turned to

look at Mark.

***

John still had traces of anesthesia flowing through his veins. That, combined with the rest he needed as his body continued to heal, caused him to nap frequently. After his prayer, he gently nodded off again.

He was hooked up to IVs that dripped painkillers that he could push to increase the dosage if he needed it. Another bag sent some antibiotics into his veins. Electrodes on his chest were wired to a machine that recorded his breathing and heartbeat. If anything went wrong, an alarm would sound and nurses would rush into the room. Of course, no one expected anything to happen. His was a routine surgery and he was in a safe and secure environment.

However, he was a participant in a spiritual battle and his prayers were a serious threat to the enemy. Though he did not know to what extent, nor did he understand the depth and power of his prayers, he prayed nonetheless, and the effect had already been felt in the spirit world. Demonic forces would undoubtedly be dispatched in an attempt to stop him. Too much was at stake.

That is why, several feet beyond the hospital window, a being hovered, sustained by its beating wings. It looked around before slowly moving through the wall and into the room where John was laying. Folding, its wings, he took a step towards John.

Out in the hall a nurse walked by and glanced in. The being watched her and took another step towards John as she studied the patient. The familiar sounds of medical equipment beeped rhythmically. After stepping in to check around and seeing nothing out of the ordinary, she left.

The being turned his attention to John and all the equipment. How fragile he was. How vulnerable to an attack. John was old and his body had been weakened by the surgery. It was a perfect opportunity to try to kill him.

The winged creature moved closer and slowly bent over the bed, bringing his face close to his. He scrutinized the man as he listened to the sounds of his breathing, aware of everything in the room. He looked at the IV, the electrical cords, and the bed sheets. How could it be done, he wondered? What would be the best way to kill him?

The angel stood close by the bed, leaned over, and gently whispered into John's ear, "I am Ramah. I am here to protect you. Rest, my friend. God is with you." Then he slowly opened his wings and spread them over John, touching his side. Light filled the room.

***

Mark was still in the garden. Enough time had passed since his near suicide that he was able to more objectively review the events and assess his emotional and mental state. The well-trained habits of methodical examination, developed during his years as an engineer, were kicking in. He was trying to figure out what it was about himself that would lead him to such a terrible act.

"This doesn't make sense," he said aloud as he shook his head.

A noise from inside the garden distracted him. He looked towards it. The moon was full and bright and dusk had not yet fully given way to the darkness. Still, the softening sunlight gave the garden an otherworldly feel. Mark listened. Did he hear something or not? He looked again towards where the sound was coming from.

Wait, there it was again. He stood up. More noise. It sounded like footsteps. He stood there motionless, alert, focusing in the direction of the sound. Steps, he thought. They were getting louder. Someone was in the garden coming towards him. Mark's heart began to race. His stomach tightened. Now he was certain that someone was there but he didn't see anyone. He tilted his head slightly and looked down along the garden path, straining to see. There! Something moved in the shadows. Mark took a step back and instinctively glanced around for an escape route.

"I am a friend," came words from the direction of the footsteps. "I am here to give you answers."

Mark slid out of the gazebo one step, ready to flee if necessary.

"I am a friend."

Mark noticed that the footsteps had stopped. He could see a figure between some bushes but couldn't quite make the person out.

"Who are you?" asked Mark.

"My name is Sotare. I have come in answer to your prayer."

That was the last thing Mark expected to hear. He thought that perhaps it was a prowler, maybe even one of his neighbors. But the voice didn't sound familiar.

"May I come closer?"

Mark weighed the options of running or staying and, since he could see no immediate threat, he tentatively answered, "Yes."

A man approached. Mark studied him. He was dressed in sandals with loose-fitting tan pants and a beige shirt; he had dark hair. He wasn't of a particular race. Instead, he seemed like a mixture of them all.

"My name is Sotare. You have been asking many questions and I have been sent to give you answers."

Mark furrowed his brow, still assessing the man and the situation, cautiously studying him.

Sotare stopped and repeated "I am here to help you in answer to your prayer."

Mark raised his eyebrows and cocked his head back a little. How did this man know about his prayer? It occurred to him that he must have been in the garden listening the whole time. This meant he had been watching him. Mark looked to the rope that was still hanging from the tree. Whoever this was, he didn't want his near suicide to get back to Kathy. He hurriedly untied the rope and jerked it down from over the limb, letting it fall on the ground.

"I know about what almost happened. It's okay. I'm here to help."

Mark started to walk backwards towards the house, keeping his eye on Sotare.

"I will be here when you need me."

Mark continued backing up until he felt comfortable enough to turn around and hurry out of the garden. He reached the back door, flung it open, stepped inside, and slammed the deadbolt home. Rushing to the kitchen window, he looked out to the garden. If the man was there, he couldn't see him.

Mark headed for the phone. *Call the police,* he thought. He took one more look out the kitchen window.

Ring!

Mark jumped. He caught his breath after a second and lifted it to his ear.

"Hello?"

"Mark?" said Kathy from the other end. "How are you doing? How are you feeling?"

He paused for a moment. He knew he had to choose his words carefully and that his tone had to be right as well. Should he tell Kathy that there was a strange man in the garden? No, that would really worry her. Then he thought about almost committing suicide and that he had felt like there was a voice in his head. Obviously, Mark chose to keep *that* to himself. He looked out the window into the garden. "I'm fine," he said into the phone. He walked over to the back door and flipped on the outside light. It chased the shadows back into the garden.

"Good. I was worried. You'll never guess what happened. I was almost in an accident."

Mark's attention was snatched away from Sotare. "Are you okay?"

"Yeah, I'm fine. I was driving along and for some reason this crazy driver swerved into my lane and almost hit me. Maybe he swerved to miss something. I don't know. But it was very close, and it nearly scared me to death."

"Are you sure you're okay?" He asked.

"Yeah, I'm sure. Everything is okay but I just wanted to call and see how you're doing all alone there. You okay?"

Mark quickly processed his concern for her and accepted that everything was okay. "I'm doing fine. I was out in the garden…" Mark paused. "…relaxing." He glanced out the window again. "I'm here in the kitchen. I'm okay."

"You sound a little weird, Mark. What's wrong?" said Kathy.

That is when Mark realized that she could read his voice as

only a wife could. He forced himself to relax and took a silent breath.

"Don't worry about me. I've been doing a lot of thinking and I got startled by a noise in the garden. It was nothing."

"A noise?"

Mark instantly regretted saying it. "You know how the wind moves through the trees. It gets noisy sometimes. Look, I'm fine. Really, I am." Mark glanced out the window again and gazed into the garden as he spoke to his wife.

"Are you sure?"

"Yes, of course." He forced himself to speak calmly, hiding the apprehension in his voice.

"I'm glad to hear it, because, you know, the way you've been lately with all the questions and everything. . ." her voice trailed off.

Mark felt a tinge of annoyance at her mothering. But he knew she was just being a good wife.

"Well, I've just been worried, that's all," she continued. "I love you and miss you and I just wanted to talk to you and hear your voice and let you know that I'm thinking of you."

"I appreciate that, honey." Mark quietly rebuked himself for mistaking her love for him to be mothering.

He wanted to get off the phone and call the police, but if she sensed he was rushing her, she might get suspicious. Besides, it was good to hear from her so he patiently talked to her while he kept his eyes on the garden. He glanced to the drawer where the knives were.

She was calling on her cell phone from the car and explained that she had only three more hours to go before she reached the hotel. She casually reviewed her plans to Mark, making small talk. She would get up early and go the rest of the way to the hospital. After that she would go to her dad's place where she would get things ready for him to come home. She told Mark how she hoped everything went smoothly so she could get back to him as soon as possible.

"I appreciate that," he said. But deep down he really didn't mind that she was gone. He just needed the rest and he wanted to be alone for a while.

They continued to talk about her drive, her father, and how he was doing. Mark was careful not to divulge anything and sound too hurried or agitated. He did, however, glance out the kitchen window repeatedly. He wanted to make sure the stranger was gone. The sunlight had faded enough to make spotting anyone out there impossible from inside. Mark figured the man was probably a drifter or something and might be gone by now out the back gate that led away from the house. But, at the same time, he could not forget what the man had said about being sent from God.

Finally, Kathy began wrapping up the conversation. "Okay then. I'll call you tomorrow from my dad's house."

"Sounds good. You take care on the freeway, all right? I love you very much."

"I love you too. Goodbye."

"Bye."

Mark hung up the phone as he stared out the kitchen window. He thought about calling the police, but by now the intruder was probably gone, so he decided to check the garden himself. Of course, he'd feel better if he had some sort of weapon with him. So, he hurried to the garage door. Next to some tools was a baseball bat. He picked it up, felt its weight, and gave it a small swing. He then headed back into the kitchen. In a junk drawer was a spare set of keys to the house and a flashlight. He grabbed them along with a padlock and headed out the backdoor, locking it behind him, the bat perched on his shoulder. He didn't want the intruder to possibly sneak in while he was in the garden.

At first, he was unsure and cautious. Was the man still there? Mark slowly walked towards the gazebo, taking care that he didn't get too close to concealed areas where he might get ambushed. The flashlight gave him confidence, but it also betrayed his location.

He took a circuitous route, repeatedly changing his direction and angle of view, making sure he had checked every potential hiding spot. Sotare was nowhere to be seen. He checked a few places again, just to make sure, until he was satisfied that he was alone. Only then did he lower the bat. He checked the back gate, which was closed and locked, and looked around a little more for good measure until he was satisfied the man was gone.

He went to the back gate and shook it. It was solid. He retrieved the padlock and secured the gate then gave it another shake.

"Just a wacko," said Mark.

He headed back through the garden towards the kitchen. His keys rattled against the metal lock as he opened the back door. Once inside, he tossed them back in the drawer, along with the flashlight, and set the bat down on the counter. He made sure that all the windows and doors were locked, just in case. He thought about getting the bat and keeping it with him, but he refused to be paranoid.

"Incredible," he said as he ran his fingers through his hair, staring blankly at the carpet. He took a deep breath, pushed the near suicide from his mind, and shook his head.

Was the man in the garden really from God? He thought about it and dismissed it as idiocy. It sure was weird. But, he figured, the guy had to have been watching for a while. That was the only explanation.

Mark dropped his hands to his side and titled his head up, then side to side, stretching, relaxing. He exhaled and he felt the first stage of exhaustion hit him.

He thought about eating but felt like changing into something more comfortable first then he'd grab something from the fridge and eat it in front of the TV.

Another long exhalation.

He plodded up the staircase slowly, letting each foot fall loudly on the steps. The door to the bedroom was open and the bed, unmade, lay before him. He headed straight for it and sat on its edge.

The day's events played through his mind. He had hoped his time alone would be productive but had found that it was anything but. Dejected, he kicked off his shoes and looked at a mirror opposite him on a wall. Staring back at him was a vulnerable, weak man who looked like he had been up for days.

"Crying really takes it out of you," he mumbled.

He was a disgusting sight, so Mark let himself fall back on the bed to look at something less nauseating, like the ceiling. He stared at the textures, finding small patterns in them.

Images of the garden, the rope, Sotare, and Kathy easily surged through his mind as though they were self-propelled and interconnected. He let them progress freely, not caring about what he thought, just relaxing, not resisting. He closed his eyes. It felt good.

Sotare sat in the gazebo in the dark. He looked over to Nomos, who stood outside the structure. Above them, the two evil creatures still sat in the tops of the trees. Why had they not attacked? What were they waiting for? And why was Mark granted the rare privilege of speaking with an angel?

The presence of the prince was especially perplexing since it meant that a principality was involved. Would the principality show itself, or was Nabal enough to do the job? They did not know. Both angels kept silent, not wanting to think the worst.

***

Mark opened his eyes and squinted. The bedroom light was still on, glaring down on him. With his feet dangling over the edge, his body had gotten uncomfortable and he had awakened. The clock said 2 a.m. He sat up slowly, stretched his back, and once again stared at himself in the mirror on the opposite wall. His hair was matted and his clothes wrinkled.

"You look like crap," he said. His reflection didn't answer, so he headed to the bathroom. He was awake, but barely. After using the toilet, he washed his hands and again looked at his reflection in the bathroom mirror. The unflattering lighting in the room was unforgiving; the mirror seemed to reveal his inner character, or at least that's how he felt.

The images of the day flooded his mind again, causing him to shake his head. *Suicide*, he thought. *I can't believe how stupid I was.*

Staring back at him was a man he saw as a failure who had

caved in over unanswered questions. Could he trust himself never to try suicide again? He couldn't be sure. He walked out of the bathroom, swatting the light switch off. He did the same with the bedroom light and immediately thought about the unnerving encounter with the man in the garden. He wandered back to the bed and sat down, too tired to take off his clothes. His stomach grumbled from hunger, but he didn't care. He looked at the gray reflection of himself in the bedroom mirror again and immediately noticed that an illumination from outside was shining through a window.

Was there a light on outside?

He walked over to it and looked down into the garden.

What the heck?

A dim light was glowing in the gazebo.

"Great," he said. "The wacko is back."

Mark hurried downstairs, went into the kitchen, grabbed the bat, and headed towards the back door in his bare feet. He paused, thought about calling the police, but decided to take care of it on his own. He needed to face this on his own. He opened the door. Mark reasoned that the intruder had turned on the gazebo light, which would make it easy for him to be seen before he was himself spotted.

Mark moved silently, bat in both hands above his right shoulder. The glow from the gazebo was oddly white and full. His heart beat fast and hard. He moved his feet with care, purposely trying to be quiet, breathing lightly, focusing on the light, listening for sounds.

What an idiot, he thought to himself. *I should have called the police. What am I doing here?*

But Mark knew why he was there. He wanted to meet this intruder on his own, facing the fear and maybe gaining back a little of his self-respect.

He tiptoed along the path. There was enough light to illuminate any stray leaves that might give away his presence should he step on them. He avoided one, and then another. He forced himself to be as quiet as possible, moving slowly, deliberately. His heart beat harder. He gripped the bat, flexed his fingers around the handle, and continued his stealthy movements. Finally, after he had woven his way sufficiently along the garden path to gain a clear view of the gazebo, he saw Sotare was sitting down, looking at him.

Mark was dumbfounded. Emanating from his body was a soft glow of white light. Shadows reached outward into the night sky like angled slivers, fragmented by the latticework of the gazebo, the trees, and bushes, until they finally disappeared into the darkness. Mark stood, bat in hand, frozen.

"Welcome," said Sotare. "I have been waiting for you."

Mark stared in amazement. Was he hallucinating? Was it a dream, or was his lack of sleep playing tricks on his mind?

"My name is Sotare. I am an angel sent by the Almighty in answer to your prayer."

Mark kept the bat elevated and stared in obvious bewilderment. He backed up a step.

Sotare stood up slowly. Mark stepped back again and raised the bat a little higher.

"Observe." The light from Sotare's body began to grow more intense. He raised his arms slightly.

Mark watched as rays of illumination forced the shadows to withdraw. The light seemed to pass through the foliage and into him. He stared with eyes wide open, hardly breathing, heart pounding. He was seeing but not believing.

Was he hallucinating? But it seemed too real for that. He focused. The light was real. Sotare was real. It was all real. Then he began to lower his arms, the light began to fade and within seconds, it was back to its original, soft intensity. Sotare sat down. Mark stood frozen.

"The light," said Sotare, "is both part of my existence as an angel and the result of being in the presence of God."

Mark was unable to process what he'd just seen and heard. He was still, silent, and could only stare. After a few seconds he began to breathe normally again, but didn't do anything or say anything. All he could do was gaze at this man whose body was glowing. It was surreal.

Sotare smiled.

Mark didn't know why, but he sensed that somehow, some way, this man standing in front of him was telling the truth.

He slowly lowered the bat.

"We can talk about Jacob when you're ready," said Sotare.

The words hit Mark like slap in the face. He involuntarily stepped backwards and let go of the bat, which fell to the ground, bouncing with a vibrato of wooden *thunks* before it came to rest. How could he have known about Jacob? Who was this person? Mark focused on Sotare's light and for a moment he wondered if it was really true. *It can't be*, he thought. He backed up some more.

"Please understand that I mean you no harm," said Sotare calmly.

Mark was still moving backwards.

"You need rest. Go up to your room and lie down. You'll go to sleep quickly and when you awaken in the morning you will be rested. Then, when you get up, eat breakfast, and, when you're ready, return here to the garden and we can talk."

Mark stopped his retreat for a moment as he seriously considered Sotare's words. Could it be real? There he was face to face with this *glowing* individual! He was right there in front of him, shining—right in front of his eyes. He focused on the light. It was unmistakable. It was real. This person was emitting light! But how was that possible?

Mark looked around quickly to see if there was some trick, some spotlight on him. But he could see nothing.

No, this was real. This man was glowing.

"I will go now and see you in the morning," said Sotare. Then to Mark's utter surprise, he vanished. The shock was instantaneous and complete. He stared at the place where Sotare had just been standing. The light gone. Sotare was gone.

Unnerved, he turned around and hurried to the house. Once inside, he locked the door, turned the kitchen light off, and made sure the porch light was on. The outer boundaries of the garden were visible, but its depths were lost in the blackness.

He stood there for several minutes while he tried to calm down. He kept looking out the window, unsure of what to expect.

It took a while, but after about ten minutes he moved into the living room.

"What the heck is going on?" He mumbled to himself as he rubbed his eyes with the palms of his hands. "This can't be real. This can't be happening."

He looked around the house and listened. It was dark except for the backyard light that filtered in through the kitchen. The pressing silence was almost foreboding and it reminded him of how alone he was.

He looked around, glancing here and there. "Unreal," he said aloud.

From the kitchen he stared out into the backyard again.

"I saw what I saw." He exhaled.

Then, out of nowhere, a rush of fatigue seemed to ambush him. The shock of the day's events was wearing off. It was obvious that he was done.

Mark didn't know what else to do, so he walked upstairs to the bedroom but didn't turn on the light. He went to the window and stood there for a while, reviewing the day's events, the light, the disappearance, all his questions, his frustration, the near suicide, the confusion, everything. It was just too much. He moved over to the bed, sat down, and let his body relax. It was good and he welcomed it.

He looked over at himself in the mirror. The dimly lit room hid his tired features. "*Am* I crazy?" He asked himself.

He sat staring at himself and periodically glancing out the bedroom window. He was tired, too tired to keep fighting so he lay back on the bed and focused on the ceiling. An image of Kathy crossed his mind and he savored its pleasant effect. Then, he closed his eyes and within seconds he was asleep.

Beside him, Sotare silently stood watch.

Chapter 3

MARK AWOKE TO SUNLIGHT flooding in through the window, dancing across the ceiling, and spilling down the wall. He stretched and, in a flash, remembered the glowing man. He reviewed the memory: light emitting from the man's body, glowing brightly, sitting calmly, and claiming to be an angel. Then more memories: Kathy had left for the hospital. He had broken down and cried like a baby. He almost committed suicide.

His heart sank.

He would have dismissed it all as a bad dream if it hadn't been so incredibly true. He got up and walked over to the window, leaning on the sill as he looked out. Sunlight bathed the backyard and a slight breeze gently stirred the trees. He gazed out at the gazebo but could not see if anyone was there.

He headed to the bathroom where he caught his reflection in the mirror. "Are you going crazy?" He asked aloud, testing how the words sounded. He knew he wasn't.

Was Sotare real? He wondered. *Was it all a dream?* He focused on his own face. "It was no dream," he said. Mark remembered the glow. It was unmistakable… unless… Well, unless the emotional duress that led him to almost commit suicide had somehow warped his mind. He *had* been under prolonged strain. Perhaps this Sotare person was a self-induced hallucination he'd concocted in order to help him cope, or maybe it was evidence that the hinges that held his mind in place were coming undone.

Mark furrowed his brow as he thought. "Maybe I *am* crazy," he said to himself. "I *have* been under a lot of stress." He listened to his own words, but they didn't ring true. He knew what he had seen. At least he thought he did. It was either real or a figment of his imagination. He visualized the garden below. He needed to get out there, but on the other hand, he wasn't exactly thrilled with what he might find or, for that matter, not find. It was a bit exasperating. Stalling, he decided to clean up first and grab a bite to eat, as that would allow him more time to think.

In the shower, the water felt surprisingly good. He let it flow over him, soothing him, and washing away his agitation. He stood in place for several minutes, breathing through the stream as it ran over his head and face. He thought about his near suicide and the man who had appeared. He thought about calling Kathy and telling her everything.

He chuckled then said, "Hi hon. Last night a glowing man appeared in the garden, said he was an angel, and then disappeared. Oh, by the way, I almost committed suicide yesterday. Other than that, I'm doing great."

He smiled mockingly. "That'd go over well."

Once finished, he dried off, threw on some old jeans and a loose shirt, and brushed his teeth, all the while casually contemplating his situation. He headed down to the kitchen, poured cereal in a large bowl, doused it with milk, and sat down at the kitchen table with a large glass of orange juice. From there he could see into the garden through the kitchen window. As he cleaned up, the familiar sound of running water and the clanking sounds of spoon, glass, and dishes helped to give him a sense of normalcy. Dishtowel in hand, he mopped up the droplets that had splashed on the countertop. He waited, stalling, preparing himself. He turned the water off and looked quickly about the kitchen. Everything was neat and tidy, just how he liked it. Just inside the kitchen door he saw his bat. It was propped up against the door.

"What the heck?" he said aloud. He walked over and picked it up. Then he glanced out the backdoor window into the garden. He distinctly remembered dropping it out there, but here it was. He checked the door. It was locked from the inside. How did it get here? He looked around nervously as he lifted the bat to his shoulder, then walked into the living room. It was empty. He went back to the kitchen and into the garage. The door was closed and everything seemed fine. He checked it quickly and then went upstairs and looked in the rooms. All empty. Returning to the kitchen, he looked out the window at the garden. "All right," he said. "Let's see what's going on." He opened the door and walked outside into the subtle warmth of sunlight and prepared himself for what he might find waiting for him.

The morning air was fresh, not too cool, not too warm. It was perfect. He looked up at the blue cloudless sky. A breeze was softly moving the treetops. He purposely breathed in the clean air as he headed for the gazebo, bat in hand.

Above him, the prince watched. The hideous creature followed Mark's every move. The slave demon crouched beside its master and with a clawed finger the prince pointed at the man. Immediately, the slave leaped from the treetops, opened its wings, and spiraled downward.

In an instant Nomos appeared between Mark and the slave, holding his wings wide open. The demon abruptly stopped and hovered. It looked up at its master. The prince opened its fanged mouth and growled. The slave continued to hover, waiting for a command. Nomos held his guard until the prince pointed to a branch next to its feet. The demon retreated in a hurry.

Mark was anxious. He heard only distant birds and the soft rustling of leaves. Other than that, the garden was silent. The gazebo was just a few feet more. There it was, empty. Mark was surprised that he was disappointed.

"Maybe I *am* crazy," he said.

He looked around and saw nothing. He leaned the bat against the gazebo entrance and stood there. At least the setting was peaceful. Yesterday had been unnerving to say the least. But, it was behind him. He sat down and looked at the seat where Sotare had sat the night before.

"Okay," he said with a skeptical chuckle. "Here I am. If you really are who you say you are, then show yourself."

Mark noticed a movement in the seat opposite him. He watched and then right before his eyes, Sotare simply appeared.

"I am here," he said.

Incredulous, Mark stared, frozen, eyes wide, until finally he let himself breathe again.

"So, where do we begin?" asked Sotare.

***

Kathy found her father's hospital room and knocked on the door softly as she slowly pushed it open. John glanced over and as soon as he saw her, he gave her a joyous smile, "Hi, Kathy!"

"Hi, Dad," she said, heading straight for him.

John reached for her hand. "I'm so glad you're here."

She leaned over and gave her father a kiss on his cheek. He held her with the arm that didn't have an IV in it, savoring her touch.

"How are you feeling?" She held his hand and looked into his eyes.

"I feel fine except for this pain in my side. Strange though, it *is* a lot better this morning." He smiled. "Better than I expected."

"I'm so glad to hear that. You always were a tough guy." She smiled.

"How was your trip?"

"It was fine except for some idiot on the freeway who swerved and almost hit me. I think there was something in the road he tried to miss, but I can't be sure since I didn't see anything. It was a close call. Other than that, the trip was fine."

John's face showed concern as Kathy told him what happened. Then after a few seconds he said, "I'm glad you're okay. How is Mark doing?"

"To be honest, I'm worried about him. You know how strong

a man he is and how he takes pride in solving everything. I guess it's an extra dose of that macho male stuff that you and he have. But since he can't find the answers he wants about Jacob's death, he's gotten so irritable and depressed... it isn't good."

"I've been praying for you two," said John. "I don't know why, but I sense that it is important that I pray for you."

Kathy stared at her father, dismissing his comment as those of an irrational but harmless religious person. She did not put any credence in his faith but knew that it was important to him, so she politely smiled and said, "Thank you."

"Did you get a hotel like you planned?"

"Yes. It wasn't too far away from here." She shifted from one leg to another. "You never did send me the new key since you changed the locks," she said, scolding him with a look.

"I know. As the young people say nowadays, my bad."

Kathy smiled. "No matter, I'm here now."

John pointed to a drawer next to his bed. "The keys are in there."

She retrieved his house key and slipped it into her purse. "Are they going to release you today or tomorrow?"

"Not sure. Believe it or not, I was able to get up and walk around this morning. It hurt, but I did it. That danged gallbladder really did give me a run for my money. I haven't felt that much pain since I stubbed my big toe back in '75." Kathy smiled again.

Behind them the angel Ramah watched and repeatedly glanced out the window. Just then, nearly a hundred yards away, the air shimmered and seemed to bend, and a rip opened in space. Darkness poured through just for a moment, and then the portal to hell closed itself.

John felt odd and stopped smiling. He looked out the window.

"What is it, Dad?" she asked.

After a moment he said, "Nothing. It must be the medicine."

***

Mark was still trying to adjust. Was he really face to face with an angel? He reflected on the previous night, when he saw Sotare emit light and watched him disappear in front of his eyes. He wasn't sure what to say. But there he was, not really knowing what to do or believe. He asked, "Are you for real?"

"Yes," replied Sotare.

Mark was both unnerved and surprised at his own composure. *I'm taking it all rather well*, he thought.

But, because he still wasn't sure he wasn't losing it, he asked, "And how do I know I'm not crazy?"

"You'll figure it out," responded Sotare with a smile. "We can begin wherever you want to begin."

Mark checked himself, wondering if he was insane, dead, or just plain hallucinating. Everything seemed normal. Mark smelled the air, listened to the soft noises of the wind through the garden. He could feel the warmth of the sun as it filtered through the trees. It was all real, all normal. He thought of the initial shock last night of seeing Sotare glow.

"Pretty cool light show last night."

"Thanks. I hope it wasn't too upsetting."

"Well, it was a bit unnerving. But I'm okay now."

"Good." Sotare shifted in his seat. "I thought the best approach was to just be direct." He looked at Mark expectantly.

Mark, obviously still adjusting, was surprised at how easily he seemed to accept the conversation.

I'm talking to an angel, he thought. *This is for real.*

He examined Sotare. He had a pleasant face, nice smile, and calming voice. "So, I just ask questions, and you answer them?" Mark was, of course, still suspicious of the situation's anchor in reality.

"Basically, yes. But please understand that some of the answers you receive may not be easy to take. Truth is not dependent upon what you want or feel. Truth is independent of your desires. It is absolute."

Profound words, thought Mark. *This guy is direct.* Without moving his eyes, he shifted his attention to the sounds of the garden once again, checking reality. He noticed the slight breeze on his skin and the sounds of the rustling leaves. This moment was almost dreamlike and he needed to let his senses inform him that he was not in some delusion. It was difficult to know where to begin.

"Well," said Mark, unsure. "I don't know what to say. I mean, I'm still trying to accept all that has happened, especially you. I still find it hard to believe, even though I watched you glow last night, disappear, and then reappear here just now. You've got to admit, it's a lot to accept."

"Why is that?"

"Because it is so incredibly out of the ordinary. I still have my suspicions that I might be hallucinating. In fact, I can hardly believe I'm so calmly just sitting here talking to you."

"But, being out of the ordinary does not mean it isn't true. I am sure that there are many things that you believe that are also out of the ordinary. Hasn't mankind put several men on the moon? This is indeed extraordinary, yet you believe it easily."

"That's because I've seen it with my own eyes…" he paused. "uh…on TV." Mark knew that it was possible that what he'd seen on TV had been faked. Of course, he didn't have any reason to doubt that it was authentic.

"Then, what is so difficult about believing that angels exist?"

Mark wasn't sure if he should continue the discussion along these lines. The fact was he was having a conversation with Sotare. He needed a reality check so he jumped into more familiar ground.

"It isn't scientific," responded Mark.

"I see. How's that?"

"Well, because…" he paused, "…because science hasn't verified the existence of angels." Mark knew he was reaching.

"Yet here I am."

Mark couldn't deny that.

"Mark, science can't be the measure of all things. Can it verify integrity? Can it measure love? Can it quantify anguish…or faith?"

"That's philosophy."

"Even science has its philosophical basis, like believing that everything can eventually be understood by science. That's an assumption. How do scientists test that science is true without first making assumptions?"

Mark thought about what he said and decided to drop this line of reasoning. "Would it be rude of me to ask you to once again appear and disappear? I would like to be prepared and actually expect it. That would help." After a pause he added an unsure, "…I hope."

Sotare smiled. "I'm not in the habit of appearing and disappearing to prove who I am. But, if that is what you want I would gladly oblige you."

Mark nodded. "Yeah, maybe it would help."

"Would you like a countdown or something?"

Mark chuckled. Somehow Sotare's question calmed him. "No, that's fine," he said with a smile.

"Okay."

Mark watched. Right before he eyes, Sotare slowly faded away and was gone. Even though Mark was expecting it, it still surprised him. He looked at the seat and forced himself to focus. "It's empty," he said to himself. Mark waved his hand into the space where Sotare had been sitting.

"Satisfied?" Sotare's voice materialized in front of him. Mark was unprepared for the disembodied words.

"Yeah," he said quickly as he withdrew his hand.

Mark kept staring in front of him and just as he expected, Sotare reappeared. Mark took it all in. "I'm either completely crazy or you are real."

"Which is it?"

"Well," said Mark with a sigh. "I would prefer to think it's not the former. I saw what I saw. So it looks like you're real."

"Thanks. I'm happy to find out I'm not a figment of your imagination."

Mark smiled. "Me, too."

Sotare relaxed in the cushioned bench and looked at him expectantly. Mark also relaxed and thought about what to say. The two of them contemplated one another for a few moments. Sotare looked up briefly, then back down to Mark. He smiled, raised his eyebrows, and nodded slightly, signaling it was Mark's move.

Mark's face grew serious. There was a single question that begged his greatest attention. He braced himself and figured he might as well dive in. "Why did my son Jacob have to die?"

***

Through the rip in space a demon slithered into the light. Ramah focused on the new menace and opened his wings slightly in response. The demon hovered in the air, waiting for the rip to close. Then it circled once before finally gaining its bearings. It turned towards the hospital and began a slow approach.

Ramah looked at John and then back at the demon. He slowly walked towards the window, studying the evil spirit, seeing if it had any wounds, any possible weaknesses. It was strong, dark, and had long black talons and large fangs, typical of its kind. It carried with it the stench and smoke of hell and would be here in seconds. Ramah prepared himself. He opened his wings wide, looked to heaven and said, "May the Lord be with me."

The demon had seen the angel through the hospital walls and was rapidly flying in to attack. It pounded its wings faster and faster against the air and, just before it entered, moved it legs forward to reveal a double set of talons that protruded from what resembled hooves. Ramah crouched down, brought his wings in close, and then leaped out through the wall into the bright sky. He braced his shoulder as he aimed himself and, a split second before they collided, Ramah tilted his wings just enough to miss the demon's claws, smashing violently into its chest. Both were dazed. Both were falling. Ramah regained his composure first and lunged at the enemy. The demon recovered before Ramah could grab it. It spat yellow bile into his face and beat the angel with a gristly wing as it moved away. Ramah lunged and struck the demon hard with a closed fist slamming its skull backwards. A string of green slime fell through the air, along with two fangs. It shook its head, hissed, and furiously attacked Ramah by digging into his back with its claws. Ramah grabbed the creature by the throat and squeezed hard. Both tore at each other, clawing and punching frantically. The demon tried to grab Ramah's wings but they were beating so rapidly, the creature couldn't get a grip. Ramah kept squeezing the demon's neck, trying to subdue it.

The demon was relentless, however. It clawed at Ramah's arm, twisting its head to bite, but Ramah punched it again and grabbed at a wing, hoping to break it. The demon elbowed Ramah in the face. The blow was hard and stunned the angel for a moment, making him lose his grip on the demon's throat. This gave it time to rise above the angel only a few feet and then it violently descended upon him, slamming its hoofed feet into Ramah's chest. Ramah plummeted through the air but regained his position two seconds later and ascended quickly. The demon folded its wings and dove headfirst. They met in another vicious collision. Ramah grabbed it in his powerful arms and drew it close to him as he tried to crush it, but the demon fought violently, kicking and punching. Ramah reached for its throat again, but the demon deflected his attempt and scratched at Ramah's face, opening his skin. The angel responded with three rapid-fire and powerful punches to the demon's face, but the creature, only slightly stunned, kept coming. It fought with fists, feet, and fury. It used its wings to beat Ramah and clawed at his legs with its talons. They hammered at each other furiously, wrestling, writhing, and punching.

In a moment, both drew back and hovered; they were damaged, weakened. Each assessed the other's condition. The angel was wounded. He had suffered gashes to his side, wing, and leg. The demon was oozing something disgusting from its neck and mouth. One of its wings was clearly injured and it labored to stay aloft. Ramah quickly rose in the air to gain the advantage and began to descend for another attack but out of nowhere a second demon struck him from behind. The stunning blow dazed him momentarily. He heard and felt the grinding crack of something in his body. Ramah fell, wings unmoving, dazed, in pain, the ground approaching. Below, another rip in space opened.

Ramah looked down and then back up at the demons. They were closing fast. He opened his wings but found that one was damaged and responded weakly.

The gash in the air grew wider. Now two demons were almost on him. With great effort, he forced his bad wing to open just enough for him to avoid being caught by the trap. Agonizing pain seared through his injured wing. It functioned, but only partially, so he closed it and plummeted downward, trying to put distance between him and the enemy. His descent increased their separation, but not for long. All Ramah could do was look for a place to hide. He glanced in every direction until he found a church. Would it be a true one? If it weren't, he'd be defenseless. With no other options, he plummeted towards it, the demons in hot pursuit. One of the demons growled in anger as it realized where Ramah was headed. Both demons flapped their wings harder, narrowing their bodies as they tried to increase their speed. They were gaining on the angel, the scent of his blood hot in their nostrils. Ramah braced himself and within seconds, he had rocketed down through the roof of the small church into the sanctuary.

Ramah threw his wings open like a parachute and, enduring the great pain in his bad wing, he braced for impact and slammed into the front of the church. Two guitars that had been resting in their stands fell over with a loud clanging. Ramah crashed into the wall and fell to the floor.

Down the hall in an office, the pastor heard the noise of the falling instruments. He looked up from his Bible, waited a few seconds, and decided to investigate.

The two demons descended through the roof and found Ramah. Almost instantly, they recoiled, in frustration and fear. This church had the presence of the truth and Ramah lay next to the pulpit where a Bible had lay open. The evil creatures howled and retreated up out of the building and disappeared into the sky, cursing as they fled.

The pastor entered the sanctuary. He looked around at the empty room and then at the two guitars. No one was there. Then he walked down the center island up onto the platform. Two guitars had fallen down.

Ramah lay on the floor next to them, unseen and injured. The pastor looked around the room again. He listened but heard nothing. The guitars were close enough where one could have knocked the other one over but it had never happened before.

"That's odd," he said aloud. His own voice echoed lightly in the sanctuary. With one more visual check around the place and being satisfied that everything was okay, he put the guitars back in place and then headed down the center aisle to his office.

"Pray," said Ramah aloud. "Pray."

The pastor stopped abruptly and turned around.

"Pray, please pray," came Ramah's words again. He was holding his side, wincing as he spoke.

The pastor listened to the silence of the sanctuary. He sensed something. It was faint, but he had felt it before. He knew from experience that sometimes the inexplicable desire to pray manifested for a reason. Though he was tired and looking forward to going home to his wife, he thought about praying. Was it from God?

"Pray," said the angel again.

The pastor felt another impression. He looked at the pulpit and then at the musical instruments.

"Pray."

He walked over to a pew, sat down, and bowed his head. He did not know what to pray for so he only asked that God would hear him and that his will would be accomplished. Then the scripture popped into his mind about how we wrestle not against flesh and blood but against principalities and powers of darkness. He began to pray for the will of God to be accomplished in the spiritual realm as well as on earth. Then a thought entered his mind about one of the church members who was in the hospital recovering from surgery. The pastor began to pray for him as well.

Ramah lay down on the ground and heard the pastor's prayer ascend to the Almighty. It soothed him and filled him with peace. He closed his eyes and rested his head against the sanctuary wall. The man's prayers would help him heal quickly.

***

"Before answering your question about Jacob, I must first explain something to you, Mark," said Sotare. "There is another world, a world about which you are totally unaware. It is the spiritual world and it is full of beings radically different from you."

"You mean angels like you?"

"Yes, and demons. It is a world where we can see you but you cannot see us. It is a world of sights and sounds of which you have no concept. We can 'sense' evil and good somewhat the way you hear sound, only we can feel it. I tell you this because you will need to see this world in order to understand more completely why things happen the way they do, so that when the answer about Jacob finally comes, you will understand."

Mark contemplated Sotare's words carefully, squinting a bit in concentration as he attempted to fully understand their meaning. The angel leaned forward. "The spiritual forces battle over mankind. We fight over all people in an ancient struggle." Sotare paused to see how the man was receiving his words.

Mark wondered what this had to do with Jacob's death, but decided to follow Sotare's lead. "How long has this been going on?"

"For millennia."

"How old are you?" asked Mark.

"You could not comprehend it. But, I am older than the earth. I was created before your world existed, as were all angels and demons."

"You mean God created demons?"

"No, he created only good beings. At first none was evil. But after a while many became prideful and rebelled. They sought their own glory instead of God's. Therefore, God gave them over to the lusts of their hearts and their minds became darkened and as a result, they became—disfigured."

"Disfigured?"

"They are corrupted not only in mind but also in form. They are hideous, evil creatures with varying degrees of strength, weakness, and abilities."

Mark felt unsettled and thought about Sotare's matter-of-fact explanations. "How could they rebel if they knew about God? I don't get it."

"Because that is what they wanted to do. Like you humans, we have the ability to make choices. And like you humans, some angels chose to do evil."

Mark nodded. It made sense.

"But I need to add that the rebellion began with one great being. God's first creation was the greatest of all in power and beauty. It was a magnificent being of light and always had a direct audience with the Almighty. It was this great being that first chose to rebel. Some say it was because of its exceedingly great beauty and power that it became prideful. It is said that this being took its eyes off of God and looked upon its own greatness and thought itself equal to the Almighty."

Mark listened intently. "Is that the devil?"

"Yes," said Sotare. "Because of his rebellion, a multitude of angels followed, seduced by clever words and that angel's incredible, splendorous form."

"They were all angels who rebelled?" asked Mark.

"Yes. They were angels of different kinds. When they rebelled, they were cast out of God's presence forever. They also lost their light. They lost the purifying effect of God's presence and so there was a kind of spiritual vacuum that resulted from being given over to their depraved souls. This vacuum was filled by everything that God is not: lies, selfishness, pride, arrogance, and rage. But there is something more. They are evil."

Sotare looked at Mark with a stern expression. It seemed that Sotare was looking for the right words, almost frustrated at not being able to sufficiently convey what he knew. At least, that's what Mark concluded.

"This evil is not a mere concept. It is an actual condition, a state of existence that permeates the very essence of these fallen creatures." Sotare shifted forward in his seat slightly and moved his hands in front of him, emphasizing each syllable.

"Mark, you have no idea how incredibly deep their hatred is. It is as though evil itself was alive and could be sensed and experienced…something like when you humans feel a cold chill slice through your bones."

Sotare sat back in his seat. His face seemed angular somehow. It was obvious that he had encountered this evil he was speaking about since he seemed to drift for a moment as though he were remembering something significant.

"They abide in darkness. They hate the light. They detest God. They abhor everything good. They despise what is right and honorable. They intensely loathe all humans, and they are completely given over to their own depraved filth."

Sotare paused again for a moment before continuing.

"The light of God is purifying. When they rebelled, they changed. All goodness and beauty left them and they became evil."

Mark was listening, hardly breathing.

"We were created in ranks. This means that there are different levels of angels and demons. Each kind possesses different strengths and abilities. The higher up in rank, the fewer there are. It is like an army. What you might call generals, we call principalities. Colonels would be somewhat equivalent to princes. The common foot soldiers, so to speak, are the most prevalent. We call them worker demons because they carry out the commands of the princes and principalities. It is these workers that are generally called demons by humans because it is they who manifest themselves the most."

"Fascinating," said Mark, finally speaking. He was trying to process it all and was momentarily distracted by a movement outside of the gazebo. There was a bird hopping along the path towards the house. As he focused on the little creature, he thought about what Sotare was saying. He hadn't believed or disbelieved in all this spirit stuff but now he was faced with it head on. The bird stopped and pecked at something on the ground. Then it hopped out of sight behind a bush. Sotare was waiting for Mark to turn his attention back to him.

"There are demons that cause destruction of life. Others possess and oppress people, imitating the dead, whispering into the mind, authoring destructive and deceptive ideas, false religions, vain philosophies, and helping to motivate people to rebel against God."

Sotare shifted in his seat again.

"The fallen ones have been given over to hatred, so their natures reflect their evil. They act on their hatred. They are vicious and vile creatures that take perverse pleasure in expressing their malevolence upon anything weaker than they. And humans are indeed weak." Sotare paused before saying, "Perhaps that is why you humans are of great interest to the Almighty."

Mark's eyes narrowed.

"Spiritual battles occur all over the world in countless ways. Multitudes of wars have been started at the hands of demonic forces: murders, rapes, thefts, lying, and all sorts of evils are due, in part, to the manipulations of demonic forces upon mankind."

"Are you saying that all the world's problems are due to these things?"

"No. They only help accomplish what is already in the heart of mankind."

Mark stiffened. "So I guess you are saying that we are evil, too?"

"Yes and no. It is a little difficult to explain. You are fallen. This means that your natures have been affected by sin, by rebellion. You're not as bad as you could be. For the most part, you do okay. You're not completely given over to it, but you're affected by it in everything you are."

"I don't understand."

"Your heart, mind, body, soul, will, emotions—everything that you are—have been touched by this evil. Every human I've ever encountered has displayed some sort of pride or selfishness, coveting, lying, or unrighteous anger. On the other hand, the great majority of you are pretty decent people—from a human perspective."

Sotare shifted his position again, marking his words. "There are wars and rumors of wars. There are thefts and murders, rapes, deceptions, extortion, and so much more. They are in the heart of man, and demonic forces need only strengthen what is already there." Sotare paused again to see how Mark was doing.

"You're not very encouraging. I always thought that basically, down deep, people were good."

"Yes, people believe that. And on the human level, most are good. But true goodness is not measured by man. It is measured by God, and, compared to God, no one is good, not even one."

Mark sighed. "I can't argue that there are a lot of problems in the world, that's for sure."

Sotare continued, "Yes. Even now, there has been a battle over you."

Mark cocked his head quizzically.

"Recall yesterday, when you almost committed suicide? Do you remember how it seemed that a voice was there?"

Mark nodded slowly, wondering how Sotare knew that, and feeling the sting of the memory.

"That was a worker demon. It was influencing you by whispering into your mind. It wanted your death. It had been sent to kill you."

Sotare leaned forward slightly and said in a measured tone. "It is very fortunate for you that he did not succeed."

Mark stared motionless and swallowed.

"If you had died, then you would have belonged to them."

Mark felt a cold shudder slither up his spine. "Are you talking about hell?"

"Yes," said Sotare.

"I always thought that hell was a fable, a myth used by religions to control people."

"No. Truth does not control people. Lies do."

Mark thought about the words and tried to shift the topic. "Okay, why doesn't God destroy all the demons?"

"That is an excellent question, and one that we angels have discussed for millennia. But I don't believe you are ready for the answer yet."

Mark was obviously disappointed. "Are you saying you know why and won't tell me?"

"I'm saying we *think* we know why and you aren't ready for that answer yet. Perhaps I will tell you after you have learned more."

Mark squinted again, annoyance evident in his expression.

Sotare continued. "The Almighty has given me instructions to answer your questions and also to grant you the ability to see the spiritual world."

"Hold on," interrupted Mark. "You mean that God himself told you to come to me?"

Sotare smiled and said, "Yes. Is that so hard to believe?"

"Well, I mean… God himself?"

"Yes. I receive my instructions from him."

"How?"

With a smile Sotare said, "Let's just say that we get a sensation, a knowledge that fills our minds. Nevertheless, you have been given a very rare privilege, even though you're not one of ours."

Mark flinched at the last few words. "What you mean by that, that I'm 'not one of' yours?"

"We will answer that later as well. But for now, I must show you what is around you. Are you ready to see?"

"Hold on, this is a lot you're throwing at me. I asked about Jacob and now you're saying God sent you, you hear from God, that I'm not one of yours—whatever that means—and now you want me to see what's around me. All this is a bit overwhelming. I'm not tracking you very well."

Mark wanted Sotare to see his expression, which was clearly a mixture of irritation and confusion. Then, after a bit, he added, "What do you mean, 'see what is around me'?"

"You are going to see the spiritual world, the world of demons and angels."

Mark felt as though he'd somehow been caught bluffing. "You mean, actually see them?"

"Yes."

Mark retreated into his seat. The concept of seeing another world where demons and angels existed and interacted had never crossed his mind. Science had not quantified or demonstrated the existence of anything other than the material world. It seemed incredible, but obviously it was true, since Sotare was right there. Mark was intrigued. "If you can show this to me, then I want to see it. I want to see it with my own eyes so I can believe it is real."

Sotare approached Mark slowly. "In order for me to show you, I must touch you. In order for me to touch you, I must have your permission."

"Touch me? What do you mean?"

"I need your permission to place my right hand over your eyes and my left hand behind your head. It takes only a moment and, when I remove my hands, you will see."

Mark's heart beat just a little harder. He looked into Sotare's eyes, trying to read them. They seemed sincere and honest. Nevertheless, he was apprehensive, but after a few seconds, he decided.

"Yes, you have my permission."

Sotare drew close to Mark and raised his right hand, placing it over Mark's eyes. He placed his left hand behind his head. Mark felt slight warmth. Then Sotare stepped back.

Mark looked at him and was immediately shocked. Instead of a man with mixed features, he saw an angel in long white robes, bare feet, with white hair falling down to his shoulders. He had huge feathered wings that emerged behind powerfully muscled shoulders. And the light! There was so much light. It was beautiful as it emanated from the angel. Oddly, it seemed to be cut by the leaves and branches as it radiated outward. Mark was beyond amazed. Sotare smiled and extended his wings slowly to full breadth.

"This is what I truly look like," he said as he slowly moved his wings up and down.

Mark swallowed hard. His mouth fell slightly open. Sotare was brilliant, majestic. Mark stood stock still, eyes wide open, hardly breathing. He studied the angel, his light, his features, his wings, everything. Then, after a short while, Sotare pointed off to the side. Mark followed and saw another angel.

"I am Nomos, your friend."

Mark shifted his posture and tensed a bit. He saw the same angelic wings and frame. Nomos had black hair and was also clothed in a white robe. A soft light radiated from his body. He, too, flexed his wings, showing their breadth and strength.

Mark was absorbing everything as best he could. It wasn't easy to assimilate this new reality. He took a deep, soothing breath.

Everything was unbelievably real, spectacular. He smiled as he glanced back and forth between the two angels, comparing them, attempting to commit them to memory. It was wonderful. Then he noticed that everything in his line of sight looked a little sharper and a bit clearer. He looked at the flowers and leaves and could see the details of their structure, almost as though he were looking at them through a magnifying glass; yet they were several feet away. He smiled. "This is amazing."

Sotare took a step towards Mark. "My friend. When you are ready, walk out of the gazebo and look to the top of the trees. You will see a demon prince and its slave. But I warn you, they are truly vile creatures, so prepare yourself, and don't be frightened."

Mark took a deep deliberate breath and peered up through the gazebo roof to the trees but couldn't see anything. Sotare walked out from under its roof. He followed. A few feet outside, he looked up and was instantly horrified. He involuntarily gasped as he stepped back, almost falling over a bush. Above him were two creatures that, to him, resembled a grotesque mix of deformed lizards and dogs. They had dark wings and canine-shaped heads with fangs protruding from their mouths. Their bodies looked as though sheets of leathery skin had been stretched over huge, bony frames. Mark's heart hammered as unmistakable terror scraped across his mind, threatening to claim sole occupancy.

The prince realized that Mark was looking right at it, so it turned to face him and opened its wings slowly, casting a huge shadow upon the garden. The prince leaned forward, extended its neck and head, and opened its mouth as it dislodged its jaw, showing rows of sharp teeth. Mark could faintly hear popping sounds. With a sudden burst of noise the prince then growled. It sounded like a human scream mixed with a lion's roar. It was so loud and horrifying that Mark stumbled backwards over a bush and fell to the ground. The prince looked at him as it leaned forward, still howling. Mark whimpered, frozen with fear.

The prince pointed a long talon at him and the slave demon leaped forward. Mark scrambled backwards over the ground.

Both Sotare and Nomos threw open their wings and quickly moved to intercept. The demon abruptly stopped in midair, growled, spat at the angels, and immediately flew back up to the treetop.

Mark cowered on the ground. "I don't want to see anymore. No more!" He threw the words at Sotare.

The prince slowly beat its wings and ascended a few feet above the treetops. It raised its hand, pointed a razor-tipped claw at Mark, and spoke loudly. "Human filth. Do you dare look upon me? I am Nabal, the great prince! Bow to me! Bow now or in hell! I claim your soul!"

Mark trembled as he crab-walked backward along the ground, moaning, almost crying. Sotare moved close to him, knelt down, and put his hands on Mark's eyes.

The vile monster continued, "I will eat your flesh while you scream in agony. You will die by my hand! Your soul is..."

Sotare removed his hand from Mark's eyes. The angelic vision was gone, as was the demonic voice. Mark looked and saw Sotare as a man again.

He could scarcely breathe. His chest hurt. He was clenching dirt in his fists as he sat on the ground. A branch from a bush poked his back, scratching his skin, the pain finally beginning to intrude into his consciousness. After a few seconds, he began to shake.

***

John and Kathy were talking about the surgery when a hospital worker brought in some food.

"Hi, Robert," said John with a smile. "Kathy, this is Robert. He's been bringing me food. He's my favorite person here, except you, of course."

"Just doing my job, John," he said with a smile. "Here is some more *delicious* hospital food for you. You make sure you eat every last bit so that you can heal up and get out of here."

"Delicious food? What? Have you been holding out on me?"

"You bet. If we give you the good stuff, you might want to

stay. And from what I hear, the nurses really want to get rid of you."

"Naw, that isn't it. You just don't like the competition."

Robert chuckled. "I guess you have me figured out."

Kathy stepped aside while Robert helped John get in position to eat. When Robert wasn't looking, John nodded towards the food and made a disgusted face at Kathy. She smiled.

"You eat all of it. It's good for you," said Robert as he walked back over to the door. "You stay away from those nurses now, you hear?" He vanished into the halls.

"I like him," said John.

"He seems like a nice guy."

"He is." John looked at the food. "My side is hurting a lot less this morning." He paused and surveyed the food. "Yuck... which bland concoction do I eat first?"

"That's great. I knew you would heal fast. You always did." Kathy looked around the room at the machines that were hooked up to her father. They seemed like a mysterious blend of technology and science fiction. She didn't understand what they were doing or what half the numbers meant on the glowing screens. But it comforted her to know that there were those who did understand. She looked at her father, who was easily handling the meal.

"Are you hungry or are you forcing yourself to eat?" she asked.

"I'm starving. I'm so hungry, even this stuff tastes good."

His voice was crisp and clear and so were his eyes. He winced slightly from the pain when he shifted in the bed, but ignored it.

Outside, two worker demons approached slowly. One of them was wounded slightly from the recent battle with Ramah. But it was still in good enough shape to be a dangerous threat. They moved effortlessly through the wall and landed on the floor of the hospital room. They hissed at John and Kathy, who were oblivious to their presence.

John was the one they wanted to kill but if they could also injure Kathy, it would be a great delight to them. But how could they do it? One demon walked over to her in the chair and placed its grotesque mouth within inches of Kathy's face. While staring into her eyes, it took its left hand and placed it over her chest. After a moment, the demon smiled. "She's safe." It then extended its long tongue into Kathy's head, just above her eyes. She sensed something very slight and shifted her position in her chair. She felt a little uneasy. The demon withdrew.

The other creature was already bending over John and was examining him closely. It placed its hand over his chest and after a moment, recoiled, almost as if its hand had gotten too close to a flame. It growled softly.

In front of John was the food. There were eggs, Jell-O, toast, and water. The creature considered how it might use the food to choke John to death. It looked at the dull knife used to spread jelly, but it was plastic and useless. It looked over the instruments, the IV tubing, and the patient-controlled anesthesia-delivery system. It moved over to the bag and studied it. If it could manage to override the dosage-delivery valve, maybe the morphine John used sparingly would pour into his vein and do the job.

The first demon was watching the electrodes that were connected to John's chest. The connection was low voltage.

"Difficult," said the first demon.

"Yes," said the second. "But we must follow Nabal's orders."

Both demons looked around. The second got an idea. "Can you pierce the veil?"

It looked at John. "His presence may prevent me."

The second looked at John, growled, and then said, "You must try. You must cross. Use your talon to slice the line and blow air into it. If the air can be forced into his vein, he might have a fatal embolism." The first agreed by nodding, then it moved over to the IV line. It would be very difficult.

The wall between the spiritual and material world is formidable. Very few things can pass between them, so manifesting a physical effect is extremely difficult. However, it can be done, in a manner the demons called "piercing the veil." The veil was the barrier between the spirit world and the physical one. It was so difficult to manifest and affect the physical world that they preferred to interact with humans primarily through possession.

The first demon extended its sharpest claw and placed it just above the IV line going into John's arm. It lowered its head and relaxed its wings. The second demon waited as the first concentrated. It strained for a full minute before it gave up and gurgled under its breath in displeasure.

"Together," it said.

The second demon moved towards the line and extended its claw. Both creatures brought their weapons to bear on a single point. They concentrated, trying to feel the fabric of space, hoping to stretch it and break through. Their breathing slowed. Both closed their eyes. Then, at almost the same time, they opened them slightly, focusing on the tips of their claws on the IV line. They pressed slowly, very slowly, only to have their claws pass through the line without damaging it. The second demon growled.

Both glared at John. "If only we had a medium," said the first. "Is there one in the hospital?"

The second stood upright and looked around through walls at the people on different floors, hoping to find a medium demon attached to a human. "I see none," it said after a minute.

Directly affecting the physical world is very difficult, especially without the help of channelers, or those who have given themselves over to darkness. But they had to try. They always tried. Neither one of them wanted to face Nabal's fury if they failed to carry out their superior's orders.

Both looked around the room carefully to see if they had missed anything. There was no other demon to help them and no demon-possessed human nearby through whom they might possibly work their evil. "I fear that we must call Nabal," said the first.

The second weighed the comment carefully and responded with a soft fearful gurgle. Nabal was a great force and it was best to stay out of its way. But the prince had commanded them to destroy John. He was vulnerable in the hospital and they wanted no more prayers coming from him. If Nabal were summoned and could not destroy John, his insane pride might bring the demons under punishment. However, if they did not call on Nabal and the prince found out later that they failed to inform it, they might suffer an even greater punishment. Both demons knew the risk was great, either way.

"I will call," said the second. The first stepped back.

The creature opened its wings. It took a clawed hand and scratched its own chest until black blood ran, glistening against its leathery skin, the drops hissing and smoking like acid where they fell onto the floor. It dipped its finger into the blood and raised it high. "Prince Nabal. We, your slaves, beckon help to aid in the destruction of the enemy. Oh great and powerful prince, your presence is needed."

Far away, Nabal turned its head to the south.

***

Mark was still recovering on the ground. Sotare knelt down beside him and placed his hand upon Mark's chest. "It is over. Be calm. Rest."

The fear inexplicably diminished. Mark looked into Sotare's eyes and realized that the angel had the ability to calm him. It gave him pause enough to blink the tears out of his eyes and catch his breath. But the memory of the gruesome creature was horribly seared into his mind. Every recollection of it threatened to ratchet up his fear, but Sotare was there with his hand on Mark's chest, calming him. Finally, after a couple minutes, he was able to get up. He put his hand out in front of him. It was shaking.

"What *was* that thing?" he said, his voice trembling slightly as he brushed the dirt from his pants. He didn't look up to the treetops.

"That is Nabal, a prince who is a very powerful and evil force. It has wounded many angels, including Nomos." Sotare looked at Mark's face, analyzing his expression, trying to determine how he was handling the vision. He could tell that Mark would be all right, so he waited. Finally, after a single long and deep breath, Mark had regained his composure enough to ask a disturbing question. "How many more of those are there?"

"There are many more workers than prince and many more prince than principalities. The principalities number in the hundreds, the prince in the thousands, and workers are in the millions."

Mark knew he would never again look at the sky or the clouds or the trees the same. He would always wonder what was behind them, in front of them, or in them. He would always wonder if he was being watched or if some demon-possessed person loitered nearby. It was not a particularly encouraging revelation.

"It seems that my quest for answers isn't turning out how I thought it would," said Mark.

"Sometimes, truth isn't very polite."

Mark started to walk towards the gazebo. "That thing was hideous."

"Let me ask you something."

Mark looked at Sotare.

"Do you really want truth, no matter what?"

Sotare's question gave Mark pause. After a few moments, he processed a possible answer. But first he had to think about how much truth he really wanted, especially after what he just saw.

What was he really after? Mark wondered. He always wanted answers. But this, this was *nothing* like he expected.

What is truth? He asked himself. *Do I really want truth, absolute truth?*

Mark thought about it for a bit. He had been presented with an incredible opportunity to learn but he knew it would probably be frightening to take advantage of it. He looked Sotare in the eyes as he continued to think. He wanted truth but, at the same time, he just wanted to rest, to avoid the difficulties that his knowledge of the truth might bring.

"People like their self deception," said Mark.

Sotare nodded.

Mark thought for a moment more and realized there was only one answer. "Yes," he said. "I want the truth, no matter what."

"Good." Sotare motioned for them to walk into the gazebo. Mark led the way and sat down. Sotare sat down opposite him.

Mark thought for a moment, a bit surprised that he was as

calm as he was so soon after the vision. "Kathy won't believe any of this. She already thinks I'm losing it and if I tell her that I spent my time in the garden, talking to an angel who showed me demons, she'll really think I flipped, especially since neither of us has really believed in this God stuff before."

"What do you believe now?"

The question penetrated his heart more deeply than he expected. The memory of the grotesque prince was still clear in his mind and even though he could no longer see Nabal, he knew it was watching him. If Nabal was real and Sotare was too, then there was a God and that meant there was a whole new world of truth to learn about.

"It's all real. I definitely believe it now." After a pause, Mark looked at Sotare warily. "What is to prevent the prince from killing me?"

"They have limits. It isn't that easy for them to destroy human life in a direct physical sense," said Sotare. "They cannot cross into this world except under the right circumstances."

"What do you mean?"

"They are spirits. This world is physical."

Mark narrowed his eyes slightly as he listened.

"They try different approaches. One way is through possession. If they can inhabit a human, then they can do a great deal in your world. But normally, they influence people more subtly using suggestion and manipulation of circumstances and use people under their control. Some of the more direct ways of influence are through cults, those involved with things as séances, channeling, trying to contact the dead, and drug use where altered states of consciousness are induced. This makes people much more susceptible."

Mark was fixated on Sotare's words.

"But most often, the demonic forces carefully and persistently work with average people, trying to influence them little by little. They don't always want to kill them because they want people to get others to become deceived as well."

"So, they are really active, then?"

"Yes," Sotare answered. "Demonic forces are everywhere."

"Does it happen very often, this demonic influence thing?"

"Quite often. People desperately want to feel good about themselves, even if it means believing a lie. They want to hear things that appeal to them. They want to gain influence and be in control. So the evil forces use people's desires against them."

"How? I mean, can they read people's minds?"

"No, but as I said, they're clever."

Mark shook his head. "This is a lot to handle. I mean, it's like we are puppets."

"Not at all. You are free to make choices. It's just that the choices you make aren't informed and since one of the best tools of the enemy is to be unseen, you remain ignorant of his tactics and can be easily influenced."

Mark sat back against the seat. He took a deep breath and slowly let it out.

"I guess ignorance is not bliss."

"That's right. You don't have to know everything, just the right things."

"And what are those right things?"

Sotare smiled, "You'll find out later."

"Figures," said Mark. "Okay, so, apparently you want me to know about the spiritual world and how demons work. Why?"

"Because you wrestle not against flesh and blood, but against powers and principalities of darkness and because it is best to know your enemy so you don't fall into his traps."

Mark paused for a moment and considered everything Sotare was saying as he concentrated on the angel's face. Sotare could tell he was thinking so he waited. Finally, Mark asked.

"Do people find God?"

"That is a very good question, Mark. It is the right question. But let me say that many think they find him when they are actually finding demonic imitations. That's why we angels have an expression: 'Humans enjoy their deception.'"

"That's a rather dismal saying."

"Yes, it is. Sorry, but people don't always want truth. They often find ways to believe what makes them feel good, even if it is wrong."

"Okay, so what about angels, do they manifest themselves to people as well?"

"Yes, we do. It's obvious, since I'm speaking to you now."

Mark smiled. "You got me on that one. But does it happen very much? I mean, have I met angels before without knowing it?"

"Yes, you have."

Mark wasn't as surprised as he thought he would be. "I have?"

"We are able to take on human form very easily. Sometimes you will meet strangers who might tell you something you need to hear, or help to change the course of your day, or prevent an accident or something like that."

"How often does that happen?"

"Not very often, Mark. We aren't going around manipulating people. That isn't our intention. For the great majority of the time, you run your lives as you see fit, without our influence. But there are times when you meet angels and are completely unaware of it. In fact, last month you met a person in the parking lot of a store. He asked you for directions to get somewhere."

"Yeah, I remember that. The guy spoke so calmly to me. I liked him. I even told Kathy about him."

"That was an angel. He was sent to delay you so you wouldn't be involved in a car accident."

Mark cocked his head back. "Really?"

"Yes."

"Was I going to be killed or injured?"

"That, I don't know."

Mark shifted in his seat, punctuating his lack of comfort with the idea of potentially being injured.

"Was that angel you?"

"No."

"How do you know all this?"

"Let's just say that we know it when we need to."

Mark half smiled as he shook his head. "Well, I guess I won't look at people quite the same anymore."

Sotare smiled. "Don't worry yourself about it. There aren't angels behind every tree."

"Just in front of them," said Mark as he looked at Sotare.

He nodded in agreement. "We angels work in the physical world as well as a spiritual one. It gets kind of complicated to explain, but when people pray, things happen, and because of their prayers, we are sent to fight against demonic forces in the spiritual realm."

"I guess it's like a giant war game, isn't it?"

"In a sense, yes it is," responded Sotare.

"And the demonic forces are out to get us?"

"Yes."

Mark finally had enough nerve to look nervously up at the treetops.

"Please, let me assure you that they cannot harm you, at least not easily. You see, even a prince or a principality cannot arbitrarily take a human life. If that were the case, there would be chaos everywhere. But the Almighty has set boundaries beyond which they cannot pass."

"Wait a minute," said Mark. "Earlier you told me that a demon was trying to get me to commit suicide but that it couldn't do anything except that which was already in me, right?"

"That's correct."

"And, the only reason it was able to work as well as it did was because I had already contemplated killing myself."

Sotare nodded.

"But, I only thought about suicide once or twice in the past few weeks and each time I rejected it."

"But it was there, wasn't it?" asked Sotare.

Mark thought about it for a moment before admitting the truth. "Yes."

Sotare's smiled compassionately.

"But, how could a demon do that? How are they able to influence us?"

"They are spiritual beings and so are you. Although you are housed in flesh, your flesh is not all that you are. When you die, you continue. Your spirit continues apart from your body. It is in your spirit, that part of you that exists in both the physical and spiritual worlds, that the demons are able to influence you.

Workers do this by exploring the mind and whispering in the ear. They strengthen in you what is already there, that part of you that is evil."

Mark's face went sober. "Are you saying I'm evil?"

"No. Saying you are evil and saying a part of you is evil, is not the same thing. You humans are different from us. We angels do not have rebellion in our hearts. We do not have fallen natures. We hear directly from God and we carry out his will. But you do not. You see, God is perfect and pure. Therefore, that which is contrary to God is not perfect and it is not pure. Your desire to commit suicide was an evil desire, a desire that did not come from God and was contrary to God's will."

The words stung a bit but they were spoken with tenderness and without accusation. Mark recognized that Sotare was not condemning him, just speaking the truth.

"To murder one's self in order to escape frustration, inconvenience, or difficulty, is an evil act because it is against God's purpose and will. That is the only reason an evil creature could get as far as it could with you, because of the evil that was already in you."

"That hurts." Mark sat up straight. Even though he could plainly hear the gentleness in Sotare's voice, he felt like a child who had just been reprimanded. "I guess you're right about truth. It isn't always easy."

"Truth is what conforms to reality," said Sotare. "Truth removes the lies."

Mark shifted his head slightly.

"We humans are capable of great evil in the world, aren't we?"

"Yes, you are," responded Sotare. "But you are not as bad as you could be, and you are capable of great good as well."

"That's nice to hear." Mark relaxed for a moment. Sotare's words weren't exactly comforting, but they rang true.

"I hope I have not upset you," said Sotare softly.

Mark looked out of the gazebo at some random bushes. "I hate to admit it, but you haven't said anything I don't already know. We may think that we are pretty good, but I guess when I look deep down in my soul I find that I'm not as good as I thought I was." He looked back at Sotare.

"True, and that is a good thing to know. Do you mind if I repeat something?"

Mark nodded.

"The standard of what is good is not found in humanity. It is found in God because God is absolute and unchanging. He is the standard by which good and bad are judged. Anything that deviates from him is not good. It would follow then that the average person's sense of right and wrong is skewed because it is based on his own preferences or the particular moral direction that society happens to have at the time."

"This is important," Sotare said with emphasis, "you must understand that feelings and personal preferences are not what determine truth. You don't create your own reality, nor do you create your own truth. You don't make reality go away if it is inconvenient. You must face it because truth is tied to reality, and reality is independent of you. Therefore, truth is independent of you."

Mark was obviously straining a little to keep up.

"Think for a moment. Whether or not you know that there is a 1907 ten-dollar gold coin buried ten inches under your feet has no effect on whether or not it is there."

Mark looked down. "Is there one?"

"Yes. You didn't know it, but now you do."

Mark looked back to Sotare.

"The wise seek truth, no matter what it is. The foolish hide from it and seek their own comfort or try to distort truth to suit their own desires. Don't be a fool."

Mark listened. He could find nothing wrong with what Sotare was saying, even though he didn't like it all that much.

"And what of the prince? What is he doing now?"

Sotare looked to the treetops. Both the prince and the slave demon were gone. He looked at Nomos, who had been standing guard.

"They left a few minutes ago," Nomos informed Sotare.

"They are gone," said Sotare to Mark. "We don't know where they went."

"That doesn't sound good."

"You're learning."

Sotare looked at Nomos then back to Mark. He was breathing slowly and a little hard. "Are you tired?"

"A little. This is taking a lot out of me." He glanced out into the garden again.

"You enjoy your garden, don't you?"

"It's my reality check," responded Mark with a smile as he looked at the trees and bushes. "The garden has always calmed me. I love it out here. It's my refuge."

"You need a rest."

"I'm okay."

"You need a rest, Mark. You haven't eaten for hours. So I will disappear for a while."

"No, please don't go. There is so much I want to know."

"I understand, but you need rest and food. Please go into the house and get yourself something to eat and then relax. It will be dark in a few hours and we can talk more this evening."

"I'm okay. Really, I can understand how you would be concerned for me, but I'm fine."

Sotare smiled. "I have only your best interests at heart. Please rest. After you eat, lie down on the couch. You'll fall asleep and when you wake up, we'll talk more."

Mark frowned and gritted his teeth slightly.

"I'm going to disappear now. Ready?"

Mark just stared at him. With that, Sotare vanished and Mark stared into empty space. There wasn't much he could do, so he sat there for a minute in quiet stubbornness before he finally got up and headed for the house. His stomach growled.

In the kitchen he made himself a large sandwich, grabbed some chips and a glass of ice water, and went into the living room. He sat down on the couch and clicked on the TV. There was a basketball game on, but it didn't interest him. It seemed so mundane now in light of recent events. He flipped through the channels and stopped to listen to the news for a few minutes. The reporter was on the scene of a shooting at a drug house. He then commented on the unsolved killing of a woman. Behind the reporter, Mark saw some trees and wondered if any demons were there. Everything was so different to him now.

More news. There was a famine in an African country and civil war in a Central American country. It was depressing. He pointed the remote at the TV and turned it off with a firm click. He finished his sandwich as he thought about Sotare.

What a day.

He downed the rest of his water and decided to prop his feet up on the couch. He laid his head on a pillow and closed his eyes. Within seconds, he fell asleep.

Beside him Sotare stood, guarding him.

Chapter 4

THE SPACE AROUND NABAL seemed to bend as the powerful creature moved through the blackness of the spirit world. The slave demon was barely able to keep up, straining hard to not suffer the wrath of its master should it fall too far behind. But the prince was unconcerned with the frailty of its slave. Instead, it was intent on answering the call of the worker demons.

In the hospital, the two fallen angels waited. They glanced at one another in fearful expectation of the arrival of the prince and watched John and Kathy, who were oblivious to their presence. The first demon cursed the man in the hospital bed.

John and Kathy talked about Mark and about Kathy's mother, who had passed away two years ago. John spoke of his hobby of building model airplanes, and, of course, his church. It was mostly chitchat, nothing too serious because Kathy did not want to burden her father with anything weighty. She realized that he was tiring and still in some pain, as his eyelids slowly grew heavy and he winced slightly, clutching his side occasionally as he adjusted himself in bed. She felt bad for him.

"So, are there any eligible bachelorettes at your church?"

asked Kathy, trying to make small talk. She knew her father still missed her mom and she was trying to humor him a little. "You're a handsome man and I'm sure you have to beat the women off with a stick."

"Actually," responded John in an overconfident tone, "I was thinking of getting two wives. I don't have enough time to train one to do everything I need so I figured that if I got two, then maybe I might have better luck."

Kathy lightly smacked him on the arm as she smiled. "Well, why don't you get three?"

"I couldn't handle three right now. I need to heal up first. Maybe after a month or so I can start looking. After all, I…" He stopped abruptly.

"What is it?"

John stared at her. He sensed something. "I don't know. I just feel funny."

"Do you want me to get the nurse?"

"No. It isn't that. It's more like a…" He paused and looked at her, carefully trying to decide what to say. "It's more like a spiritual thing."

Kathy slumped her shoulders. "Oh Dad, I thought it was serious. You scared me."

Outside the window, an ominous, evil creature glided towards them. Nabal had arrived. The demons bowed low to the floor.

Preceding the monster was the stench of death and decay and it reminded the demons of The Cavern. Nabal billowed its wings to slow its descent and skillfully folded its wings as it slipped through the wall. It crouched slightly to fit in the confines of the hospital room. The slave demon remained outside, hovering. The two demons cowered in a corner.

"Master," said the first. "We need your strength. We are too weak to accomplish your commands. We are your servants and bow before you. Great One, the enemy is weak and vulnerable, and we knew that such an opportunity is best used by such a one who is as powerful and wondrous as you are. Therefore, we fearfully requested your presence."

Nabal accepted the sycophantic flattery, then looked at the second creature, which still crouched with its head bowed almost to the floor. "You are fortunate that I do not crush you for summoning me away from my prey." Nabal stepped towards John, and the two demons quickly bowed lower.

"Something's not right," said John to Kathy. "I can't explain it, but I feel as though… as if something bad…"

"It's probably the antibiotics and the narcotics they're giving you," interrupted Kathy. "Let me get a nurse."

"No," he said as he put his hand on her arm. "It isn't like that."

John knew that she would not be able to relate to what he was sensing and, even though he was concerned, he was also cautious about saying too much to her. She simply wouldn't understand. Besides, maybe she was right. After all, he did have a lot of medicine running through him, and it could be playing tricks on his mind.

"Maybe you're right," he said. "This old body can't handle these newfangled medicines."

Kathy nodded approvingly and relaxed a bit. He smiled as he tried to reassure her, but he could not shake the feeling. He suddenly had the urge to pray but he could not because Kathy began to talk to him. She was trying to distract him.

"Dad, I've been concerned about you being all alone in the house without someone else there. I know you've told me you've been fine, but I really want to know how you're doing."

John realized that he could pray after she left, so he decided to engage her in the conversation.

"I'm doing great. I have my model airplanes, volunteering at the church, working in my garden, and worrying about you." He smiled.

"You and Mark and your gardens, he's just like you and loves to putter the hours away out there." She knew that was one of the things that first drew her to Mark, an obvious attraction born from seeing her father work in his garden when she was younger.

"Yes, he's done a fine job. I still remember the first time I found out he also liked to garden. I knew he was the right man for you. That was all that mattered." John smiled. They had had this conversation before, and he liked to lovingly rub it in that he knew Mark was going to be her husband before she did. Kathy rolled her eyes as she smiled. They continued their loving banter.

Nabal moved closer to John. It examined both of them but focused on him. Neither of them knew that pure evil was only a few feet away, watching them, lusting after their destruction. Nabal leaned down to John's face and opened its fanged mouth very close. It exhaled slowly. Then it turned to Kathy and put its hand over her chest. It bent down close to her ear and whispered, "I will pull the flesh from your bones and drink your blood." Kathy broke from her conversation and shivered slightly.

"What is it?" asked John.

"I don't know. I just felt a chill."

It wasn't a chill, but that was the best way she could describe it.

"Probably a vent open or something," responded John.

Kathy didn't answer. She couldn't shake the odd, uncomfortable feeling that was mixed with a twinge of anxiety. She wondered momentarily if there was something more to her father's feeling of unease than she realized.

Nabal saw the IV bag that was dripping into John's arm. The first demon began to speak very carefully, raising its head only high enough to look at Nabal's feet. "Oh Great One, we thought that if we could force air into the veins of this mortal creature, it might cause his heart to stop." With that, the demon returned its head to a downward position.

Nabal considered the possibility but only after first examining the room carefully. The electronic devices only reported information. They were useless. The antibiotics were not potent enough to harm him, even if the prince could manage an overdose. It looked at Kathy. She hadn't been cultivated for use so Nabal dismissed her. There was nothing suitable. It realized that the first demon was right.

Without confirming the demon's recommendation, Nabal raised its clawed hand towards the line that led into John's arm and drew its face close. Piercing the veil is difficult even for a prince, but it could be done. Nabal grasped the line with two talons and extended a razor-sharp claw from its other bony hand. Both the demons crouched, motionless. The prince closed its eyes, feeling the line, sensing its existence. Its breathing slowed and, after a few seconds, it opened its eyes to focus. Then it moved the tip of its talon forward slightly. The fabric of space around it sliced open and the tip of the razor sharp talon emerged into the room.

If John or Kathy were to glance at the line, either would have seen only the tip of Nabal's claw. But the prince had selected a place where it dropped down beside the bed, so it was not visible to either.

Nabal aimed at the soft plastic tubing, moving slowly, pressing its claw onto the plastic. The line tugged slightly. Nabal carefully tried to keep it as still as possible so as not to draw attention, and managed to press it against the bed frame. Then the tip of the claw began to compress the plastic and a visible dent formed. Nabal moved deeper into concentration, ignoring external noises and movements as it slowly and inevitably ensured its ability to pierce the line. The small indentation was growing, deepening. Soon, the tube would give way under the pressure. The next step would be to force air into John's veins with its own vile, poisoned breath.

There was a knock at the door. John and Kathy looked up.

"Come in," said John.

A man stuck his head inside.

"Hi, Pastor Tim," John said with a smile. He tried to sit up a little but the pain prevented him.

"Hi, John. I was at church and I had the strongest urge to pray and then you came to my mind. Since the hospital was on the way home, I thought I would stop by and see how you're doing."

The two demons shuddered and stared at their master, who was deep in concentration, eyes closed, breathing slowed. They moved along the wall, away from the door, and towards the window.

"I'm doing great," said John. "Oh, this is my daughter, Kathy, who I was telling you about."

Kathy stood up, walked around the bed, and shook Pastor Tim's hand. As she did, she passed through Nabal's body and noticed that odd chill again. She ignored it.

"You are as beautiful as your father said you were."

Kathy threw an embarrassed look at her father.

"Well? It's true," said John.

Tim was smiling. "It really is a pleasure to meet you."

Nabal was having difficulty forcing its claw into the tubing. The pastor's presence was weakening its concentration.

"It is nice to meet you, too," said Kathy. "My father has mentioned your church many times."

"Yes, and he has mentioned you as well. We have all been praying for you and your husband."

Kathy shifted her weight. She felt uneasy about strangers praying for Mark and her. "Thank you," she said politely and let it go.

"Well, look," said Pastor Tim as he picked up on her body language. "I don't want to disturb you two but I really did have a burden to pray for you, John. Can I do that quickly and get out of your hair?"

"Of course. I'd love it. Kathy, do you mind?"

"No, I don't mind. I can go outside in the hall and wait."

"You don't have to leave," said Tim. "If it makes you uncomfortable, please feel free to go out but, well, I'm sorry. Maybe this isn't a good time."

"Oh no," said Kathy. "It's fine. I'll stay right here. I guess prayer never hurt anyone."

With that, Tim and Kathy moved back towards John. She went to her chair and Tim moved to the bedside. As they did, both inadvertently passed through the same space in which Nabal was standing. The demon prince shuddered.

"That's strange," said the pastor. "I just felt a chill."

Kathy and John looked at each other.

Nabal was deep in concentration, but faltering.

Pastor Tim gently grabbed John's hand. "I'll make it fast."

The two closed their eyes and Tim began to pray. "Lord, I lift up John to you right now and ask that you would protect him and guide him as he heals from this surgery."

The prince reeled as if it had been struck. The tip of its claw slipped back into the spirit world.

"Please let him recover fully and completely so that he might serve you once again. We thank you that you have given us this hospital through which you have worked your healing hand and we give you thanks for your everyday provision. And Lord, please protect John and Kathy from evil as well…and draw her to yourself. In Jesus' name, Amen."

The pastor's prayer reverberated into the spiritual realm and ended with a seismic shockwave produced by the mention of the Savior's name. Nabal shuddered as if it had been violently struck. The two demons cowered and backed away. Nabal shook its head trying to clear its mind, and then in an instant, realized what had happened. Nabal had been in immediate proximity of a pastor's prayer. The prince threw its head back and roared. The two demons had been backing away, but now they both leaped out through the wall, trying to escape the inevitable wrath of the immense demon. Nabal was enraged and opened its jaw full-breadth, jutted its head forward, and shrieked deafeningly into the hospital room at the pastor. Kathy felt an uncomfortable wave pass through her, but she said nothing. The pastor and John had both stopped talking as well, and were both looking at Kathy.

The prince lunged out through the window. The two demons were trying to escape, beating their wings rapidly, fearfully glancing behind them. They flew as fast as they could, but the prince was faster. They split into different directions. Nabal focused on the closest demon servant and with lightning speed, fell upon it and grabbed it, instantly changing direction to find the other, which was still flying frantically. Nabal crushed the throat of its victim and grabbed its wings. With a single movement, it broke them both and threw the wounded demon downward, racing towards the other.

The second growled in terrified defiance, drastically changing its direction, hoping to escape Nabal, but it could not. Each time it dodged, Nabal followed. The demon ducked, but Nabal kept up. It flew upward and bolted to the left, but Nabal tackled it in midair with a thud. The demon screamed but its shriek was cut short by the crushing pressure of Nabal's talons piercing its throat. The demon shuddered violently and beat Nabal with flapping wings. The prince responded by immediately breaking both its wings and ripping a gash in its chest. The demon gurgled; frothy black blood erupted from its mouth. Nabal brought its face close and peered into yellow eyes until their glow faded. When all movement stopped, Nabal loosened its grip and the demon fell downward, disappearing into the earth.

Then the prince turned its gaze upon its own slave demon, who had fallen behind but was now approaching. It bowed its head in submission as it hovered in the air, awaiting its fate. Nabal considered crushing its frame, but thought it best to let it be, only because it liked having a slave nearby. The prince turned towards the garden and flew, the demon following at a safe distance.

***

Mark opened his eyes. The room was dark except for the light from the TV. There was a war movie on. He immediately felt sad as he realized the futility of fighting and killing and wondered about demonic forces again. He stretched, sat up, picked up the remote and clicked the TV off. The room was dark except for the faint shadows cast from the streetlights outside. He looked at the clock on the wall and could barely make it out. It was just past 8 p.m. Then it hit him. "Wait a minute. I turned the TV off earlier." He looked around. "Sotare?"

Nothing. He sat there. "Hello?"

Still silence. Mark's scanned the room.

"How am I going to tell Kathy about this?" He picked up his glass and plate, went into the kitchen, and put them in the sink; then he headed to the downstairs bathroom to freshen up.

In the mirror, he saw the same man he had known for so many years. But he wasn't the same anymore. Sotare had changed everything. He ran some water and splashed it on his face. It felt good. He looked in the mirror and watched the water drip off his chin.

After he dried his face he decided to head for the garden. On the way out, he glanced at the TV. It was still off. At the entrance to the kitchen he stopped and listened carefully to the empty quiet of the house. The solitude was almost palpable. He missed Kathy more than ever.

He turned his attention to the garden, he said, "Here we go," and headed out the back door. It was cool and comfortable outside and as he looked up at the stars he took a fresh pleasure in seeing their light. The moon was almost full and a soft breeze moved through the trees. Mark headed down the familiar path and approached the gazebo.

Sotare was waiting.

Nabal was also waiting in the treetops, watching Mark walk from the house to the garden.

"How do you feel?" asked Sotare as Mark casually entered the gazebo.

"I feel fine, rested."

"Good. I am pleased."

"Did you turn the TV on?"

"Yes, to wake you."

"Thanks."

Mark sat down opposite Sotare and smiled. "So you angels can turn things on and off?"

"Yes and no. Since I've been granted the privilege of appearing to you, I've also been granted a few other abilities. Pressing a button on a remote is one of them." Sotare smiled.

Mark was rapidly tapping his right index finger on his thigh; then he chuckled lightly.

"Yes?"

"Sorry, I just find it amusing that I walked out here to the garden and casually sat down here with you, an angel, and it seems so natural. It's unbelievable, yet at the same time so real."

"I guess it isn't every day that you meet an angel and see demonic forces, is it?"

"You got that right." Mark shifted in the seat and then asked in a measured tone, "Is Nabal back?"

"Yes."

Mark looked up and was glad he couldn't see anything.

Nabal stared down at Mark and drew its head back as it thrust its chest forward. Then it convulsed as if it was choking on something. With a single jerk, Nabal spat forcefully. Green bile hurtled downward. "Bile!" said Nomos.

Sotare stood up quickly and turned to face Nabal. He saw the spittle heading towards Mark. He raised his hand and blocked it, then flicked away the mess remaining on his hand

Mark saw Sotare unexpectedly stand and turn as he raised his hand. "What was that?" He asked.

"Nabal spat at you, and I blocked it." Sotare lowered his hand and Mark could see a wound in the palm.

"Are you injured?" asked Mark.

"It's nothing. It will heal within minutes."

As Sotare sat down to face him again, Mark studied the blistered hand of the angel and couldn't help but wonder how much Sotare would be willing to suffer for him. "I thought you said it couldn't hurt me," said Mark. "So, why would you block it?"

"It would not have injured you. I stopped it because it is a great insult to have bile spat at you. You are made in the image of God and the spit is really an insult aimed at God. So, I stopped it."

Mark raised his eyebrows. "I don't get it. God's image?"

"Mankind is the creation of God. You are made in his image—not a physical image, since God is not a physical being. You are made in his spiritual image in that you can be rational, think, love, hate, make choices, and such. This is why all people should be shown respect...because they reflect God's image."

"That's like from the Bible, right?"

With a smile, Sotare added, "Because you are made in God's image, to honor you is to honor God."

Mark knew there was a lot to learn.

***

"Thank you for spending time with us, Pastor Tim," said John

"I'm sorry I stayed so long. Heck, it's almost been an hour. I was only supposed to drop in, not invade your family time."

"You didn't invade anything," Kathy reassured him. She didn't mind the conversation. After all, the visit had helped her to see that Tim was a good man, even wise. She liked him and considered talking to him about Mark.

Maybe another time when the opportunity was right, she thought.

He stood up. "I hope our spiritual time didn't bother you," Pastor Tim said to Kathy apologetically.

"Not at all. I've heard it all from my father for the past few years, ever since he got religion. It doesn't bother me."

"Well, I'm glad. You're very gracious."

John chimed in from the bed. "My daughter doesn't believe in all of this God stuff, Pastor. But she's a good girl."

Tim looked at her, "If only a tenth of the things your father has said about you are true, then you're a wonderful woman."

Kathy smiled politely at the pastor, but gave her father a look of slight embarrassment.

The pastor moved towards the door. "I know you'll be up and around in no time, John. It looks like you are in good hands." He smiled as he looked back at Kathy and said, "Goodbye."

"Yes, I'm in the best of hands," said John.

The pastor grabbed the door handle and began to open it, but he paused. Both John and Kathy waited for him to say something. He stood there for about ten seconds, motionless. They watched him, both curious, glancing at each other, and then back to him.

The pastor turned around to face John. "Uh, I am not sure... but I...I have a feeling that something significant is going to happen." He looked at Kathy. He let go of the door handle and took a few steps towards her. Bewildered, Kathy stared back at the pastor, who was obviously trying to figure out what to say. He looked into her eyes.

"Please, forgive me. I hope this isn't out of line, but I have such a strong urge to tell you something and I don't believe I should go until I have said it."

Kathy was motionless.

"You can take this or leave it, but I feel as though I'm supposed to tell you something about your husband." He paused. "Your husband…" He stopped again, looked at John, and then back to Kathy. "Your husband is important. I don't know how or why. But he is." He paused again and after a few seconds looked at John in the bed. "What have you been praying for regarding Mark?"

John was caught off guard by the question, as was Kathy. Pastor Tim didn't wait for an answer. He stood up straighter, now more confident. "It's because of your prayers that a great battle is coming." He paused yet again and directed his next words to the young woman he had just met. "Kathy," he said. "I'm not trying to scare you and please don't be offended by anything I'm saying here but your husband is special. I believe that God is going to call him to serve him in a mighty way…but first, he must prepare him."

Startled and perplexed by the pastor's puzzling statement, Kathy raised her eyebrows slightly in astonishment.

Tim turned to John. "The life and soul of your son-in-law is at stake. You must continue to pray." He looked up towards the heavens, staring past the ceiling. "Something's coming."

He glanced back at Kathy and then to John. "I will tell everyone in the church to pray."

It was an awkward moment for them all. John was not sure what to say next and Kathy was speechless. After a moment, Tim headed for the door, paused once more as he grabbed the handle, turned to them again and said, "I'm sorry for the melodrama. But I had to tell you." He nodded as he said, "May the Lord be with you." Finally, he opened the door and disappeared into the hallway.

Both watched as the door slowly and quietly closed. The click of the closing latch seemed to punctuate the moment. Kathy looked at her father who was obviously a little surprised.

"Does he do that often?" she asked.

"That's the first time I've ever heard him talk like that. Sure was different, wasn't it?"

"Yeah, a little too different for my taste."

Out in the hall, the pastor continued to walk. But he could not escape the aftereffect of what he had just said. A great spiritual battle was coming that would somehow also involve him. He did not know how he knew, but he was sure that his own life was in jeopardy.

As he continued, he noticed a conveniently empty patient room, ducked inside, and closed the door. A chair was next to a wall, so he sat down. His breathing was a little labored and he had been clutching his Bible firmly. He put it in his lap and lowered his head into his hands. Light from outside streamed through the window onto the floor. Tim noticed the shadowed pattern at his feet.

Light and dark. Black and white. Good and evil.

He began to pray.

Back in the church, Ramah felt a surge of healing. He knew that someone was praying directly for the strength and work of angels and people to prepare for spiritual battle. He savored the warmth of healing that flowed through him. It was good and powerful. It was what he needed to heal.

He stood up in the church and flexed his wings. The pain was gone and the damage was healed. He flapped three strong strokes. It felt good. But he noticed something else. He felt very strong, much stronger than before.

*** *

Nomos continued to keep an eye on the prince. The powerful demon did nothing but wait and watch. The angel stood outside the gazebo keeping guard. He knew he could not defeat the prince, but he stood guard just the same.

Sotare sat opposite Mark. "One of the things I enjoy about taking human form is the breeze. It is so pleasant."

Mark was amused. "Is there anything else you like or don't like?"

Sotare smiled. "When I'm in human form I miss my wings.

They are there in the spiritual world but in yours they are not and since my consciousness is in this world, I miss them. Also, gravity. Right now I feel its pull on me and am reminded of how limited and anchored to this world you are."

Mark smiled while Sotare described sensations with which he himself was so familiar but to which he rarely gave a thought.

"You do not know the great pleasure of being able to fly through space with an almost effortless movement. Nor can you understand what it means to see two worlds instead of one. Mark, I can see you and to my right is Nomos. I see him but you cannot."

Sotare turned his head and looked out to the landscape. "I can see great distances. I can see angels flying about, carrying out the Almighty's plans, going to and fro. From here they are specks of light, but I can see them. They are everywhere."

"Can you also see the demonic forces?" asked Mark.

"Yes." Sotare's countenance changed. "I can see blackness moving. It is difficult to describe, but it is possible to see very far and very clearly and know where concentrations of evil are at work. I often wonder whose souls are being redeemed and whose are being damned."

Sotare's comment was provocative but Mark let it pass.

"How far can you see?" He inquired.

"Sitting here in the gazebo, not very far. But when I am above the trees, I can see great distances."

Mark sat still as he listened.

"Do you feel that?" asked Nomos. Sotare turned his head and concentrated for a moment, "Yes."

"Yes, what?" asked Mark.

"Would you please wait a moment?" asked Sotare politely.

Mark nodded, wondering what was happening.

Sotare opened his wings and began to work them slowly. All Mark saw was Sotare stand up and slowly ascend through the gazebo roof. He quickly ducked his head outside the structure and followed the rising figure. Sotare hovered above the trees. Mark's mouth hung open, eyes wide.

Both Sotare and Nomos hovered above the trees, a safe

distance from Nabal. They looked towards the city and then both of them gazed off in another direction, into the distant horizon.

After about 30 seconds, Sotare began to descend slowly back through the gazebo roof, where he came to rest on the floor and sat down in the seat.

Mark was half smiling. "Can anyone else see you do that?"

"No," said Sotare. "Just you."

Mark sat back in his seat, enjoying the memory of the spectacle. He pressed his lips together as he prepared to ask the next question. "What was that all about?"

"Both Nomos and I sensed an increase of darkness. I needed to get above the trees for a better look." Sotare pointed off toward the southern sky. "In that direction there is a dark cloud hanging over that part of the city. It tells me there is a demonic stronghold at work. It has been there for a while and has been slowly growing."

Mark knew that the area the angel had pointed to was several miles away, the bad part of town, known for crime. It was an area that he always tried to avoid.

"Is something going to happen?"

"That is a rather open-ended question. But we sometimes sense an increase in darkness around us."

"There's a lot of bad stuff over there," said Mark. "That area is getting worse."

"Many areas are," responded Sotare as he looked in a different direction. He sat back in his seat, wanting to get back on the previous topic. "The thing that intrigues me the most is how the Almighty is orchestrating everything for a purpose. Through the millennia I have learned there is so very much beyond my comprehension. The greatness of knowledge that the Sovereign holds is infinite."

"Who is he?" asked Mark.

"He is God, the creator of all things. He is the one who is without beginning, without end, who does not change, and who knows all things. He is infinitely wise, pure, perfect, and complete in himself." Sotare looked at Mark and leaned forward to emphasize what he was about to say. He spoke slowly.

"When you are in his presence, you are undone, made low, filled with awe. It is a wondrous experience." Sotare leaned back, but his words drew Mark in.

"Who is he? I mean, which religion is he in or are they all correct or all wrong?"

As Mark asked, he realized that he was now a firm believer in God's existence.

Sotare responded, "God works with truth, absolute truth. God does not leave truth to man's discretion."

Mark noticed the rather cryptic answer. "Can't you just tell me which religion is true?"

"It is not an issue of which religion is true. It is an issue of *who* is true."

"What do you mean, 'who'?"

"Exactly."

Exasperated, Mark exhaled loudly and asked, "Does that mean you're not going to tell me?"

"You will learn the answer for yourself later."

Mark was both intrigued and a little annoyed, but he was getting used to Sotare's semi-cryptic, conversational style. "Am I right in assuming that there is a lot you can tell me, but that there are things I must learn first?"

Sotare smiled. "I apologize for not being as direct as you would like, but I don't think it is wise to give you all the answers just yet. In part, I want you to draw conclusions for yourself. You need to experience them."

Mark's face became pale. "Experience?"

Sotare looked up at the treetops to check on the prince. Nabal glared back at him and slowly opened his mouth, showing long, formidable fangs. The slave demon still cowered at its master's feet.

Mark watched Sotare look up to where the prince was perched.

The angel looked back at Mark and continued. "Yes, experience. In the meantime, ask questions."

Mark took a deep breath and slowly exhaled. Their conversation had been circuitous, so he thought he'd get it back on track by being direct. "Why did Jacob have to die?" He steeled himself in preparation for Sotare's response, but before that was delivered, Mark added, "You said before that answers are not always that simple. Are the answers related to my son's death like that?"

Sotare nodded once. "If I give you a simple answer, would you be willing to wait for a more complete one later?"

Mark nodded once.

"Please forgive my bluntness and also please understand that even though I have never been nor can I ever be a father, I am familiar enough with humans to know that losing a child is extremely difficult. I do not mean to be insensitive to the great tragedy in your life. But, the simple answer is that your son was allowed to die in order to bring you here."

Mark stiffened. Was he somehow the cause of his son's death? It was a painful answer and one that Mark did not like. But he was learning enough to not jump to conclusions.

"Wasn't there another way to get me here? Was it necessary for Jacob to die so that I could learn?"

"Different events teach us different truths and truth equips us for service." With that, Sotare stopped and watched Mark's reaction.

Mark was obviously not satisfied.

The angel continued. "There is great mystery in the suffering of the innocent for the benefit of others."

"But my son. Why my son? Wasn't there another way?"

Sotare leaned forward slightly and repeated himself with a measured pace. "There is great mystery in the suffering of the innocent for the benefit of others." He leaned back into his seat.

Mark considered the deliberate tone and repetition. He tapped his chin with a forefinger, contemplating the response. "Was there no other way?"

"I suspect that there are most certainly other ways to bring you to this place, but this is the path that has been chosen for you."

"What do you mean that a path has been chosen for me? Is this what God has decided?"

"Yes."

"You mean God is the one who decided my child would die?"

"Would you rather that your son's death be a random and purposeless accident or would you prefer to know that the infinitely wise Sovereign of the universe has a plan and that your son's death is in that plan?"

Mark shook his head slightly. "You mean God killed my son?"

"No, he did not. Mark, I know this is hard. Please understand that I am not trying to be insensitive, but I know you want straight answers. Let me say this again. God did not kill your son. He permitted your son to die."

Mark didn't like what he was hearing. It was emotionally difficult to say the least. But he had seen demonic forces, was talking to an angel, and was quickly realizing that there were truths about himself, the world, and God that he didn't particularly like.

"It kind of makes God a little cruel wouldn't you say? I mean, he permitted Jacob to die when he could have saved him. I have to admit, as a father, it is not comforting to hear that God arbitrarily let my son die."

"Nothing is arbitrary with God."

"Then is it a game he's playing to see how I will react?"

Mark's tone was hard. He was getting more agitated so Sotare let the moment soften before saying, "Mark, my friend. I hurt for you, for your loss, and for the unsatisfying answers. But, sometimes we have to face the unpleasant things before we can accept something of greater value."

"No, I'm sorry; I'm having a tough time here. This is something that has always bothered me. If God is all-powerful and there is suffering in the world and he chooses to do nothing about it, then something is wrong. How can he be good if he lets so much bad happen when he can stop it?"

Sotare stared at Mark, obviously forming an appropriate response. Mark stared back.

"God does stop suffering, just not all of it," said Sotare. "There are many instances where suffering is prevented, but you wouldn't know about that because you, and others, don't experience it."

"Why not stop all of it, then?"

"To do that would require removing your freedom. It's like this. You have the ability to choose among different options. If God were to stop all suffering he'd have to stop you from making your free choices that have bad consequences." Sotare paused and then asked, "Do you want to be free?"

Mark hesitantly answered, "Yes."

"And do you think others want their freedom, too?"

"Yeah, I suppose so."

"People make bad choices that lead to suffering. Do you want God to stop people from making those choices?"

Mark didn't answer.

"Then there is the issue of belief," continued Sotare. "You can choose to believe something like a lie that can end up bringing suffering. Should God stop you from freely choosing to believe what you want? Should he step in and *make* you believe something to the contrary of your desires?"

Again Mark was silent.

"Remember what I said earlier about being made in God's image?"

"Yes."

"Part of that image means that you are able to make choices, are responsible for your choices, and need to face the consequences of those choices."

"But if God is all powerful then can't he arrange it for us to be free and also to not suffer?"

"I guess you want it all, don't you?" responded Sotare with a tilt of his head. "You want God to take care of all of your problems while you're completely free to make choices, even choices that are wrong."

Mark looked back at Sotare as he thought about it.

"It sounds to me like you want to be a child. You want to be comforted in everything and have no suffering, all while you are free to choose whatever you want, even if those choices are wrong. It seems to me you're asking for the impossible."

There wasn't much more Mark could say at this point. He'd

been cornered again and was feeling a little insulted.

"Your bedside manner leaves a little to be desired," responded Mark a bit defiantly. It was obvious he didn't like the answers. "You're quite direct."

"Would you rather that I tell you what you want to hear with nice-sounding words so you can feel satisfied and fulfilled—even if those words are not true? Or do you want the truth?"

Mark knew the answer to that question. He wanted truth, even if it was uncomfortable. He exhaled, resolved to see this through.

"You know something?" said Mark.

"What?

"Truth is uncomfortable. No wonder we try and find things that make us feel good."

"Yes. Humans enjoy their deception."

Sotare relaxed into his seat and straightened a fold in his pants. "May I say something that is just a little difficult?"

Mark shook slightly his head with a half smile, preparing himself for another hard truth. "Go right ahead."

Sotare swept his hand as he emphasized, "People don't like it that God allows bad to happen, so they complain. They have no problem accepting good from God but they reject the adversity he may send. Yet, both are part of God's plan, a plan that is infinitely complex and old." Sotare stopped and stared a Mark.

"So," began Mark in a measured tone, "God is in control, and we need to trust him, right?"

"Right, even if it is difficult at times."

Mark thought about it and rubbed his chin.

"So, basically, you're saying we have the free will to screw up and yet God is still in control?"

"That's one way of putting it. But think about this. Since God knows all things, nothing that exists can exist outside of his knowledge, whether it is the past, the present, or the future. This means that every action and choice that you make is known beforehand by the Almighty. In turn, since this knowledge is eternally known by God, the interaction between God's control and your freedom is already known by him as well. Though you are free to make choices, God is also free to be sovereign. It is as though they work together, yet you are taken where you go and you are still free."

Mark was trying to understand what he was hearing. "It sounds like philosophical mumbo-jumbo."

Sotare smiled. "Is a fish in a fishbowl free to swim wherever it desires?"

"Yes, within the limits of that bowl."

"And if you were to pick up that bowl and move it to where you want it to be, have you forced the fish to swim in a different place or a different way?"

"Well, I suppose not."

"Your life is that fishbowl. God moves it where he wants it to go, yet you are still free to act as you desire. It's just that God knows your free will choices before you do."

Mark was following Sotare. "If God knows what I'm going to choose, then how can I be free to make the choice? I mean, I can't really make a different choice then the one that God knows I am going to choose, right? Isn't he restricting my choices by knowing them ahead of time?"

"I'm glad to see you can think through these issues. But, God is not restricting your choices. You are. You are the one who freely chooses and thereby it is you who excludes other possibilities. God just knows how it's going to work out. And, just so you know, he does some nudging as well."

Mark relaxed a little. But he was still unsure. "I think this confusion is going to be a regular occurrence for a while."

Sotare laughed lightly.

Mark realized this was the first time that Sotare had laughed. It made him more personable. "Okay, so I guess this means that God has a reason for why he allowed it, but I'm unable to understand it completely now, right?"

"Yes, to put it simply." Sotare turned around and looked up to the treetops. The prince was staring down at them. The angel sensed something. He turned back to Mark. "Please hold on. I will be right back."

Sotare looked up, flapped his wings, and again ascended

just above the treetops a safe distance away from Nabal as he looked out to the west. After a little bit, he descended back to the ground.

"That's going to take some getting used to."

"I apologize. I have become comfortable speaking to you and I thought nothing of ascending." He looked over at Nomos, who had been standing quietly on guard the whole time. Nomos said, "I have sensed the same thing. Are you going to tell him?"

Sotare was looking at Nomos. All Mark saw was him staring into an empty part of the garden. He heard Sotare say, "Yes," and then he turned to Mark. "Something is coming."

The way Sotare said it sent icy chills down Mark's spine.

"What is it? What is coming?"

"I am not sure, but it might be a principality." Sotare looked at Mark. "You are very important. I do not know why, but you are the reason it is coming."

Mark swallowed hard and tasted the fear rise up in his throat. He forced it down.

"A principality?" asked Mark cautiously. "That doesn't sound good."

"No, it isn't. It's bad, very bad." Mark's expression went blank.

"There is no easy way to say this, so I suppose that being straightforward is best. A principality rarely leaves its abode. It commands princes such as Nabal, and the princes carry out these commands without hesitation. The prince who is above us on the tree could easily defeat both Nomos and me. In fact, it might take twenty angels like us to match it. As it is, there are only two of us here for you." Sotare looked at Nomos then back to Mark.

"If Nabal is so great, why hasn't he attacked?" asked Mark.

"If he were to attack us, he could defeat us. Then you would be far more vulnerable to him. But as I said before it cannot arbitrarily harm you. It can make your life miserable. It can make fear come over you, influence others to harm you, cause you to have horrible nightmares, and even make you sick. If it were allowed to work on you unchecked, it could end up killing you."

Mark recoiled slightly and frowned. He had seen the fierceness of the ugly prince and did not doubt Sotare.

"But a principality," continued Sotare, "can rip a hole in your spirit and influence your mind not only to hurt yourself, but also your wife, and others."

"There is no way I would hurt my wife. No way!"

Sotare looked at Mark with a quick and direct examination. "Your suicide would have hurt her deeply."

That stung.

"Mark, my point is that you must always keep guard over your heart. Don't be so confident and boast about things you cannot guarantee. You don't know what really resides in your own soul. Let me ask you, would you have ever suspected that you could commit suicide?"

Mark did not like Sotare's reasoning, but he already knew the angel was correct.

"No, you're right. I guess you never know what you'll do until you are in the situation."

"Exactly," Sotare concluded. "Anyway, let me continue. A principality is so strong that it can defeat many princes. It is a monstrously hideous and awesomely powerful evil force, and if it is coming, then things are going to get much, much worse."

Mark swallowed hard. He frowned and pursed his lips. Fear hit Mark's soul with the thud of a large rock hitting the ground. He managed to ask, "And are you worried that one of these principalities is coming here for me?"

"I don't know," said Sotare straightaway. "There are other people involved in the battle. It might be coming for someone else. But it could be coming for you."

Mark's chest grew tight and his heart thumped with the fear that seemed to have crawled down into his stomach and taken hold.

"But," said Sotare, "it is also possible that it is coming to open the door for a larger demonic presence, I don't know. There are many possibilities."

Mark couldn't say anything. He sat motionless, his full attention on Sotare.

Above them in the trees the prince opened its wings and held them outstretched as it threw back its head and howled into the sky.

Sotare instinctively flexed his wings, causing him to vanish. The unfortunate timing was disturbing, yet Mark had to force himself to stay calm, accept it, and wait. A moment later, Sotare reappeared.

"I apologize again, Mark. I know that if I tell you not to worry my words might seem meaningless. But, still…don't worry. Though a battle is coming, the fact that I have been given the privilege to appear to you means that God is working. I doubt very much that he will let anything too serious happen to you."

Mark found the words comforting as well as disturbing. He looked up to the treetops and visualized Nabal, then back to Sotare. "Too serious?"

Chapter 5

BACK IN THE CAVERN, the creatures moved restlessly among the well-worn paths that snaked around boulders. In a large, open flat area groups of beasts congregated according to their kind. They gathered there because the recent portal opening above had excited them and they were hoping another might open among the ground creatures. They wanted their turn in the world of people.

The Cavern was a dangerous place even for them. There were occasional skirmishes and battles for position and territory. Sporadic screams, growls, and scuffles echoed off the walls as creatures of one kind would clash with those of another. The stronger would attack the weaker and the weaker would return in groups to exact revenge. The cycle was ongoing, ages-old, and relentless. Any sign of weakness was an invitation for pain, so they stayed in groups according to rank and kind.

None of the creatures knew what opened the portal, though they assumed it was controlled by the worst of evil forces, called Satan. This horrendous creature possessed no compassion, no love, no kindness, and no beauty. Instead, in the black void of

Satan's soul flowed pure evil—utter and complete evil—the depth of which was matched only by its tremendous power.

No demon, no worker, no prince, and no principality ever dared to challenge the angel known as The Great Fallen One, the Deceiver. All the demonic forces cowered in its presence and greatly feared its ability to exact unimaginable pain upon any who did not instantly obey its commands. But the devil never came to The Cavern. It had its own place of dwelling that no creature here had ever seen, nor had any ever desired to visit.

Near a dark fissure that had ripped a gaping hole into The Cavern's side, a lizard-like thing was licking a frothy liquid that had spilled upon a stone. Unexpectedly, a cool wisp of air brushed up against its wet leathery skin. It paused and turned, dropping its guard for a moment. Then, a second wisp, almost imperceptibly cold, barely brushed against its torso. In this place of fire anything other than heat was out of place. The creature stood up straight and peered into the blackness from which the cold emanated.

Nearby, a skeletal beast, with loose black skin, huge shoulders, and massive jaws watched the first creature drop its guard. It crouched and immediately lunged upon it, thrusting its fangs deep into its victim's leathery back. The first growled, reached back, and grabbed the assailant's head with its claws. But just before the second was about to inflict another wound, an intense wave of cold swept over them both. They instinctively stopped and cowered. The second fled. The first tried to run, but quickly discovered it could not. A huge gash in its lower torso made it impossible to run. It fell to the ground, wounded, only able to feebly hobble away from the icy cold that now was washing over its entire body.

The frozen air moved like a wave, flowing over rocks, filling crevices, moving around boulders, and reaching like fingers deeper into The Cavern. As it did, more and more creatures paused and stared out into the dark cave before falling silent and running. The first to flee were those closest to the outside. They felt the presence first. Then, as it swept inward, more and more demons felt the chill and they, too, finally erupted into a panicked race to flee through the numerous fractured corridors that scarred the landscape. They clawed and growled at each other as they ran, until finally the last darted into a deep crevice and The Cavern fell silent.

Soon, two faint points of light appeared. They seemed to move slightly back and forth as they approached. There were soft, rhythmic tremors in the ground as the creature walked and a low-pitched growl, like that of a prowling lion, almost inaudible. The cave funneled the sound outward into The Cavern, gradually increasing its intensity.

The foreboding sound and dense cold swept into The Cavern ahead of the mighty beast that lumbered forward until finally, the principality known as Paraptome entered The Cavern. It stopped and looked around; its huge black, shiny form was illuminated by the soft glow of numerous golden fires. It surveyed the landscape through deep-set, red eyes.

Paraptome was an immense hulking mass. It had a huge bony head topped by several immense, sharp saber-like quills pointing backward where hair would have been. Its red eyes were sunk deep into its skull, which was separated by a shallow cleft running from its nose up past its forehead and back down its neck. Its cheekbones were abnormally large, as were its brows and sloped forehead. On top, two huge horns twisted upward and outward. In its massive jaws, two teeth protruded forward from the bottom and curled upward slightly, ending below its eyes. Its neck seemed an impenetrable mass of muscle that led down to a hulking black chest that moved as the creature breathed. On its back, two inconceivably huge bat-like wings were partially extended. A barbed tail the size of a tree trunk rested on the ground behind it and the talons on its two hoofed feet dug deep into The Cavern's earthen floor.

It looked down at the wounded and terrified creature that had managed to drag itself only a short distance. Paraptome approached it, the ground thudding with each step. Then, slowly, it extended a giant clawed hand, palm forward. The wounded creature rose into the air and floated towards the hulk. It kicked wildly in suspended motion and snarled in sporadic bursts of fearful growls until it was finally in the giant's hand. Paraptome brought the creature close to its face and gazed upon the fragile demon. Then with a rumbling gurgle it squeezed until the creature fell silent in the steel grip of the principality. A dark liquid oozed forth and fell to The Cavern floor.

Paraptome let the mangled carcass fall to ground before it continued its lumbering movement forward.

Once deep into The Cavern, it stopped and looked around slowly. It took a deep breath and exhaled. A river of cold fell downward, distorting the light that passed through it. Then it took another breath, this time larger than the first, bent down slightly, and began a drawn-out howl as it stood up straighter and straighter until finally, a deafening roar filled the rocky cave.

Then Paraptome stopped. The remnants of the scream echoed and took half a minute to give way to an eerie stillness.

It stepped forward a few feet, each footstep thudding under the weight of its mass. It stopped and looked around then extended its two clawed hands. With the back of each touching together, it then flattened its fingers so its talons pointed forward. Paraptome took another step and thrust its razor-sharp claws into the fabric of space and by sheer force, ripped open a hole. A metallic bending sound filled the void and emanations of light from somewhere in the hole reflected off of its chest.

Paraptome stepped closer and ripped the hole larger. More metal tearing sounds filled The Cavern. It held the rip in space open until, with a single effort, the monster stepped through and disappeared. The tear closed behind with a pounding thud.

***

Nabal howled one more time, extended its wings, and looked upward. The slave demon cowered among the tree branches. Then, above them both, the fabric of space ripped open and from within a wave of intense cold poured out and fell like a waterfall.

From the rip Paraptome emerged into the clean air. Then behind it, the rip closed with the sound of rapidly moving wind before falling silent. The principality hovered in the air using long powerful strokes as it surveyed the landscape. Finally, looking below, it saw the garden with Nabal on the treetop. Paraptome glided downward and stopped its descent just above the prince, hovering heavily in the air. Nabal bowed its head and dropped its wings.

Sotare and Nomos instinctively opened theirs defensively. "A principality!" shouted Sotare. Mark saw him turn as he spoke the frightful words, only to vanish. He felt a chill and was once again glad he could not see into the spirit world. He wanted to panic, to run into the house. But he couldn't. He wouldn't. Then he felt it, a presence. It was a foreboding manifestation that seemed distant, but somehow detectable. He looked to the tree tops.

Paraptome looked at Mark and growled.

Mark felt a wave of fear brush against his mind.

Three birds sitting in one of the trees suddenly took to rapid flight. Then he felt a misty coolness brush up against his skin.

His heart began to pound. With Sotare being invisible he felt alone and vulnerable.

"What's happening?" he asked in a controlled alarm. But Sotare did not respond.

Mark looked around the garden and again to the treetop. He could see nothing, but he knew something was happening. It was quiet. The sensation of aloneness struck him hard and he realized how utterly weak and fragile he was. There was nothing he could do. He again thought of running into the house, but he knew it would do no good. He considered hiding behind some bushes but quickly dismissed it. He could only wait motionless, quiet, looking to the trees, and hoping Sotare would soon reappear. All he could he do was try to control the rising fear crawling its way into his pounding chest.

Sotare and Nomos stood between him and the demons, wings spread wide. Sotare glanced back at Mark and could see he was afraid. "We are here, Mark. You will be okay."

Mark could not see Sotare but he heard the disembodied voice utter the comforting words. He looked around at the trees and the bushes and tried to focus on what he knew was familiar. He wondered what would happen, if anything.

Paraptome looked down at the two angels. It saw Mark alone, a weak man, vulnerable. But it knew that even though it could squeeze the life out of this tiny human with the slightest effort, it was not permitted.

Paraptome spoke to Nabal. "The two angels."

"Yes, master. They are weak and can easily be defeated."

"Their names."

"One is Sotare and the other is Nomos."

Paraptome let a deep base rumble show his displeasure as it said, "The names tell me much."

"Master, there is more."

The principality looked at Nabal.

"Master, the human has seen me."

Paraptome moved his head slightly and flexed his jaws open enough to show more rotting fangs.

"Master, the human was granted the privilege of seeing our world."

The principality looked down at the man and said nothing. Its red eyes narrowed. Nabal kept its distance and tried to bow even lower. "There is yet more."

This time the principality did not look at Nabal and made no response, but Nabal knew to continue. "Our forces have told us that the pastor of the man's father-in-law is now involved and he will soon seek the aid of his congregation in praying directly against us. He has been called to the battle and he has been granted knowledge that this man is important."

Paraptome did not remove its eyes from Mark as it listened to the prince and then said, "That is why I am here. Our great master sees all."

"We are here to do your bidding." After that Nabal fell silent, lowered its head further, and waited for its master to speak or move. Sotare and Nomos stood, holding their ground. They could see that Paraptome was watching Mark.

Without looking at the prince, it said in a guttural base voice that echoed like mild thunder, "We cannot lose this battle. This man must die. But be careful. He is protected. Do not move against him at this time, lest you be injured. I will need you later.

Stay and keep watch. I am summoned to kill the pastor."

Nabal bowed again in complete submission.

Paraptome had been hovering but now with slow, heavy movements it lifted its hulking mass into the blue sky and hurried off.

Sotare and Nomos watched.

Nomos looked at Mark. "What is this that a principality is summoned?"

Sotare said nothing.

***

After praying in the hospital for a half hour, Pastor Tim ducked out of the room, thankful for not being disturbed. Once at home he talked to his wife, Suzie, about John and Kathy and how he couldn't leave without telling them that Mark was somehow important. He told her that he had an unusually strong sensation to spend more time in prayer, and that he would be getting the congregation involved on Sunday, just a couple of days away. Of course, he didn't tell his wife that he felt his own life was somehow in danger.

"Do you have any idea why Mark is so important?" She asked.

"None. Maybe I'm wrong about it all, but down deep I believe that the Lord is going to use him."

After that their conversation drifted to other things. She fixed him a sandwich and sat at the table with him. Being a pastor was sometimes very stressful, and they would frequently sit at the table and talk about the ministry and its pressures. Tim would use his wife as a sounding board. She knew that he needed to talk to her and she considered it part of her ministry to him to be available. He never disclosed private things about people in the church, but he still needed to talk to her. She was such a good listener, and it helped him.

"I know it's a bit late, but would you mind if I head back to the church to get some books on spiritual warfare? While I'm there, I'd like to spend some time in prayer at the office."

"Of course, dear." She stood up and grabbed the plate and

glass as she headed to the sink. "Do you know how long you might be?"

"I don't think I'll be more than a couple hours, if that's okay with you." He was right behind her.

"Of course it is."

She stopped at the sink and he gently pressed his body to hers as he hugged her around her waist.

"Thanks for listening," he said tenderly.

"Any time."

He kissed the back of her neck and she relaxed under his caress.

She watched him as he headed towards the front door, grabbed his keys, and put on his coat.

"See you later," he said. "Love you."

She responded with a smile. "Love you, too." She watched him until he disappeared. Going back into the kitchen, she sat down at the dinner table and began to pray.

It only took ten minutes to get to the church. Once in the parking lot, Tim turned his car off and sat there thinking about the unusual feeling he had regarding Mark and the accompanying impression that he needed to pray. He glanced over at the marquee, which had Sunday's sermon title: "The Spiritual Battle Between Light and Darkness. Eph. 6." He wondered if this was a coincidence. Had the Almighty orchestrated what he would speak on in preparation for the impending spiritual battle? He got out of the car and headed inside.

Above him on the church steeple was a large cross. It was white, about eight feet tall and could be seen for miles. Pastor Tim didn't think to look at it, but if he had, he would never have known that Paraptome was perched upon one of the horizontal beams.

Pastor Tim unlocked the front door and went inside. He never did like the idea of locking the church, but it was an unfortunate necessity of the times. Paraptome looked through the church roof into the building, watching the pastor until the man got to his office. Then it opened its wings wide, and let itself slowly glide down through the roof and into the church.

Paraptome was in the sanctuary. The principality did not like being there but, unlike the weaker demons, it was able to endure the revulsion. It looked around at the pews and the stained-glass windows. It glanced at the pulpit where there was an open Bible turned to 1 Peter 5. It immediately glanced away, not wanting to see its pages. Then it turned its attention to the pastor's office and looked through the wall. There sat Tim, motionless, resting back in his chair. He was praying. Paraptome growled.

***

Back in the garden, Mark had been waiting patiently for a while.

"Please tell me what's happening," said Mark. "I can't see you. What's going on?"

Sotare heard Mark's voice. "We are still here. We are watching Nabal."

"What is happening?" Mark asked.

"Right now, nothing. A principality was here, but it is gone now."

Mark could feel the cold sting of fear pierce his chest. He glanced over at the house and once again thought about going in to hide.

"Do you have any idea what he wanted?" Mark peered above the treetops.

"We do not use personal pronouns when referring to demonic forces. We always say 'it' since we do not want to give them even the slightest respect."

Mark thought about the words and quickly realized that was exactly how Sotare had referenced demonic forces. He rephrased his question. "Do you have any idea what it wanted?"

By now Sotare felt comfortable enough to turn his back upon Nabal and answer. As he did, he reappeared. "I do not know if I should tell you what I have heard because I'm not entirely sure what it means. But, I believe that you are entitled to know what it said about you."

Mark was suddenly frightened at being the topic of such a

powerful evil force.

"It said that you must die."

He stiffened at the words and straightened up. He opened his eyes just a little wider and swallowed hard.

"It also said that you are protected. This is what I'm confused about and perhaps this explains why they have not attacked us." Sotare looked into Mark's eyes and continued, "The principality also said that the pastor at your father-in-law's church must die. It left to go kill him."

Mark lurched forward. "We have to warn him!" He surprised himself with the words. *So much so fast,* thought Mark. "I can't believe how quickly I have accepted all of this." Then he balled his fists as he dismissed what he had just said. "Shouldn't we warn the pastor?"

"He has already been warned and is praying." Sotare looked at Mark in such a way that Mark paused, expecting something serious. He prepared himself.

"Those given the burden of knowing are the ones called to pray."

Mark raised an eyebrow. He wasn't quite sure what to make of it, but the words rang true. It suddenly occurred to him that he should be praying. But there was a problem.

"I don't know how to pray or who to pray to," said Mark.

"You will soon enough." The angel turned back and looked at Nabal who was still watching. "What do you think, Nomos?"

Nomos turned his attention from Nabal to his fellow angel. "I do not know." Then he looked at Mark as he spoke to Sotare. "This human is not one of ours, yet so much rests on him."

"Yes," said Sotare.

Yes, what? Mark thought.

Nomos continued. "The Almighty must have a great plan for him. I have not seen a prince for many years and now we have seen not only a prince but also, in the same day, a principality."

Sotare said, "I do not know what to think."

"You don't know what to think about what?" asked Mark.

Mark was watching Sotare, who appeared to be staring at nothing, but he knew that Nomos was speaking to him. Sotare turned his attention from the treetop to Mark.

"I don't know what to think about you."

***

John was getting tired as he lay in the hospital bed. He and Kathy had talked about the pastor's cryptic words and had chitchatted for quite a while since then. John had tried once again to convince Kathy that she needed to trust in Jesus. She politely listened and thought of other things while her father spoke, as was her custom. She was not interested. John knew he wasn't getting anywhere and didn't want to push his daughter, so he smiled and squeezed her hand as he changed the subject.

"You know, I don't mind if you take off for a while and go get something to eat. You've been here long enough, and, besides, I'm getting sleepy. Why don't you go to the house and relax? You can come back tomorrow. Besides, the doctor isn't going to release me tonight anyway."

"Yes, I suppose you're right. I *am* getting hungry and I could use a rest. Tell you what. I'll take you up on that. But, if something happens, just call home and I'll come running."

"Sounds like a plan," smiled John lovingly.

She got up from her chair and collected her things before she leaned over the bed and gave him a kiss. "You're looking good," she said. "You'll be back to your old obnoxious self in no time."

"All the more to irritate you."

"I love you, Dad," she smiled.

"I love you, too."

For a few pregnant seconds, Kathy considered the mortality of her father as she looked into his eyes. Then she slipped out of the room and paused just outside the door. The perfectly clean corridor smelled of medicine. She thought about how she loved her father and hated to see him like this. Then after a moment, she gathered herself together, readjusted the purse strap on her shoulder, and headed off.

She had a nagging urge to talk to God about her father. But she dismissed it as a reaction to acute desperation.

Fatigue began to overtake John. His eyelids grew heavier. As he released himself to the call of sleep, just before closing his eyes and drifting into unconsciousness, he thought he saw a large figure in the room. It hovered in that gray area between consciousness and sleep. He wanted to focus on it, but couldn't. Sleep took him.

In the corner of the room, a demon stood, staring at him.

***

Paraptome had been watching the pastor while he was in prayer. As weak and as frail as this mere human was, prayer to the Almighty was a powerful deterrent to attack. It kept the monster at a safe distance. So Paraptome patiently waited in the church as it watched the man through the wall. It regarded him and reflected on eons of memories, many of which involved destroying ministers. They were, after all, only human. The pastor had been praying for twenty minutes. Paraptome continued to linger, growing more impatient. It stared at the pastor through hate-filled eyes, sizing him up, thinking of how to destroy him. The fact that the pastor prayed regularly meant that he was protected spiritually. But still, he was a sinner like all the rest and was not invincible.

The principality considered its favorite option, invoking the aid of people who had given themselves over to evil. There were plenty of them in the city and many could be easily manipulated. Yes, that seemed the best way. Still, this was a pastor and although it was possible to influence someone to take this man's life, the short timeframe needed to accomplish this task would make it very difficult. This left paraptome with one further option, possession, so it could be done quickly.

Find a human possessed by a lesser demon. Yes, that would work. Expel the possessor, take over that person, and bring him to the church. "Yes," said Paraptome aloud. "A Sunday murder in the church."

With that, it opened its wings, lurched forward, and glided through the wall, stopping just inside the pastor's office. It slowly approached the pastor. Paraptome then exhaled its icy breath that mingled with the thick cold that fell from its body.

Pastor Tim felt the wintry chill in the room. He shivered. Then his prayer was violently interrupted as his mind filled with images of mutilated carcasses of dead animals and tortured people. They flooded into his brain, accosting his heart and soul, drawing his attention towards evil. The images were strong. He tensed his muscles and shook his head as he tried to dispel the images.

"No," he said aloud. "No."

Paraptome stepped closer and breathed again.

Tim felt fear scratch across his soul, growing, feeding off the horrible images. He found himself virtually hypnotized by their intensity and horror. Then in an instant he shook his mind free again. "No," he said. "Lord, Jesus, protect me. I need you. Lord Jesus, rebuke the evil one."

Instantly the images left.

Paraptome felt an invisible blow against its chest that set it stumbling backwards out of the room. The creature retreated further after recovering. It growled angrily, showing its fangs as it leaned forward with one step, clenched its clawed hands, and cursed at the pastor. Then it said angrily. "You will die! This Sunday, you will die!" It lifted its wings and in a quick and powerful movement ascended out of the church.

The pastor exhaled slowly. "Please Lord. I'm weak and a sinner. I need you. You are my strength. You are my hope. Even if I am slain, in you I will trust." He prayed intensely, purposefully.

Peace fell upon him. He opened his eyes slowly and looked around the room, half expecting to see something. There was nothing but the cold remnants of the demon's presence. He could see the fog of his own breath. It was obvious and undeniable. He was under demonic attack, and this was only the beginning.

***

Mark looked at Sotare. So much had happened so quickly. It was as if the shadows of the surreal were interfering with reality.

He examined his own sense of wonder as he experienced this new knowledge. It was amazing, yet also disturbing. Just a couple days ago he was depressed, wondering about the death of his son and the purpose of life, and now he found himself talking to an angel, seeing demons, being told how important he was and that his life was threatened. As he reflected, he glanced again at Sotare, who was the proof that there was so much more than the physical world. He had seen this angel appear and disappear several times. He had seen another world. It was undeniable. He knew he would never be the same. He forced his mind to focus.

"I can't believe how I missed all of this," he said to Sotare. "I feel like I have wasted so much of my life pursuing…" he strained to find the right word until he realized what it was. "…pursuing my own desires, my own self interests."

Sotare smiled and nodded.

"I mean, there is so much more to life than what I was able to see."

Mark thought about what he had just said. It was a revelation into his own soul and he didn't like it. He needed a moment to reflect. "Would you mind if I went into the house and got something to drink? I'm thirsty."

For the first time since their encounter Sotare reached out and rested his hand on Mark's shoulder and said, "Yes, of course." After a pause, he continued. "Do you mind if I go with you? I would like a drink of water as well."

Mark raised both eyebrows and after a moment asked, "Are you thirsty, too?"

"No, but I would like a drink nonetheless."

Mark thought about it and realized Sotare's real motive. "You want to stay close to me and protect me?"

"Yes."

"Of course." Mark walked out of the gazebo and headed for the back door. Sotare followed. Nomos watched them both, intermittently glancing at the treetops.

Mark felt a little odd leading an angel into his house. But he did so without letting his mind wander too far from his immediate goal. Focusing on getting a drink was a needed and familiar break from all the new experiences that were flooding his mind. He marveled at his own experience, at merely walking to the back door of his house, such a mundane and common thing, yet somehow it wasn't anymore. He listened to the footsteps of Sotare behind him as they arrived at the back door. Mark pulled it open.

"After you."

"Thank you," said Sotare as he entered. Mark studied Sotare from behind, noticing his broad shoulders. He gently closed the door, headed to the fridge, and pulled out a cold pitcher of water. After retrieving two glasses from the cupboard, he turned to Sotare, "Do you actually want a drink?"

"Yes, please," said Sotare, smiling.

"I didn't know angels got thirsty."

"We don't."

Mark looked at Sotare, "Then why are you having a drink of water?"

"When I am in a human form I feel human experiences such as gravity and wind. I don't get thirsty, but since I am in this form, I thought I would like to take a drink. It is more like experiencing something unusual for me."

Mark realized the irony. A drink of water was nothing extraordinary for him, but Sotare considered it something uncommon enough to want to experience it. On the other hand, seeing the spirit world was commonplace for Sotare, yet extraordinary to Mark.

"Okay," he said as he poured Sotare a glass and handed it to him.

Sotare nodded politely and lifted it to his lips. In one long drink, he emptied it. Mark watched.

"Aaahh," said Sotare, smiling. "That hit the spot."

Mark smiled back at him, amused and impressed by Sotare's use of idiomatic English. He knew the angel was putting on a display for his benefit. Mark poured himself some water and drank it all in one gulp, same as Sotare. "Aaahh," said Mark "You're right. That hits the spot."

Sotare smiled.

Mark took both glasses and set them in the sink. Then he walked over to the refrigerator and returned the pitcher of water. Sotare was watching. Mark turned to him. "I'm curious. Do you have all the human body parts when you're in this form?"

"Well, yes and no. I have real hair and real skin, but this is only a shell, an appearance, and I don't need internal organs to keep me alive."

"Then where did the water go that you just drank?"

"Into my stomach."

"But, you just said you don't have internal organs."

"Actually, what I said was that I did not *need* internal organs to keep me alive. Not needing them and not having them are different. If I drink water, it would be a good idea to have a stomach, so I have one."

"Okay. So, are you telling me that you just manifest a stomach when you need it?"

"Yes."

"The water went into your stomach?"

"Yes."

"Are you going to need to go to the bathroom in a little while?"

"No," replied Sotare with a smile. "There is a lot about us you do not understand."

Mark agreed to that understatement with a grunt of acknowledgement.

"All I need to do is disappear and the water will fall to the ground."

"That is an interesting visual."

"Hold on." Sotare disappeared for a few seconds, and then reappeared.

"What was that about?"

"I went into the garden and got rid of the water."

Mark exhaled slowly, nodding. He chuckled slightly as he smiled. "I can see it now on the phone. Honey? Did you know angels go to the bathroom? Well, not exactly. They just disappear and the water drops to the ground. One just did it in our garden. Oh, and by the way, I've seen some ugly demons, too. But don't worry, hon, I'm feeling fine." Mark was obviously amused by the whole thing.

Sotare was smiling. "Think that'd work for you?"

"Yeah, right."

"Okay, well, let me continue. We are able to take human form. You wouldn't be able to tell the difference between us and humans. But we can see two worlds at once. We can fly and see through walls. Compared with your strength, we are very strong. We also have the ability to learn hundreds of languages, and to learn more in minutes. Our essence is nonmaterial, but because we are able to control material manifestations regarding our own presence, we can take almost any form we want."

With that, Sotare morphed into a smaller man, about a foot shorter, with black hair. His clothes even changed into jeans and a jacket. Then in an instant, he was back to normal.

Mark wasn't quite ready for that and he shook his head briefly. "Whoa. That was a head rush."

Sotare smiled again.

"You know, two things surprise me. First, I find it difficult to believe that I'm here talking to you, watching you do this, and it somehow seems so normal to me now. On the other hand, I can't quite get used to your changing forms and disappearing. It's a bit distracting."

"Would you prefer I not do it?"

"Actually, I kind of like it. In a strange way it is entertaining as well as reassuring. It helps me continue to believe that all this is real. All this angel and demon stuff is still settling in my mind."

"Yes, I can see your point. Some people don't handle it very well, but you're a natural."

Mark smiled. "Thanks." He paused for a moment and reflected. "These demons and angels have always been around us, right? I mean, they've always been around humans, haven't they?"

"Yes, we have. We were made before you and there are millions upon millions of us working in and through the world in both kinds of people."

"Both kinds of people?"

"There are two kinds of people in the world: the slaves and

the free. The slaves are the ones who are ultimately in the service of demonic forces. Some slaves are possessed while others are merely manipulated; most don't realize it. The free are those who are no longer slaves."

Mark was curious. "And which one am I?"

"Let's just say that you are not free."

From feeling good to feeling bad, the quick change was unsettling. Mark took a deep breath and shifted his weight to one leg. After a few seconds of letting Sotare's words sink in, he said. "I don't understand. If I am not free, as you say, then that means I am a slave to demonic forces. But how can that be since you are here with me and I want nothing to do with them?"

"Whom do you serve?" asked Sotare. "There's only God and the devil. Which one do you follow?"

"Well, I like to think that I follow God."

Sotare stared at him. "Were you following God a week ago, or a year ago?"

Mark looked down momentarily. "Okay, I guess it is obvious that I have not really believed in him very much. But, I wasn't out killing anyone or stealing anything."

"This is true, but we do not measure who you follow by what you do *not* do. We measure it by what you *do*."

Mark knew that he hadn't really given much thought to God's existence. He didn't go to church and he dismissed God as an unknowable concept. But now with the stark reality of the spiritual world staring him in the face, he had nowhere to escape, no ignorance to hide behind anymore.

"But, I'm not following the devil. I mean, I don't lie and cheat and steal."

Sotare stared calmly at Mark. "Have you ever stolen anything? Have you ever lied?"

Mark felt his heart sink slightly.

"When you were twelve, you stole two dollars from your best friend's mother. When you were seventeen, you lied to the police officer who stopped you when you were speeding. In college, when you were a junior, you deliberately got hold of the answer sheet to an upcoming test. You obtained it from someone you knew had stolen it. Remember when you got drunk in college with Rebecca and what happened afterwards? Your first job out of college you would take extra-long lunches and not report it on your time sheet."

Mark lowered his head and set his teeth on edge. He tapped them together. "All right. You made your point."

"There's much more. I could go on for hours and work my way up to this week."

"No, that's all right," said Mark as he waved Sotare's suggestion aside. "You're right. I have not followed God. I must be serving the only other option, right?"

"Yes. If there are only two options, and you are not with one, then you are automatically with the other."

"Even if I don't want to be with the other?"

"Your actions reveal your wants and whom you serve."

Mark felt a wave of despair. "This isn't good. It's confusing. You're telling me I'm in league with the devil. This isn't helping me at all."

"Mark, please understand that on a human level you are basically a good man. You've been faithful to your wife. You don't try and hurt anyone, you work hard, and you're honest. But, all of what you are, your heart, mind, soul, and body, has been touched by pride, selfishness, and envy."

"My wife lets me know that often enough." Said Mark as a weak attempt at humor.

"Remember what I said before about truth and how it is independent of what you feel or what you want?"

"Yes."

"This is what truth is. It is absolute. Unfortunately, most people don't want real truth. They want to feel good about themselves. They want the world to fit their needs and preferences so they adopt all sorts of self-deceptions to support or bolster their delusions. They imagine they are divine, or can become divine. They think they are worthy of being with God based on their sincerity. Some people even deny his existence so they can take his place. Mark, truth may not always be pleasant and you may not always want to hear it, but truth is what it is."

"All right." Mark had already dropped his shoulders and, in a defeated tone, said, "Then why are you bothering with me if I'm really serving the devil?"

"Well, you aren't deliberately serving the devil. It's more like you're accidentally doing it."

"That's good to hear," said Mark sarcastically. "But still, why are you here helping me?"

"Because I was told to."

Mark stared silently for a few seconds. "By God?"

"Yes."

Sotare looked intently at Mark.

"You said you wanted answers. I'm giving them to you."

Mark remembered what he'd seen out in the garden and what had happened. He could not deny that there was a reality he had been unaware of, a truth he had closed his mind to before, but now it was profoundly real. He knew he wanted the truth no matter how difficult it might be.

He quickly realized what he needed to say. He nodded to himself before speaking. "All right. I want to know who God is, what I have to do to please him, and what I have to do in order to get through all of this. I suspect that it won't be easy, but that's the way it has to be."

Sotare smiled and once again put his hand on Mark's shoulder. "I'm going to enjoy teaching you."

"I'm not sure if that's good or bad," responded Mark with half a laugh.

"Ultimately, truth is always good, though not always easy." said Sotare. "You will be experiencing more of it later."

Mark noticed the words "experiencing more of it later" and wondered what was in store for him.

Chapter 6

HUGE BLACK WINGS CARRIED Paraptome's dense mass towards the south. From above, the creature peered into two worlds: the spiritual and the material. It could see countless lost souls milling about, aimlessly walking, unaware of the forces around them. They were drawn to this area where demonic forces had a stronghold, blissfully unaware of their own state of slavery as they went around fulfilling their passions.

There were, of course, angels surrounding the dark area but they kept their distance. Paraptome ignored them. It was on a mission to find a human slave and take possession of it in order to quickly carry out its plan.

The principality flew slowly through the drug-infested area of the city and found a dilapidated building where many demons moved among the slaves of darkness. It drew attention. Paraptome hovered and peered down through the walls. It did not know exactly what it was looking for, but it would know when it found it. The creature lessened the beating of its wings slightly so that it could descend closer to the building, but not so close as to be noticed by the forces deep within. The bitter cold that fell from its hulk cascaded downward, away from the building, away from the demons. Paraptome liked surprise.

Demons were scurrying about, manipulating the minds of the lost. Two young men had a demon assigned to each of them. One had its hand in the mind of the older. On a corner, a prostitute leaned against a wall. A demon stood next to her, and fifty feet away another demon manipulated the mind of a passing man. He stopped to talk to the prostitute. Both of them shivered slightly from the unexpected chill that fell to the street from above. But Paraptome was not interested in mere manipulations. It wanted possession.

This particular building had a strong spiritual darkness. There was plenty of activity. Paraptome peered around, looking through the walls. Below, in an alley, walked three young men. Two demons were following them. In an apartment across the street, a man and a woman were arguing. A demon was manipulating the mind of the woman, its claw embedded in her skull. People were milling around on corners, smoking, drinking, and swearing. Among them mingled demons who were constantly whispering into their minds.

Paraptome saw a prince resting on a building across the street. It would know the layout and location of the lost since it was in charge of this territory. It descended. The prince was already aware of its superior's presence and knew not to flee. It waited, afraid; not knowing what would bring a principality to this place.

Paraptome landed on the roof, close enough to be a threat, but not so close to convey imminent danger. "Speak!"

"I am Dreglord, your servant." The prince bowed low. Paraptome studied the creature. The prince had thin, bony hand-like digits that supported long curved claws. One of them had been broken, which meant that it had recently been in a battle.

"Are you the lord of this city?" demanded Paraptome in a deep guttural tone.

"Yes, Master," said Dreglord as it bowed further. "I was told to assist you."

Paraptome noticed that it was shaking.

"I need to find a host in which to dwell."

So unusual was the command that Dreglord momentarily raised its head and looked at Paraptome.

In an instant, it jumped forward, grabbing the prince by the throat, and lifting it off the ground. With a slow, growling rumble it said, "You dare to look at me without my permission?"

Dreglord was choking and, although its face was pulled up close to Paraptome's, it averted its eyes and forced out the words, "My master, you should destroy me for my insult. But if you do, I cannot tell you which host is here."

Paraptome looked at the creature for a few seconds before throwing it to the roof. The prince crawled backwards as it kept its head low, then massaged its bruised neck and choked away the pain. After a couple of seconds, it lowered its head further in submission.

"Your cowardice has saved you," said Paraptome. "You may rise and speak to me, but take care where you look."

The prince stood and faced its master but did not to look any higher than its taloned feet. "Great One, there is a man who is host to one of our kind. We have used him many times. Master, this human is a servant, easily controlled. Even now he is obeying our command." With that, Dreglord pointed downward to a nearby street.

Paraptome turned its head to the left, following Dreglord's skeletal finger. In the alley at the edge of the shadows stood a lonely male figure, silhouetted against the dimly lit walls. It was obvious to Paraptome that the human was possessed. There was coldness and darkness around the man that only angels and demons could see. Paraptome watched.

Walking along the street was an African-American woman and her teenage son. He was carrying two bags of groceries, one in each hand. The man was lying in wait for them. Without facing the demon, Paraptome said, "Explain."

"Master, this human calls himself Leech. He has desired to join a street gang so he can have a steady supply of drugs. We have demanded, through our servants in that gang, that he kill someone in order to be accepted. This man also desires power and influence. He believes he will receive both. This is our test for him."

"He will receive more than he asked for," said Paraptome, studying the man.

The woman and her son continued their walk. She was a single mother, a waitress, and they were going home together after getting off the bus. It wasn't a good neighborhood, especially this late in the evening. They had no choice but to live there because it was all they could afford. Their life had been difficult ever since her husband had abandoned them for another woman and they were forced to fend for themselves. They walked slowly, close together, trying to avoid the menacing shadows and alleys. She appeared to be fatigued, thin, and had sunken eyes. She seemed to labor to walk. Her son was obviously slowing himself to stay with her.

Just as they reached the alley, Leech stepped out of the shadows and out into a dim storefront light that illuminated that part of the sidewalk. The light cast an eerie, menacing shadow across his face.

They stopped and took a couple steps backwards.

Leech raised a gun and pointed it at the woman. She put her hands in front of her and said something about not having money. Leech took a step backward and tensed his arm. "Take our money," she pleaded. Leech watched her eyes. He heart was pounding hard and his hand was shaking. "Take what we have," she said. "Take it all."

Leech's hand stopped shaking. He gritted his teeth.

The boy dropped the groceries and quickly lunged in front of his mother. Leech fired. The crack of noise echoed through the streets in the alley and numerous bystanders turned to look. They saw the boy fall to the ground and a man running across the street, the sounds of his footsteps fading into the blackness.

The mother screamed, sending echoing shards of shrieks among the buildings. Two men, who had just emerged from a bar, had heard the shot and saw Leech running away. Both bolted towards the commotion. She was on the ground on her knees, crying, cradling her son's head as she begged for help.

Two men stopped and stood over her and one of the men

accidentally kicked one of the bags of groceries spilling it across the sidewalk. The other said, "I'll get help," and hurried back into the bar.

The boy lay sprawled on the cold cement. His mother sobbed, calling his name over and over again. "Bobby, Bobby…"

He stared into his mother's eyes, hardly moving, coughing. Then blood began to bubble from between his slightly parted lips. He grabbed his mother's blouse.

"No! No! No!" she screamed, sobbing. She yelled out again, "Somebody please help me! Please help!"

The prostitute and the man were now there.

The woman clutched her son, "Please God, no. Save him. Please God."

Ramah stopped and heard a call. He turned and began to fly quickly.

She sobbed, calling her son's name over and over, "Bobby, Bobby, Bobby." The boy closed his eyes. "No!" She yelled out. "Bobby, please don't die!" Her tears poured down upon his face and she wiped his hair with a bloody hand.

"Bobby! Baby! Mommy's here, baby!"

Bobby looked into his mother's eyes.

"Yes, baby! That's right. Look at me. Look at Momma!"

Ramah arrived and quickly circled twice before landing near them. He then moved to a better vantage point and looked into the boy's eyes. The boy looked back at Ramah.

Paraptome saw the angel but did not care. It opened its wings and descended in a slow arc as it followed Leech through the dark alleys.

The killer was running. Paraptome kept its distance lest it alert the demon inside him.

Leech ducked into an alley, ran across a street, and then down another alley. He stopped to catch his breath and frantically looked around to see if anyone was following him. No one was.

He turned and started running again, then ducked down another alley where he kicked open a door to a building and ran up some stairs, knocking over an old man carrying a garbage bag. He hustled through a hallway, around a corner, and down more stairs, slamming his body against a door and then almost tumbling to the ground as he missed a step before finally emerging into another alley. There was a garbage dumpster there, so he bolted towards it and ducked into its shadow, and lowered himself, sitting on his heels. Leech could hear the hard pulse of his blood in his ears. Between hurried deep breaths he swallowed, then looked back and forth, listening for anyone that might be close by.

He jumped up and sprinted down the alley and across a street and into another building where he ran up two flights of stairs. A cleaning lady was unlocking a door to an office, so he stopped running and casually walked past her as he forced his breathing to be calm. She glanced at him. His hand gripped the gun that he hid in his pocket. She opened the door and quickly entered to avoid him. Leech kept going.

He went down the hallway and climbed through a window to a fire escape where he ascended two flights of stairs before entering another window and another hallway. It was quiet.

He passed two doors and drew out his key, barely able to work it into the lock with his sweaty and trembling hands. Finally, it clicked open and he hurriedly slipped through the door and slammed it shut, sending an echo into the hallway. He was breathing heavily and sweat ran down his face. Backing away from the door, he pulled the gun from his jacket pocket and tossed it on the couch.

He had just shot someone and there was the weapon.

Leech buried his face in his hands, then raked them through his hair. He then went to the other side of the living room and peered out the window. He didn't see anyone. He was too fast and took too many turns to be followed

Leech turned around and slowly walked over to a mirror; for the briefest of moments, he thought he saw another face looking back at him. He blinked hard and examined his reflection. A couple beads of sweat moved down his temple. He went to the kitchen sink and splashed his face with water, then peered outside through the window.

His heart was still racing but his hands were shaking less. He moved to the door and peered through the peephole. Nothing. He listened. Only silence. He waited by the door for a few minutes, then checked again. Still nothing. If anyone knocked on the door he could quickly wipe the gun clean of fingerprints and toss it out the window. He listened. Everything was quiet.

"I did it. I passed the test," he said to himself. "I did it."

He realized the water was still running so he went to the sink and turned it off. In the quiet he heard three things: his own breathing, his heartbeat, and the faint sound of a distant siren. *It is either the police or the paramedics - or both,* he thought.

For a moment a twinge of guilt rose up in his soul, but it was quickly suppressed by the demon.

Leech went to the mirror again. The more he gazed, the more confident he became. He started to feel powerful and self-assured. He looked into his own eyes. They were dark and bloodshot but he felt good. He smiled and savored his freedom and his guilt-free independence from manmade morals.

"I did it," he said with a smile. "I did it."

But what he could not see, looking out at him from within, was Grawl, a demon that had been cultivating Leech for years, finally possessing him three months ago. The man was now a willing slave, although he did not know that he was.

Leech had long ago given himself over to the depravity of his own heart and mind, seeking sensuous pleasures, drugs, and power. He had learned to deny God's existence and felt the false freedom that comes from that lie. Grawl had tweaked his mind and whispered in his ear for years, gradually influencing Leech to move further and further into darkness and now the man had just shot someone and what was better still, he felt no remorse.

Leech looked at his face in the mirror and reflected on how easy it was to shoot the boy. He felt powerful. "Morals are for the weak," he said contemptuously, and then he chuckled. A drop of water fell from his chin. He liked what he was feeling.

"I feel so free," he said with a smile.

He stood still and listened. The sirens outside suddenly stopped and he knew that he was the cause of the turmoil. He knew they were helpless to find him. It was so easy. It had been a clean point-blank shot.

Inside him, Grawl, intertwined in the man's mind, was experiencing every thought and feeling that Leech did. Likewise, Leech could feel the desires of the demon, though only in a dull way. With nothing more than the exertion of its own will Grawl was able to manipulate Leech's thoughts. It spoke through the man, "They are fools."

Leech listened to his words and smiled again. He knew they were all helpless reactionaries who scrambled to pick up the pieces left over by his powerful actions. It felt good to savor the memory of the shooting and realize that he felt no remorse, no guilt. Inside, the demon resided, watching, controlling him, yet making him think that it was he who was in control. The demon liked it. Leech felt good.

Grawl was a dirty greenish, bony demon with growling yellow eyes sunk deep in its skull. It was sinewy, with tendons stretched across thin leathery skin. Its wings were compressed, folded and wrapped around its own chest so as to be fully encased within Leech's body. Talons protruded from its hands, and claws extended from its feet, curling downward. It used them to anchor itself in the body of the man. The demon resided in its human host with its arms stretched down the length of Leech's arms and likewise its own legs stretched down into his legs. Its head was in his head and its mind in his. The demon saw what Leech saw and felt what he felt. What it thought would be his thoughts, and whatever Leech thought, the demon knew. Leech's possession was complete. He was an ignorant slave who believed himself to be free and in control of his own life.

The demon turned its head, walked over to the window, and looked outside. It listened. It could see the faint reflections of red flashing lights off a building three blocks away. It had manifested its will through Leech and relished the idea of accomplishing more through its slave. The demon walked Leech over to the refrigerator and opened the door. Although it was in control, the man needed to eat and it would do no good to the demon to starve him to death. As exceedingly tempting as that prospect was, the demon had worked far too hard and long to gain its possession. No, it was not time kill him yet. There was much more to be done with the man. Besides, there would be plenty of time in the future after his death to feed off his soul. The demon was extremely pleased. It smiled.

Leech smiled as he looked in the refrigerator. He thought he would celebrate with a beer, a reward for his bravery. Besides, it would help to calm his nerves.

***

Traffic wasn't too bad. Kathy maneuvered through the streets, following the blurred memories of previous visits. With only one wrong turn, she managed to find her father's place. After letting herself in, she found the guest room and unpacked her suitcase. She went into the kitchen, intent on making a sandwich. But her father, not the neatest person in the world, had left the place in a condition not quite up to her standards. She smiled. "Same old dad." She cleaned up before finally fixing some food and then headed out to the living room, where she flipped on the TV and propped her feet up on the sofa. She reached over and grabbed the phone to dial home.

***

After drinking their water, Mark had excused himself to use the bathroom upstairs. Sotare settled down at the kitchen table. Mark was a little tired, so he took his time as he carried out the mundane biological functions of life while reviewing the facts concerning Sotare, Nomos, the demons, and everything else he could remember. It was difficult at times to follow Sotare's teaching, to absorb the new truths, and make it all fit. He looked in the bathroom mirror. The man staring back at him had changed. It wasn't visible on the outside but it was incredibly obvious to him.

Sotare was sitting at the kitchen table, waiting patiently, when he heard Mark's footsteps.

"The phone is going to ring," said Sotare. "Your wife is

calling. Are you going to tell her about me?"

Mark glanced at the phone and back at Sotare. With a slightly confused look, he wanted to ask Sotare how he knew this.

"Sometimes we know what's going to happen," responded Sotare preemptively and with a smile.

Mark accepted the explanation without further inquiry. "Well," replied Mark cautiously, trying to go with the flow. "I don't think I'll tell her. After all, she'd probably think I was crazy."

The phone rang. Mark looked at it, then back at Sotare, before picking it up. "Hello?"

"Hi, hon. It's me. I'm calling to see how you're doing and to let you know how Dad is."

"I'm doing very well," said Mark as he looked at Sotare again. "Things are going great here and I'm feeling like a new man." He changed his gaze to the garden, clearly visible through the kitchen window.

"I'm really glad to hear that." Her voice had an obvious tone of relief. "I've been worried about you and, with Dad the way he is, well, it's all been a little stressful."

"I know it hasn't been easy for you, but things will be fine. But trust me. I am doing so much better now." He glanced at Sotare, who was sitting at the table examining a saltshaker. "So many things are beginning to make sense and I have an awful lot to tell you when you get back. So don't worry. I'm doing great."

"Are you sure?" She asked. "I mean, I don't want to upset you by questioning you over and over again but, well, you know, I just want to make sure you're okay."

Mark smiled at the humble and humbling love of his wife. It was comforting as well as reassuring. "Honey, you know that I love you and that I have always been truthful with you. So please believe me when I tell you that I am doing so much better. I'm not in denial. I really needed this time alone to get my head on straight." He looked back at Sotare. *I'm not really alone,* he thought.

"That's great. I'm so happy to hear that. I have to admit, you do sound better."

"See? There you go."

She decided to change the topic. "Well, Dad is doing *much* better. I'm surprised at how quickly he is healing, and he might be home from the hospital tomorrow. At least, that's the rumor. I was hoping it would be today, but it'll probably be tomorrow." She yawned. "Anyway, I'm at his place resting. I fixed myself a sandwich and was going to take a nap. But before I did, I wanted to call you."

"I appreciate that."

She continued. "But, you know something, Dad's pastor came into the hospital room to pray for him and the weirdest thing happened. As he was leaving, he turned around and told us that you were very important. I mean, it was the weirdest thing. There we were, sitting in the hospital, and he came in and prayed for Dad and then, out of the blue, he just starts talking about you. I mean, it was so strange."

Mark looked at Sotare who was nodding at him knowingly. "Yeah, that *is* strange." Mark tried a little humor. "Well, I always thought I was really important."

"You sure are important to me," she said.

"And you are to me, too."

Each paused as they both enjoyed the love they had for one another. Sotare understood this bond even though he was an angel. He sat there and watched Mark and found himself intrigued by the husband-wife relationship that he had seen so many thousands of times throughout his long life. *Marriage is a privilege*, he thought to himself. *It is a wonderful thing, such intimacy and fellowship.* Sotare looked out the window into the garden. He could just see Nomos, who still stood in the same place. Above him, not too far away, Nabal remained vigilant, but still and quiet.

He looked around the kitchen and through the walls into the home as he waited for Mark to finish his conversation. He did not want to appear rude by eavesdropping, so he motioned to Mark that he would be in the garden. Mark nodded and smiled.

Sotare disappeared and was in the garden in a moment. He looked back through the foliage, through the kitchen wall, and kept his eye on his charge.

After fifteen minutes of chitchat, Mark hung up the phone. He turned and looked out the kitchen window. Beyond its glass, among the trees, the flowers, and the bushes were angels and demons.

He was about to walk back into the clutter of newly discovered truths. But he waited, staring out the window. It was a new world out there. He purposefully and slowly took a deep breath. Putting his hands to his face, he rubbed his eyes and leaned against the kitchen counter. He took another deep breath.

"Here we go again," he muttered as he headed towards the back door.

He pulled it open and once again walked the short path through the garden, where Sotare was patiently waiting, seated in the gazebo. Mark sat down opposite him.

"Was talking to your wife helpful?"

"Yes, it was. It is always good to hear from her when she's away."

"I'm glad."

"You mind if I ask you a personal question?"

"Not at all," said Sotare.

"You angels don't have anything like marriage, do you?"

"No, we don't get married. In fact, we are neither male nor female. We are spiritual beings. Gender does not apply to us."

"Then why do you appear as a man?"

"That is our custom from ancient times."

Mark pondered the answer but thought better than to ask for clarification. He decided to change the subject. The remnants of the conversation with Kathy prompted him to ask, "Is my wife in any danger?"

Sotare thought for a moment. "Mark, you must realize that the demonic world does not play fair. It *always* seeks to harm people. And because something very significant is going on here and you are at the center of it, we can conclude that demonic forces will be sent to attack your wife."

Mark felt a spasm of panic. He sat up straight as he leaned forward. "No. Not Kathy." He was anxious and confused; not knowing what else to say, he blurted out, "I have to do something."

"There's nothing you can do for her right now." Sotare said gently.

"Then you, can't you do something?"

"Yes and no."

Mark slumped his shoulders, exasperated. He already knew that many of Sotare's responses were cryptic, but now was not the time for that. He forced himself to be calm. "Please tell me how this works. I want to know if angels will be sent to help her."

"They will be sent because the right people will pray for her."

Mark squinted slightly. "The right people?"

"Yes."

Sotare's one-word answer carried a tone of finality. Mark wasn't in the mood for any more cryptic answers, so he decided not to pursue it. "But if it is true that I am as important as you say, then won't *strong* demons be sent to harm her?"

"We do not know for sure, but that seems reasonable."

This time Mark balled his fists and unconsciously pounded one of them on his thigh. With a strained but controlled tone he asked, "Is there anything we can do?"

"For now, no. Mark, while you were on the phone I spoke with Nomos. It's a little difficult to explain, but he told me that a demon, a strong one, will be dispatched in an attempt to harm your wife."

Mark's heart skipped a beat. He stood up automatically, almost frantic. "No!" he said, "No! I need to go to her!"

"No," said Sotare. "You would not reach her in time."

"What do you mean? Is she in danger now?"

"Yes," responded Sotare softly.

Mark took a step forward. Almost yelling, he said, "Then go do something. Go to her!"

"I am supposed to stay with you."

Mark exhaled angrily. "I don't care about that. You need to protect my wife!"

"I cannot, nor can Nomos."

"Why not?" asked Mark in a definitely raised voice.

"Because our instructions are to remain with you."

"Then I'll go to her and you can come with me." He started walking out of the gazebo.

"No, Mark, don't do that."

He froze in his tracks without turning around.

"Mark, it isn't wise for you to go right now. You're safe here.

"My wife needs me."

"You're wife needs what you need and you're not the one to give it to her."

Mark clenched his fists.

"Besides, you'd not reach her in time."

Mark turned around slowly. He glared at Sotare.

Sotare stood up and approached him. "I know this isn't easy. But this is what it means to have a fuller knowledge of things. The more you know, the more you must trust."

Mark's mind scrambled for options. "Maybe if I call her and warn her." But he realized that wouldn't work. What could he warn her of? Besides, she'd think he was crazy. "Okay, if I call the pastor, my father-in-law's pastor, he might believe me. Would he pray for her? Would that help?"

"Yes, but you won't be able to reach him now. He is in prayer and he will also be under attack very soon."

Mark felt powerless and frustrated. "I hate this. Why tell me all of this if I can't do anything?"

"You asked me. But, don't worry. Your wife will be okay."

Mark glared at Sotare, more than a little irritated. But, he was relieved.

"You're sure she's going to be okay?"

"Yes."

Mark was visibly less tense with Sotare's affirmation. "Why didn't you tell me this sooner?"

"Please sit down." Sotare motioned with his hand towards the seat opposite him.

Without responding Mark pressed on. "Can I drive there and be with her at least?"

"Mark, you are supposed to stay here in the garden. You will be safer here."

"Why here?"

"Because it is a garden."

"And what has that got to do with anything?"

"Because life began in a garden. Your life had its beginning when your father proposed to your mother in a garden. You and Kathy were married in a garden. This garden is where you come for peace and relaxation. It is a place of peace for you."

Mark weighed the words and considered Sotare's calm tone. It was true. The garden was always a place of peaceful refuge. He slowly sat down, reluctantly complying. Sotare sat down, too.

"Wait a minute, if this is such a good place for me, then how come I almost committed suicide here?"

"Peace and safety aren't the same things."

Mark's expression was puzzled.

"Remember, the demon was only able to accomplish what was rooted in your soul. Suicide was already in your own heart. The demon merely helped you and attempted to strengthen your resolve further. Suicide was something that you were already capable of carrying out."

Mark had to admit that he had occasionally entertained the idea of suicide as a way of escaping the turmoil of unanswered questions. The emotional agony had fueled suicidal thoughts but he had dismissed them each time. He knew it was something he would never really do, no matter how bad things got. At least, that is what he had always thought.

Sotare leaned forward slightly and looked into Mark's eyes. "How deeply have you examined your heart?"

Mark tightened his lips and swallowed. "What do you mean?"

"The deeper you look into your own heart, the more honest you must be; otherwise you won't see what is really there. Those who look and find nothing but purity and goodness don't look very deeply. But Mark, you know that down in the depths of your being, there is pride, selfishness, and arrogance. I'm not trying to be insulting, just truthful." Sotare leaned back in his seat and continued.

"I'm not saying these things to hurt you. On the contrary, I'm trying to help you. But, you must know yourself according to truth, not according to your own desires."

Mark contemplated the angel's words, absorbing them. Sotare had touched some deep-rooted chord. But Mark automatically fought back. "I'm not that prideful."

Sotare leaned forward again. With his right hand, he pointed to Mark's chest and said with directness, "Pride and humility are similar. They both hide themselves in the heart and cannot be seen except by others. Saying that you have no pride is proof that you have it. Not knowing that you are humble means that you are." Sotare sat back in the seat, lowering his hand.

Mark knew better than to argue with him. It would be futile. Mark conceded silently by slumping back into his seat.

"I'm glad we agree," said Sotare confidently. "Now, you need to know that we are always fighting against the demonic forces. But our battles are tied to prayers and to the commands of the Almighty."

Mark welcomed the change of topic. "Well, then, I need to pray. If I prayed for her, would angels be sent to protect her?"

"No."

Mark choked out an exasperated breath and closed his eyes for a couple of seconds as he waited for his frustration to subside. "Wait," he said in a clearly irritated tone. "You just told me that prayer would help. Then, when I ask you if my praying would work, you tell me no. So which is it?" Mark gently pounded his leg with the last syllable. "You aren't making any sense. You have to tell me something I can understand. You're confusing the crap out of me."

Mark took a deep breath. "What am I missing? What is it that I need? Why do you keep telling me I'm not of God and yet here you are sent from God to speak to me? Why do you tell me that prayer works, but *my* prayers won't? All this makes no sense."

Mark's anger got the best of him. "How do I know you're not a demon sent here to deceive me?"

"That is a fair question," Sotare responded calmly with a nod. "I suppose there is no real way to prove it to you. For all you know, I could be a demon imitating something good. That happens all the time without people knowing it. How *would* you know?"

Mark said nothing. The possibility struck him hard, so he took a moment to seriously reflect on it. But then he thought *What if it was all a trick? What if Sotare could read his mind and was manipulating him?* He sat there dejected, confused, and unsure. How would he know what the truth was? How would he know?

"You're beginning to doubt, aren't you?" asked Sotare.

Mark's answer was a simple blank look.

"I understand. You have to be able to find the truth on your own. But the problem is, would you recognize it if you saw it?"

"I suppose that is the million-dollar question, isn't it?"

"Yes, it is. Discovering absolute truth is perhaps the most important issue you will ever undertake. So let's start with that. Let's start with truth. What is truth?"

Mark raised his eyebrows. He didn't feel like getting into a philosophical discussion, especially now. Sotare could see it, but he persisted.

"Of all that you've experienced lately, tell me what you believe to be true."

Mark thought about the idea that Sotare might be a demonic force in disguise. He reviewed the facts quickly. He had watched him appear and disappear. He had seen him in the spiritual realm as an angel with wings and he had certainly seen hideous creatures on top of the trees. Sotare was a bit cryptic but had also told him truths, the kind that Mark didn't want to hear but knew were correct. But, then again, if demonic forces were as powerful as they seem to have been, they were also probably highly intelligent. This meant it was possible that he was being deceived. On the other hand, all he had to work with was what he had seen, what he had experienced, and how clearly he could analyze it all. But he knew one thing for sure. He wanted the truth, no matter what it was.

"Well," Mark finally began to answer. "I would say that what is true is that you are here and that you are a spiritual being. You claim to be an angel and so far I have no real reason to doubt that, though I'm beginning to. It is also true that you're confusing me. I saw Nabal, and it scared the crap out of me. But, even though I can't deny it, I know that just because something looks good, it doesn't mean it *is* good and I suppose that just because something looks bad, it doesn't mean it is automatically bad."

"Very true." Sotare crossed his legs and shifted topics. "Do you believe there is a God?"

"Yes," responded Mark. "Yes, I definitely believe there's a God now."

"And do you believe that God is greater than you?"

"Yes, of course."

"Good. You're a human, right?"

"Yes."

"Does your nature change? Do you stop being human?"

"I will stop being a man when I die."

"Notice that I said 'human', not 'man.' The reason is that man and woman deal with gender. I want to talk about human nature of which males and females are a part. Okay?"

"Alright, no problem."

"If you lost your arms and legs would you still be human?"

"Well yes, I suppose."

"And if you lost your eyes and ears, would you still be human?"

"Yes."

"And if you were also in a coma, would you still be human?"

Mark thought for a moment. "Yes, I guess so."

"Then being human is more than the physical. It is more about nature and essence, an essence that is transmitted to you from your parents at your conception. This nature doesn't disappear with death. You continue on."

"So you're talking about life after death."

"Yes. Though the physical part of you will eventually die, the spiritual part, that part that makes you human, will continue."

Mark looked quizzically at Sotare and thought of pursuing that tangent, but he didn't give him a chance. "Does God die?" asked Sotare.

"I suppose not."

"Do you think God's nature changes? Do you think that he stops being God or somehow his nature varies?"

"What if it is possible for God to have a nature that changes?" asked Mark.

"If that were the case, then that would be God's nature to change, which would mean his nature wasn't really changing."

Mark thought for a moment. "Okay, I can see that. But, the nature of a piece of wood is changed when it is burned up. It stops being wood. What about that?"

"Within the nature of wood is its ability to be burned up and stop being wood. In that sense, different objects can be altered by an outside force—in this case, fire."

Mark was still exasperated and paused for a moment before saying with a mocking chuckle, "I just realized that I'm talking philosophy with an angel."

"Philosophy is, to an extent, a tool of logic that, if used properly, can help find truth. I'm glad you're enjoying it."

"Well, 'enjoy' isn't a word I would use to exactly describe this. I'd rather be helping Kathy."

Mark was, of course, still concerned about her and his comment registered his unease. But, he knew he had to wait, to be patient and continue on in this student-teacher relationship, at least for now.

Sotare nodded. "I understand. But, can we continue?"

Mark just looked at Sotare.

"God is not like a piece of wood. He can't be burned up. He can't have an outside force alter his existence. Otherwise, he wouldn't be God."

"Okay, I'm following you."

"Good. Would you agree with me that if God is unchangeable, then it means his nature is absolute?"

"Yes, that makes sense."

"Would you also agree that God has no defect in him? That he is perfect?"

Mark thought for only a moment before conceding. "Yes. I don't have a problem with that, at least conceptually."

"Okay, that's fine. Would you also agree that the attributes of something reflect what that something is?"

Mark had to concentrate in order to follow and the pause

let Sotare know to explain a little further. He pointed to Mark's right at a small bush nearby. "That bush has a nature and characteristics. It is a plant. It can convert sunlight into food. Therefore, it grows." Sotare waved a hand theatrically towards the sky. "The stars are immense and intensely hot; therefore, they give off light as an attribute of their nature, right?"

"Yes, I'm following you."

"If the nature of God is that he is absolute, then it follows that his attributes are also absolute. Since God can think and know and speak, then his thinking, his knowledge, and his speech are all absolute. If they are perfect and complete, they are true because they cannot contain error, as they represent God's absolute perfection. After all, truth is not self-contradictory." He paused once more, awaiting Mark's response.

After a few seconds, Mark nodded.

Sotare continued. "Then, in a way, isn't absolute truth itself a reflection of God's nature, since both truth and God are absolute?"

Mark thought about it and offered a tentative, "That would seem to make sense."

"And if truth is a reflection of God's nature then, as I just said, truth could never be self-contradictory because if something is self-contradictory, it cannot be true. Do you agree?"

Mark nodded his head slightly. "Yes, I agree."

"If truth cannot be self-contradictory, then truth has an absolute quality about it. But, if someone says that truth is relative or that truth depends on what you believe or think about reality, then that would be wrong because it would mean that truth is not absolute."

"You mean like when someone says that what is true for you is not true for me?"

"Kind of. It can be true that you like one flavor over another where someone's tastes would differ from yours. In that case, what is true for you about a flavor might not be true for another person. But that isn't what we are talking about. You see, if people believe that truth is relative, that truth as it relates to reality and to God is not absolute, but depends on your perception or wants, then they cannot find God, can they?"

Mark shook his head slowly. "I guess not."

"Therefore, to find God you must first believe in absolute truth, right?"

"Yeah, I suppose so."

"Also, if you find truth, absolute, pure truth, won't you to some degree be finding something that reflects God's existence?"

Sotare paused again to allow Mark to absorb the words.

Mark was squinting slightly, focusing. He took a deep breath and said, "The words 'head-rush' come to mind about now."

Sotare smiled. "I know it is a bit heavy."

Mark nodded and looked out into the garden passed Sotare. He was obviously considering what the angel had been saying. After a few seconds, Mark asked, "Alright, I guess then we should we try and find what truth is, shouldn't we?"

"Very good," said Sotare with a smile. "Let me work with that. Truth is a statement that agrees with reality. For example, if I tell you that I am here, I am making a statement that is true. If I say that we are in a garden, then that is also true. If I say we are not in a garden, then that is false. Therefore, truth is a statement or set of statements that properly reflect reality. But, truth is different than reality. Truth represents reality. A truth is a statement *about* reality."

Mark nodded. "Okay. I'm following you."

"But, the thing I want you to realize is that truth also requires a mind. It can't exist without a mind."

Sotare shifted in his seat as he studied Mark's expression. "Are you following me?"

Mark tilted his head and asked, "How does truth require a mind?"

"Simple. Truths are statements about reality like when I said that we were both sitting here. Statements are sentences, communications. Such communications require minds."

"Okay, I see what you're saying."

Sotare leaned forward. "But wait, there's more."

Mark smiled courteously.

"Think about this. It is always true that 2 + 2 = 4 which,

incidentally, is a conceptual truth. Also, it is always true that something is what it is. It is always true that something cannot be both true and false at the same time and in the same way. Do you agree?"

"Yes, that makes sense."

"These, among other absolutes, are universal truths. They are always true and are not dependent on people's opinions or preferences for their validity otherwise these truths would change and wouldn't be universal or absolute. Likewise, their truth is not dependent on when or where you are. 2 + 2 = 4 doesn't become true at a certain time when before it wasn't. 2 + 2 = 4 isn't true if you're on a mountain but not in a valley. It is absolute. Absolutes truths that relate to reality are universal truths. But, if there are universal truths, doesn't it follow that there is a universal mind since each truth statement only exists if a mind exists?"

Mark sat up just a little straighter. "Whoa. That was good. I never thought of that."

"You see Mark, I'm trying to show you that the very basis for truth, universal truths, the truths that support logical thought, even universal moral truths, require a universal mind. That mind is God. He is the necessary and foundational requirement for the nature of all universal and absolute truth."

Mark sat back in his seat and let the words sink in. "Deep stuff. I see you've been thinking about this for a while."

"For millennia," said Sotare with a smile. "I just wanted to reach you where you were at. I know that as an engineer you work with truth in physics, mechanics, and mathematics. You use logic a great deal and you depend on truths being there so you can build on them. I wanted to show you that without knowing it, you were depending on God, but you were never acknowledging him."

Mark raised his eyebrows at the realization. "I'll admit I've never thought of that before." He stared out into the garden as he contemplated the conversation. The foliage made him remember why he was there, which brought his mind back to Jacob's death, to pain, and finally to suffering. He looked at Sotare.

"What about suffering? What if it is absolutely true that

someone is dying of cancer? Does that mean that God is somehow in the cancer, bringing it about?"

"No. It means that you know the truth that someone is dying of cancer. It means that things such as that unfortunate reality can be absolutely known."

Mark was busily sorting through the sequence of logical concepts. It was taxing, but he was able to follow. A leaf fell behind Sotare. Mark focused on it, watching its rhythmic swaying motion towards the ground. Then another fell and another. He watched them until they had finished their descent then turned his attention back to the discussion.

"And what does all of this lead us to?"

"Why, Mark, it leads us to truth and to God." Sotare smiled slightly and sat back.

Mark slumped his shoulders a bit. "You're not getting off that easily. You just said before that God is unchangeable and that whatever he tells us is always true or absolute, or something like that."

"Yes."

"Okay. Then where does God speak to us, so that we might know his truth?"

Sotare narrowed his eyes. "That is a great question, Mark. If God encompasses the universe, then how would you, a mere man, recognize his words? What words would he use? What language would he speak? What form would he take? He is so magnificent that if he were to manifest even a sliver of his greatness, you would be destroyed."

"Then God is unknowable."

"That would seem to make sense, but the truth is, he is knowable. For example, we can know that he exists and that he is true and absolute."

Mark realized he was in a battle of wits with Sotare, and he felt very inadequate. But Mark wasn't dumb, and he also knew that Sotare was engaging him for a reason. He suspected that ultimately this dialogue would lead to more answers.

"Okay, God is knowable, at least to some degree. But that still does not answer the question I asked. Where does God speak to us so that we might know his truth?"

"Let me answer by asking you something. Does it seem logical to you that if God is going to communicate to us, he would have to lower himself to our level to do so?"

"Okay, that makes sense. So, did he speak out of heaven or inspire someone or some people with his words?"

"More or less. But, in actuality, he did something even greater than inspiring someone and speaking *out* of heaven. He came *from* heaven." Sotare stopped and stared straight into Mark's eyes. "He did something more profound, more absolute."

Mark returned Sotare's gaze, knowing that he wanted him to think. Sotare sat silently, waiting. Then Mark finally said, "So, are you saying that he became one of us?"

"Yes."

It was Mark's turn to stare into Sotare's eyes. "How is that possible?"

Sotare took a breath. "It is possible because God is God. All he would have to do is voluntarily limit himself to a human level. He would be, so to speak, both God and man at the same time."

Mark tightened his lips, cocked his head, and said. "Then who is he?"

"Don't you know?"

Mark thought for a moment more as he tried to think about who or what might be the conclusion of Sotare's leading questions. "I would guess that God has manifested himself in many forms and in many ways. I would say that he is found in every religion since so many religions point to God."

"What if those various religions contradict each other about who God is? Can they all be true?"

"I suppose not, not totally, maybe partially. But don't they all seek the one true God?"

"No."

Mark raised both eyebrows. "They don't?"

"No."

"People in these religions are very sincere. Doesn't that count for something?"

"No."

"What do you mean, no? Are you telling me that millions upon millions of sincere seekers of God are all wrong?"

"No, not all. But being sincere doesn't make you okay with God."

Mark shook his head. "That's ridiculous. I can't accept that."

"That is correct, you can't."

Mark dropped his shoulders, frustrated yet again. "Wait, that isn't fair. There are just too many people all over the world who are sincerely trying to find God. You can't possibly tell me that because they don't have the exact right truth, or are born in a place where they can't know the *right truth,* that they're all somehow wrong and going to hell."

"Why can't I tell you that?"

"Wait, is that what you're saying?"

"Not exactly. But Mark, remember; do not subject truth to your feelings. You *must* be willing to accept the fact that what you want and what you desire have no bearing on what is true, no matter how much you don't like it."

"Sorry, Sotare, but I just can't accept the idea that God rejects people even if they are sincerely trying to find him."

"Then why not walk away? You can close your ears. You can stop listening if you don't like what is being said. It's your choice."

"I'm glad to know I have a choice. But still, this is about what is fair. It is wrong to condemn sincere people for believing a few things wrong. That isn't right."

"Who said?"

"Well, me. It just isn't right."

"And who are you to say what is and isn't right?"

"Come on, this is silly. It's common sense."

"It is?"

"Would you stop that? Why don't you talk to me instead of answering everything with a question?"

"All right, then. Tell me about what is fair."

Mark settled down for a bit, finally feeling he was getting the upper hand, if only a little. "Sincere people shouldn't be condemned for innocently believing in something false if they are really trying to find the truth. It just isn't right to say otherwise."

"Would you say that sincerity lies within a person's heart?"

"Yes," replied Mark, cautiously already suspecting a trap.

"Then if you are appealing to sincerity, are you not appealing to what is in you, to something good in you, to something worthy in you, that somehow merits favor with God?"

"Well, yes. I mean, that is only fair."

"Then, Mark, you are really being prideful because you are appealing to self-value, to self-worth, to something good in you in order to merit favor with the Almighty. That is pride, is it not?"

Mark found himself trapped. It was an unpleasant experience. But it didn't stop him from resisting.

"No, pride isn't the same thing as sincerity."

"I didn't say it was. But when you appeal to something in yourself that you think is of value so as to be worthy enough before God to be accepted by him, then that *is* pride because you're appealing to the goodness in yourself as a reason that God should accept you. That, Mark, is exactly what pride is."

Mark shook his head slowly without saying anything. Sotare continued.

"*Your* idea of what is fair and what *is* fair according to God are two different things. You are appealing to what is in a person as a standard to judge what God should and shouldn't do. But that is wrong. God judges all people by the same standard: his own holy, perfect standard. That is why everyone falls short, no matter how sincere they claim to be."

"Then God needs to not have such a strict and impossible standard."

"I see. So you want God to judge people by a standard that is less than perfect?"

Mark shook his head in disagreement. "Well, no, but they believe in God. Isn't that enough?"

"No. The devil believes in God, too. It doesn't help him any."

Mark stopped. Sotare watched him.

"But…" Mark paused. "But they believe in God."

"Which God?"

"The only God."

"And who is that?"

Mark shook his head. "This is a bunch of crap. Look, people have faith in God, whichever God they believe in. That is good enough."

"Faith is only as good as who you put it in. If you put faith in something false, then it is the same as no faith at all. So if people put their trust, their faith in false gods then it is the same has having no faith at all."

"I just can't accept that."

Sotare smiled.

"Why are you smiling?"

"Because you're right. You *can't* accept it. You don't want to. It isn't an issue of what is right. It's an issue of what you like and don't like."

Mark exhaled strongly in frustration as he rubbed the palms of his hands on his thighs. "If it weren't for you being an angel and everything I've seen, I'd just bail on this whole conversation and walk away."

"Exactly. You'd run. You don't like the truth, so you would want to find something else more comfortable and you'd leave."

Mark's face adopted a straight, bland expression. "You're making me angry."

"Good."

"Good?"

"Yes, good. Absolute truth does that to people."

Mark shook his head and looked at the ground. He clenched his jaw for a moment and released it. Sotare continued. "Be a man and face the truth whether you like it or not."

Mark looked up at him straight in the eye. "You're trying to make me angry, why?"

"I'm trying to make you see. Sometimes it means we have to be strong not only to deliver truth, but to accept it."

"Well, you're pissing me off."

"Would you prefer I tell you what you want to hear so you feel better about yourself and everyone else? Maybe we can go into the house and sit in a comfortable chair and I can tell you how wonderful you are."

Mark let out a single long exhalation and balled his hands

into fists. He looked out of the gazebo at some bushes, anything to focus his mind away from the immediate topic. He shook his head again and said, "You're being rude."

"It is not my intention to be rude. But Mark, I perceive you as a strong man who desires the facts even if it is uncomfortable. This is how you do your engineering work and this is why you're good at it. You don't hide from the tough problems. You don't ignore them and hope they go away. You face them. You grumble a little, but you tackle them and solve them. You can't do that by ignoring what isn't easy. And, as you already know, you can't do that with finding real truth either."

By now Mark was staring intently at Sotare. The angel was obviously right and Mark knew it. He *did* tackle problems head on. He *did* enjoy the challenge. Why should he be any different here?

"You're a good engineer because you're strong enough to face difficulties and not be undone by them."

Sotare's affirming words had calmed Mark a bit. Sotare could see that he was reaching him. "There is much more to this than you know, Mark."

"Apparently," said Mark cynically.

Sotare smiled.

"You're good at frustrating me. You keep giving me cryptic answers and not telling me the whole truth. This is difficult and I don't like it."

"I don't blame you for being frustrated. But, you'll understand later."

"I don't care for being kept in the dark." He thought for a moment about everything that had happened in the past couple of days and he knew that there was a great deal he needed to learn. He pondered the idea of Sotare being a demonic deception, but it just didn't fit. He reasoned that if he were being tricked, he would be told things that he liked rather than disliked. Then he had an idea.

"Are you being so blunt with me in order to convince me that you are from God?"

"Partly, and also because you're a man."

"What?"

"Be a man, Mark. Face the truth; embrace it. Leave childish things behind. Don't seek to be coddled and babied with easy words and comfortable feelings. Those things aren't wrong in themselves, but if that is how you carry yourself through life, then you'll never know the real truth that surrounds you. You'll only find what you want to find, what is comfortable, and what tickles your ears. That is how people abide in self deception, by not facing the difficult truths around them."

"Does truth have to be so hard?"

"No, Mark. It is people who are difficult. Truth is just that, truth. It corresponds to reality. But as you already know, sometimes difficulties are necessary so you might learn greater truths."

Mark pinched his lips together and exhaled forcefully through his nostrils. He looked out at the bushes again.

"All right," said Mark carefully, not knowing if he would get a straight answer, "Tell me, which religion is true?"

Sotare smiled, "Well, I guess you could say that none of them are."

***

Towards the edge of The Cavern a terror-demon sat gnawing on a rotting tangled carcass. Its strong arms moved under its wings, which had been brought around to conceal the carcass from others. Another creature approached, obviously looking for an opportunity to steal the gruesome remains. The first growled threateningly at the approaching challenger and arched its back, sending the intruder into the shadows. Resuming its meal, it gnawed on some small bones, crushing them in its powerful jaws. It snapped another and was about to swallow the fragments when, quite unexpectedly, a rift in space opened next to it. In a single motion, it jumped through. The rip closed.

Above John's house, the fabric of space twisted open and the creature fell into the sky. It opened its wings and gaining its bearings, it hovered as it surveyed the area, looking for angels.

Seeing none, it glided down through the roof and into the kitchen to rest on the floor. It quickly assessed its environment and tuned in to the sounds coming from the living room. In a kind of smooth, swinging motion it walked towards the living room; in so doing, its left side passed through the refrigerator and then the edge of the doorjamb. Stopping just beyond it, the demon stared at Kathy with black, empty eyes.

She had settled into watching television and was flipping through the channels. A cold chill brushed across her face and she automatically tucked the comforter tighter around her chin. She glanced at the thermostat and thought about turning it up. She was comfortable, but the room was definitely colder.

She threw the comforter aside, marched to the thermostat, and turned the gauge up a few degrees. Before she returned to the couch, she retrieved another blanket from a nearby closet. The extra layer helped. But the room grew colder still.

The demon had short arms that ended in bony hands and long talons. Its ribcage was easily visible through the thin skin of its chest, and small gaping holes resembling unhealed wounds revealed rotting internal tissues. Its face was a distorted deep-red mass of translucent skin draped over protruding bones. Eye sockets were dark and deeply set. Two small horns angled up in the top of its skull and a gash revealed what looked like decomposed brain matter. From its mouth, long sharp teeth forced its lips apart, allowing thick green drool to drip from its chin. It let its wings drag on the floor as it drew closer to examine the woman. It positioned itself between her and the television so that as Kathy watched the TV she was looking directly into its eyes. The creature stared back and moved closer. Kathy shifted under the blanket, getting more comfortable. The demon shifted as well, causing their eyes to meet again. It tilted its head slightly to the left and then straightened.

"I am Crasak. You belong to me."

Kathy shivered once, although she wasn't cold. She frowned and, without thinking, glanced towards the front door to make sure it was locked. She thought about the chill in the room, then about her father in the hospital, and the encounter with the pastor. She looked around some more, feeling a little anxious.

It feels like someone is watching me, she thought.

She looked around again and returned her attention to the TV.

"Get a hold of yourself, Kathy." she said aloud. The sound of her own voice comforted her, but the reassurance was fleeting. The feeling that she was being watched grew stronger. The air felt wrong. She flipped through the channels in an attempt to distract herself. The demon crept closer and extended its clawed hand, pointing a single talon at her forehead.

"Maggots in your clothes," spoke the creature. "Rats at your feet."

Kathy shifted on the couch. She was trying to focus on a news program, but the odd sensation wouldn't go away. She muted the TV, glancing around at the windows. They were all covered by drapes. It was dark outside, which didn't help.

"He is watching you. He wants to get in the house."

Is there a prowler out there? she wondered.

She looked over her shoulder to the kitchen and down the hall, flipping through more channels, paying no attention to what was on the set. The only lights on were in the living room and kitchen. It didn't help that she was alone. She thought of Mark and wished he were there.

Darn that cold.

She kicked the covers off and returned to the thermostat which was set to 76 degrees. She figured it would take a little while before the place warmed up. She thought about brewing a cup of hot coffee. That would help. She headed into the kitchen to the cupboard and remembered that next to the fridge was the knife drawer. Forgetting the coffee she opened the knife drawer. Inside were three stainless steel blades with wooden handles. The beefiest was around ten inches long and two inches wide. It looked like a long, flat thin mirror with a razor's edge. She reached down and fingered the handle as she withdrew it from under the other knives, listening to the sound of metal sliding on metal. Its weight and balance felt good.

Crasak had shadowed her closely. "Vomit, death, hate,

murder." It whispered, close to her ear.

A strong, uneasy feeling leapt on her. She focused on it as she tensed her muscles. Was it the lack of sleep and worries over her husband and father that had combined to make her feel so bad? Or, was there really something wrong?

She turned towards the living room.

"I will kill you," said Crasak slowly.

Her heart began to pound hard.

Is someone here? She thought.

She carefully moved forward setting each step down on the kitchen tile as quietly as possible. The light from the TV flickered silently on the walls ahead of her. The knife was pointed forward, gripped with both hands.

She looked down the dark hall and pointed the knife in that direction. Another quiet step, then another. She listened as carefully as she could to anything that might clue her in on the presence of someone else. Was her mind playing tricks on her? She didn't know. The uneasiness grew.

She switched on the hall light and the shadows disappeared. There was a bathroom and two bedrooms to be checked. Then, of course, she had to look in the garage. That would be last.

Crasak followed her.

She entered the hallway. "This is ridiculous," she whispered to herself as she stopped and looked at the doors.

The creature spoke loudly into her ear, "Die in hell." She turned around quickly, sudden anxiety stealing her breath. Did she hear something or was that her imagination?

It smiled and walked through her to the other side. She felt a brief twinge of nausea. It spoke again. "He sees you." She twisted around, jerking the knife in front of her. *What was that?* She stood motionless, not breathing, just listening. Crasak smiled again.

Kathy stood there for a full minute, checking back and forth, looking behind her into the living room, then back into the hall. Did she really hear something or was it the house creaking? She forced herself to take another step, then another. On the right was a bathroom door. It was slightly ajar, so she slowly pushed it open with her foot. The hall light flooded the room, and she was greeted by an empty stillness. At the far end of the bathroom, the shower curtain was pulled to the side. She was relieved she wouldn't have to look behind it.

She continued down the hallway and slowly walked a few feet further to the guest bedroom, her room. The door was open, just as she had left it. She pushed it open and flicked on the light. Empty. She went in and pulled the closet door to one side. Nothing there, either. She bent down and lowered her head to look under the bed. The room was empty.

Kathy went back into the hall and approached her father's room. The door was closed. She aimed the knife at it and with her left hand turned the knob and pushed it open. Upon turning on the light, she saw a nice, neat room. The bed was made, and there were some slippers neatly placed side by side on the floor. On the dresser were some coins and a Bible. On the other side of the room was a closet. She opened the door and turned the light on. Empty. Relieved, she lowered the knife.

"I'm losing it big time," she mumbled to herself.

She turned around and walked back into the hallway, still a bit nervous, she again noticed the chilling air. Just as she was about to enter the living room, Crasak opened his wings and flapped once.

What was that? Did something move near the couch? Instantly raising her knife, she stopped dead in her tracks. She could see the whole living room.

Did she see a shadow or not? Was it her mind playing tricks on her again? She bit her lip as she contemplated the options. Then she remembered the garage.

She headed out through the kitchen, knife in hand, breathing shallowly. She stopped in front of the garage door. Would there be someone just inside waiting to attack her? She felt the thump of each heartbeat as she slowly inched her way forward, silently putting one foot in front of the other. Finally, she grabbed the knob, gulped, and threw the door open while hurriedly turning on the light. The garage, too, contained no surprises. Her father's car was in the driveway outside, so she had a complete and unobstructed view of everything in the garage. With a sigh of relief, she lowered the knife, closed and locked the door, then headed back into the kitchen.

It had been a nerve-wracking few minutes and she was glad it was over with.

She slid the knife drawer open and slipped the knife into the drawer. Everything seemed normal, but she still had an uneasy feeling.

"I think I need a good night's sleep."

She walked into the living room to the couch, and with one final look, she scanned the room. The phone was sitting on the end table and she imagined calling 911 if necessary. But everything was fine. She turned up the TV sound, plopped down onto the cushions, and put her feet on the coffee table.

The demon had followed her through the home; now it again positioned itself in front of her. She looked around the living room once more for good measure.

"This is ridiculous," she said aloud. The chill was still in the air so she glanced at the thermostat again and then around the room. Everything seemed to be okay. She turned her attention to the TV.

The demon was right in front of her, two feet away. It moved closer, raising its clawed hand as it pointed a single bony finger at her forehead. It tilted its head to the left, smiling slightly as it pushed its sinewy hand forward through the air towards her. But it stopped. Changing its mind, it withdrew the claw.

Kathy still felt uneasy. The air was cool and oddly damp. "Get a grip on yourself, Kathy," she said as she tucked the blanket under her chin again, forcing herself to focus on the TV.

The demon kneeled in front of her and stared into her eyes. It opened its mouth and what looked like a small black snake whipped around its fangs. But it was no snake. It was its tongue.

Crasak leaned forward some more.

Kathy shifted in her seat.

Then, with its face almost touching Kathy's, it slowly extended its tongue forward. It whipped slightly back and forth. But, the closer it got to Kathy's mouth, the less it moved, until it entered her mouth.

Kathy frowned.

Crasak raised the claw on its skeletal left hand and moved it forward until it was just in front of her skull. The demon extended its tongue until it was moving down her throat.

Kathy rubbed her stomach.

Then, Crasak pushed forward a little more until its talon pierced her skull, just above her eyes. As if physically sensing the intrusion, Kathy rubbed the spot on her forehead absentmindedly.

The demon slowly withdrew its tongue, opened its mouth, and breathed into hers, synchronizing each of its exhalations with her inhalations. It moved its claw deeper, looking for a spot to tweak, hoping to find a place of fear. With each movement, Kathy found her mind effortlessly wandering from thought to thought. They were random, unrelated memories that darted in and out of the periphery of her consciousness. They appeared and disappeared, one after another as the demon searched through her mind, looking, feeling, exploring.

At first she was curious about the recollections that seemed to come out of nowhere, but Crasak diverted her attention by touching that part of the brain that released endorphins. It worked. She was distracted by the soft pleasure that seemed to push away her uneasiness.

She welcomed the relief.

The demon was careful not to be too bold. It did not want to cause Kathy to become curious about what was happening to her, so it moved slowly, periodically touching the pleasure center as it continued to search.

Then it found something. When Kathy was seven, she was riding in the car with her parents on a summer day. The police were up ahead and her dad had followed a detour around an accident. But John was late for an appointment and, because he knew the area pretty well, he tried to take what he thought was a shortcut. Unfortunately, it brought then back upon the gruesome accident, from a different vantage point. Kathy found herself staring at the mangled and burned body of a man who had died in the inferno of a car wreck. Kathy screamed and her mother quickly tried to cover her eyes, but it was too late.

It took five minutes for her parents to stop her hysteria. The next few nights were filled with nightmares of burning bodies and the dreams were accompanied by her screams. She ended up sleeping with her parents and for five weeks she could hardly stand to be out of their sight. They were naturally concerned and after a few days they took her to a child psychiatrist, who prescribed some mild sedatives and told them to stay close and to comfort her as much as possible. He said it would take a few weeks for the trauma to subside and that she should eventually recover. He was right. After a couple of months, the memory faded, along with the nightmares, and she finally returned to her own bed.

It was a gut-wrenching ordeal for John, who had scolded himself repeatedly for what had happened. It was one of those unfortunate regrets that parents sometimes can't avoid but wish they could take back. It took him many months before he was finally able to forgive himself. He tried never to think about it again.

For a young child like Kathy, the whole incident was very confusing and painful. As an adult, she reflected upon the unpleasant memory each time she saw an accident or heard about one. Her childhood trauma didn't terrorize her anymore but it wasn't completely gone, either. She had simply stripped it of its ugliness, leaving only a shell of emotionally bare facts to review on occasion. Still, she knew better than to dwell on it too long.

The demon had what it needed, but it kept probing just a bit more until it found something else: an abortion. It happened while in college. Crasak smiled. Perhaps it could use this to stir up guilt.

It probed further into that time period. There were memories of cheating on a test, flirting, cooking, movies, nothing of real value.

There! In college Kathy had a girlfriend who was into white magic and, as a result, Kathy had also dabbled in drugs and séances. This open door to the occult was just what Crasak needed. It looked at the woman's chest and could see her breathing was deep and slightly fast. Then it listened to her heartbeat. It was a little loud. The creature smiled again and with its other hand took a talon and slowly forced it into her mind.

She felt nothing.

It tweaked the memory of the abortion to see her reaction. Her heart pounded harder and she tensed slightly. Kathy still felt guilt over it, especially after she'd given birth to Jacob. Crasak thought there might be more emotion hidden within her about this. As the memories surfaced, Kathy tried to push them away. The inner struggle had already begun.

It would serve Crasak well.

The nightly news on the TV was conveniently showing images of earthquake-recovery efforts in a Third World country. They were unpleasant pictures of crumbled buildings and dead bodies. Crasak removed its talon from the pleasure center and found the part of her brain that processed images; it then tweaked her mind to help her focus on them. With its other hand, it lightly scratched at the memory of the car accident.

Kathy stiffened just a bit.

The demon moved closer until its nose and mouth met hers in a kind of mocking kiss. Then it matched its exhalations with her inhalations again. The breath from the creature passed into her mouth and her breath into its. The demon drew closer until its eyes passed through hers and its mind entered her mind.

Then it drew its legs up around her hips and hooked its feet around her back. Likewise, it wrapped its wings around her, enveloping them both in a cocoon-like embrace.

Kathy felt suddenly tired but she still focused on the TV. Crasak moved and aligned itself with her mind. Since it was now inside her, it let itself flow like water down into the void of her spirit. It intertwined its essence with hers. Though not the same as being possessed, it was a temporary imitation and Crasak's special talent.

The demon could feel the flow of increased adrenaline in her system. Her breathing quickened and her heartbeat grew stronger. She was agitated. So, it tweaked the part of the brain that made her susceptible to manipulation and whispered, "You are alone in the house. You are vulnerable and weak."

Kathy moved her head slightly and frowned. She pressed her hands down on the couch, her fingers gripping the cushion. She tried to clear her mind, but it was useless. She couldn't focus. The demon was working hard to control her.

"Someone is outside, watching you. He sees you. He followed you here and knows you are alone. He's waiting until you fall asleep."

Kathy felt a ratcheting up of faint, cold fear in her spine. Crasak moved its talon and prevented her mind from reacting, subduing her flight response. Then it tilted its head downward and opened its mouth. With a small convulsive movement, it coughed up bile and took aim as it looked downward and let the liquid fall from its black tongue. The slime fell slowly through her throat and stomach. A wave of nausea washed through her stomach. She grimaced. Crasak tightened its grip on her mind, keeping her desire to panic at bay. Then it exhaled a whisper, "The man is going to kill you." With each word it manipulated her emotions with its talons, canceling her resistance with its skill. It was in control, not Kathy.

Crasak strengthened the image of the body at the car accident with one hand and with the other it caused her to focus on the images of destruction on the TV. Then quickly, it forced the memory of the abortion to the surface.

Kathy remembered. She saw the burned body and with it experienced the revulsion, terror, and guilt all mixed into a tangle of distress. She tried to force the memories and feelings away, but she couldn't. She wanted to flee but was too weak to resist.

Crasak continued to exhale its vile breath into her body as it slowly whispered, "Murder. Torture. Rape. Death. Pain."

Kathy swallowed. Her heart pounded. She was vaguely aware of her emotional struggle, but she was lost in a daydream, being carried along by the images and manipulations, exploited by Crasak's considerable skills.

She gripped the couch fabric with both hands.

It tweaked her mind again and let more bile drip down into through her stomach. Again the nausea and then an intruding shadow of fear touched her.

She fought back.

The creature adjusted its grip, trying to keep control, deflecting her resistance. Simultaneously, her instinct to fight surfaced and began to grow stronger.

Crasak, aware of this, focused all the more to keep control for as long as possible before it finally released her.

Slivers of determination pierced her consciousness, trying to pry her free from Crasak's hold. The demon held strong, controlling her brain, holding on tightly, breathing into her mind, and began whispering over and over, "Release yourself to me. Release yourself. Let go."

The creature knew what to do. It squeezed itself tightly around Kathy's body until its arms, legs, and wings all entered her, bringing its putrid filth into full contact with her spirit. Kathy began to convulse involuntarily, but Crasak would not let her go. It squeezed tighter and gripped her mind with its clawed hands. He shrieked into her consciousness, "He is behind you!"

Kathy's head began to sway. She wanted to look behind her, but Crasak would not let her move. She was panting. Her heart pounded and she pressed her back against the couch. She clenched its fabric with both fists as she fought panic and the rising terror within. But the creature was still able to control her. Crasak spoke intensely, "Die! Die!"

Kathy twitched. She blinked hard and managed to look away from the TV. She moaned slightly, then again. Crasak wrestled to sustain its control.

She was fighting hard to break free from the intrusive haunting. Aware but unaware, it was as though she were being carried along a powerful river, helpless to get free of the current, but fighting nonetheless.

Crasak knew it could not hold on much longer.

Kathy felt cold fear permeate her veins, her bones, and muscles. She could almost taste its agonizing intensity as it seemed to flow within her. She opened her eyes wide. Her chest heaved with gasping breaths as she broke free from the TV and glared at the ceiling.

Each breath was quick, short, and hard. Her body was tense.

Her mind could not comprehend what was happening. She felt on the verge of panic, but Crasak skillfully held it in check in order to increase its final and sudden release.

"The killer is behind you. He is reaching for you."

A chaotic tornado of emotions was twisting her mind into a knot, forcing her instincts to the surface. Crasak knew it was about to lose control so it screamed, "He is going to kill you! Run! Run!"

Kathy began to shake. Her head bobbed downward, then jerked back up. She managed to force out a muffled, weak groan. She closed her eyes and then opened them wide. Her heart hammered against her chest. Adrenaline poured into her veins. Kathy blinked hard, shaking her head, almost convulsing. She was fighting.

Crasak yelled, "The murderer is behind you," Kathy shuddered again.

She wanted to scream.

"His hands are on you! He is here. He is going to kill you!"

Kathy began to straighten her legs, which pressed her back into the couch. Then, finally, with great effort she forced out one word, "No."

The demon's grip was giving way.

"No," she cried again. "No."

With that, Crasak released itself from her and, in an instant, it left Kathy's body and placed itself directly in front of her.

There was nothing to stop the eruption. The sudden release of her mind and will allowed all the pent-up terror to detonate. It was like a shock wave that carried with it emotional debris as it scraped across her mind and heart and swept her into the realm of pure panic.

She screamed at the top of her lungs.

In that instant, Crasak reached back into her mind and tweaked her vision center so that it became visible to her for a split second.

At the same time Kathy had already begun to bolt up from the couch and, as she did, for one fleeting moment she

saw the hideous creature inches from her face. It flashed into
her consciousness almost imperceptibly, yet it was real, and
terrifyingly ugly. The shock was too much. Her long, hard
scream stopped. Her eyes rolled back and, like a rag doll, she fell,
slamming her head on the corner of the coffee table.

Pain ripped through her skull. She struggled against the pain
and panic, fighting the blackness that was overcoming her sight.
Her mind drifted between consciousness and unconsciousness.
Pain came and went, as did the light and dark. Then everything
went black.

Crasak smiled and took a step closer. It knelt down and put
its face just above hers. Rotting saliva dripped through her mind.
She began to move. Crasak smiled and lowered its face closer.
With both hands close together, it slowly began its reach into her
brain. It opened its fanged mouth wider as it drew closer, closer.

A streak of white crashed into Crasak and sent it tumbling
through the living room wall and into the yard outside. Dazed,
it tried to recover but quickly found that Ramah had gripped
it around the chest and neck and was digging his fingers into
its throat with all his strength. The evil spirit fought, growling
and clawing at the angel. It kicked ferociously and tried to beat
him with its wings, but Ramah had Crasak from behind and
was locked on the demon's back. The demon fought fiercely. It
bucked, kicked, and clawed at the angel, but Ramah held on.
Crasak grabbed his arm and dug its talons deep. Ramah ignored
the pain and began to crush Crasak's throat, but the demon was
too strong. It kicked violently and clawed at Ramah's hands until
finally it was able to force itself free. They broke apart, but Ramah
instantly thrust himself at the demon again. Crasak punched at
his head. Ramah turned just enough to deflect most of the force,
returning with a crushing blow to Crasak's face. He grabbed the
demon's wing with both hands and quickly broke the main bone
in it. Crasak growled in pain, twisted, and then kicked Ramah in
the chest. The angel fell back a few feet, giving the demon enough
time to thrust its hands forward and downward as it descended
into the earth.

Ramah did not follow but immediately turned his attention

to Kathy. He knelt beside her. *Was she alive?* He checked her neck and felt the artery pulsing rapidly. There was a nasty bump on her left temple. He put his hand on it and slowly removed it as if caressing her head. She moved a bit, moaned, and blinked.

Ramah knelt down and looked into her eyes. The panic, which had been temporarily silenced by unconsciousness, rumbled to life as she regained her senses. When she opened her eyes, it came forth like a volcano.

He backed away.

The memory of the fear and hideous image erupted in a terrifying tangle. She started to kick and scream. She pushed the coffee table over as she flailed her arms about.

Ramah spoke out loud, "It is okay. You are all right. You are safe."

Kathy shrieked and squirmed on the ground, blindly groping in the air.

The angel spread his wings over her and spoke into her ear, "You are safe. You are okay. It is over. You are safe now." He put a hand on her chest.

Kathy was still screaming, but the angel's touch had an immediate effect. Even though the fading remnants of terror were still strong, the panic decreased and her mind began to clear.

Ramah continued to speak with a soft and comforting voice, "You are safe. You are safe. It is okay. There is no danger. Relax. Calm down."

Ramah's words worked their calming effect. After a few moments, she managed to stop screaming and force her mind to focus. She clutched the leg of the overturned coffee table and stared at the ceiling, eyes wide open.

"You are all right. You are safe," whispered Ramah repeatedly. His words soothed her and the panic quickly melted away. Finally, she was able to force herself to calm down, although her chest continued to heave with each breath.

"Calm down. Everything is okay. You are in no danger."

Kathy felt the effect of his calming words as they washed over her, ministering to her. Her breathing slowed and she let her legs fall flat on the floor as she stared upward. After a minute more, she managed to steady her breathing. She lay there. Ramah moved away.

Then, quite naturally, she began to cry. At first she convulsed slightly with each sob, but they soon gave way to full, rhythmic heaves. One after another, they came, accompanied by groaning wails. She put her hands over her strained face. She coughed out moans and sobs and wept hard. The tears poured down her temples and into her hair.

Ramah watched, paining over her ordeal.

She cried for a while lying there, venting her emotions until her strength was finally spent. She was able to take one final huge, cleansing breath before regaining full composure.

She rubbed her scalp and jerked her fingers away at the painful throb. Then she managed to sit and look around.

"No one is here," said Ramah. "No one is here." His voice was masculine, but also soft with a soothing, comfortable resonance.

Kathy felt herself grow inexplicably calm.

"You are all right," said Ramah.

Then, as if the last tear of her life had finally fallen, the urge to cry completely stopped. Her mind cleared. With both hands she whipped her hair back over her head, then slowly got up and sat on the couch.

What happened? She asked herself.

It certainly wasn't normal. She couldn't explain it, and she had no previous experience with which to compare it. But she knew something strange had happened. The TV caught her attention. She forced herself to watch a commercial for a local car dealership and let herself relax, even though her body was still trembling slightly from her recent surge of adrenaline. She slowly, laboriously stood up and looked around. Her breathing shuddered twice. Her heart was still pounding, but not quite so violently as before. She walked back into the kitchen and retrieved the knife before going back to the living room. She felt better with it in her hand. The TV was the only sound she heard. She grabbed the remote and punched the off button. Silence seemed to fill the house. Her eyes and ears were attuned to survival mode, aided by the remaining adrenaline coursing through her system.

She stood there, shaking slightly, pointing the knife forward, and looking around cautiously. She believed she was alone, but that nagging doubt wouldn't leave.

She headed for the front door to make sure it was locked, then went into the hallway, from which she proceeded to search every room for an intruder once again, leaving lights on everywhere, even in the garage. The place was empty. Everything was clear.

Back in the living room, she examined the overturned coffee table. She touched her temple again and a shard of pain forced her hand away. There was no blood, but there *was* a very tender lump. She glanced back at the coffee table and the corner where she hit. Suddenly, the image of Crasak's ugly form flashed into her mind again. She responded in revulsion and cried out, "No," as she forced her eyes shut and tried to will the image away. It persisted. She dropped the knife on the floor and grabbed her head in both hands, twisting her hair with her fingers. The urge to cry returned once more and a few tears managed to run down her cheeks, falling onto her blouse. Then, like a ruptured barrier, their presence signaled the coming flood. She began to sob.

Ramah stood by and looked into the spiritual world to see if any other dangers were approaching. There were none. He placed his hand near Kathy's forehead. "You will be okay," he said aloud. His voice was soothing, full of care and compassion. "You are all right Kathy. You are all right. You are safe."

Kathy's sobs subsided into cries and in a few short minutes, they were reduced to an occasional whimper, until they disappeared altogether. She looked around the house again to reassure herself that she was alone. Walking over to the coffee table, she set it upright. Then she sat down on the couch, and for several quiet minutes, she gathered her thoughts.

"Mark would think that I am the one falling to pieces," she said to the empty room. The urge to call him was strong, but she knew it was not a good idea. Not now. She didn't want to worry him and add to his stress. Besides, he'd think she was crazy for sure. She'd tell him what happened, but not now, not until he was better.

She let her head fall back on the couch and stared up at the ceiling. It made no sense. Why the panic? Why the memories? And that face, that horrible face. Was it all her imagination? She shuddered as she remembered the experience. She grabbed the remote and turned on the TV again, pulling the covers up on the couch and propping her feet up on its cushions.

She glanced at the clock. It was approaching 11 pm. Her father would be asleep. Anyway, she had neglected to jot down the number for his bedside phone and she was sure that the hospital switchboard wouldn't put her call through at this hour. She wanted to talk to him, but that would have to wait until morning. She stared at the phone and thought again about calling Mark.

My dad will believe me, she thought, but Mark sure won't.

Chapter 7

MARK AND SOTARE SAT in the dark, their faces faintly lit by the moonlight. The droop of Mark's eyelids betrayed his fatigue.

"It's late," said Sotare. "You need rest."

"Yes, you're right. This is all very demanding and my brain feels like mush." He stretched in his seat and looked at Sotare, who smiled at him. Mark got up, surprised at how willing he was for the evening to end.

"Tomorrow is Saturday. I've always loved Saturdays," he said as he looked absentmindedly into the garden. Mark took a few steps out of the gazebo and turned back to Sotare, but the angel was gone. He looked around and then up to the treetop and imagined that Nabal was watching him. He averted his eyes and dismissed the thought as he headed towards the back door. The full moon cast weak shadows on the ground. At the house, Mark took one last look at the garden and went inside.

He rummaged through the refrigerator and found some leftovers. After eating and cleaning up, he headed towards the living room and thought about watching TV. It seemed pointless.

The place was so empty without Kathy there, especially now. He looked into the kitchen, the hallway, and out through the front window. A car passed by. Across the street, a tree full of leaves rustled softly in the wind, its movement barely perceptible under the moonlight. Everything seemed normal.

He walked down the hall and into his office. His computer was off. He saw the phone next to it and thought about calling Kathy but figured that she would either be tired or asleep. He remembered how Sotare had said she would come under attack. Not being able to be there for her made him feel all the more helpless and alone, even though he knew he was not.

"Sotare?" He said aloud. "Thank you for speaking with me."

He waited for a moment but heard no response. *I wonder if he heard me*, thought Mark.

He walked down the hallway and back into the living room. The TV didn't hold any interest for him, and he was sure the radio wouldn't either. So he just stood in the living room, not sure what to do. He thought about Kathy and about John in the hospital. He wanted to talk to them both about what he was experiencing. John might believe him, but he was certain Kathy wouldn't.

He headed upstairs to his bedroom and to the closet. He tossed his shirt into the clothes hamper, kicked off his shoes, and took off his slacks. As he pulled his robe off its hanger, something fell from the shelf above and slapped on the floor. It was a Bible.

Mark stared at the cover. "Did you do that?" asked Mark as he glanced out the window towards the garden. He tossed the robe over his shoulder, picked it up, and headed to the bed, where he lay down and propped his head on the pillow. He flipped open the cover to the first few pages and found the table of contents: the list of books of the Bible was long and he had no idea where to turn to. He had attended a couple of churches a few months ago in his search for spiritual insight and someone had given this to him. He had looked at it before and found nothing of particular interest so he had tossed it. Kathy must have put it up on the shelf along with the other stack of books that were infrequently used. But now, considering everything that had been going on, he thought he'd look at it again.

Mark read the first few chapters of Genesis and then skipped around. He read a little about Jesus and then went through a couple of Psalms. A lot of it made no sense, although there were some obviously wise teachings within the pages. He was familiar with a lot of it from various TV shows he had seen over the years. He was glad for that. After about half an hour, he was too tired to continue, so he put the book on the nightstand and headed into the bathroom to get cleaned up. It wasn't too long before he was back in bed and under the covers.

The ceiling seemed like a familiar companion as he lay there in the dark, staring upwards. He looked out the window at the two trees in the garden. They were still. He knew Nabal was there, at least he assumed he was there. The memory of that hideous creature disturbed him, so he pulled his mind away from it and turned his back on the window, idly stroking the pillow on Kathy's side of the bed, then cradling it in his arm. Kathy's favorite scent was still fresh on the case.

From outside, Nabal watched him. The creature had orders to observe and report to Paraptome. So it waited.

On both sides of the bed stood Sotare and Nomos. Nabal hissed at them.

***

Leech paced nervously around the apartment for a couple of hours, halfway expecting a knock on the door and the police to come and take him away. The demon in him caused him to feel confident and secure in his actions, so he quickly became convinced that no one would connect him to the shooting. It had been dark and he'd left too quickly for anyone to identify him. The ghetto was a safe place to hide. With another self-assuring smile he decided to settle down and watch TV, finally deciding on a horror movie.

Grawl was savoring its accomplishment through its human host. Shooting the boy had driven Leech's soul deeper into darkness, making it that much easier for the demon to control him. Grawl stared out through the man's eyes and practiced moving them. Possession took effort but, once accomplished, the spirit of Grawl and the spirit of the man were intertwined. Grawl could direct him. It was a kind of symbiosis, moving together, and Leech never suspected that he was being influenced. Grawl's goal was to gradually control the man's thinking so much that he would be completely under its control, all the while letting the man think he was free. Grawl laughed.

Leech thought the horror movie was funny and laughed out loud. "This is great," he said.

Grawl reached for the remote control. Leech changed the channel.

Grawl led the man, testing him, seeing to what extent he could influence and control its human host now that a new level of treachery had been accomplished. Leech was flipping through the channels. Grawl decided to return to the horror movie. Leech went back to it. Grawl smiled and so did Leech. Grawl looked out the window and listened. The commotion outside had faded. Leech knew that the police would file a report, and a few questions might be asked, but in the ghetto, shootings were rarely solved because no one ever saw anything. It was a success for the evil forces in this area.

The demon continued to explore the mind of its host. It felt what Leech felt, experienced what Leech experienced. That is why it sensed pain, a feeling of both sickness and hunger as the pangs of drug addiction manifested themselves in the man's body. Leech shifted in his seat and knew that he needed a fix, and soon. He got up, went to his bedroom, looked under the mattress, and retrieved a small plastic bag of pills. He grabbed three and hurried to the kitchen, where he filled a dirty glass with water and swallowed them. Relief from the soft pain would come soon. The pills, he thought to himself, were merely an appetizer meant to take the edge off. He'd enjoy the main course, the injected drug of choice, a little later. Leech headed back to the living room and waited. He still felt good, even confident about what he'd done.

Paraptome had been watching from above before it finally, slowly descended into the living room. Leech was back to watching the movie, and Grawl was relishing every moment of its possession, unaware of the presence of the principality. Because Leech was not able to see the spiritual world, it would take time before Grawl, so deeply entwined in the body and soul of its host, could fully regain its own spirit-world awareness. But it was well worth the inconvenience. It might take months before it was able to train Leech's mind to hear voices and see things and think they were normal.

The principality moved closer behind the man and peered inside. Grawl noticed a presence, and momentarily wondered if the drugs that it was vicariously experiencing were having an effect on it. Paraptome moved closer. It would have to be careful when ripping Grawl out of Leech because it did not want to unintentionally kill the human. Even though Paraptome could easily crush the demon, to do so would most probably kill Leech. Paraptome would have to be careful.

The principality leaned forward and whispered, "I am Paraptome."

Grawl spun around, instantly startled by the voice. Leech convulsed and twisted. He thought he heard something. A split second later, Grawl growled in terror and Leech felt a wave of cold fear crawl up the back of his neck. His mind filled with the thoughts of the police knocking on his door. He tried to get up and get his weapon, but Grawl, terrified, froze, as did Leech. The fear flooded Leech's mind. Did he hear a voice or not? He tried to move, but he couldn't. He struggled to lift his right hand but it seemed sluggish, heavy, and uncooperative. Then it occurred to him that the drugs he had just taken might be bad. There were plenty of people who wanted him dead and perhaps this was payback time for earlier crimes.

"I claim this human," said Paraptome. "Leave him or I will destroy you."

Grawl knew that it was no match for this vastly superior force; under different circumstances, it would obey instantly. But the insanely evil pleasure of possession forced it to risk defiance.

"Leave him," commanded Paraptome.

Leech felt fear sweep over him. He tried to move but couldn't.

"He is mine," said Grawl. "This one belongs to me, and I will not let him go."

Leech's mind began to fade in and out. Grawl was intertwined within him and, although Leech did not know why, he felt his own mind participating in another conversation. It seemed that he could almost hear it, and then not, then hear it again.

"Bad drugs," he said aloud. Again he tried to get up, but still couldn't. He was dizzy, getting nauseated, and was feeling an increasing uneasiness.

Paraptome reached down into the neck of the man and grabbed Grawl by the throat. The demon kicked and the man began to choke. Grawl clawed at the massive hand but Paraptome was careful not to crush it. Grawl tightened its grip on Leech's spirit, wrapping its tail more tightly around his spine and gripping with its talons deeper into the human's brain. Leech convulsed and shuddered. Voices disappeared and returned. His eyes were open wide; he was confused and fearful. His breathing was rapid and harsh. His muscles tightened.

Paraptome took its other hand and, with its long claws protruding from its fingers, reached into the man and grabbed the human's spine just below the neck. Then, carefully and slowly, it began to pull as it tried to separate the demon from the human. Leech crumpled on the couch, and then arched up, his eyes blinking wildly, looking and seeing nothing but the ceiling. He felt the twisting in his spine and the cold and pure evil that washed through him. He felt the terror that Grawl felt and became, for an instant, aware of its presence. Leech almost passed out from sheer terror and for a moment he believed the drugs were poisoned and going to kill him.

Grawl kicked and scratched into the air, fighting against the hand that held it. Leech's mind was foggy, unfocused. Fear grew as he thought about the drugs in his system. Grawl resisted but Paraptome squeezed its throat with precision.

Leech felt the threat and punched the air in front of him, above him, in every direction. He gasped for breath and gurgled out a groan of pain. His eyes seemed to lose focus and regain it. He felt dizzy and nauseous, and then he fell to the floor. His legs kicked and his body bounced as he twisted. Foam spattered from his mouth. The pain was intense, his muscles stiff and twisting wildly. He could not control himself and he feared he would die under the onslaught of convulsions.

Paraptome gripped hard onto Grawl's throat, causing it to suddenly stop moving. Leech was motionless, dazed. Then it leaned down, opened its huge jaws, and encased the head of Grawl in its mouth, gently closing on its skull, but not biting. It forced three fangs to bear down upon the demon's head. Grawl continued to resist. Paraptome began to slowly apply pressure, then more pressure.

Leech grabbed his head with one hand and screamed out in pain. It was a piercing intense sting. He arched his back, every muscle ripping with agony. Then he fell limp again. Grawl had weakened for the moment.

Paraptome applied more pressure. Grawl screamed as one fang pierced its eye.

Leech screamed. His eye was searing as if a hot shard of metal had stabbed him. The pain fired into his brain. He struggled as blackness grew, and he slipped slowly into unconsciousness.

Grawl continued to resist, striking out at Paraptome. But with Leech out cold, it made Grawl's efforts more difficult. Grawl had to move the weight of the man from within instead of influencing his mind to do it. Leech loosely flopped on the ground as the two spirits fought within him. Paraptome squeezed his jaws upon Grawl's skull. The demon screamed and arched, causing Leech to arch. Grawl continued to resist, clawing into Leech's soul, trying not to let go.

Paraptome applied more pressure. It squeezed and let one fang slip further into the eye and face of its opponent. The demon violently growled and clawed at the huge monster, but it was no use. Paraptome continued to use its strength to slowly, inexorably separate the demon from the human. Grawl could feel its grip loosening, and tried to dig its talons into the man's spirit as tightly as it could. But Paraptome was far too strong and Grawl's claws gradually began to give way, scraping across the man's soul, damaging it. Paraptome could see that Grawl was determined. It knew that a prolonged struggle would probably kill the human. So, the principality decided to risk the man's life with a quick move.

With one fang protruding into the face of Grawl and the other upon its skull, Paraptome squeezed, causing both fangs to pierce deep into Grawl's brain. The demon flinched horribly. Leech was convulsing on the floor, every one of his muscles in spasm, moving in slow motion as his body arched.

Grawl's strength was fading fast. First its bony left hand released, then its right. Paraptome squeezed harder on its neck, applying more pressure and driving its fangs deeper into Grawl's skull. The demon managed a faint growl and finally after a single violent twist, it went limp. In an instant, Paraptome ripped it out of Leech. The principality opened its mouth, withdrawing its fangs from the demon's skull. The man fell still and Paraptome stood up, holding Grawl in its clawed hand. It was terribly wounded and had only enough strength to open its eyes and look into the face of its hideous master.

"I will deal with you later," growled Paraptome as it pierced Grawl's chest with its talons. The demon flinched weakly, barely aware of its own pain. Paraptome grabbed the wings and with a single movement ripped them from Grawl's back. The demon groaned weakly. Then Paraptome hissed at the creature, opened its clawed hand, and let the creature fall limp through the floor, disappearing into the earth.

Leech was still unconscious. Paraptome looked at him and stared into his body. It was bruised, but he was alive. It moved its nostrils up Leech's torso, stopping at the man's face and stared. It watched Leech's breathing and matched its own to his. Paraptome opened its mouth and slowly extended its tongue into the mouth and throat of Leech. It bowed low and moved its face into the face of the man, its hands into his hands, its legs into his legs, and, its body into his body. But, in order for this huge demon to possess the human shell, it had to compress itself and contort its muscles and frame into the smaller cavity of Leech's body. The principality explored the mind of the unconscious man, reading his memories, feeling his depravity and, finally, taking full possession. Paraptome growled out loud in a kind of victorious howl. The possession was complete.

Leech lay still on the floor. He was dreaming of being eaten alive.

Chapter 8

PASTOR TIM AWOKE AND looked over at his wife. He loved to see her next to him in the morning. It didn't matter that her hair was messed up, or that small wrinkles moved out from her eyes. To him, she was beautiful. He adored her and considered himself blessed.

I don't deserve her, he thought.

In fact, just a week ago, when they were at a friend's house discussing marriage, Tim told everyone in the room that if it weren't for his wife's taste in men, he would have a lot more respect for her. They all chuckled, and she lovingly swatted him on the shoulder. He smiled when he thought of it.

She opened her eyes. He said nothing. She looked at him. Tim could feel his heart beat just a little stronger. He looked at her lips and the shape of her nose. He loved the way her hair rested on the pillow and how the morning light made it glow. She looked back into his eyes, smiled, and scooted over close to him. They held each other and rested for several more minutes without saying a word.

Finally, outside the bedroom, the sound of hurried footsteps grew louder until there was a knock at the door.

"Yes?" said Susan with a smile. The door opened and a small, five-year-old freckled boy with a button nose appeared. "Mom, can I have some cereal?"

"Yes, dear," she said as she began to get up. "I'll be there in a little bit and make breakfast." The head disappeared and rapid footsteps faded down the hallway.

Susan exhaled and she said, "That boy never stops eating."

Tim smiled, "And he's growing like a weed."

She got up and headed into the bathroom. "You feeling any better?" she asked.

"Yes. I think praying helped a lot last night. Thanks for being so understanding."

She stuck her head out the bathroom door. "My pleasure," she said with a smile and ducked back into the bathroom.

Tim stretched in bed and threw his legs over the side. He forced himself up and headed into the bathroom to get ready for the day. "I'm going to spend some time on my sermon and then go to the church to take care of some stuff, if you don't mind."

"Okay, I'll just do the grocery shopping all by my lonesome." She was teasing.

"You don't mind?"

"Not at all. Sometimes it's nice to have time alone. I'll just see you later when you get back."

The little freckled boy appeared again at the door, "Mom? I'm totally starving."

"I'll take care of it, hon," said Tim as he slipped into his robe.

***

Leech opened his eyes. He stared at the ceiling until his head cleared. It was light outside. Saturday morning. He'd been asleep on the floor all night. He tried to move, but an intense soreness ricocheted throughout his body.

"Crap."

He forced himself up, wincing, dragging the dead weight of his body onto the couch. It was difficult to move. "Bad crap," he said, referring to the drugs he remembered taking the night before. "I'm going to find the guy who sold them to me and kill him." He rubbed his hair, wincing from the dull pain permeating his body. His mouth was dry.

Leech sensed that something in him wasn't right. He felt heavy. He tried to move and, although he could, it required a lot of effort.

Stinking drugs, he thought.

Leech forced himself up and headed to the kitchen. He stopped halfway and leaned against a wall. The room seemed to move. He shook his head and lifted his left arm. It was heavy. "I've never had a reaction like this before," he muttered to himself.

He continued into the kitchen, dragging his feet slightly. With a tug on the refrigerator door, he managed to open it and grab a beer. He twisted off the cap and tossed it behind him as he headed back to the couch. It felt good to let his body fall into the cushion.

"Man! This is bad."

Leech leaned his head back, tilting it from side to side, trying to assess the degree of soreness in different muscles. He looked out the window. Instantly reminded of the shooting last night, his heart skipped a beat.

Paraptome had remained patiently silent within him but now decided to test its new possession. With the memory of the shooting freshly brought back to his mind, Paraptome tweaked the part of Leech's brain that gives pleasure. Leech felt good. Paraptome stroked it hard so that each time Leech thought of it, it was exceedingly pleasant.

Leech welcomed the thought of killing someone else, and with each malevolent contemplation, pleasure surged through him. He was a very willing and easy subject to control. He smiled, but it was a not casual smile. Behind it was wickedness, the kind that takes morbid pleasure in seeing others suffer. Paraptome laughed maliciously and so did Leech. He felt good, relishing the satisfying emotions that flowed through him. He dwelt on the memory of the shooting, reliving his actions, enjoying it.

Paraptome raised the beer to Leech's mouth. Leech took a drink. The evil creature stood up and walked him over to the window. The massive hulk inside of Leech caused him to move laboriously but Leech thought it was due to the bad drugs. Paraptome stared out through the man's eyes, towards the direction of the shooting. Leech felt powerful and confident. He smiled and laughed out the window in complete defiance.

Paraptome whispered into Leech's mind, "You need to kill again." With these words, it caressed Leech's mind, sending endorphins flooding into him. That's when Leech realized he had a new addiction: killing. He smiled and closed his eyes for a moment as he slowly exhaled in pleasure, savoring the thought, the new realization. *I wonder how many people I could kill and not get caught.*

Paraptome walked Leech over to the mirror. The evil creature used its power and presence to manipulate Leech's mind, knowing it would be easy to bring him to murder once more.

While looking in the mirror, it continued to massage the pleasure centers of his brain and whispered sinister, evil thoughts in Leech's mind and mixed them with a wicked pleasure. Paraptome found memories and sifted through them, quickly discovering what naturally pleased the man and what did not.

Leech was staring back at himself, liking what he was seeing and enjoying the memories that were flooding through his mind. He saw himself as handsome and powerful. He thought of the murder as a kind of baptism, an initiation into a new world of freedom. He could take a life and not care. He had the power to extinguish a living being and enjoy it. He felt so free and alive. He smiled again. Paraptome spoke and Leech said, "I should have done this a long time ago." Leech smiled.

The man walked back to the couch and sat down. Still feeling the effects of the repossession, he noticed he was beginning to feel more than soreness. Acute pain emanated from his muscles. Then Leech realized he should have been awake all night from the drugs, instead of being unconscious.

"I'm gonna kill the guy who gave me that junk," he said aloud.

He tucked the beer between his legs and rubbed his eyes. After another swig he closed them and rested his head on a dirty cushion. Paraptome wasted no time.

"No one can get in your way. You can take whatever you want."

Leech listened to his own thoughts. "All I have to do is kill anyone who gets in my way." He listened to the noises outside the window, thinking of what people were doing and how vulnerable and weak they were. He knew that he had power over them. He liked it. It felt good, very good.

"Killing is freeing," said Paraptome softly into Leech's mind. "It is the greatest of power." Leech felt his body fill with pleasure. He let his arms drop heavily to his sides and savored the moment.

"Kill again," came the voice from within. Paraptome spoke in the first person to mimic Leech's thoughts. "I can do it again. I can get away with it again because I am smarter than other people. They are all weak and stupid." Though the words came from Paraptome, Leech believed they were his own.

He thought of the gang. Undoubtedly some of its members would have heard of the killing by now, and when he took credit for it, they would give him the proper respect and position in the group that he deserved.

Paraptome spoke into to his mind again. "How will they know it was me who did this? Do I have proof? Or will they think that I am taking credit for what someone else has done?"

Leech snapped his eyes open. There was no way to prove he was the killer. He could claim it, but that didn't prove it. He forced himself upright on the couch, trying to think through what to say to them. But the more he thought, the more he realized that there wasn't any proof.

"There is a way to prove myself to them," said Paraptome, still imitating Leech's own thoughts. "If I tell them who I am going to kill tomorrow, then they will have to believe me."

Leech thought about the idea. But who? Who would he kill? It would be difficult to plan to kill someone just walking down the street, unless one of them was with him. But they probably wouldn't want to risk that. They always wanted to protect themselves. No, it would have to be someone special.

"A pastor," whispered Paraptome.

The idea surprised him. It was a great idea. He could hardly believe that he thought of it. "Yes, a pastor," he said aloud. "A pastor, yes! That would show them."

Paraptome searched Leech's mind to see if the man knew of the church where Pastor Tim was preaching. But as the creature expected, Leech did not. So Paraptome put it into his mind to look in the phonebook and pick a church. Leech's heart leapt with a sinister joy. Paraptome tweaked his pleasure centers again and Leech very quickly decided to do it.

"Get the phonebook," said Paraptome into Leech's mind.

Leech struggled to get up, still feeling the noticeable weight within him. He went over to the cupboard next to the phone in the kitchen. Inside the local directory were listings by category. He began leafing through them looking for churches in the area. It was not difficult for Paraptome to guide both Leech's eyes as well as hands and lead him to the church where Pastor Tim was. "Here it is," said Leech aloud. "This is the one." Paraptome had manipulated Leech so easily.

Christian Community Fellowship, 1461 Twelfth Street, the City of Arbor, service at 10 a.m., Sunday Mornings. Pastor Tim Doulos. There was even a picture the pastor.

Leech smiled with the discovery of his new victim. It was a wonderful plan. It would ensure his entrance into the gang, which meant a better supply of drugs, good ones. Paraptome again massaged Leech's mind, causing pleasure to flow into him. He laughed out loud, enjoying how self-assured he was with the idea of killing a minister.

Leech thought for a moment. How would he do it? Maybe if he went in early the next morning it would be easier. But he didn't know what time the pastor would get there or if he would be alone. He could wait across the street and follow him home after the service. But he might not see him and even if he did, he might lose him in traffic. If he was going to give the gang a date and location, he better not mess up. Then it hit him. Kill the pastor during the service right in front of everyone! Just come in late, put on a mask without anyone seeing him, walk down the aisle, shoot the pastor, and escape. Everyone would be too shocked and terrified to do anything, and he would be gone before they knew it. It would be spectacular.

He liked the idea. It was bold and dramatic. Paraptome continued to tweak his mind and feed Leech ideas. He was nodding slowly as he smiled. But, he would have to find the church first and case it. He would have to know if his plan was possible. "Go to the church and check it out," whispered Paraptome. "That way, you could make sure."

Leech decided to go. He would check the place from the outside and if he was lucky, he could even get inside and take a look around. Churches were often open on Saturdays. Leech smiled. Paraptome, of course, was already smiling.

He got up and walked over to the phone and dialed. After a few rings a voice responded. Leech recognized who it was and said, "It's me. Did you hear about the killing on 13th street?"

"What killing?" responded the monotone voice.

"The boy. I did it."

"That was you?"

Leech waited as the phone was muffled for a few seconds.

"Oh. He's not dead," said the voice.

"What?" Leech almost yelled into the phone.

"The news said the paramedics brought him back from death or something. He's in the hospital recovering."

For a moment panic erupted in Leech, but Paraptome quickly calmed him and said, "He will never identify you," and then it caressed Leech's pleasure center. It worked.

After a few seconds Leech said, "Well, it was me. I did it."

The other end of the line was silent.

"I did it."

"Anyone can make claims," came the voice.

"I thought you'd say that so I will prove it. Tomorrow I'll do a pastor at the Christian Community Fellowship on Twelfth Street over in Arbor. You'll have your proof then." He waited for a response but there wasn't one. "Tomorrow you will have your proof. Just remember Twelfth Street in Arbor," said Leech again as he hung up.

Physically he was beginning to feel better, more clearheaded and awake but his body was still a little uncooperative as he turned away from the phone.

"That kid should be dead. I shot him point blank in the chest."

He walked over to the window and thought about the pastor. Killing him would go a long way to demonstrate his worthiness to the gang. They were his drug connection, and he wanted in. Besides, selling drugs was a great way to make a lot of cash, too. Initially, they were suspicious. He was too eager, so they were watching him. But he didn't mind and he figured that they would *have* to let him in after he killed the minister.

Leech labored to change his clothes. He ran a heavy comb through his matted hair, grabbed a jacket, and stuffed his gun into the pocket. He opened the apartment door, checked both ways, and headed downstairs. The only way anyone could connect him to the boy's shooting was by the gun. He had to hide it. He went down into the basement. There was a stack of boxes with rags in them and old tools that had been sitting around for years, rusting. He found a box full of old oilcans and trash. He took the gun and wiped it off with a rag. After destroying all fingerprints, he slipped it underneath the cans. He put the lid back on and made sure that no one saw him as he left the basement. The police were all too familiar with him and if somehow they ever ended up asking him any questions about the shooting, there was no way they could pin it on him without the weapon, unless the boy and mother somehow identified him. "But that will never happen," said Paraptome. "They can't connect it to you. It was dark." Leech believed the lie.

Paraptome led him outside to his car. Leech drove off towards Twelfth Street.

***

Kathy didn't sleep well even though she had taken a sleeping pill. She woke frequently and had to force her mind to calm down. The terrifying memory of the night before was still too fresh. But morning finally came, and after eating a quick breakfast, she left for the hospital. As she drove, she remembered the hideous face and the paralyzing fear she had felt. It was too real, too different. She tried to focus on something else, so she concentrated on the traffic. She wondered if anyone else had experienced something similar. That caused her to think about the nightmare again, so she shook her mind away from it. All she wanted to do was get to the hospital and talk to her dad.

Every red light tested her patience and every slow driver seemed to purposely be in her way. She gripped the steering wheel tightly, and rapidly tapped her fingertips while she waited at red lights. By the time she finally walked into her father's room, she was agitated. She pushed the door open. John was awake and watching TV.

"Hi, Kathy," he said cheerfully.

As anxious as she was to talk about last night, she decided to suppress her anxiety and inquire about how he was feeling before she dove in. She wanted to make sure that he was up to it.

"How are you feeling, Dad? You look great."

"I *feel* great. My side hardly hurts and the doctor says that he probably will let me go home today. That is good news."

Kathy sat in the chair next to his bed and held his hand. Somehow, her father made her feel safe.

"That's great." Her voice was a little strained. Her eyes drifted away as she realized how much she wanted John to be released today and home tonight because she did not want to be there alone again.

"What is it?" asked John.

Kathy brought her eyes back to him and paused to consider what it was she was actually going to say. She sighed and scooted the chair closer to the bed and looked deeply into his eyes. He became concerned.

"Is Mark okay?" he asked.

"Yes, he's fine." She waited for a moment. "But I don't think I am."

John instinctively tried to sit up to be more prepared. He

winced slightly and abandoned that idea as he gripped her hand and waited for her to speak.

"Dad, I know that you believe in God and all this church stuff. You know that I haven't put any credence in what you've been telling me. But something happened last night at your place that I can't explain."

"What happened? Are you all right?" He studied her face.

Kathy wanted to tell him everything that happened, the terror, and the vision of the creature. But she was unsure of what to say. "Yes, I'm fine. I'm fine."

She looked down at the strong, weathered hand holding hers, then back to her father's eyes. She did not want to cause him any discomfort by being too suspenseful, but she just didn't know how to begin. She figured the best thing to do was just say it. Just get it over with.

"I… I think I saw some sort of demon last night."

"What?" John raised his eyebrows.

"It was horrible. It was the most hideous thing I've ever seen in my life."

John moved himself in the bed to face her more directly. He ignored the pain. "Please, tell me what happened."

"It was the strangest thing. I was sitting on the couch watching TV and…" She was staring blankly at the bed sheets, not seeing them. "Now that I think about it, it was as though there was another person there, but there wasn't. I was feeling a little paranoid because I thought someone was watching me, so I checked out the whole house." She looked back at John. "Everything was fine, but I couldn't shake the feeling that I was being watched. The feeling went on for a while and then… then… these images…the images of that car accident we saw when I was a little girl."

John knew exactly what she was talking about, and immediately, it brought back the discomfort and guilt he felt over it. His heart sank.

"Those images of that body kept flooding my mind. I don't know how to describe it because it was so strange. But it was weird, too. They kept coming and coming. I couldn't stop it. And, then, this intense feeling of fear came over me and I became very agitated and started to get scared. It was horrible. I kept getting this idea there was someone who wanted to kill me, that there was someone in the room with me but I knew there wasn't because I had just checked everything."

John was listening intently, motionless, holding her hand firmly.

She looked at him. "The feeling grew stronger and stronger and horrible images kept coming into my mind. I couldn't shake the idea that there was something wrong and I felt like my life was in danger. It was so bad, so awful that I ended up screaming and that's when I saw it. Dad, I saw it. I saw this horrible thing. It was only for a second, but I saw it. It was so ugly and I was so terrified that I passed out." She was throwing the words out rapidly as she became more and more agitated.

John examined her face with its raised eyebrows and wide-open eyes. Her voice had quavered slightly, and then the corners of her mouth dropped before she abruptly stopped talking. She had been gripping his hand tighter and tighter, shaking it with each syllable. But now she was still and quiet.

John tightened his grip on her hand and ached as he watched the tears well up in her eyes.

"You passed out? Are you okay?" She didn't say anything so he decided to wait and see if she was going to cry or not. She didn't and after about a minute, he sensed she was better.

"Can you tell me what you saw? Can you describe it, if that's okay?"

Kathy took a breath, preparing herself. "It was horrible. It was red and had horns. It had lots of bones with ugly skin stretched over it and..." She paused for a moment. "It had holes in its head and I, well, it was like I could see into its brain." Her voice was becoming strained again and her expression was full of revulsion. She paused, obviously having difficulty. Then she continued.

"It had lots of teeth and..." Kathy stopped abruptly again, but this time the tears came. She laid her head on the bed next to John's chest. He put his hand on her head and gently stroked her hair as she cried. It was obvious to John that something traumatic had happened. He prayed silently and held his daughter with both arms. She wept for about half a minute and then forced herself to stop. She sat up. Her father gripped her hands.

John handed her a tissue box from the table next to the bed. She took a tissue and dabbed under her eyes.

"I know I saw something, but was it my imagination? I mean, I could have been dreaming it. After all, I was a little tired and maybe because of all the stress…" she faded off. "I just don't know."

"Kathy," he said tenderly. "Do you think what you saw was real or not?"

Kathy closed her eyes again and shook her head. She did not like the answer she knew she was going to give. She exhaled hard and said, "I think it was real. I have never experienced anything like that before. It was looking at me. I can still see it. It was hideous. I will never be able to forget it."

John held her hand. He knew it was difficult for her and he didn't want to offer some lame, "I know how you feel," kind of comment. She did not believe in God, or at least she hadn't shown any interest in knowing anything about spiritual things. John knew that this was a great opportunity, so he silently and quickly asked God to guide him.

"Why me?" asked Kathy. "What did I do? I mean, I don't get it. I didn't hurt anyone. I am a nice person and I do good things for people. Why would…?" she stopped. She was going to mention God and ask why he would let something like that happen to her. But to do so would mean she was acknowledging his existence, and the ramification of that, combined with what she saw, made her instantly reconsider the validity of her father's faith.

She looked him in the eyes. "Am I crazy, or did I really see something?"

John could see the stress and bewilderment in her face. He wanted so much to say the right thing, but the words failed him.

"Maybe it has something to do with Mark," she said. "Remember how your pastor said Mark was important? Maybe something is happening with him or maybe your pastor knows something. What do you think? Should we call him? Do you think he'd believe me?"

John looked at her with mixed emotions. On one hand, he was thrilled that something had happened and caused her to talk to him about this but, on the other hand, he was deeply saddened that it had hurt her.

"Yes, Kathy. I think he will believe you. I know *I* do."

Chapter 9

LEECH DROVE TOWARDS THE church. He figured that the pastor might be there, so he developed a plan just in case. He would tell him he was new in the area and was thinking about coming to his church. Then, he could ask the pastor to show him around. It would be a perfect ruse to be able to case the place and check out all the exits. He smiled. Thinking about killing the pastor brought Leech both fear and pleasure. It was a big risk to do something like this in the middle of the church service. But he wanted to impress the gang so he knew he had to do something bold.

As he drove to the neighboring town, he realized that the next day he would have to steal a car and park near an exit at the church. He figured he could wear a mask and run in through a door, shoot the pastor, run out, get into the car, and disappear. He could then drive it to a parking lot filled with other vehicles. That way, it would be harder to find. About that time, he noticed a large grocery store in a strip mall. There'd be a car in the parking lot he could steal tomorrow morning. He could park his vehicle there and retrieve it when he dumped the other one off.

He figured that getting to the church and back would take no more than ten minutes from this location. So, if he were to spot someone who had just entered the grocery store, he could steal the car, shoot the pastor, and maybe get it back before anyone knew it had been taken. If he did it right, the owner would never know the car was stolen and would drive off with it. Leech knew how to pick locks and hotwire just about anything, so it would be easy. He had done it many times before.

It didn't take him long to navigate the streets. "There it is," said Leech as he spotted the church. He parked across the street. There was only one car in the lot. "I'm in luck." He got out and quickly scoped the building. It wasn't large and had double doors in the front with a lobby visible through the window. Leech walked to the side and could see an alley behind the church and a door at the other end. He could park the car in the alley and escape through the rear.

"May I help you?"

Leech didn't see Pastor Tim open the front door.

Paraptome was repulsed. Leech felt the same revulsion and had the urge to kill him right away. Paraptome retained control. Now was not the time. He had no gun, the pastor was not a small man, and he didn't know if anyone else was in the church.

"I'm sorry, I didn't see you come out," responded Leech as he struggled to control his disgust and appear casual.

"I hope I didn't startle you. I was just coming back from the restroom and saw you walking outside. Is everything okay? Do you need anything?"

Leech was approach Tim, sizing him up, hating him. "Well, I'm new to the neighborhood and was checking out different churches. I hope you don't mind me looking around."

"Not at all. Why don't you come on in and I can answer any questions you might have?"

"That would be great," said Leech with a smile that didn't quite reach his eyes. He walked up the steps to the church where Tim was waiting and holding the door open. The pastor extended his hand to shake Leech's. "I'm Pastor Tim."

He shook Tim's hand and thought to himself, *you're dead.*

"My name is David Smith," said Leech, offering a false name. "I just moved here from out of town."

"It's nice to meet you, Mr. Smith. Please come in."

Leech squeezed in through the doorway as Pastor Tim held it open for him. "Please, call me Dave," said Leech with fake politeness.

"Okay, Dave."

The pastor let the door close and for a few seconds he looked Leech over. He was poorly dressed and a bit unkempt. Tim looked into Leech's eyes and saw that they were slightly bloodshot. He was thin and seemed weather worn. It took only a moment for him to surmise that Leech might have had a rough life. But it didn't matter. He was glad to see him.

"Can I get you a drink of water, or a soda or something?" asked Pastor Tim.

"No, that's okay." Leech didn't want to touch anything and leave any fingerprints. "Well, I was just wondering what time your service was and if you had Sunday school or not."

"Service begins at 10 a.m. and goes to 11:15. We have a time of fellowship where we have cookies and coffee for fifteen minutes and then at 11:30 we have a Sunday school class. You are welcome to join us."

"I appreciate that," he said. "Can I look around?"

"Of course," said Tim automatically as he started to walk towards the sanctuary door.

Tim watched as Leech scanned the windows and hallway. Leech seemed normal, but there was something odd, something wrong that Tim couldn't put his finger on.

Paraptome was seething with revulsion. It wanted to rip out the pastor's heart, but it knew that now was not the time. Leech was still recovering from the repossession and didn't have his weapon. He wasn't in good enough shape to ensure killing the pastor.

Tim watched as Leech seemed to focus on the location of the door and then look back to the street where he peered down both directions. It seemed a little odd, even a little suspicious and it caused a small spark of fear to spring to life. Tim knew that he was alone in the church with a stranger. Was he there to rob him? Tim dismissed the notion and offered a quick prayer of forgiveness for judging this man without cause. Then he entrusted himself to the care of the Lord.

Pastor Tim opened the door and Leech walked in. Immediately, he surveyed the sanctuary which was a typical rectangular room with a pulpit at the far end on a slightly elevated platform. Leech could see an exit to the left that led out next to the alley. There was an exit sign over the door. He smiled.

"Well, here it is. It isn't much, but the Lord has blessed us with it. Over to the right down the hall, we have Sunday school classes. The kitchen is down there as well. It's a good facility, not too big, and not too small."

Leech had seen enough. He figured the place probably held at most maybe two hundred people. The only problem was whether or not that exit was locked from the outside. "How many people are in your congregation?"

"I would say we have around one hundred fifty on a typical Sunday morning."

"I guess the parking gets kind of crowded out there doesn't it?" said Leech with a smile, trying to make small talk but also trying to get information.

"That hasn't been a problem. I wish it were, but we have just what we need." Pastor Tim smiled.

Leech didn't know how to shrewdly find out if the door would be locked during the service, so he thought he would get a little more direct. "I suppose people from the neighborhood walk here too, right?"

"Yes, we have many people from the immediate area who attend."

"Do you unlock all the doors so they can come in from everywhere?"

Tim thought that was an odd question and he again thought of being robbed. "Yes, we unlock them all during the service, but afterwards we lock up. It's a shame that we have to do that at all. Unfortunately, for insurance reasons, we have to. We don't have much here except some musical instruments and some food supplies in the kitchen. But that's the world we live in."

"Yeah," responded Leech sympathetically. "The world is really getting bad out there. If only more people went to church." He looked at Pastor Tim and smiled, but it was a smile of mockery and contempt. Paraptome growled silently.

"Well," continued Leech. "I need to get going. It was nice talking to you."

"It was nice talking to you too, Dave. I hope you come back tomorrow for the service and, if not this church, I hope you find another you like."

"Thanks," said Leech as he headed towards the inner door of the sanctuary. It was still open so he walked through it towards the front. He noticed the horizontal bar that you could press against in order to open it, so he put his hip on it and pushed it open. Leech had touched nothing and left no clues that he was there. He walked down the steps of the church and through the parking lot, heading across the street to his car. He didn't look back.

Pastor Tim watched him walk away. There was something disturbing about the encounter. He pulled the door closed and turned round. The inner doors to the sanctuary were open and he could see down the center aisle to the pulpit. He'd always enjoyed seeing it from there and it comforted him. It meant so much to preach the Word of God to the congregation. He truly loved it and counted himself blessed to be able to do what he did. But, there were always battles and, considering what happened in the hospital and the increased desire to pray that had recently come over him, he figured he'd better pray some more. He turned to watch Leech out the window. For some reason, his visitor had been unsettling.

"Lord," he said aloud as he turned to look back to the pulpit. "Please forgive me for my thoughts concerning Mr. Smith. Let my heart and mind be pure before you and let me not judge another man by his appearance. But Lord, I feel that something is not right. If it is my own flesh that has been prejudiced against this man, please forgive me. And by your grace, please direct me how to pray for him."

From inside the sanctuary Ramah stood between the pulpit and the pastor so that as the man prayed, he was looking right at Ramah. The angel was warmed by the humble man's entreaty. He flexed his wings as wide and as high as they would go and then raised his arms to the heavens. He glowed brighter. "My Lord," said Ramah aloud. "I am ready."

Pastor Tim felt a warmth come over him and a peace flow into his heart. He smiled. "Thank you, Lord."

Tim walked toward his office, talking to God the whole way. The church was silent. Ramah followed him, walking through the walls and into the office. As Tim sat down, Psalm 37 flashed into his mind. He didn't have it memorized so he turned to it. "Do not fret because of evildoers. Be not envious toward wrongdoers. For they will wither quickly like the grass and fade like the green herb. Trust in the Lord, and do good." The words struck Tim hard. He pushed his chair away from a desk, slid out of it, and fell to his knees. He began to pray.

Ramah again spread his wings, lifting his hands and head upward.

***

Mark had slept surprisingly well and unexpectedly late into the morning. It was around 10 a.m. when he got up. He was concerned for his wife and wanted to call her but thought it best to wait until after he'd spoken with Sotare. So he hurriedly got dressed and went out into the garden. He drank in the sunshine. It was another beautiful morning with a perfect, soft breeze that made everything clean and fresh. He walked along the short path between the trees and towards the gazebo. He stood in its doorway.

"Good morning," said Sotare. "I trust that you slept well."

"Yes, I did. Maybe a little too much, though."

Mark moved into the gazebo and sat across from Sotare. The angel waited patiently.

"I want to call my wife, but for some reason I thought it would be best to wait until I spoke to you."

"Why is that?"

"Well, to be honest, I'm not so sure of myself right now."

"I see. I can understand that. All of this is a bit much to process."

Mark nodded.

"I suppose you want more answers."

"Yes. But if I might make a request, would it be possible for you to give more direct ones? I've noticed that you've kept me in the dark a little bit. I'm not trying to complain, but I just want to know the truth about my son, about God, about purpose, the meaning of life and all that. I want to know why you're talking to me and why, as you say, I'm so important."

Mark crossed his legs as he sat back in the seat.

Sotare thought about his student. There had been a lot of questions and answers, but Mark had not received an understanding of the whole picture yet, so Sotare wasn't sure how much he could tell him. He needed to learn so that things would make sense.

"Is Kathy okay?" asked Mark.

"Yes, she is fine. But last night, a terror demon was sent to attack her."

Mark immediately scooted up on his seat and leaned forward, frowning. "She's okay, though, right?"

"Yes, she is fine. She had quite a scare. It appears that she has seen a demon and she is even now talking to her father about it in the hospital."

"Why would they attack her? I mean, I thought I was the one they were after."

"It is not just you who are important in this battle, though you are the center of it. The enemy will attack your wife in order to get to you."

Mark sat back in his chair. He was surprisingly calm, and it seemed so unnatural a thing considering the circumstance. But he had a complete peace about it. "You know what's interesting? I can't explain it, but I am not worried at all. I feel as though everything is going to be okay." Mark paused, looking at Sotare quizzically. Something entered his mind about his father in law's pastor. "Pastor Tim is in danger. There will soon be an attempt on his life."

Mark sat back in the chair and found himself intrigued by what he had just said. He was confident yet confused. He looked into Sotare's eyes. "I don't know how I know, but I just know."

Sotare glanced over at Nomos who was a few feet away. Nomos had heard Mark and said, "This is most unusual. How can one who is not ours know this unless the Almighty has told him?" Sotare looked back at Mark.

"What were you looking at?"

"Mark, it seems that we both have unanswered questions."

***

The phone in Pastor Tim's office rang. He was at the end of his prayers so he quickly said amen and answered it. "Christian Community Fellowship. This is Pastor Tim speaking."

"Pastor. This is John in the hospital. Your wife told me you were there. I hope I'm not disturbing you. Do you have a few minutes to talk?" John's words seemed a little hurried.

"Of course I do. Are you feeling all right? Is everything okay?"

"Yes, I'm feeling fine and I'll probably get out of the hospital today. But, it's Kathy. I'm not sure how to tell you this, but I think that she may have seen a demon last night."

Instantly Pastor Tim reflected on the odd feeling he had about Leech coming to the church and the unusual desire for increased prayer. John's words were, somehow, only a confirmation to him that something spiritually significant was in the works. "Can I come over to the hospital now?"

"Yes," said John. "That would be great." John looked over at Kathy and said, "He wants to come here. Is that okay with you? Do you want to talk to him?"

Kathy nodded.

"Yes, that's fine. We'll be here waiting."

"Okay, I'll be right there. Goodbye."

"Goodbye," John replied.

Pastor Tim sat back in his chair for a moment and looked at

his Bible. He thought about the recent events. "Lord," he said. "I don't know what's going to happen, but I ask that you guide me and teach me that I might be used for your glory." With that, he contemplated what his role might be in the unfolding scenario and grabbed his Bible. A minute later, he was in his car heading to see John and Kathy.

***

Mark knew instinctively that Sotare would be more forthcoming now.

"May I ask some questions?" said Mark as he looked into Sotare's eyes. His tone was sober.

"Of course," responded Sotare.

"What do you know about my involvement in all of this?"

Sotare took a breath, more for effect than anything else. "We don't know how involved you're going to be or what's going to happen. This is all very unusual. In fact, it is extremely unusual for an unbeliever in your situation to be given the knowledge that you have had concerning your wife and the pastor."

"Unbeliever? I believe in God. Why do you call me an unbeliever?"

"Because you have not yet turned to God."

"I don't understand. I believe in God."

"So does the devil."

The words stung and once again Mark was irritated. "Why compare me to the devil?"

"I only compared your belief. You are not like that evil thing. You're a human. You believe that God exists. In this you do well. But the devil also believes that God exists."

Mark thought about this, unsure which direction to take. "Okay, I'm listening."

Sotare exhaled once again and let himself fall just a bit more into the cushioned seat. "It goes without saying that neither you nor I can truly comprehend the incredible stature and presence of the Almighty. He is simultaneously conscious of every star in the entire universe and of your every thought. He does not exist in time and his nature is so different from yours and mine that we have no means of truly comprehending what he is." Sotare leaned forward.

"As an angel I am able to see into the spiritual world and I have been graced with the privilege of very close encounters with God. I'm many thousands of years old and have had great opportunities through the millennia to observe his hand… and yet, I am aware of how very little I know of him. He is completely *other*. We exist in time and space; he does not. We experience reality one event after another; he does not. We learn; he does not. This is the necessity of his unchangeableness and his presence as he dwells in all places at all time. You see, Mark, because of who he is in his vastness and in his nature, he cannot change. He is, therefore, completely perfect and utterly pure." Sotare paused for a moment and then said, "Let me ask you, Mark, are you perfect and pure?"

Mark squinted slightly as he responded, "Of course not."

"Would you agree with me if I were to say that because God is perfect whatever, he says is also perfect?"

"That makes sense."

"Would you also agree that he is the standard of perfection?"

"Yes, I suppose that would also make sense."

"Good. Now, God can do no wrong. Correct?"

"Well, I suppose not, considering what you're telling me. But there sure are a lot of people in the world who think that he has done plenty of things wrong. There's way too much evil in the world. People die of diseases and suffer through all sorts of tragedies. There's famine and earthquakes and sickness. If God doesn't want these things, then why does he allow them? It would seem that his standard of perfection isn't all that perfect."

"I see. So you think that God makes mistakes?"

"No, but I wonder why he allows so much misery to exist in the world."

Sotare stopped to consider Mark's words.

Mark stared back, aware that Sotare was weighing the pros and cons of his next decision. Then finally he broke the silence, "Would it be okay with you if I touched your eyes again so that you might see into the spiritual world once more?"

Mark tensed up. The thought of seeing Nabal in the trees was not something he wanted to experience again. "Is Nabal still there?"

"Yes, but this time you won't see him. You'll see a vision. You will be safe and what you see will appear perfectly real. I will be with you in this vision and we will be able to speak together."

Mark was a little apprehensive. "Why do you want to do this?"

"In order to answer your question on why there is evil in the world. As before, I need to have your permission."

Mark was intrigued as well as a little cautious, but he knew that he wanted answers. "All right. Go ahead."

With that, Sotare got up and approached him. "When you open your eyes you will probably want to hold on to me. But, don't worry, you'll be safe."

"You're not exactly reassuring me," said Mark with a nervous smile.

Sotare placed his right hand over Mark's eyes and his left hand on the back of his head. He felt warmth and then a strange sensation that faded quickly. Sotare removed his hands. Mark opened his eyes.

Light was everywhere. There was no ground, no trees, no sky, nothing: just light emanating from a faint blue, vast background. Mark instantly felt vertigo and the fear of falling. He reached his hands out instinctively to steady himself. As he did he noticed a figure to his right. It was Sotare in angelic form. He grabbed Mark by the arm to steady him and Mark reacted by holding on to Sotare with both hands.

The angel was beautiful and glowing with light. His wings stirred slowly and gracefully. They both seemed to hover in nothing. He felt no movement and no gravity.

This is a vision, thought Mark. *This is a vision. I am okay. I'm not going to fall.*

Mark looked around. Everywhere, in every direction was the white light and that soft blue background. He was enveloped in it. He looked down and noticed his own clothing had changed.

They were dirty, torn, and stained. He was in rags, filthy rags. Confused, he looked at what Sotare was wearing and saw him dressed in a beautiful white robe. Mark looked back to his own clothes and was about to ask why he was in them when Sotare pointed off to the left, ignoring Mark's confused expression.

Mark followed his hand and looked into the distance but could see only a blue-and-white mixture of light. There was nothing distinguishable where Sotare was indicating. He looked back at the angel, who continued to point in the same direction. So, Mark looked once again. Then, there it was, movement. Mark saw something, but it was barely detectable. He could see that it was very far away. "What is it?" he asked. Sotare said nothing as he lowered his arm. Mark followed his lead and looked on in silence.

From the great distance Mark could see what seemed to be an approaching glow of radiant, brilliant color that stood out from the background. He could see glimmers of red, green, blue, and violet, all shooting out in different directions like rays of sunlight that pierce through clouds. It was absolutely beautiful. The glow resembled a sphere, but it had no distinguishable borders. Instead, it seemed to change its contour with each emanation of colored light, yet remaining constant in shape.

Mark was intrigued, almost hypnotized. He watched calmly as the shape approached, spellbound by the growing and dazzling drama of dancing lights that moved in every direction. It shimmered with intensely colored lights that appeared and disappeared, spiraling outward like slivers, and then fading out of existence only to be replaced by other gleaming rays of beauty. The colors seemed alive and pure, growing in intensity the closer the shape came.

Mark could not have moved his eyes away even if he wanted to. He was captivated by the intense beauty of this magnificent radiance. He found himself taking in its brilliance, barely able to comprehend its exquisite form. Then he realized he was seeing colors he had never perceived before.

Sotare gently took hold of Mark's arm, and, with a single movement of his wings, the two glided from the path of the approaching orb until they were what seemed to be a few thousand feet away.

"Is that God?" asked Mark aloud.

Sotare said nothing.

The moving rays of light flared outward. Ripples of rainbow-like shapes curved in undulating, flowing movements. Ribbons of color seemed to explode and dance, only to fall back into the orb and erupt again. The details of its beauty became clearer as it approached, and its glory intensified as it came closer.

Then Mark began to hear music: wonderful, ethereal music. But it was not in the form of singing or instruments. It was something else, something he could not wrap his mind around. It was musical, but it was unlike anything he had ever experienced before. The sound seemed to be part of reality, part of him, yet he did not know how he could hear it inside his mind. The sound somehow reached into him and touched a piece of his soul he didn't know was there. It was enthralling, wondrously experiential as the melody streamed forward into him and through him. Mark then realized that the extraordinary music seemed to match the undulating colors in a perfect ballet of sight and sound. It was magnificent, absolutely astounding—an orchestra of perfection.

Mark was enthralled. His breathing became deep, almost labored, and his knees weakened. He wanted to fall into its wonder and be swept away by its beauty. He had the urge to release himself completely, to follow the light wherever it would go. Tears began to well up in his eyes as the awesome spectacle overtook his soul.

Mark was surprised to find he was feeling good, but, at the same time, much more than good. He analyzed the feeling and quickly realized it was a combination of pleasure and assurance, no, it was more than that. It wasn't assurance. It was profound confidence. Then, unexpectedly, he felt the profound urge to bow down. The mixture of sensations of sight, sound, and feeling was both overwhelming and marvelous. He savored it and willing relaxed as he gave himself to the all encompassing sensation. Automatically, he began to bend his knees to bow low, but Sotare would not let him and pulled him up by the arm. This angered and confused Mark, but the angel's grip was too strong.

All Mark could do was watch as the orb moved closer until he realized that the marvelous array of sight and sound was passing them by, moving away, and with it, immediately the beauty and music began to fade.

"No," pleaded Mark. He wanted to go after it. He desperately wanted to pursue it and stay in its presence. But Mark could not move. He had no ability to follow the object that had just given him the greatest experience of his life.

"No," he said in a shaky voice. "No."

He tugged free of Sotare's grip.

Sadness overcame him as he realized the sensations were fading. But all he could do was watch it move away until finally, agonizingly, it disappeared and with it all the marvelous sensations that had caressed his body and soul. Mark stared into the void left in its absence. Everything seemed profoundly empty and dead. He was dismayed at its disappearance.

"Why didn't you let me follow it?" pleaded Mark.

Sotare said nothing. Instead, he took his right hand and placed it over Mark's eyes and quickly removed it. Mark expected to see the garden. Instead, he saw what looked like clouds below and above. In the very great distance another brilliantly white light was shining, but this one was intense, possessing a clarity and purity that was unlike the orb he had just seen. It was pure white, absolutely pure. Though there was no point of reference to judge its size, Mark somehow knew it was immensely greater than the orb he had just seen. That was when Mark realized that they were very far away.

"The great distance is for your protection," said Sotare.

Mark heard the words but only stared straight ahead. He saw rays of light hovering in space like shimmering, flowing beams that seemed almost alive. They changed their shape and intensity, always shining outward and lighting space in such a way that it seemed as though the radiance became part of the surrounding area. The light and the purity moved into the very fabric of existence.

All around in every direction, there were smaller specks of

moving light. He looked at them from his distant viewpoint. *What are they?* He wondered.

They flowed, moved, and glistened in minute beauty like facets of a diamond reflecting the magnificent source of light that surpassed them. They stirred closer, then further away from the center like the ebb and flow of a slow tide. Some were brighter than others and, as Mark gazed out again at the distant rays, these flecks of light were everywhere. It was a dazzling beauty on an incomprehensible scale that extended far beyond his ability to perceive.

Then Mark noticed something. He wasn't sure what it was at first, but he soon realized there was an absolute purity emanating from that Great Light. It moved through him even as it fell upon him. It was pure, subtle, complete, and superbly good. He was amazed and intrigued by the sensation as if another sense had awakened from dormancy and was letting him experience a whole new reality. But, although beautiful, it was not entirely pleasant. This new sense seemed not only to convey the wondrous sensation from the outside, but it also revealed the negative from within. It caused him to see himself, to sense his own impurity and selfishness. It was as though a light had illuminated a hidden, dark corner of his soul that was only now revealed. In that corner was pride and arrogance. He saw and felt how unholy and impure he was and with this realization came an overwhelming sensation of shame. Once again, but for a different reason, he wanted to bow, this time motivated out of humility.

Though there was no ground below him, he still felt the urge to bend his knees and lower himself. So instinctively he did. He looked over at Sotare halfway expecting him to grab him by the arm and lift him up again. But Sotare was already bowing.

Mark could not help but feel unworthy and unholy in the presence of this majestic and colossal purity. He felt dirty because that which was shining on him was so holy and absolutely clean in its very essence. It pierced into Mark's soul and ripped him open, exposing him. He was completely unworthy, totally undeserving to be in such a magnificent being. Mark could not bow low enough. He began to cry. Yet, at the same time, he felt goodness, purity, and righteousness flow upon him and into him. Then he understood why he was wearing filthy rags. In fact, he felt the rags were too good for him.

He was in the presence of God.

Mark's head was low, eyes averted.

Sotare spoke one word, "Look."

Though Mark did not feel worthy enough to raise his eyes, he obeyed Sotare's command and saw that he was pointing towards the Great Light. Near it, moving away from God was that orb of iridescent beauty he had just seen seconds earlier. But, it was tiny compared to the Great Light. As it moved away from God, thousands upon thousands of the diamond-like points moved with it. Somehow Mark knew about one third of them were following the iridescent orb. He watched the great scene unfold, glancing back and forth, absorbing the unfolding majesty.

But then, he noticed that the orb was changing. The rainbow effect dimmed a bit and he noticed that all its splendor and beauty was turning, right before his eyes, into shades of darkness. Then, one by one, each fragment of beauty that was following also changed from light to dark creating a huge white canvas with speckled bits of darkness scattered about.

He stared at the orb as it slowly changed and became a black hole in the realm of light. Then he could see what looked like fire. Mark did not know how he knew, but it seemed as though this orb was in agony as its shape contorted and twisted in response to the flames that seemed to erupt from inside. Likewise, the specks of light that were following also changed. With their luster gone, they became black dots against the repelling purity of God's brightness. Together the now ugly orb, along with thousands upon thousands of dark specks, moved away from the presence of God.

Mark was awestruck. He wasn't thinking or analyzing. He was only watching in amazement as the scene unfolded before him. The vision was breathtaking and surreal. He watched the creature move away.

Then he heard something far away and faint. They were distant screams of agony emanating from the multitude of dark splinters so far away. Sadness washed over him.

There was no music coming from the orb now. Its splendor had vanished and all that was left was a wretched shell of misery. Mark inexplicably sensed hopelessness and evil as he watched the ugly thing flee from the presence of the light. He then knew what it was.

Sotare placed his hand in front of Mark's eyes once more and when he removed it, Mark and Sotare were back in the gazebo.

***

Pastor Tim arrived at the hospital and quickly made his way up to the room where John and Kathy were waiting. He entered and saw her in a chair next to John. He was sitting up and looked much improved.

"I'm glad you made it, Pastor." John extended his hand. Tim quickly took it with both of his.

"I hurried over here, as fast as I could," he replied.

"I hope you didn't speed."

"Nah, I tried to obey the speed limit, but there were a couple of streets there where I was moving pretty well. At one point a little old lady walking across an intersection had to dive into some bushes to get out of my way. I think she'll be okay. If the cops show up here later, tell them you never saw me." He smiled and looked over at Kathy. She was smiling too.

"All right then," said Tim as he grabbed a spare chair and moved to where Kathy was sitting. He sat down and put his Bible in his lap.

There was a slight moment of awkward silence. Tim decided to get things moving.

"Well, I guess I'll just jump right in. So, your father tells me that he thinks you may have seen a demon. Is that right?"

She nodded. The expression on her face showed just a bit of strain. Obviously, the memory was unpleasant. Since she professed no real belief in God, she felt a little embarrassed about talking to Tim who was, essentially, still a stranger. Tim could see the tension in her face and immediately regretted jumping in so fast.

"I'm sorry. I didn't mean to be so direct."

Kathy smiled slightly. "Oh, that's okay. I suppose we have to start somewhere." She adjusted herself in her seat.

"Well, I'm not sure what I saw." She adjusted herself again. "Last night…" she trailed off and became silent. Both John and Tim waited patiently.

"Last night, when I got home after visiting Dad, I was watching TV, and the place got real cold. I turned the heat up, but it didn't seem to help. And then, it's kind of hard to explain, but I got this feeling. It was as though I was in danger, that there was someone watching me. And…" she paused again. "And… then I started to feel really bad. It doesn't make any sense because I just sat there and I was getting more and more afraid for no reason. This feeling was getting worse and then," she looked at her father, not wanting to bring up a painful part of his life. "As this feeling got worse, a memory flooded my mind." She paused again. "The accident."

Pastor Tim looked over at John, whose face had fallen. It was obviously an unpleasant memory for him, too. He looked back at Kathy.

"Go ahead," said John.

Kathy took a breath and let it out slowly. "Pastor, when I was a little girl there was a terrible accident, and I saw a badly burned body."

John groaned slightly and looked at the ceiling.

"It's okay, Dad."

John continued to look away.

"You see, my father blames himself for this. He tried to take a shortcut around an accident and unfortunately it led us onto the scene and I saw a body. I had nightmares for a long time and Dad really beat himself up over it for a long time. It wasn't his fault, though. It was just one of those things." She looked at her father. He was still staring at the ceiling.

She reached out and grabbed his hand and gave it a gentle squeeze before she returned her attention to Tim.

"Well, last night, for some unknown reason, that memory

flooded my mind at the same time that this intense fear was growing in me. I mean, it was really intense. I tried to break away from it. I tried to not think about it, but I couldn't help it. I mean, these memories just… they just came out of nowhere and I couldn't stop them. And then there was the fear, this incredible fear that someone was going to kill me. It grew and grew and images of that body kept forcing themselves into my mind. I couldn't get rid of them. I wanted to, but I couldn't."

Kathy was animated in her speech, her hands moving quickly, and her voice carried the tension of the experience.

"And then, when I didn't think I could take it anymore, when it was so awful, I finally managed to scream, that's when I saw this face in front of me. It was horrible. It was the most hideous thing I've ever seen and that's when I passed out. It was all too much for me, so I fainted." Her voice was shaking and slightly higher in pitch. She stopped again to calm herself. Both John and Tim were watching her, obviously concerned.

"I woke up after a little while on the floor. As soon as I started to regain consciousness I began to cry really hard. I felt like panicking. But then, and I can't explain this either, I felt this peace suddenly come over me. It was strange. I mean, after what just happened, you'd think I'd be terrified but there was this peace, as if it came out of nowhere. I mean… it makes no sense." She stopped abruptly, slumped in the chair, and stared blankly at the floor. John and Tim looked at each other without saying a word. Kathy raised her head and looked at her father, then the pastor. Her voice shook slightly.

"I feel a little embarrassed talking about this. But it was so real. I've never felt anything like it." She looked at them both, her expression gently pleading for an explanation.

John was not sure what to say. The ball was in the pastor's court and, after a brief pause to process what she had said, Tim finally responded. "Thank you very much for telling me about this. It certainly sounds as though something spiritual has happened. Exactly what it is, I'm not sure, but it does appear to be demonic."

With that, Kathy stiffened. The pastor noticed it.

"Kathy, I need to ask something, and I want you to know that I mean no offense whatsoever." He adjusted himself in his chair. "Are you on any medications?"

She cocked her head back.

"Kathy, I have to ask this. I need to find out if this might have been chemically induced. Please forgive me if I'm being rude. I don't mean to be."

"No, that's all right. I understand. No, I'm not on any medications. I don't do drugs and I wasn't drinking, either. I was just sitting there watching TV."

"Thanks Kathy, but one more thing. Have you been getting enough sleep lately?"

Kathy knew the pastor was trying to rule out other possibilities. His face showed genuine concern.

"I hope you understand why I have to ask. I'm not trying to be offensive."

"No, don't worry. I know why you are asking and yes, I've been getting enough sleep lately."

The pastor nodded approvingly, shifted in his seat, and calmly said, "Now that that's out of the way, it sounds to me that the best explanation is you were attacked by a demonic force."

Kathy was obviously displeased to hear these words and Tim picked up on her body language.

"I know this is probably pretty weird to you, huh?"

"Yeah," she said with a smile. "It's just that I've never given this spiritual stuff much thought. I mean, no offense, but it's so foreign to me."

"That's understandable. Maybe there is another explanation, and if there is, I'm open to hearing it. But, from what you've told me it seems the most logical conclusion is that you had a real spiritual encounter."

Kathy bit her upper lip slightly as she contemplated the pastor's words. "Okay, let's assume for a minute that it was like you say. Then, why would this happen?"

"Pastor?" interrupted John. "When you were here the other day, you mentioned something about Mark and that he was important. Do you think that he has anything to do with this?"

Tim looked at Kathy. "Well, to be honest, I've never really had a feeling about anyone like I did about your husband. It was definitely unusual. As a matter of fact, now that I think about it, in my office at the church recently, I had a strange sensation as though another presence was there." He looked at John and paused. He knew he had to weigh his words carefully, especially since Kathy had her doubts. It was obvious to him that there was something extraordinary going on.

Tim spoke carefully. "Look, I know that this whole God thing is probably a bit confusing for you, maybe even ridiculous. I certainly would understand if you are hesitant to believe what I have to say, or accept even what you saw last night as a reality. But, for what it's worth, I believe that we're all here together for a reason and that God has his hand in this."

Kathy took in his every word. She didn't know what to think, and though she had hoped for a more definitive, scientific answer, she realized his comments would have to do for now.

"What about my husband? Do you think this has to do with him, like my dad says?"

"I don't know *how* I know, but I know that your husband is very important, and he is the reason this is happening." With that the pastor lowered his head and clenched his hands together, intertwining his fingers.

He looked at her. "Kathy, there is a God and he has spoken to us in the Bible. He's told us that there is a spiritual world and that there are demonic and angelic forces. He also tells us that prayer can be very effective and that nothing comes to us unless he permits it. Therefore, we need to be alert and in prayer." He looked at John. "Have you told her about the Lord, and about receiving him?"

"Well, Pastor. You see, Kathy and I have this understanding that I won't push Christianity on her and she will respect my belief." He adjusted himself in his bed once again, and again the pain reminded him where he was. "I have witnessed to her before, years ago, but I don't know how much she remembers."

"Okay, I understand," said Tim. He turned to Kathy again. "Kathy, in no way do I want to put you on the spot. I'm not here to pressure you, but if you have any questions, I would be glad to answer them. Please feel free to say and ask anything you want."

Pastor Tim was trying to find out where Kathy was spiritually. There was much he could tell her, but was she ready?

"I appreciate that. My dad is right, we have come to an agreement, and we really don't talk about this religion stuff because, well, we just don't agree. I believe that as long as you are sincere and believe in God, you're good enough. But, my dad tells me that Jesus is the only way to God and I just can't accept that. It would mean that all the good and sincere people in the world who don't believe in him are all going to hell."

"I see," said Pastor Tim. "A lot of people have the same objection. But, if you don't mind, can I read you something Jesus said? I won't bug you about it. It is something that he said that relates to what we're talking about here."

Kathy inhaled and exhaled slowly. "Sure," she answered, only to be polite.

The pastor could sense her hesitancy, so he flipped through the pages of his Bible quickly. "Here it is." Though he had the verse memorized, he wanted her to see that it was there. "John 14:6 is where Jesus says, 'I am the way, the truth, and the life, and nobody comes to the Father but by me.'" With that, he closed the Bible. "Kathy, Jesus said that. Now, I don't know about you, but I find myself unable to say he was mistaken, no matter what I might feel."

Kathy looked at her father. The words were a direct contradiction to what she believed, and that obvious fact was amplified by the silence. The pastor's point was made. But Kathy could sense no arrogance in his tone. He was sincere. After a few seconds he spoke.

"Well, when are you going to get out of the hospital, John?"

"Believe it or not, the doctor said I may get out in a few hours."

Kathy looked surprised. "Why didn't you tell me that?"

"Uh, maybe because we were a little preoccupied?" John had raised his eyebrows along with his tone while he motioned with his hands to the hospital room. Then he smiled.

"You got that right," she responded.

"My side is still hurting a bit, but the doctor said that everything is healing up very well and that, if I want to, I could head out of here sometime this evening."

"That is pretty fast, isn't it?" asked Kathy.

"Yep, praise God. I'm healing up very well. It has to be all the prayers. And, of course, that laparoscopic surgery sure makes recovery easier."

He looked at the pastor, then back to his daughter. "I wanted to surprise you, but what happened last night was more important. Besides, the doctor told me just this morning before you got here. He said I was doing great." John smiled and flexed a bicep. "Yep, this old body still has what it takes." Tim chuckled.

It was obvious to everyone that John was trying to relax his daughter with some humor.

Kathy got up and grabbed his hand. "I'm so glad to hear that. I know how you are, wanting to get home and work on your garden."

"Yep, and I want to get to church tomorrow, too." He looked at the pastor. "What is your sermon going to be about tomorrow?"

"Well... coincidently," he said as he pointed up, "It's going to be about spiritual warfare. I'm going to be talking about angels and demons and how they can affect us."

"Oh, I have to be there for that. If I get out tonight, I'll be sitting in my usual spot in the morning. I wouldn't miss it for the world."

"Dad, you aren't planning on driving yourself to the church tomorrow are you?"

"I don't see why not."

"But Dad, I don't think you should be driving so soon. I can take you home tonight, but you're still pretty sore and maybe you should take it easy for a day or two longer."

"I appreciate that, but I really do want to go to church."

Kathy sighed, realizing that the only thing she could do now was to offer to drive her father to church. She quickly resigned herself to that predicament and then volunteered, "All right,

Dad, if you get out of the hospital today, I'll take you to church tomorrow." It was obvious she wasn't happy about it.

"I would love that. You're such a good daughter."

"That's only because I had such a good dad," she offered with a fake smile.

With that, the pastor took the opportunity to stand up and excuse himself. "Well, I think I'll get going and head back to the church and do some more prep for tomorrow's service." He looked at John and said, "I hope that you get out of the hospital this evening and…" he looked over at Kathy, "…I hope to see you tomorrow, as well." He smiled and moved towards the door.

"I'm glad you confided in me, Kathy. Don't worry, everything will be all right."

He gently pulled open the door and disappeared into the hallway.

Kathy took a long look at John and exhaled hard. "I'm getting hungry. This spiritual stuff is a lot of work."

John snickered a bit, "Yep."

"Dad, if you don't mind I would like to go to the cafeteria and get something to eat and then maybe head to your place afterwards. I'm a bit stressed, and I wouldn't mind relaxing for a while. Is that okay with you?"

"Of course. You just take as much time as you need and I'll be here waiting for you. Who knows, maybe the doctor will give me an early release. If he does, I'll call you at home."

With that, Kathy got up and gave her dad a kiss on the cheek, squeezing his hand yet again. She looked at the IV and the machines all over the room and headed out the door. "See you in a little while," she said, disappearing into the hallway.

John lay back in his bed and looked up at the ceiling. He relaxed and let himself fall into its comfort. On a stand to his right was a Bible. He reached over and brought it to his lap, where he opened it to Ephesians 6, a chapter dealing with spiritual warfare. He read for a few minutes, and then closed his eyes as he began to pray for his daughter and the pastor.

In a corner of the room, a demon watched him. It could not stand to be in the presence of a man who was praying to the true and living God, so it slowly turned its face to the wall, stepped through it and let itself fall downward, opening its wings, and gliding away.

***

Mark found himself having difficulty expressing his feelings. Ever since the vision of the fall of the devil, he had been unable to speak. It wasn't that he couldn't. He just didn't want to. He looked at Sotare through intense eyes and said nothing. The memory of the incredible sight of countless angels, of the glorious light of God emanating and filling the universe, of the beautiful and immense being that fell and became ugly, left him without words.

Why had he been allowed to see such an incredible thing?

Mark turned his eyes from Sotare and looked past him into the garden. A small butterfly had landed on a flower and was slowly beating its wings. He focused on it, studying its colors, memorizing it. He remembered the one he had recently crushed. A twinge of remorse surfaced. He had taken a life, a small one, needlessly. Somehow, the butterfly wasn't insignificant anymore.

Mark saw past the garden and visualized the realm where God dwelt. His desire to have questions answered had mysteriously vanished. He had discovered that hard questions had hard answers.

Mark thought again of the vision and the indescribable majesty of the glory of the light that radiated from the presence of the Almighty. He contemplated his insignificance, his utterly minuscule stature in the grand scope of creation. He felt like that butterfly. He felt like he deserved to be crushed. Yet, the Almighty had sent an angel to speak to him. It made no sense.

Sotare broke the silence. "What you have seen is remarkable and you are highly privileged."

Mark didn't feel special. On the contrary, he felt unworthy. "Why would God be concerned with me?" asked Mark, his eyes still focused on the butterfly.

Sotare responded carefully. "He is concerned with you because of who *he* is, because he loves you. It is not because of who *you* are."

Mark was gleaning from these experiences that his own fragile and helpless life was not for his own enjoyment: it had purpose. Only, he didn't know what it was.

Mark slowly slid out of his seat and dropped to his knees. Tears welled in his eyes, not because he was in anguish, but because his heart was humbled as he reflected on the greatness of the vision and the exceedingly rare, perhaps unprecedented privilege he had just experienced. With his head bowed, he allowed his tears to fall without the slightest desire to hide them or wipe them away.

Sotare knelt down beside him.

Chapter 10

KATHY HAD RETURNED TO her father's house and was sitting on the couch, endlessly flipping through the TV channels. Occasionally, she would check behind her, a little uncomfortable with the memory of last night's events so fresh in her mind. Somehow, she knew that whatever had happened had passed and she was able to relax. She dozed off a couple of times, only to be awakened by some obnoxious commercial on the television set. Just when she was getting overly bored, the phone rang.

"They are releasing me," said her father, happily. "I'm ready to leave when you get here."

"Great, I'll be right there." She gathered herself together and hurried out the door.

When she walked into the hospital room she found her father already dressed and in a wheelchair. A volunteer hospital worker, a woman around John's age, was sitting in a chair next to him waiting to wheel him out. He was smiling and tapping his feet impatiently. "Where have you been?" he kidded. "I've been waiting here for hours."

The woman smiled, as did Kathy.

Kathy said, "I thought you'd be out of here a lot sooner than this. You must be slipping." Kathy enjoyed her father's continual good nature. He had always been that way.

They chided each other for a bit as the volunteer began to wheel John out and towards the elevator. In a few minutes they were at Kathy's car. John stood up, wincing a little bit in the process, but managing to get himself inside. Both Kathy and John thanked the hospital worker. "Thanks, Angela," said John cheerfully.

"My pleasure. Now you take care of yourself." She smiled and disappeared back into the building, pushing the wheelchair ahead of her.

They both buckled up and after Kathy made sure that her dad was ready to go, she headed out of the parking lot.

On an outside ledge of the fifth story of the hospital, a demon was looking their way. As the car drove off, the creature leaned forward and fell. Plummeting, it opened its wings and arced downward towards the car. As Kathy navigated the turns, the demon followed until it quickly was at their car. Bracing against the wind by opening its wings wide to slow down, it latched onto the roof with its clawed feet and folded its wings in close to its body. It tucked low and then it peered down through the roof, growling and spitting. The spittle passed through John's chest and disappeared.

John felt a twinge of nausea in his stomach, but ignored it. He was happy to be going home.

***

After Pastor Tim arrived at home, he greeted his wife Susan and told her about meeting Kathy at the hospital and what she had said. He also mentioned Mr. Smith's visit to the church.

"That is certainly unusual about Kathy," responded Susan as she made Tim a snack. "And I hope Mr. Smith comes to church tomorrow."

Tim didn't tell her how uneasy he felt being alone with him. "I'm going to the study for a bit, okay?"

"That's fine. I'll bring this to you when it's ready."

"Thanks." Tim headed off.

Susan watched him as he walked away. There was a feeling of foreboding in the air and though she didn't know why, she was concerned for his safety.

Tim was having difficulty concentrating. So much had happened in the past few days and with Kathy's description of a demonic being, he was all the more convinced that something significant was on the horizon. *But what?*

He looked at his sermon notes on the computer and read for a bit. He began to rewrite a sentence when an urge to pray for Kathy and John popped into his mind. He hurried to finish the sentence and then sat back in his chair as he stared at the computer screen and then at the Bible which was open on his desk. "It's all in there," he said.

Tim knew that the Spirit of God was always with him, but he was still feeling particularly vulnerable. Through the years he had learned not to trust his feelings, and it did not matter whether he felt close or distant to God. He knew that such emotional ups and downs could be deceptive, and he had learned long ago not to trust them. Instead, he had always relied on the Word of God. Through his years as a pastor, he had discovered that sometimes the dry spells were precursors to spiritual struggles and victories. As he thought about it, it became more and more apparent that this battle was going to be different.

He sat there in his office and thought about tomorrow, about the church service, and the more he thought, the more he had an indescribable and acute awareness that "something" was going to happen, something significant. He decided to open his Bible. As he brought it to himself, it slipped from his fingers. He tried to catch it and as he groped for it he inadvertently ripped a single page from its binding. The Bible thudded on the ground.

"Great!" said Tim, exasperated. He'd had this Bible for years. It was like an old friend to him. Upset with himself that he had damaged it, he placed the single page on his desk and retrieved the book from the floor. He took the ripped page. It was Psalm 23.

"Hmm," he said contemplatively as he slowly slipped it back in place. He frowned at the damage and fought back the soft wave of disappointment coursing through his heart. He exhaled hard and stared out the office window.

He was a stickler about books, especially this well-read and lovingly worn Bible. It was his constant companion. Damaging it irritated him greatly. He pounded his fist on the desk gently, then after a moment he sat back in his chair and closed his eyes. Immediately, he envisioned the church and himself standing in the pulpit preaching. He would not let this minor incident get the best of him, so he began to pray for John and Kathy.

From outside his office window two demons hovered, waiting and watching.

***

John was having a little difficulty staying comfortable.

"What is it, Dad?" Kathy was concerned.

"My lower back hurts a little. I think it's from lying in that hospital bed for too long. It's a little difficult sitting up now. Don't worry, I'll be fine. It's nothing."

"Would you like to stop at a convenience store? We can get some aspirin."

"Naw, I have some at home, and besides, the doctor gave me a prescription for stronger medicine for when the over-the-counter stuff doesn't cut it. If I need it, you can go fill the prescription for me. But right now, I'm okay."

They continued to talk about the operation, Mark, the pastor, and whatever else flowed to their minds. Kathy was glad to have her dad out of the hospital, and, of course, John was glad to be going home. He was watching the scenery pass by and realized how much he missed it, having been cooped up inside the stale medical environment. He looked out the window and enjoyed the scenery. The trees were particularly enjoyable to look at.

"It's going to be great being home," said John.

Kathy glanced at him but she was wondering how Mark was doing and had already begun to plan when she might be able to return home.

The demon continued to peer at them through the roof. It let more spittle fall into and through John.

John laid his head back on the seat and closed his eyes.

"Tired?"

"Yeah, just a little," he replied, rubbing his stomach.

Kathy kept driving and let her father relax. She thought about Mark and wondered when would be a good time to call him.

The demon knew that Kathy was unprotected and that she was susceptible to its influence. But, she was also very concerned about getting her father home safely which would mean she'd be careful about driving. The creature realized attacking her directly was probably not the best option. Should it wait until they got to John's home and look for something there or should it try and use the vehicle or another driver to hopefully cause an accident? It did not know which was best, so it raised its wings, caught the air and lifted away from the car. With several quick flaps it rose above the traffic and looked around. If it could find a demon assigned to a person in another car, perhaps it could persuade that demon to use the driver to cause an accident. Or, perhaps there was a pedestrian somewhere that it could influence to jump out in front of the car. But this was difficult to achieve, especially on such a short notice. Perhaps, something in the home could be used: a poison, a gas line, or medicine. Its assignment was to kill both or either, and, at the very least, stop John from praying. There wasn't enough time to plan a car accident, so the demon headed towards the house, frantically flapping its wings.

John opened his eyes and looked at Kathy. She glanced over at her father, "What?"

John stared at her, saying nothing. He turned and looked ahead.

"Are you okay?" she asked.

He did not respond. He just looked at his daughter and nodded slowly. He turned his attention back to the road.

"Dad?"

He didn't respond. She kept glancing at him as she drove.

"Dad? Are you okay?" She began to pull to the side of the

road.

John was looking straight ahead, but he did not see the street. Instead, he saw Pastor Tim in the pulpit of his church and a masked man with a gun nearby. He raised the gun. John could see that Kathy was there. Tim looked at the gunman and John saw the gun go off. The vision ended and John could see the street in front of him again.

"Dad? Dad? Are you okay?" She had pulled off the road and was now shaking her father's shoulder. "Dad! Dad, are you all right? Dad?"

John slowly focused on her eyes.

"Pastor Tim is in danger," he said. "We need to warn him."

***

In the garden, Mark had been sitting silently for quite some time. His heart and mind had calmed enough for him to sort through the clutter and he had finally managed to quell the emotions that were so vividly left over from his vision.

Sotare had been waiting patiently. Finally Mark spoke.

"I'm beginning to really see that this world is not limited to the one I am living in. The real world consists of both the spiritual and the physical and the only right way to view things is to know them both." He glanced at Sotare, surprised at the clarity and assurance of his new understanding.

Sotare nodded slowly.

"It is a war between good and evil and if we are not prepared and aware, we become vulnerable, even defenseless."

Mark gazed into the fading light of the evening and saw softly swaying shadows of gray shift beneath the plants. He looked at Sotare.

"I want to do what is right. Teach me. Teach me what I need to know. I don't care what it costs or how difficult it is." His voice was emphatic.

Although Sotare was an angel and did not need to breathe, he slowly let out a sigh, nodded, and smiled faintly as he looked back into Mark's eyes.

"May I touch your eyes again?" asked Sotare.

Mark paused for a moment.

His heart had softened. "Of course," he said calmly.

Sotare stood up and placed his right hand over Mark's eyes and his left hand on the back of his head and then lowered them. Mark found himself in Pastor Tim's church on Sunday morning. John and Kathy were sitting in the pew and there was a man in the pulpit, the pastor. From the rear of the church another man entered. He had a mask and a gun and began to walk towards the front. The pastor was speaking, and it appeared that he was introducing Kathy to the congregation. She stood up as the gunman raised his weapon. Sotare removed his hands from Mark's eyes and the vision stopped.

Mark bolted up. "No!" he exclaimed loudly. "No!"

"Go to her," said Sotare.

Mark was taken aback. "I thought you said I had to stay in the garden."

"I did, but now it is time for you to go. You're supposed to go." Sotare handed him a piece of paper.

"What's this?"

"The church's address."

Surprised, Mark looked at the angel. "What about you? Will I see you again?"

Sotare smiled. "Go to her. She is going to need you."

Mark didn't like that. "Is she going to be okay?"

Sotare said nothing. He just stared at him. Mark tried to read Sotare's blank face.

"I should call the police and warn them," said Mark.

"And what would you tell them? Are you going to let them know that you had a vision? Or maybe you could try to convince them that you know there's going to be a gunman in the church tomorrow. The police would want to know how you know, what your involvement would have been. Remember, as far as anyone knows you've been having serious problems at work and are on a much-needed vacation due to emotional stress. It wouldn't look good for you to call the police and say a gunman is going to shoot someone. You might even be implicated."

"Implicated? Implicated in what?"

Sotare didn't answer.

Mark was obviously agitated. He forced himself to remain calm as he looked at Sotare.

"Am I supposed to go alone?"

Sotare looked at him again with the same enigmatic expression and remained silent.

"All right," Mark broke the silence. "I'll run upstairs and get some clothes and head to the airport."

"Drive," said Sotare.

Mark stared at his teacher. Sotare knew things he did not and arguing with him would only waste time.

"Alright, if I hurry, I can be there early in the morning." He started walking towards the house. As he went, he remarked, "I'll call Kathy and let her know I'm coming."

"No," said Sotare. "Don't call her. Don't let her know."

Mark stopped dead in his tracks. He turned around quickly and frowned, his agitation finally getting the best of him. "Why not?" he asked.

Sotare said nothing and vanished.

Mark stared into the emptiness, feeling suddenly alone, and angry. Sotare's abrupt departure was unsettling, especially with his instruction not to call Kathy. He didn't like being kept in the dark. But it didn't matter. He'd go to her as fast as he could.

He turned around and headed towards the house. As he left the garden, he thought about Nabal at the top of the tree. He stopped and took one last glance upward...

Above him, looking down through eyes filled with loathing was Nabal. Mark was looking right at the creature without knowing it. Turning, he hurried into the house.

Nabal slowly opened its wings. In one slow, massive movement it allowed itself to fall forward and downward into the ground below. The slave demon followed fearfully.

***

John and Kathy arrived at his house without incident. He

exited the car slowly and with a few grunts he managed to punctuate a few painful movements. Kathy carefully helped him plod up the few steps to the front door, opened it, and let him in.

"Boy, it's good to be home," he exhaled noisily. "But I have to get inside and call Pastor Tim." John had not told her about his vision. She would probably think he was losing his mind.

Kathy closed the door and quickly walked to the couch, making sure that the pillows were in the right position for John. She put the remote control within arm's reach and turned back toward her father, who was standing behind her.

"I see you didn't have any wild parties while I was gone," he said. "That's good." He was trying to be lighthearted as he slowly lowered himself to the couch, trying not to let his expression reflect the decreasing but still-present pain still jousting with his side.

"Can I get you anything?" she asked.

"No thanks. You've done enough already. Why don't you just sit down and relax?"

"I think I will, but first, I need to call Mark. Do you mind?"

"Not at all. I'll call Pastor Tim while you're talking to him."

Kathy disappeared into the kitchen. She retrieved her cell phone from her purse and dialed Mark.

John reached for the phone on the end table by the couch.

At home Mark was quickly gathering some clothes and putting them in a small suitcase. He knew he wouldn't need much and he wanted to get to his wife quickly. The phone rang. He briefly toyed with the idea of not answering it before walking over to pick it up.

"Hello?"

"Hi honey, it's me. How are you doing?"

Hearing from Kathy was unexpectedly precious. "I'm doing fine," he said, as he closed his eyes.

"Are you sure? Are you sure things are okay?" She was unknowingly projecting her own anxiety onto him.

"Yes, I'm doing very well. This time alone has been surprisingly helpful." Mark knew that was quite an understatement.

Kathy wasn't as convinced as she wanted to be, but she continued. "Dad is out of the hospital. We just got home. He's getting better fast, and I hope to come home as soon as I feel he's well enough to manage by himself."

For a moment Mark hoped that she might be able to leave tonight. He wanted to tell her to leave now, to get away. But he knew that he was supposed to be there just as much as he knew that trying to warn her was not the right thing to do. "Can you come home tonight?" he said obligatorily, even though he knew it wasn't practical.

"Oh, no. It's too late for that and besides, I don't feel comfortable leaving him alone just yet. I mean, he just got out of the hospital. Maybe in a day or two I can come home. I don't want to abandon him just yet. But I really want to be there with you." She paused.

"Me too," he said as he continued to pack.

"I know that you say you're doing well, and you sound as though you are, but I'm still a little worried and am anxious to see you. Are you sure you're doing okay?"

"Kathy, you know that I wouldn't lie to you. In all seriousness, I'm doing well. Really. In fact, I'm doing a lot better than you might think." Mark entertained the idea of telling her about Sotare but, of course, he couldn't.

Kathy knew his voice. His reassurance seemed genuine. "Good," she responded. "That makes me feel better."

Mark wanted desperately to confide in her, but it wasn't the right time.

"Dad is doing so well. The doctor was really surprised at how fast he is healing. Now, you know I'm not into any of this God stuff, but maybe all the prayers from the church and the pastor have helped."

Mark froze. "Maybe," said Mark, staring out the bedroom window. "I've heard that it does."

"Yeah, me too. Well, it'll be interesting tomorrow at church. I know that my dad will want to go so I'll have to endure it with him because I don't want him to drive right now."

Mark felt the ache of fear rise in his heart. He did not want her to go, yet he couldn't tell her not to do so. It wouldn't make any sense, and it would undermine her confidence that he was doing better. It suddenly made more sense to him why Sotare had told him not to call her. On the other hand, she had called him. Still, he knew that the only real option he had was to get to her. Should he tell her that he was on his way? He thought about it for a moment while she spoke about her dad's recovery. He threw in the few statements like, "That's great" and "uh huh," but his focus was more on getting to her than her words.

Once he showed up at the church tomorrow, she would want to know why he hadn't mentioned that he was coming. He figured that all he would have to say is that he wanted to surprise her. Besides, she would know soon enough when he told her everything, whenever that would be.

He turned back to the conversation. "Anyway, the pastor seems to be a nice guy, but I'm still not looking forward to going to Dad's church tomorrow. He needs me, so I'll go. But I really don't want to. I guess it won't be that bad."

"It might be good for you," he said in a happy tone.

"What? Are you finding religion during your vacation?"

He froze with her question and changed the subject.

"I really am looking forward to seeing you soon."

"Me too."

They chatted a little longer until John appeared in the kitchen behind Kathy. "I'm going to make myself something to eat," he said. "You hungry?"

"Hold your horses, Dad. Just go back to the living room and I'll fix you something." She made a hand movement towards the living room. John went to open the refrigerator but Kathy intercepted him and gently slapped his hand.

"You're serious," he said.

"You bet." She turned him around and gently nudged him out of the kitchen. "I have to get going, Mark. Dad is getting hungry."

"Okay, I understand. Love you."

"Love you, too."

She hung up the phone and followed her dad into the living

room. She stopped just past the kitchen door, and with a fake, irritated tone, she asked, "Okay, what would you like to eat?"

Mark sat staring at the phone and looked out the window into the garden. He wondered where Sotare and Nomos were. For that matter, he thought to himself, where is Nabal?

***

Pastor Tim sat at his desk, trying to recover from John's phone call regarding his vision. It was upsetting to say the least. But what did it mean? Was there really going to be a gunman in the church or was it symbolic of the spiritual battle that he was under? There was a gentle knock at the door. His wife stuck her head in. "Dinner time."

"I'll be there in a couple of minutes." He returned his attention to John's vision. Dread and apprehension flowed into his heart. He thought about the sermon, about spiritual warfare, about how the invisible battle around him was so very real. Perhaps John's vision was nothing more than an attempt by the enemy to stop him from preaching. It was certainly a possibility.

Tim tapped his fingers on his desk and thought about tomorrow's message, about how society offered so many distractions with its promotion of sexuality, moral relativism, the killing of the unborn, evolution, and an increasing irreverence towards anything sacred. There were far too many politicians with no moral fiber who seemed more interested in self-gain, power, and popular opinion than in showing character in the service of the people. He considered the liberal and anti-Christian agenda that was flowing through the schools and universities, and how the denial of absolute truth was undermining rationality and ethics. These were some of the points of his sermon, but he was also going to speak about the demonic and angelic realms and how the spiritual forces were at work undercutting decency and goodness in the world as well as in the Christian church. It would make sense that such a sermon would be opposed by the demonic realm and the forces of darkness would be dispatched to hinder him.

He slapped his hand down on the desk lightly and determined to preach the truth no matter what. His message had the potential to be depressing, but people needed to hear it. He remembered an adage he heard in seminary: The gospel that offends no one is not the Gospel of the Bible.

He needed to preach the Word of God with conviction and without compromise. As he thought about the many false preachers that have done damage to the faith, he became more convinced of the need to speak the truth, no matter what the cost.

He looked over at his Bible and thought about the cross of Christ and what Jesus went through, how his teaching the truth and standing for it got him killed. Was he willing to do the same? Was he willing to speak the truth to that degree? He hoped he was.

He knew that tomorrow was an important day. Maybe the gunman would be real. Or maybe it was a symbol. He didn't know. Should he call the police and have someone there tomorrow? What would he say? Would he tell them that an old man who just got out of a hospital had a vision and that he was afraid? That would fly like a ton of bricks.

He drew the Bible near him and touched it to his lips. He closed his eyes. "I will do whatever you want me to, Lord. Let my life be for you. I trust you. I ask for protection tomorrow and that you would give me the strength to speak your word in truth and power. In you alone I put my trust. In Jesus' name. Amen."

He sat quietly for a couple of minutes before setting his Bible down. His wife was waiting, so he headed out to the dining room.

Outside his office window, demons sat, watching him.

***

Mark was hurriedly gathering a few items for his trip. He was reviewing what he would tell Kathy when he got there. Telling her that an angel had given him a vision in the garden wouldn't sound like he was fully anchored in reality, so that was out. He decided not to worry about it now, besides he'd have plenty of time to think during the drive. He did not know what was going to happen when he got there but, the more he thought about it, the more agitated and desperate he became. He shoved shirts and pants into his suitcase along with some socks and underwear. He grabbed a toothbrush and shaving items, tossing them in as well. He checked his cell phone, got his charger, and headed downstairs to find some snacks to munch on the way. He wanted to stop as infrequently as possible.

Inside the garage, three demons were kneeling inside the engine compartment of his car. Each of them had its hands directed towards one particular area. They were almost motionless.

Mark entered the garage, swatted at the garage door opener, opened the car door, and tossed his suitcase in the backseat before getting in. The demons did not look away from their task. Instead, their effort became all the more intense. Mark inserted the key into the ignition, turning it. Nothing happened. He groaned aloud and said, "Crap!" as he hit the steering wheel. "Come on, start!" he yelled as he turned the key once more. Again nothing. At that point, the demons all stood up and moved away. Mark instinctively tried one more time and the car started easily. He turned the engine off and restarted it two more times. It ran perfectly. The thought occurred to him that maybe, just maybe, some demonic force was involved. He had no idea if it was true or not and he wondered if he was just paranoid, but he couldn't help thinking about it. He sat there for a second and then thought, *I should pray*. Surprising him, it made sense. The only problem was he didn't know how.

"God," he began aloud. "I don't know how to do this."

One of the demons jumped upward, rising through the rafters as it beat its wings. The other two growled at Mark, and one spat at him.

"All I know is that I have been wrong about a lot of things and that…" he paused and looked around. He thought he heard something. To the side of the car, one demon remained, hissing ferociously at him. Dislocating its jaws, it screamed out a growl, fangs showing. Opening its wings wide, it leaned forward with its fists clenched. In the spiritual world its hissing was loud and formidable and Mark, surprisingly, heard a faint noise. He looked around. The creature stopped. Mark decided to close his eyes. "God, please protect me and my wife and keep me safe as I travel. Teach me what you want me to know. Amen." The demon fled.

He put the car in reverse and carefully backed out. He closed the garage door with a click of the remote and was on his way.

***

As the evening drew to a close, John and Kathy finished their casual conversation over dinner. John was fading fast. He was going to retire early. Kathy thought she would stay up for a little while. After John went to bed, she turned on the TV. She was a bit nervous and apprehensive, and looked around the room once just to be sure there was nothing there.

Sotare stood in the living room. Nomos was hovering above the house and they could see each other through the rafters. Kathy propped her feet up on the coffee table and snuggled down between two oversized pillows positioned on the corner of the couch. To her right was an end table with a lamp. She clicked through the channels with the remote and thought about going home. She missed Mark.

Sotare moved close and stood next to her behind the couch.

There wasn't much to see on TV except a couple of war movies, a cooking show, and some documentaries. The news was depressing. She clicked past a shopping channel and a game show that had an overly exuberant blonde jumping up and down. She clicked another channel but each program was as boring as the previous. She wasn't in the mood for the same old thing. As she was about to give up, she stumbled upon a religious channel.

A man was standing silently behind a pulpit. He wasn't saying anything, which surprised Kathy. She let her thumb hover over the channel button and was immediately reminded of Pastor Tim and what he had said about Mark. Her father seemed to do well with this religion stuff, so she thought she'd see what this guy had to say. The man on TV moved but remained silent. This was odd and Kathy figured that he must be pausing for some dramatic effect before trying to say something profound. Or, she thought, maybe he lost his sermon notes. She chuckled. After five more seconds, he spoke.

"And this is why you must believe what Jesus says over anyone else. No one but Jesus has fulfilled detailed prophecies. No one else has commanded a storm to be still and it obeyed. No one else has walked on water. No one else has raised people from the dead. No one else has changed water into wine. No one else fed five thousand people with a few fish and a little bread. No one else has spoken such words of truth and power that they reach in the heart and cause us to truly see ourselves. And no one else claimed to be God in the flesh and proved it by performing numerous miracles and rising from the dead as he predicted he would."

Continuing with a serious tone, the preacher said, "Jesus was crucified on the cross, died, and was buried, but he did not stay dead." With each syllable of the last sentence, the preacher gently pounded his hand on the pulpit, sending a low, reverberating, emphasis with every word. The man was not angry. He had a gentle but firm tone.

Kathy was intrigued.

"My people, you must listen to the words of Christ. Do not trust your own feelings. Do not trust your own preferences. Do not trust your own wisdom. Do not risk eternity by failing to heed the words of Jesus."

"Jesus said in John 14:6 that he alone was the way, the truth, and the life and that nobody comes to God the Father but through him. Jesus said in Matt. 5:29 that it is better for you to lose one of the parts of your body than for your whole body to be cast into hell."

He paused and looked out at the congregation and then stepped out in front of the pulpit.

"Can we trust this man from so long ago? How can we *not*? Remember, Jesus claimed to be divine. When Moses was on Mt. Sinai, he asked God what his name was and God answered him in Exodus 3:14 by saying, 'I am, that I am.' Jesus said in John 8:58, 'Before Abraham was, I am.' The false religious leaders wanted to kill him for claiming the very name of God for himself, but

Jesus hid himself because his time to die on the cross had not yet come."

He paused and in a calm voice asked calmly, "People, do I have your attention?"

He looked around again. The place was silent and every eye was on him.

"Let me speak plainly and directly, for what I am about to say is very important."

He turned around, picked up the Bible, and then he faced the congregation. "Please understand that God is holy and perfect and his standard of righteousness is also perfect. If you have ever lied, then you are not perfect. You are a liar. If you have ever stolen, then you not perfect. You are a thief. To lie and to steal is to break the Law of God. It is to commit sin against God. Now, please understand that laws have punishments. Therefore, all who have broken the law of God must face the punishment of his law. This is why the Bible says in Roman 6:23 that the wages of sin is death and Isaiah 59:2 says that such death is separation from God."

The preacher again stopped and looked out at the congregation. Kathy realized that it must be a Saturday night service. She watched as the cameras panned across hundreds of people before cutting back to the preacher.

"God is holy and he must punish the law breaker. If he did not, then he would not be righteous. But, my brothers and sisters, God is not *only* righteous. He is also love. This is why God has provided a way for you to escape his punishment. In his great love and mercy, God the Father sent his Son to take your sins upon himself by bearing your sins in his body on the cross, as it says in 1 Peter 2:24. All you have to do is receive, by faith, what Christ has done and you will escape that holy judgment. Again, you accept Christ's sacrifice on the cross by faith. You must receive him as it says in John 1:12. You must believe and accept what Christ did for you there on the cross the same way you would accept a free gift. Ask Jesus to forgive you and to give you this gift of eternal life with him. Rely on nothing in yourself. Trust completely in him."

He again paused, looked down, and then back to the people.

"In Matthew 11:28 Jesus tells us to come to him so that he can give us rest. In Luke 5:20, Jesus forgave sins. In John 10:27, Jesus said he gives eternal life to those who trust him. Eph. 2:8 says we are saved by faith. That is, we are saved from damnation by faith in Christ's sacrifice on the cross, the sacrifice that removes your sins if you receive, by faith alone, what he has done."

"My people, it is only through the cross of Christ that you can escape the wrath of God. Yes, I know, God's wrath is not a popular thing to preach on and far too many pastors ignore it. It is not comfortable to hear that God is a righteous and holy God and will pass judgment on all who have sinned against him. People don't want to hear about unpleasant things. They want to hear what makes them feel good, sometimes even at the expense of truth."

With the last syllable, the preacher firmly planted his fist on the Bible and the low thud served to emphasis the following moments of silence. After a few seconds, he began again.

"But if I only tell you what makes you feel good, then I would be doing you a disservice. Woe to me if I do not speak all the truth."

The preacher again paused for dramatic effect. Kathy was unaware of how intently she was listening.

"I am not trying to make you all feel bad about yourselves. And I'm not trying to bring fear upon you. I'm only trying to speak the truth." He stepped down from the pulpit towards the congregation.

"There is a spiritual war going on around us, and there are demonic forces that seek to undermine the truth of the Gospel. But there are also angelic forces at work. Above them all, is the supreme God of the universe, who allows what he will for his purposes. He has spoken to us through his son Jesus Christ. If you fail to trust in him, if you fail to receive his sacrifice on the cross, and what he has done for the forgiveness of sins, then you will have no hope and instead of the punishment *you* deserve falling on Jesus, it will fall upon *you*."

He took a few steps to his right.

"You cannot rely upon your goodness because your goodness just isn't good enough. Nor is your sincerity good enough to please God because your sincerity is an appeal to God based on the goodness of your heart—and this amounts to pride. You cannot do enough good things to bring God's favor. You cannot be sincere enough to make things right with him. Salvation isn't found in church membership or rituals. It isn't found in traditions and habits. It is found only in Jesus, only in what he has done on the cross."

"Galatians 2:21 says that if there were any way to God through your own efforts, then there was no need for Jesus to die for our sins. But he did die, didn't he?"

The preacher moved a few steps to the side and raised the Bible in his hand.

"If you want your eyes opened, your sins forgiven, and a new life given to you, then you must acknowledge that you have sinned against God. Turn away from your sins. Confess them to God. Ask Jesus to forgive you of your sins. You must seek him. Put your trust, your hope, your life, and your eternal destiny in his hands. Trust him. Receive him. Turn from your pride. Turn from your sins and come to Jesus. He is the only way."

The lights suddenly went out as the TV flickered off and the house was immersed in darkness. Kathy was startled. She looked around and listened; everything was still and quiet.

"Power outage," she muttered to herself.

She thought about her father. He was asleep and the darkness wouldn't matter to him. So, she sat there a little while as she waited for her eyes to adjust. "Where does Dad keep the flashlight?" It comforted her to hear her own voice. Then she remembered that there was one in the kitchen junk drawer so she got up to retrieve it.

Sotare looked up through the rafters at Nomos. Nomos spoke to him saying, "It is only this house that is dark."

In the garage, three demons were crouched in front of the electrical panel. They had emerged from beneath the earth and had somehow remained undetected by the angels.

As Kathy moved towards the kitchen she could see out the

living room window across the street. The house lights were on, and she noticed that the streetlights were, too. She glanced out the kitchen window towards the back and could see lights in a neighboring house. "Great," she said. "It looks like we blew a circuit breaker."

She headed into the kitchen, easily managing with the filtered light from outside and rummaged through a couple of drawers until she found the flashlight. She clicked it on and headed towards the garage.

Nomos had drifted down through the ceiling and was standing next to Sotare in the living room. "The timing is too coincidental," he said.

"Agreed," replied Sotare. "We should sweep the house."

Each angel spread his wings and quickly moved through each room. Sotare spotted the three demons near the electrical panel in the garage. There was a fourth that had its wings spread over the other three. "Nomos!" he cried out. The demons were not fighters, but they could present a problem if they decided to try. Nomos appeared in an instant, and both angels launched at the creatures that immediately fled down into the ground and disappeared.

The lights flickered back on. "A cloaker demon!" scowled Nomos. "They used a cloaker to hide from us."

Kathy was out in the garage when the lights went back on. She slumped her shoulders. "Of course."

Sotare and Nomos followed Kathy as she headed towards the kitchen. She returned the flashlight to the drawer and went back to the living room couch, where she plopped down, wanting to hear more of what the TV preacher was saying.

The TV had come back on, but it was a different program, something about the Bible lands. She sat there thinking about what the preacher had said.

Sotare leaned close to her ear and whispered gently, "The Bible. Pick up the Bible."

Next to the couch was an end table with a Bible on it. Kathy had seen it before but ignored it. This time she was curious. She had no idea where to look, so she fanned through the pages.

Sotare focused on her, looking at her fingers, watching the pages, and then he said into her ear, "Stop."

She did and scanned the pages at the end of Luke chapter 22.

"And when it was day, the council of elders of the people assembled, both chief priests and scribes, and they led Him away to their council chamber, saying, 'If you are the Christ, tell us.' But He said to them, 'If I tell you, you will not believe; and if I ask a question, you will not answer. But from now on the Son of Man will be seated at the right hand of the power of God.' And they all said, 'Are you the Son of God, then?' And He said to them, 'Yes, I am.' And they said, 'What further need do we have of testimony? For we have heard it ourselves from His own mouth.'"

The passage was interesting but perplexing. Down at the bottom of the page were some notes. She read them. They explained that Jesus was on trial for claiming to be the Son of God, a term which meant equality with God. The notes cross-referenced John 5:18 for support of this statement. Furthermore, to be seated at the right hand of someone meant to be in the position of authority and Jesus would have the authority to judge all people, even those who condemned him. But to the Jewish leaders of the time, this was blasphemous and when Jesus said what he did, it was just what they needed as an excuse to get rid of him. The Jews did not have the authority under Roman rule to kill Jesus, so they would have to send Jesus to the Roman ruler in the area.

She decided to keep reading about Jesus going before Pilate and then to Herod. She read how Barabbas was released instead of Jesus. She looked at the note at the bottom of the page, which stated that Barabbas was a combination of two words "bar" meaning Son, and "abba" meaning father. Barabbas meant son of the father and that Barabbas was condemned for being a thief. The note then quoted John 10:10, where Jesus said that the thief comes to "steal, kill, and destroy."

This coincidence really caught her interest. Jesus, who had done nothing wrong, was being sentenced to death, and the thief, who came to kill and destroy, was being set free.

As a young child she had seen many films on TV about Jesus and had gone to Sunday school a few times, but as she got older and went to college, she dismissed religion. She considered her college education to be an eye-opener since it explained evolution as a fact. It had been presented with so much evidence by Ph.Ds that she finally accepted it. Anyway, she could recall the films of her youth and the stories of Jesus. She returned to the pages and read how Simon of Cyrene helped to carry Jesus' cross. She continued through to the end of the book of Luke and read where Jesus was crucified, buried, and rose from the dead—just like the TV preacher had said.

She finished and set the Bible down on the end table. Her mind was filled with images and ideas. She could not help but wonder if what her father had found was worth believing in. He was at such peace, and she had noticed a good change in him over the past few years. He loved his church, always speaking about the great people in it. But, there were good people everywhere.

The TV was still showing a special on the Bible lands and there was a man walking around explaining some historical facts found in the New Testament. She decided to watch it.

For the next hour, she learned about the Ancient Near East, Jesus, and some Old Testament characters. Many of the things touched her heart and she kept reflecting back on Jesus claiming to be the Son of God. He spoke with authority and without compromise. Yet, he was not harsh or unkind. He just spoke truth, and they killed him for it.

The evening finally grew late and Kathy became tired. She headed off to the guest bedroom after turning off the TV, checking the doors, and turning off the lights. The quiet in the house seemed to make her contemplation of spiritual things all the more serious. Although her father had told her these things before, and she had known the basic story from youth, it felt different. This time both her heart and mind had been stirred.

She got ready for bed while she thought about the day, the pastor, her dad, and Mark. It would be great to be back home.

Finally, after changing, taking off her makeup, and getting out her clothes for tomorrow, she tucked herself beneath the covers, safely snuggling under their warmth and comfort.

Sotare stood beside her. He looked up into the rafters to Nomos who, once again, was on top of the roof surveying the spiritual world. They eyed each other and nodded. Sotare opened his wings, rose through the rafters, and disappeared into the night.

***

Mark had been driving for hours, and it was now around 5:00 AM. He was, of course, quite anxious to get to where Kathy was, especially after the vision. So far, fatigue hadn't been a problem since it had been kept at bay by a large coffee which was, by now, less than warm.

When Kathy made the trip, she stopped at a hotel. She didn't like to drive long distances. But Mark liked to drive straight through, especially tonight. He pushed himself and forced away every approaching sliver of fatigue. He was on a mission.

By now Mark was on a lonely road between two cities. He was doing about seventy on cruise control, relaxing in his seat, listening to the radio, and of course, thinking about everything. He was on autopilot.

Up ahead was a curve, Mark remembered from a couple previous trips that he and Kathy had made, that brushed up against a river thirty feet below. He would have to suspend the cruise control and drop down to forty to safely navigate it. Mark reached for the button to disable it. Nothing happened. He hit it again. Still nothing happened. He tapped the brakes to disengage it but that didn't work either. The curve was coming up quickly. He hit the brakes harder and the car slowed just a bit as the engine raced, countering the speed decrease. Adrenaline dumped into his system. The curve was just a couple hundred feet away. Frantic, Mark applied both feet to the brakes and, although the car slowed, the engine raced in defiance. All he wanted to do was slow it down as fast as possible. Then it occurred to him, shift into neutral. He grabbed the shifter and took it out of drive. He engine raced wildly.

He slammed on the brakes and finally the car began to slow quickly but it wasn't enough. He turned the wheel to the left trying to lessen the impact. A moment later he slammed into the metal rail. The airbag burst open and then deflated. Crashing and scraping noises filled the compartment. Another jolt smashed his body against the door. He felt the strong tug of the seatbelt keeping him in place. The car slid along the guardrail, sparks flying into the darkness, the grinding and scraping ringing loudly in his ears. Mark did his best to muscle the steering wheel until the car finally ground to a stop. The engine had finally quit racing and the sudden silence was almost as disturbing as the crash.

He sat breathing quick and shallow breaths in the driver seat and watched as one headlight shined into the darkness, illuminating the dust kicked up by the accident. He looked out the dark window into the cold blackness, spotting the moonlit whitewater below in the river. The thought of careening over the side skidded across his mind. He rebuked it.

What was going on? Was this Nabal attacking him or was it just a coincidental mechanical problem? He didn't know. Would Sotare appear and tell him what was going on? Was he alone, really alone? Maybe the angel was watching. Maybe there were demons around him. He looked out into the darkness and listened. All he heard was the faint sound of the river crashing against some boulders.

He opened the driver's-side door, stepped out, and looked himself over. Surprisingly he wasn't hurt, just shaken up. As he walked to the front of the car he could see that the right fender was badly damaged and steam was billowing from under the hood with a faint hiss. He looked both ways on the road. Not a car in sight.

"This can't be happening," he bellowed into the night air.

He got back in and turned the ignition. The headlight dimmed a little and the engine cranked miserably but didn't start. He rolled down the window so he could hear better and tried again. It grumbled. He tried a third time, and a fourth, and a fifth. Nothing but the droning rasp of the engine as it cranked.

He slammed his palms against the steering wheel. "Sotare? I need some help!"

He sat back in the seat, enveloped by the silence and darkness, the lone headlight faintly shining into the black. "Crap!" He tried the engine again. It still wouldn't start.

He remembered his cell phone. All he had to do was call for help! He scolded himself for not thinking of it already and unclipped the phone and flipped it open. The display read "No Service".

"Not now!" he cried angrily, realizing his phone was of no use to him. "This is great. This is just great." He gritted his teeth, clutched the steering wheel until his knuckles turned white. The cool air was wafting through the window, and he could see his breath faintly before him. He checked the rearview mirror, realizing that he was halfway around the curve and that someone coming along the road might not see him. If they swerved out too far to the right, he might get hit.

In the trunk there were some roadside reflectors for just such an emergency. He popped the trunk lid latch, hopped out, and retrieved three triangular reflectors. He hurried back up the road about fifty feet in direct view of the oncoming road. To his surprise he saw headlights in the distance.

"Yes!"

He unfolded one of the triangles and put it about twenty-five feet from his car and then another one further back on the road towards the straightaway. The third he held in his hand and began to wave. About a minute later the headlights were upon him. The car was slowing down. The sound of its tires crunched on the gravel as it moved off the side of the road and dust wafted into the headlights, casting an eerie haze upon him. That is when it occurred to Mark that he was very alone. Mark hated that he was now becoming paranoid and suspicious of everything.

The car door opened and a figure appeared in dark silhouette created by the headlights. The person started walking towards him. The dust from the road was mingling with the headlights and when the man stepped in front of the car, a heavy lined shadow moved as he approached, making him seem unusually large and menacing.

The man stood there, motionless and silent for a moment. It made Mark just a little nervous.

"Need some help?" asked the dark figure.

"Yes, my car, I don't know what happened to it. I was using cruise control coming up to this curve and when I tried to turn it off, it wouldn't work. I turned off the engine to slow the car down but I hit the guardrail and wiped out the front right." Mark waved a hand towards the mangled fender. "Now it won't start. It's in a bad position, too." Mark stopped, realizing he was just rambling on, feeling awkward and apprehensive.

The man took a few steps closer to him. It was difficult for Mark to make out the man's details. Remembering that one can tell a lot by looking at someone's face and clothes, Mark realized he couldn't see the stranger in the dark. He put his hand forward for a handshake.

The man put forth his hand to shake Mark's, seemingly hesitant, "I'm Reggie."

"My name is Mark," he said, not wanting to give his last name.

"Let's take a look at what's up." Reggie walked on ahead of Mark towards the car. Mark followed.

"I don't mind leaving it here. But I'm worried about this location. If someone comes round the corner too fast he might hit it."

"No problem," said Reggie. "I have a rope in my trunk. Tell you what. We'll hook her up and tow your car out of the way. By the way, where are you headed?"

"I'm heading to Destiny to visit my wife. She's taking care of her father."

"That's where I'm headed. Small world." The man started to head back towards his car and stopped. "You're lucky I'm passing through."

"Yeah," said Mark, still unsure of the situation.

Reggie headed back to his car, and just as he promised, drove it ahead of Mark's. He got out, popped the trunk, and retrieved a thick rope about twenty feet long. Within a couple minutes, they had it tied to both cars. Reggie drove his car while Mark steered his. In no time they towed it up the road a quarter mile and safely out of the way.

Mark retrieved his suitcase and once in Reggie's car, Mark felt a lot better. "If you would drop me off at a hotel or at an airport, I can rent a car and contact someone in the morning to get my car towed in."

"Sounds good," responded Reggie.

By now, Mark was able to size up his rescuer. He seemed nice enough. There was a skull tattoo on his left forearm and the car was a bit dirty, but Mark was grateful. They talked for another forty-five minutes, but he was careful not to reveal any details to this stranger. For some reason, he didn't feel comfortable with him. A couple of times, Mark could feel Reggie staring at him in an odd manner.

"There," said Reggie as he pointed up ahead. "There's an airport. See that plane coming in for a landing? We'll be there in about five minutes."

"Yeah, I see it. Thanks, you saved my rear."

"No problem." said Reggie. "I like helping people out. Besides, who knows how long you would have been there."

"You got that right." Mark gazed out of the window at the descending plane. "I really appreciate the lift, Reggie."

"Call me Leech. All my friends do."

***

Pastor Tim was not sleeping well. His tossing and turning reflected the nightmare accosting his mind. He was in his church, in the pulpit preaching, when a demon suddenly appeared in the church aisle. It was huge and bony with sharp quills pointing backwards on its head. It had red eyes and a skull that had a vertical cleft running down to the nose. Its forehead was sloped and two huge horns twisted upward from its head. Two large bottom teeth curled towards its eyes and two large wings dragged behind it on the ground. It had hoofed feet and clawed bony hands. No one in the congregation seemed to notice it. Tim felt the hatred emanating from the dark, evil, creature.

His heart was racing as he dreamed. It pounded hard, almost matching the rhythm of his shifting head.

The demon pointed at him. Sharp pain pierced his chest. Tim looked down to see three holes with light from the outside passing through a stained-glass window behind him, continuing through him, and resting on his open Bible.

He looked up and noticed the congregation was gone. He turned his attention back to the three rays of light on the Bible. It was burning. He beat the pages with his hands until the fire was out. As the smoke cleared, he saw three charred holes in the Bible. From each, blood began to flow.

Tim twitched while adrenaline seeped into his veins. His heart pounded like a hammer. His breath was shallow and quick.

He looked at the demon. It leaned forward, opened its mouth and what looked like worms fell down to the ground. It growled in a low, rumbling gurgle before it spoke: "Die!"

Tim burst into consciousness, gasping for air, his chest pulsing with the hammer blows of his heart.

It was a dream! It was just a dream.

He was clenching the sheet with his hands.

Fear hovered over his soul for a few seconds until he was finally able to calm himself. The nightmare was over. He let go of the sheets and forced himself to calm his breathing. He looked over at his wife. He was surprised to see that she wasn't awake.

Tim looked at the ceiling. *Oh Lord,* he prayed silently, *please be with me in this hour of darkness. Please deliver me from the evil one.*

He slowly slid his legs to the side of the bed and onto the floor, and then he got up and headed into his office where he knelt down on the floor.

"Lord, I don't know what the dream means. But I know that you have allowed it for a reason. Here I am—your servant. I ask to be used for your glory and according to your will. If I'm to die in your service, then I praise you and thank you. I know that your will is perfect and that my death would be what is best should you deem it necessary."

He paused for a moment and considered the seriousness of his prayer. "As your Word says, we wrestle not against flesh and blood but against powers and principalities. I ask in the name of your Son that you fight for us in the spiritual realm and that you send a host of angels to protect us and guide us." He paused again, trying to sense the direction and calling of the Lord. Then Mark flashed into his mind.

He waited. Mark again came to mind.

Tim began to pray for him and also for Kathy but within a few seconds, quite unexpectedly, he sensed the words, "Go the church now, and pray." It was very strong and very clear. He waited for the impression to come again. It did. "Go to the church now, and pray."

He rose and hurried to the desk where he grabbed the phone and quickly dialed one of the elders of the church. The phone rang five or six times.

"Hello?" said a man in an alert voice.

"Allen, this is Pastor Tim. I'm sorry for waking you up this early, but I believe the Lord has spoken to me about getting the church to pray for today's service."

"I've had the same feeling," he said. "In fact, I had a disturbing dream about you. It woke me up."

Tim had expected to hear the groggy response of a half-awake friend, but not this. "You did?"

"Yes, it was about you in the pulpit. I was sitting there listening to you preach and suddenly three holes appeared in your chest. Light shone through your chest from outside the church onto the Bible and then it caught on fire." Allen paused for a moment and then asked, "Did you have the same dream?"

Even though Tim believed in the miraculous, Allen's apparently identical dream left him speechless for a few seconds. "Yes, but mine had a horrible demon in it."

"Mine didn't."

After a pause Allen said, "I'll start making calls right now and we will get the prayer chain started. I don't know what's going to happen or what it all means, but we'll be praying."

"Thank you. Oh, and I don't know if you are aware of this,

but there is a man, an unbeliever that is somehow significant in this whole thing. His name is Mark. I believe the Lord is calling him and will use him greatly. I don't have time to explain it all right now, but pray for him, too. His wife is Kathy, and his father is John Creed."

"John? I heard he's out of the hospital."

"He is. Please pray for them. I'll fill you in later at the church on all the details."

"Okay, no problem."

They hung up and Tim went back to his prayer.

Allen dutifully made several calls and in a very short time, the church prayer team had been activated.

Angels turned their heads as they heard the prayers rise up to the heavens. Ramah heard it, too. Hands were lifted high.

Tim stood and went to wake his wife.

***

Paraptome peered through Leech's eyes at his passenger. It knew about Sotare, Nomos, and the garden. It knew that Mark had been targeted for death. Here was a great opportunity. His possession was alone in the car in the dark with this man. Should Paraptome risk using Leech to try and kill Mark now? Would doing so jeopardize his assignment to kill the pastor, a far more important target? Paraptome weighed the options. Its orders were to kill the pastor and it knew better than to allow failure. The penalty would be harsh indeed. But, this opportunity was too important to pass up. There was no one around. Leech could kill him and dispose of the body and still have plenty of time to steal another car, get to the church, and kill the pastor.

Paraptome stared at Mark and as it did, Leech felt intense loathing. He was returning from a connection in a nearby city where he had picked up an untraceable revolver. It was under the driver's seat. Leech knew he could retrieve it and shoot this stranger easily. He didn't know why he had the urge to do it, but he did. He despised Mark. He took his left arm and set it down between his legs, close to the gun, tapping the seat, contemplating his actions.

Paraptome whispered, "Kill him." Leech felt a surge, a wave of desire to destroy Mark's life. It was seductively powerful. He looked in the rearview mirror to see if any cars were nearby. He saw no lights. He glanced over at Mark to size him up. Leech would have to surprise him, which would be easy. He could kill him and the pastor later. He inched his hand a little bit further downward.

Paraptome was focusing on Leech, gently moving him to action. But, it was distracted by a bright light out in the darkness that was moving in a slow arc. Paraptome focused on it and Leech found himself gazing straight ahead. Ramah was coming.

"I think that is the off-ramp," said Mark as he looked at Leech.

Leech said nothing. He was still staring forward.

Ramah arrived quickly, arched upward in a loop, reversed his direction, and quickly matched the speed of the car. He folded his wings and dropped onto the hood, slipping through the windshield, and sat next to Mark. Ramah leaned forward and stared into Paraptome's eyes.

Leech felt inexplicably troubled. He grabbed the steering wheel with both hands and looked at his passenger.

Mark was beginning to get nervous.

"Do nothing," said Paraptome.

"Yeah, that's it. That's the off-ramp," said Mark.

Leech slowly looked at him without speaking.

"Right there," said Mark again as he glanced to Leech.

Leech flipped on his turn signal.

"Let him go," whispered the creature into Leech's mind.

Now is not the time, thought Leech.

"There's the car rental," said Mark as he pointed to a sign. Leech was still quiet as he steered towards it and quickly came to a stop, his tires squealed a bit on the pavement. Mark opened the door, and before he stepped out, he turned around and obligatorily extended his hand. Leech automatically took it and while they shook, Leech felt a strong surge of anger and hatred rise within him. Mark, on the other hand, looked into Leech's eyes and thought he saw something odd. He couldn't place his finger on it. Something was wrong. He released the grip, retrieved his suitcase from the backseat, said thank you one more time, and walked towards the entrance.

Leech kept his foot on the brake as he watched Mark.

Ramah was walking right beside him, though Leech did not know it.

Far away, in the dark, starry night a single speck of light moved downward in a slow arc. It grew in size as it approached and within seconds Sotare arrived. "I came as swiftly as I could." He landed softly on the ground next to Ramah.

"It was close, but Mark is safe for now."

"I thank you, my brother. May we fight for our Lord together yet again."

Ramah lowered his head humbly, extending his broad wings, and lifted himself into the night sky, arcing in the direction from which Sotare had come.

Leech continued to glare at Mark, imagining what it would have been like to kill him.

Paraptome whispered, "Your purpose is to kill the pastor. Leave him."

Leech smiled as he thought about his task of murder in a church in front of everyone. It would surely be on the news and he would be an anonymous celebrity. The gang would have no choice but to believe that he was a determined and dangerous man, worthy of their respect and fear.

He looked out into the darkness ahead of him and smiled as he drove off.

Chapter 11

MARK ENTERED THE RENTAL office after he watched Leech drive off. Something about him wasn't right, especially his quiet stare before they took the off ramp. *Was it a spiritual thing or just nerves?*

"May I help you?" asked a nicely dressed young woman behind the counter.

Mark turned and approached her. "Yes. I got into a fender bender about 15 miles back and need to have the car towed. Is there a tow truck service around here?"

"Sure is."

"Great, oh, and I'll need to rent a car, too."

She gave him a look.

"The cruise control wouldn't turn off and I ended up denting the fender pretty good coming around a curve. It won't start. I got a ride here."

"Okay," she said as she glanced down at some papers. "All I will need is some identification and a credit card and we will have you in a car in no time."

Mark nodded. In a few minutes he had a set of car keys in

hand. As they finished their business, she dialed a number, and handed the receiver to Mark.

"I just dialed Frank's Towing. He's the best guy in town and he knows where to take your car."

At the other end of the line a voice answered. "Frank's Towing. This is Frank."

Mark introduced himself and explained how he had lost an argument with the guardrail.

"Ah, yes," interrupted Frank. "I know exactly where that is. It's about 20 minutes from here. Believe me, you're not the only one who's met his match at that bend. Where are you? I'll come pick you up."

"I'm at the airport car rental office. But, can you get my car by yourself? I have a very important appointment in town and I can't miss it."

"Well, yeah, I suppose so. You can give me your car keys and the license number to your car. I'll head out there and take it to the shop down the street from my yard. Shotsky's Garage is close by. They can take a look at it."

"That would be great," responded Mark. "I appreciate it."

"No problem. I'll be at the airport in about ten minutes. See you then."

"Great. I'll be here in the lobby."

Mark heard a click and the phone went dead. He handed the receiver to the girl behind the counter, who smiled dutifully. There were some comfortable-looking seats over in the corner, positioned just right for viewing outside, so he meandered over and examined the magazines on a coffee table. He picked one up and sat down and fanned through the pages, not paying attention to what he saw. His mind wandered. He was agitated and exhausted.

I hate this, he thought to himself. He stopped and looked up, hoping to see Sotare. He thought about the vision he had had, about Kathy and the gunman… the gunman. He reviewed the memory. There was something familiar about him, something…

He stopped and, in an instant, it hit him. Leech, the man who had dropped him off, was he the man in the vision? The walk, the clothes, they were the same. At least he thought so.

Mark stood up and looked out the window in the direction where Leech had driven. His heart raced. He crumpled the magazine in his hands. "What is going on?" he said aloud.

The girl behind the counter was watching him. Mark noticed her reflection in the window but his attention was directed elsewhere. After determining that he needed nothing from her, she went back to her business.

He stood gazing off into the rising sun. A strong wave of fatigue hit him. He rubbed his eyes in an attempt to brush it away and forced himself to focus on the events that had led him here. He thought about calling Kathy but he knew it wasn't the right time.

God, he thought to himself in prayer. *God, I know you can hear my thoughts. I know that you have plans and you are in control, but please keep my wife safe. I don't know what else to say.*

He was frustrated and confused. Then, softly, he whispered into the air, "Sotare, where are you?"

Next to him, Sotare, invisible, listened, but did not respond. He glanced around, keeping guard, taking care of his charge.

"Where are you?" Mark called out. "Where are you, Sotare?"

He tossed the magazine back on the table. That is when he noticed a Bible. He looked around to see if there was anyone else there. The book seemed out of place lying on a table in a car-rental business. He leaned down and randomly opened the book and his eyes were drawn to two verses. Jeremiah 23:23-24, "'Am I a God who is near,' declares the Lord, 'and not a God far off? Can a man hide himself in hiding places, so I do not see him?' declares the Lord. 'Do I not fill the heavens and the earth?' declares the Lord."

The words struck Mark intensely as an answer to his prayer. Intrigued, he picked up the book, sat down, and started reading.

About ten minutes later Frank showed up with his tow truck. The sound of country-western music at high volume blared from what looked like a well-worn flat bed with a tow hitch bolted on. The side of the door said "Heaven's Tow Service." Mark chuckled at the name. "Is this for real?" he said to himself.

Frank was a potbellied man in his fifties. He wore stained overalls, a Chicago Cubs baseball cap, and sported a toothpick hanging out of the corner of his mouth. There were a couple of days of accumulated stubble on his face. Frank offered Mark his grease-stained and calloused hand. Mark shook it and could not help but notice Frank's stereotypical appearance.

They chatted outside the rental office next to the truck. At one point, Frank looked past Mark into the office, waving at the girl behind the counter. She smiled and waved back.

"I guess you've done this before," said Mark.

"Sure have. You ain't the only one wrecked out there on that road. It happens on that curve more than anywhere else in the county. I think it's a bad combo of both the long stretch and people trying to make it through the night. Anyway, sometimes an accident can get pretty bad." He sized up Mark with a single long look. "The good Lord was watching over you."

Mark had heard other people make such comments, invoking the name of the Lord in such a way, but it had never meant anything to him before. This time he understood.

"Just sign right here," said Frank as he pointed with a pen at a space on a clipboard. "It's a standard release so I can get your car." Mark signed it and handed the keys to Frank.

"All I need is the ignition key. Does the trunk open from the inside?"

"Yeah. I appreciate you doing this." Mark removed the key and handed it to him.

Frank nodded politely and started towards his tow truck, stopped, and turned around. "Do you know your way around town?"

"A little. I've been here a few times before. My father-in-law lives here and I'm going to visit him."

The man stared at Mark for an extra couple of seconds and then said, "Well, there's a good motel up on Seventh Street called Seventh Heaven Motel. If you just tell them that Frank sent you, you'll get a discount. That way, you can get cleaned up for your appointment if you need to." Frank turned and got into his truck. The door squealed loudly as he closed it.

That was odd, thought Mark. Heaven's Tow Service and Seventh Heaven Motel? He looked up into the sky and chuckled.

Frank's noisy truck sputtered onto the highway.

Why did he suggest a motel? Mark wondered about that as he watched Frank drive off. That's when he noticed someone sitting in the passenger seat. As Frank turned onto the road, the person in the passenger seat looked back at Mark. It was Sotare.

Mark locked his eyes on the truck as it sped off down the highway. What was he doing? Did Frank know Sotare was there or did he just show himself for Mark's benefit? He continued to watch the truck until it was gone. He looked at his watch. It was just after 6 a.m.

Mark turned around and was instantly startled.

"Hello, Mark."

"Sotare!" Mark smiled. "I'm so glad to see you."

"I'm glad to see you, too. Please take Frank's recommendation." With that, Sotare smiled slightly with a nod and disappeared.

The brief and unexpected encounter left Mark bewildered and a bit exasperated. Why would Sotare appear and encourage him to go to a hotel? Mark shook his head and retrieved the car-rental keys from his pocket as he hurried to the vehicle. Somehow it all seemed normal, Frank's comment, Sotare's sudden appearance and equally hasty disappearance.

"Seventh Heaven Motel, here I come."

***

Kathy lay awake in bed, thinking about the events of the past few days. Her dad had been in and out of the hospital. Pastor Tim had said that Mark was important. She had possibly seen some sort of demon and, to top it all off, she was away from Mark, who was having some kind of emotional problems. She thought about her dad's faith, about Christianity and what the preacher said on TV. She never took any of it seriously before, but the past 24 hours were beginning to change that.

Through the slightly parted curtains, Kathy could see two

maple trees in the front yard. Then it struck her. There were two trees, just like at home in her garden. The one on the right was swaying very gently in the breeze; the other one was oddly still. She turned back to the ceiling, letting her mind wander.

There was a soft knock at the door.

"Yes?" she said as she started to get out of bed.

"You up?" asked John with a muffled voice.

"Yes, Dad. I'm up."

"Okay, I'll be eating cereal in the kitchen. Do you want any?"

Kathy smiled as she remembered how her father had always liked cereal for breakfast. "Yes Dad, that would be great."

John walked slowly to the kitchen, still hindered by acute pain, but managing quite well. Kathy started getting dressed and went into the bathroom to make herself presentable before finally heading to the kitchen.

"There you are. I thought you fell in to some girl-make-up-void. How'd you sleep?"

"I slept surprisingly well," she replied with a glare of her eyes as her response to his feeble joke. "How about you?"

"I had one of the best night's sleep I think I've ever had." He smiled briskly as he poured some orange juice for Kathy. "I had the most wonderful dream."

"Really? What was it?" Kathy was playing along.

"It's when you're asleep and you imagine and experience something and…"

"Dad!"

John adjusted his chair carefully towards her and with an excited smile began to tell her. "I dreamt that both you and Mark became Christians and that Mark was going to be used of God in a mighty way." He stared at her, waiting for her reaction.

Normally she would dismiss what he said, but now it seemed a little bit more meaningful.

"That is very interesting," she said. "But it was only a dream." Secretly, she couldn't help but wonder if there was something to it.

"It was a dream, a good one. And, if you don't mind humoring this old man, I think I will relish it." He reached over, grabbed Kathy's wrist, and lovingly squeezed it. He got up slowly from the table, supported himself on it, and gave her a kiss on the cheek. "Church is about a half hour away. I can drive myself if you want to stay here."

Though that sounded a appealing, she'd have none of it. "No, I'll come with you." She was surprised at her newfound eagerness. "I don't feel comfortable with you driving by yourself just yet."

John washed out his bowl and glass in the sink and set them on the counter. Kathy watched him and could easily tell that he was joyful, in spite of his occasional pain and slowness of movement.

"You know something?" he said as he looked at Kathy, "I really am surprised at how good I feel and how much I have healed so far. This really is a miracle from God." He tried clumsily to hop slightly in excitement, but the grimace on his face revealed how bad an idea it was. He looked at Kathy and with a smile said, "Ouch."

Kathy grinned back, wondering what the service would be like.

***

A rip in space opened and a demon emerged, then another, and another. For about a minute, several distorted and grotesque creatures came flying through. Then the gap closed and they headed for the church.

***

Paraptome did not like inhabiting this insignificant carcass of a man. But its instructions were to kill the pastor, and it knew better than to resist the unholy one from whom it had personally received its orders.

The devil was a maliciously evil creature that could deliver the severest of punishments for the slightest infraction, without an iota of remorse. The last time Paraptome had been summoned by the vile master, it had been careful to always look down, crawling as it obeyed every command. If wickedness was a force like gravity, then Paraptome had felt the intense black hole of evil itself. The principality was completely given over to hatred, malice, and corruption. But its own wickedness paled before the undulating waves of cold, calculating malevolence that emanated from the great Fallen One. Its evil intensity was matched only by the its power and ability to inflict agonizing pain in ways that Paraptome feared in the deepest part of its being. To be summoned to the devil's lair was terrifying, but it was nothing compared to the wrath that followed if the Evil One was disobeyed.

So, Paraptome was enduring this fool of a man for the time being; that is, until the killing was done. Afterwards, it would free itself from the wretched creature and fall back into the dark pit, maybe taking Leech with it.

As it thought about the pastor, a seething repugnance filled its dark soul. It desired desperately to lash out in unrestrained anger against Leech, just to satisfy its own cruel appetite. But it would not, lest it damage the man and fail its master. For the time being, Paraptome needed this slave unharmed.

Leech had found a car in an alley behind the grocery store he had spotted the day before. It was an old Ford and was a model he was familiar with. He knew how to hotwire it quickly. Parking his own car a couple hundred feet away, he walked a circuitous path to the sedan, making sure he wasn't being watched. This would be easy. As he approached the vehicle, he put on some thick latex gloves so as not to leave any fingerprints. He wore a baseball cap and overalls. Once he had killed the pastor and fled, he would take the gloves, the overalls, and his shoes and throw them in a trash bin on his way back to pick up his car. He was wearing pants and a T-shirt underneath the overalls and had another pair of shoes in his vehicle. He had planned well.

Leech used a Slim Jim to unlock the car door. He quickly slipped inside, closed the door, and bent forward under the dashboard. In just about a minute the car spurted to life. He checked to see if the coast was clear, put the vehicle in reverse, backed out of the space, and headed off towards the church. He wanted to find a strategic place to park before anyone else got there, to ensure an easy escape.

***

Mark was heading into town when he finally saw the Seventh Heaven Motel. It was about 7:30 in the morning and although he was tired, he still felt awake enough to go straight to the church. It was a typical motel, nothing special about it. The sign was a bit ragged and weatherworn, but the place seemed nice enough. He parked his car and headed into the lobby. The bell rang loudly on the counter. From the back room, an elderly woman slowly made her way forward. She used a cane.

"May I help you?" she said in raspy voice.

"I'm from out of town and need to get cleaned up for an appointment this morning. Frank, the tow truck driver, told me to stop by here and mention his name. He said you'd give me a discount."

The woman nodded, expressionless, and turned around to a rack full of keys. She selected one and slowly made her way back to the counter. She held out her hand as if asking for Mark's. He extended his. "May the Lord be with you," she said as she dropped the key into his hand. "It's room number seven. It's outside, three doors down on the right. No charge." She smiled and said, "I'll be praying for you." She turned around and slowly disappeared through the same door she entered.

Mark stood there staring at the empty doorway as he tried to make sense of things. He looked out the window at his car and back to the empty door. Everything was completely silent.

He retrieved his bag from the car trunk and found the room. It was tidy, nothing special. He tossed his bag on the bed. "Sotare? I'm here."

Silence.

He checked in the bathroom and even looked under the bed. Why was he sent here? Would Sotare appear or would someone knock on the door and give him some mysterious instructions? The clock on the desk next to the TV read 7:35. He didn't have much time before church started, according to what Kathy had told him over the phone. Sitting down on the bed, Mark thought about what would happen in the next couple of hours. He was filled with a mixture of emotions and an increasing need to sleep, not mention his great concern for his wife. Would anyone get hurt? Would he? Would the pastor be okay? Would Kathy be alright? The questions were like keys opening doors of confusion and despair. He forced his mind away from them and shook his head to fight off the sleep that was so perpetually seeking to master him.

He unzipped his bag, pulled out his toiletries, a fresh shirt and pants, laid them on the bed, stripped, and headed into the shower. Five minutes later, he was drying himself off.

The mirror bore the grim image of his tired face. He was unshaven and baggy-eyed and his lack of sleep was clearly visible. How easy it would be to lie down on the bed and drift off to sleep, but he knew he couldn't risk even a moment's rest. There was no way he would miss the church service. He shook off his growing exhaustion while he shaved, and continued to wonder why he was sent here. In a few minutes, he was dressed and ready to go.

He packed his bag and set it on the floor next to the bed. He sat down on the covers and waited. He closed his eyes. *God, why am I here?* He prayed silently. *Do you want me to stay here? Will my wife be okay? Where is Sotare?* He had a laundry list of questions.

He sat on the edge of the bed, pondering where he was, what had happened, and why he was there. His breathing slowed. The bed was soft. It felt good. With his eyes still closed, he continued to offer prayers to God, feeling inadequate and awkward. His breathing slowed even more. His head drooped a little. He shook it off and focused on a point on the opposite wall while he thought of Kathy. After a few moments the soft edges of fatigue began to overtake him. He resisted them, but they were pleasant and welcome. He tried to offer up another prayer, but it was disjointed and unfocused. His breathing was shallow. He tried to utter a few more words of silent prayer, but his mind was too foggy, too tired focus. He opened his eyes and looked at the door, halfway expecting a knock. He closed his eyes again and tried to pray a little more. He thought of Kathy, of surprising her of…. Kathy and her father… driving… the church… He needed to… He exhaled in short breaths… It felt good to relax… Then, without realizing it, he very slowly fell back on the bed, asleep.

***

Pastor Tim had arrived at the church early. Shortly afterwards, Allen showed up and went straight to his office.

"Good morning, Pastor."

Tim was leaning back in his chair, holding a football trophy he'd gotten in college.

"Are we playing football after church today?" joked Allen.

Tim smiled and set it back on a shelf. "Just thinking about challenges and what it takes to be victorious."

Pastor Tim's Bible was on the desk on top of the neatly stacked sermon notes.

"Everyone on the prayer team has heard about our dreams. The good Lord has gotten an earful this morning." Allen smiled.

"Thanks. I believe we really do need it, especially today."

"Yep," said Allen casually.

The two men looked at each other, not sure what to say. Allen broke the awkward silence.

"You said that you are going to fill me in on some details. Is now a good time?"

With a sigh, Tim replied, "Yeah, now is as good a time as any. Pull up a chair."

Outside the church, a host of winged demons hovered like vultures, circling slowly over the church, waiting for the arrival of Paraptome.

***

"Come on, Kathy. I don't want to be late."

"I'm right behind you, Dad," she said rather crisply. "For someone who's recovering from surgery, you sure are revved up."

They both headed out the front door. Though John was sore, he was doing quite well, politely motioning his daughter through the door so he could lock up. He was always the gentleman. Reassured by the clank of the deadbolt that the door was securely locked, he carefully negotiated the front steps.

Kathy had already made her way down them and hurried to open up the passenger side of the car for her father. She watched him as he approached the steps. Below them, a demon was crouching next to some bushes. It stood up, opened its wings, then took a step towards John, extending its clawed hands as it reached for John's head. Just as the demon was about to touch him, Ramah swooped from the sky, crashed into the demon from behind, and sent both of them rolling into the yard. He gripped it behind the neck and held it in a headlock. The creature growled and clawed at the angel's arm, violently kicking and flapping its wings. But Ramah clasped it powerfully, squeezing tighter and tighter, wrapping his legs around the waist of the demon and bending its head back further and further. Then he reached for the demon's wings and with deliberate and intense determination wrenched one of them until it cracked. The creature shuddered in pain and growled with a roar. Ramah released it abruptly and the creature fell to the ground, shuddering convulsively as it slowly sank beneath the grass. He turned in time to see John and Kathy driving away.

***

"That's quite a story," said Allen. "This Mark fellow must be an important person to the Lord, even as an unbeliever."

The pastor smiled, "Well, I'm sure glad he was interested in us when we were unbelievers, aren't you?"

Allen returned the smile. "Sure am. He saved us in spite of ourselves."

"You got that right," said Tim.

There was a knock on the door and a woman stuck her head in. "Pastor Tim? Is everything okay?" It was Fran, one of the members of the prayer team. She was a great prayer warrior and oversaw the women's ministry. She slipped in further.

"Yes, everything's fine."

"Pastor?" she said in a tone that told him she wanted to say something.

"Yes?"

She looked at Allen. "After you called me this morning I called others on the prayer chain and told them what you had said, about the dream. Well…" she paused. "Three other people said they had the same dream about you. All three said they dreamed that there were three holes in your chest with a light shining through them on the Bible."

Tim was shaken. He didn't like admitting it to himself and he didn't want them to know, but he felt fear. He deliberately tried to speak calmly.

"It looks like the Lord is going to do something today. Let's trust him as we find out together what it is."

Fran looked at Tim with a combination of sympathy, love, and concern. He noticed it and even though he knew she meant well, her expression caused him more unease. He got out of his chair, approached her, and placed his hands gently on her shoulders.

"Why don't you two go on out there and fill in the rest of the prayer team. I'll stay in my office and pray through the worship. When it's time for me to preach, I'll come on out. Oh, and when you see John Creed and his daughter Kathy, could you please have them sit in the front row?"

Pastor Tim was always with the congregation during the song service. He sat near the front so everyone could see him. They would, of course, be curious to know why he wasn't in his usual spot but, considering the circumstances, both Allen and Fran nodded.

"Sure," said Allen. "We'll let everybody know." He got up and politely escorted Fran out of the office and closed the door. Tim looked around. In the corner was a fishing pole. "*Fishers of men,*" he said to himself, bowing his head.

"Lord Jesus," he said, "I do not know what you have in store for this morning. But I will trust you and I ask that you give your servant the words to speak without fear, without compromise, and with power. I confess that I'm afraid and I ask that you forgive me for that fear. But, in the name of your Son, I ask that you send forth your servant to speak your word without compromise. Give me the grace to hear you and to do your will."

He fell silent for a moment, then reached over for his Bible and turned to Psalm 23, the page that he had accidentally ripped from the binding. It was tucked back in place. He read it carefully and felt the renewing and strengthening comfort of its words. He then bowed his head again and continued to pray.

***

The angels had gathered in the air just to the east of the church at a safe distance from the demons circling above it. There were more of them than there were angels, so, for now, the vile creatures dominated the area.

The demons seemed to be everywhere—some were standing on nearby buildings, the rest were flying. They had their instructions: be ready, and stand guard. One demon tucked in its wings and slowly descended onto the roof of the church. Another followed, then another. Like grotesque birds, they perched, peering down through the wooden shingles into the sanctuary. Six demons in total gathered, the first one opening its wings, falling down into the sanctuary, followed by the other five. Above them, the rest of the demonic horde waited.

The six creatures in the church had a special talent. They were able to mingle with the people during the worship service, speaking hatred and fear into their minds. One large and muscular demon, Grat, slowly flew down the center aisle above the heads of the people. Its job was to enter the pulpit area and disrupt the pastor as he preached. The other demons would likewise speak evil to the members of the congregation, trying to influence any susceptible person. But for now, until they were called into action, they slowly surveyed the gathering congregation and waited. They knew that Paraptome possessed a man and that this man was on its way to kill the pastor. Their job would be to prevent any angelic intervention, disrupt the service, and prevent further prayer.

The crowd increased as more people entered the sanctuary. In the confines of this church, the demons would need to avoid getting too close to the people. Since Christians were indwelt by God, it meant that demons could not pass through or enter them and the resulting collision was extremely uncomfortable. So, like bugs, they climbed the walls and studied their enemies from afar.

The demons crawled along the walls and roof of the sanctuary like huge, monstrous insects, scurrying back and forth. However, when the congregation began to sing in worship to God, the demons would not be able to stay. They would fly out of the church to join the circling horde above, only to return once the worship had stopped. Grat was one of the few demons who possessed the ability to work in a congregation during its time of worship. This horned creature with its leathery wings and three claws at the end of its hands was incredibly skilled at deception and fear.

***

Across the street, a tan Ford drove slowly by. Leech examined the area. He turned left at an intersection and circled the block, looking for the best place to park.

Above him creatures circled, two descending onto the car's roof. They knew that Paraptome had arrived and that this human fool would soon kill the pastor. They let their wings fill with air as they were pulled along by the vehicle. One of them stuck its head down through the roof to get a look at Leech. Inside the man, Paraptome sensed the demon's presence, quickly reached its hand outside of Leech, and grabbed the demon by the throat. Caught completely off guard, the creature flapped its wings frantically, and gripped the powerful hand that held it at bay. Paraptome squeezed lightly and let it go. Immediately it retreated back into the sky, coughing, humiliated. The other demon likewise withdrew lest it receive the same treatment.

Leech felt an unexpected surge of anger as he finally found a place to park. "There," said Leech. He spotted a place in an alley behind the church. It took only a moment to turn the car around and back it in, positioning it for a fast getaway. It was more or less hidden, but close to the church. The only problem was a six-foot high chain-link fence between the church property and the alley. Being agile and quick, Leech figured he could scale it easily.

One last check of the surroundings and he was satisfied. He reached down under the dashboard, where two wires were twisted together. He pulled them apart and the car instantly stopped running. He got out, took the handgun from under his seat, and tucked the weapon in his pants, making sure his shirt covered it.

He looked around and listened: the only sound and movement were those of an occasional passing car on the street. He got out and started walking, glancing in different directions, his paranoia in full swing. He planned to case the church one time and come back to the car. He did not want to be seen any more than was necessary. All he would have to do was to wait for the right moment, enter the front doors, put on his ski mask, walk down the center aisle of the church, and shoot the pastor. He knew that the exit door would be easily accessible and that, in the mayhem that was sure to follow the shooting, no one would know who he was. He would escape via the side door, scale the fence, get to the car, and make his escape. When he dumped the car, he'd wipe down the steering wheel, the wires, and the dashboard and he'd be set. It would all be so easy.

Paraptome smiled.

Leech did, too.

***

"I don't know why, but I feel as though today is going to be a special day." John was smiling as he looked at Kathy. She was driving and hadn't been saying much. She was thinking about Mark, what the TV preacher had said, Pastor Tim's comments, and that frightful vision—or whatever it was—from the other night. Everything was a jumble of disparate experiences that all seemed to be related somehow.

"Hello? Earth to Kathy."

She broke from her thoughts and turned to her father. "Sorry, Dad. I'm just thinking about everything…and I'm missing Mark too."

John empathized automatically. "Why don't you just drop me off at church and go on home to Mark? I can find someone to drive me back to my place. Really, it would be no problem."

She put her hand on her dad's hand. "Thanks, Dad, but I need to make sure you're okay. I see you hiding the pain. You're not fooling me. You still need me."

"I always need you. My heart is always with you." He was looking straight into her eyes.

She took in his loving gaze.

"I've just been thinking about everything, you know?" she said. "Last night after you went to bed, I listened to a TV preacher. Now, don't get your hopes up, but what he said really stuck with me. Normally I wouldn't have considered it at all, but there was something about it. And with all the weird stuff going on, I figured that maybe God is trying to tell me something." She looked at her father, expecting him to start praising God.

John, knowing that this was an important breakthrough, chose to remain silent rather than be overly zealous. Instead, he said, "I'm glad." Then he prayed silently: *Lord, please give me the words.*

He hoped that some answer, some appropriate comment would fill his mind. But nothing came. So he said nothing. He just squeezed her hand gently.

"I didn't expect you to be speechless," she said.

"Me, either," responded John with a smile. "I wish I had something profound to say, but I don't."

"That surprises me." Her tone was full of friendly teasing.

"Well," he said. "I have to agree with you that the past few days have been very strange." He looked at her, considering the weight of what he wanted to say. "I have a feeling that something important is going to happen. I don't know what it is. I just have this feeling."

Kathy looked at her father. "Yeah, I get the same feeling."

***

People were in the church, milling about, catching up on the latest news of the week and, of course, talking about the pastor and the dream. The place was almost full fifteen minutes before the scheduled start of the service.

Normally, Tim would sit with the congregation during the entire service, but this time he would wait until after the singing was done before coming out of his office. He needed time alone, time to prepare and reflect, time to pray. So, for now, he listened to the muffled voices of almost two hundred people as they echoed down the hallway. He sat alone, thinking, trying to calm himself; yet he was eager to speak. Was his ministry on earth coming to an end? Was the dream a precursor to something bad or something good?

He did not like being afraid, so he prayed a simple prayer out loud. "Lord, into your hands I commit my life, my soul, my will. I trust you, no matter what."

Ramah stood beside him.

Tim sat at his desk, silently praying the same prayer. As he repeated it, a gentle peace began to fill his heart. He knew the Lord was with him.

Finally, the song service ended. It was time. He entered through the sanctuary doors and walked down the center aisle. Everyone was standing and his presence brought the congregation to a quick silence. It seemed an unusually long walk. Upon reaching the pulpit, Tim tapped on his lapel mike and after hearing the reassuring *thump thump* through the speakers, he surveyed the congregation. Every eye was on him. He saw John in the front row with his daughter Kathy. He smiled and nodded to them.

A man in a ski mask entered the back of the church. The pastor did not notice him because he was so accustomed to people moving around.

Tim addressed the congregation. "We're glad to announce that John Creed is back from the hospital." He nodded to John who smiled. "In fact, his daughter is here taking care of him." He smiled at Kathy.

"John, if you don't mind, could you introduce your daughter?"

Kathy immediately felt embarrassed.

Leech reached under his shirt for the gun.

John stood up and gently nudged Kathy, who reluctantly rose to her feet.

The gunman approached.

John turned to face the congregation. As he began to introduce Kathy, he saw the man in the ski mask walking down the center aisle. Then, unbelievably, he saw a gun. Pastor Tim had already started to come down from the pulpit. There were murmurs in the back part of the congregation.

Someone yelled, "He's got a gun!"

Instinctively, John stepped out into the aisle to shield his daughter. Kathy saw Leech. By now, the pastor was down in the aisle, trying to get out in front of them both. John, oblivious to the pastor's intention, remained steadfast, with one arm pushing Kathy behind him and the other firmly planted on a pew. Closing fast, Leech raised the gun, nerves strained, adrenaline pumping, the gun shaking in his hand. John and Kathy were in the way and, in the panic of the moment, he fired a shot into Kathy. A second shot rang out, hitting John in the chest. Both collapsed on the ground. The reverberating echo of the gunfire caused pandemonium in the congregation. Screams and a cacophony of noises filled the sanctuary as people scrambled for safety.

Leech raised the gun, firing once more. A bullet hit the pastor square in the chest. He instantly dropped and joined John and Kathy on the ground. Without mercy, Leech stepped closer to him and fired two more shots into Tim's body.

People were screaming. It was chaos. Some were running and others were ducking under the pews. Leech turned and ran out the side door.

Inside, Kathy, John, and Pastor Tim all lay bleeding on the floor. Kathy was coughing up blood. John was motionless....

...something was ringing. There it was again.... and again.

Leech was running as fast as he could.

…ringing again, and again.

Mark opened his eyes, sat up, and gasped for air. "No!" he screamed out. The image of Kathy on the floor had wrenched his mind and heart into agony. The phone rang again. It scared him. It rang again, forcing him to wake up.

It was all a dream!

The phone rang again. He looked at it, then at the clock. It was 8:20. The service hadn't begun yet. They weren't dead. It was a dream. Immense relief washed over him, even though he could still taste the anguish. His heart was still pounding heard.

The phone rang once more.

He had dreamt it all. Relief! "It was a dream," he said aloud.

The ringing was his cell phone. He shook his head to clear his mind. Where was the cell phone? It rang again. The bathroom. It was in the bathroom. He jumped up and hurried to retrieve it. He flipped it open. "Hello?" Nothing. The line was dead. He could see from the display that it was Kathy. She had called twice.

Mark looked in the mirror and was angry at having fallen asleep. "Idiot," he said to himself sternly. "Idiot!" He looked back at the cell phone. Should he call her back or not? *No*, he thought, *don't call her back.* He'd see her at church.

He bolted out of the bathroom and was startled by the unexpected figure standing in his room.

"Mark," said the figure.

It took a moment for him to regain his composure. "Sotare? What are you doing here?"

"I came to ask you a question."

Stunned, Mark stared at the angel. His hands were shaking, his heart still pounding.

"What is true love?" Sotare stared at Mark for a moment and then smiled. "I envy you," said Sotare as he disappeared.

Mark stood in the room, dumbfounded. Why had Sotare appeared just to ask that question? And why did he say he envied him? Couldn't he have said it in the car? Why was he instructed to go to a motel room? Was it so he could fall asleep and have Sotare mysteriously appear and pose yet another cryptic question before going away again? He knew it had to be important. Frustrated, he forced himself to think about it for a few seconds. Did it have anything to do with the dream, with Kathy, with…? Then in a flash, Mark thought he knew what the answer was.

He grabbed his bag, threw all his stuff in it, and headed out the door. The church, fortunately, was close by.

Chapter 12

THE SERVICE STARTED JUST a few minutes late. As soon as the congregation began to sing, all of the demons fled, except Grat. It hovered above the people, moving and weaving among them until it approached the front of the church where the pianist was playing. It leaned over towards the woman and spoke, "You are going to die." The pianist missed a single note. Then Grat swiftly moved to the guitarist and said the same thing. He seemed unaffected so Grat leaned closer and yelled, "Murder." The man's concentration was broken. He, too, missed a note. The communion of worship was weakened, if only just a bit. Grat moved to the drummer and, within moments, he missed a beat. The subtle missed notes were picked up by members of the congregation. A few people noticed it enough to lose just a bit of focus. Grat had been watching them to see which ones showed any signs of receptivity to its craft. With a quick eye and a quicker movement, it slid into the congregation among the people who seemed to be vulnerable. It spoke loudly into the ear of a woman, "You will die horribly," then to a man, "Your wife is committing adultery." To a grandmother it whispered, "You have cancer."

And to a pair of newlyweds it said, "Lust, hatred, evil." They both stopped singing for a short while.

It moved quickly, found a woman, and said rhythmically, "Rape, rape, rape." The woman stopped singing and frowned. Grat smiled and moved to another and another and another, whispering and shouting into the ears of as many people as it could reach. It circled back to the pianist, "Rats are eating your flesh." The pianist again missed a note. Moving back to the guitarist and the drummer it spoke words of evil. The worship team lost its rhythm and stopped in confusion.

The church fell silent. The guitarist apologized, "Sorry folks, even the musicians mess up sometimes." Turning back to the worship team, he said something that only they could hear, and they started on a new song. It was obvious that things weren't right. Grat worked quickly, moving from person to person, speaking vile descriptions of murder, rape, molestation, infections, and disease into the ears of as many people as it could. Though the music continued, it was slightly disjointed and out of synch.

Outside, the circling demons could faintly hear the musical discord. They became energized and began to dip and rise, striking each other, growling and spitting in their excitement.

Finally, after two more songs, the congregation was finished. As they sat down, people were looking around at each other, aware that something was wrong. Most of them felt a little unsettled.

The five original demons knew it was time to move. They entered through the roof and clung to the walls of the sanctuary. They watched Grat as the demon continued its malevolent work and then they joined in, slithering to the floor and mingling with people, speaking words of evil, filth, and hatred into their ears.

Right on cue, the pastor entered through the door of the sanctuary and walked down the center aisle. He was surprised that it was filled to capacity. There were people there whom he hadn't seen in weeks. They watched him. He could feel their curious eyes upon him.

After ascending the three steps to the platform at the front of the congregation, he moved behind the pulpit. He laid his Bible down quietly and then tested his lapel mike with a gentle *tap*, *tap*, *tap*. He picked up the bulletin and opened it, the crackle of paper amplified by the mic. Grat approached him from behind, and spoke into his ear, "Today you die." Tim experienced an immediate flashback to his dream. He glanced down at the Bible and then up at the familiar faces in his congregation. They were all looking attentively at him.

Tim adjusted his sermon notes and Bible on the podium. He was having difficulty concentrating, "Today you die," came the words again from behind. A trickle of fear began to scrape across his spine. He tried to ignore it.

"Today is the day of your death, vile pig."

Pastor Tim's heart began to beat faster. His mouth was dry. So far, he'd not said anything and the congregation was waiting. He prayed quickly and silently. *Lord, please give me the strength. Please give me the strength. I need you.*

Grat jerked back suddenly, as if slapped. It kept its distance and retreated to the congregation where it began again to speak words of fear to whomever was vulnerable. The other demons were there as well, mingling among the people.

"Please be seated."

Everyone sat down slowly and quietly.

Pastor Tim finally began to read the bulletin announcements.

***

Mark was at a stoplight, waiting impatiently for it to turn green. He knew where the church was. At least he thought he did. He'd been there a couple years before on a visit to his father-in-law. Had he missed a turn? Things weren't looking familiar. Was it because he was so tired and having trouble concentrating? Heavy, heavy eyelids and shallow breaths were testament to his fatigue. The lack of sleep made his mind drag. He shook his head to clear it.

The light turned green. He hurried through the intersection, anxiously examining the streets, looking for the right one.

"There it is," he said to himself. He turned onto Twelfth Street. Just a couple blocks down on the right would be the sanctuary. He could see the white cross brightly reflecting the sun as it pointed upward into the blue sky.

Above it the demons were circling. They saw him approach, but they were more interested in Leech, who was walking towards the church.

***

Pastor Tim finished the announcements. Opening his Bible, he took his notes out and placed them on the right side of the pulpit. He cleared his throat. It was time to talk about why the prayer team had been activated so early in the morning. Of course, the collective dream had been related to everyone by now. That was obvious. He looked to the congregation. Everybody sat silently, watching, waiting. Nervously, he cleared his throat again.

In the front row sat John and Kathy. Tim nodded to them and smiled politely. John nodded in return.

"As many of you know, just a few hours ago we activated the prayer team. Normally we don't do this in the middle of the night, and, since everyone is curious about what is going on, I thought it would be best to fill you in." He paused for a moment as he considered where to start. He gulped a drink from the fresh water bottle inside the podium.

"A few days ago, John had emergency gallbladder surgery." He looked at John. "I stopped by the hospital Friday afternoon to pray for him. His daughter, Kathy," he nodded towards her and smiled, "was in the room visiting. We talked for a little while. It was nice to meet her, as John had told me so much about her. We chatted and I was about to leave when I felt I received a word from the Lord. It was about Kathy's husband, Mark. As I was leaving, I had this distinct impression that Mark was somehow important spiritually. This struck me as odd since Mark isn't a believer." He looked at Kathy, "I mean no offense." Kathy smiled back politely. Tim continued, but only after weighing whether or not to tell them what happened next.

"After I excused myself from the room, I was walking down the hall when I had the strong impression that my own life was in danger." He glanced over at Susan, his wife. This was the first she'd heard of this and she showed obvious signs of concern.

A soft murmur erupted in the congregation. He raised his hand towards them and waited for it to die down.

"Don't worry. I have committed everything to the Lord and am in his hands."

***

Leech entered the front door of the church. He fingered the ski mask he had in his back pocket and looked around. Luckily, no one was in the foyer. He peered through the windows of the doors that led into the sanctuary. He could see Pastor Tim at the pulpit. Leech reached under his shirt and felt the gun. He swallowed hard and focused momentarily on his pounding heart. He licked his lips nervously and checked around the foyer again. It was still empty. From his vantage point, he could see most of the congregation and, so far, no one knew he was there. He swallowed again as he thought about what he was about to do. Did he really have the guts? He moved away from the doors and looked at his hands. They were shaking.

Paraptome sensed his doubt and immediately spoke into Leech's mind. "Do it. It is the right thing. You will not get caught. Do it." Paraptome tried to numb the place in Leech's brain that dealt with fear. "Do it. Do it."

Leech started to feel better, more confident. He reached for the ski mask. Unexpectedly, the door to the sanctuary opened and a young girl, perhaps six years of age, entered the foyer. She glanced at him, smiled, and headed off down the hall where she disappeared into the bathroom. He had been seen.

She was young, but she saw him. He thought about killing her but he knew it wasn't a good idea. Besides, he would be far away after it was all over and what could a little girl tell the police? He decided to take a chance and wait until she went back to the sanctuary. He found a corner with a table and literature on it. He walked over and picked something up, blankly staring at it, pointing his face away from the sanctuary and out a window.

***

Mark had trouble finding a place to park. "Come on," he said to himself as he kept driving. He gripped the steering wheel frantically, peering through the windshield looking back and forth. "Not now!" he exclaimed in frustration. He could see only a few spaces at the far end of the lot. "Of all the bad luck!" Maybe he could find a spot closer to the church on the street.

***

"The dream I had," said Pastor Tim, "was very disturbing. Normally, I wouldn't wake anybody up in the middle of the night to ask for prayer. But this was different, so I called Allen, the head of the prayer team. To my complete surprise, he told me that he'd had the same dream."

Tim could hear another low whisper move through the congregation.

"Needless to say, that shook me up. But Allen was very kind and said he would activate the prayer team. We both thought it was important enough to do that. So, to those of you who lost some sleep, I hope you'll forgive me." He took another drink of water.

"When I got to church this morning, I began to pray. Allen showed up and we talked about everything." He looked over to where Fran was sitting. "Fran, who is on the prayer team, also came in early. She had been calling others to pray, as had been Allen, and she said that three other people had had the same dream."

The congregation again began to murmur. Tim had to wait for about fifteen seconds for the sanctuary to become silent again.

"Who was it?" asked someone in the congregation. "Who were the others who had the dream?"

Tim looked quizzically at Fran. He nodded. She stood up

and turned towards the congregation. "Could those of you who had the dream raise your hands?" Two women and one man responded. Tim decided to let everyone talk for a bit until they were ready for him to continue.

***

Mark saw a spot on the side of the road. He pulled into it quickly and within seconds was jogging towards the church.

***

Leech was growing apprehensive. He did not like waiting in the foyer. He began to think about leaving, about forgetting the whole thing. Leech glanced back at the hallway, hoping that the little girl would come back. He didn't want any surprises. "Forget the little girl," said Paraptome. "She's nothing." Paraptome tweaked Leech's mind, subduing his fear and caressing the pleasure center. "You can do this," said Paraptome. "You are strong, and this will prove to everyone just how strong you are."

Leech realized he didn't need to wait for her to return and that his nerves were getting to him. That's it! He had decided. He was going through with his plan. Just then, the door opened. The little girl skipped down the hall and disappeared back into the sanctuary. He watched as the door slowly closed behind her. He strode to the doors and peered through the windows into the main sanctuary.

***

Pastor Tim looked at John and Kathy and then back at the entire congregation. "I don't know how all of it works, but the good Lord has it figured out. It seems to have a lot to do with Mark, Kathy, and John." He looked at them again. "John, Kathy, would you two mind standing up?"

Kathy felt a bit embarrassed, but she complied with the pastor's request. John moved more slowly, still hampered by the soreness from his surgery. Pastor Tim decided to step down from around the pulpit to stand beside them in order to make the discussion more personable.

***

Leech saw the pastor step down. "Perfect."

He slipped on the ski mask. It wouldn't take long before someone spotted him. But, if he moved quickly, that wouldn't matter.

Mark was just outside, about to open the door to the church. Leech's heart was pounding and has hands began to shake. "Go!" said Paraptome. "Become free. Kill him!"

Leech pushed the sanctuary doors open and charged in.

Mark opened the outside door and entered the foyer. He saw the doors in front of him closing slowly. The church was quiet except for a single muffled voice. He surveyed the foyer before walking to the sanctuary door.

Leech strode quickly. A few people noticed him but could only see him from behind so they didn't know his face was covered.

Mark peered through the sanctuary door's window in time to observe a man walking down the center aisle. He glanced beyond the man and saw John and Kathy standing next to the pastor. *Why were they all standing there?*

He watched them as he tried to decide what to do. Should he walk in and surprise Kathy, sit in the back of the church, or wait here?

Mark was tired and his mind wasn't functioning at its best. He strained to find clear thoughts.

Leech reached into the waistband of his pants and fingered the revolver.

Pastor Tim was only now realizing that Leech was approaching and that he had a ski mask on.

Mark was still gazing through the door, trying to make a decision. Nervously, he looked behind him into the foyer.

Pastor Tim immediately thought of the dream. His heart

skipped and he took a step backwards. Instinctively, he wanted to run, to hide himself, but he knew that he could not. He watched the masked man reach under his shirt and pull out a gun. Someone in the congregation screamed and Leech nervously reacted by swinging the gun towards the shriek. Everyone saw it. Someone shouted, "He's got a gun!" And that is when chaos erupted. Another woman screamed and people nearest the aisles started to move towards the walls, scrambling past each other. Some indistinguishable cries of fear rose in the sanctuary as the erratic rumble of moving bodies cascaded through the church. The mayhem caused Leech to look around frantically. He did not want to be jumped.

Leech pointed the gun back and forth from the pastor to the crowd. The screams and commotion continued to cause him to jerk the weapon in different directions.

"Kill the pastor!" yelled Paraptome into Leech's mind. "Shoot him now!"

Leech actually heard Paraptome's voice inside. It startled him. Confused, he looked around, waving the gun. He was panting heavily, his hands shaking.

"Kill the pastor!" came the words again.

People were yelling and scrambling, making it difficult for Leech to focus. He had to shoot the pastor and get out. But he saw the people running out of the door that was to be his escape route. He wouldn't be able to get out cleanly. For a split second, he scanned the room in search of another exit.

Mark had seen the commotion and heard someone shout something about a gun and instinctively reacted to protect Kathy. He forced himself into the sanctuary and was fighting against the flow of exiting people.

By now, Pastor Tim had put himself in front of John and Kathy and was backing up with them. Paraptome yelled into Leech's mind, "Kill the pastor! Kill him!" Leech turned. He took aim and pulled the trigger.

A tremendously loud crack echoed in the sanctuary above the screams and scuffling. But something was wrong. The pastor was still standing.

Leech had missed.

From the rear of the church, shards of a stained glass window fell noisily to the ground. Leech aimed his gun again and, as he began to pull the trigger, he felt a hard blow on his back. The gun went off but this time it discharged into the floor. Mark had launched himself through the last few feet separating him from the gunman, and caught Leech just as he pulled the trigger. The impact almost sent both of them to the floor, but Leech was surprisingly nimble and managed to remain on his feet.

Pastor Tim extended his arms in a protective stretch in front of John and Kathy, who were quickly backing away. Kathy was shocked not only by the mayhem and the gunfire but also by seeing Mark. It didn't register. It was impossible for him to be there. "Mark!" she cried out and instinctively started to run towards him. Pastor Tim held her back.

Mark and Leech struggled over the gun. Mark punched Leech once, but it didn't do much. The gun was waving in all directions. John took a step forward but Pastor Tim pulled both him and Kathy out of the way.

Paraptome, realizing that it was about to fail its mission, cursed into Leech's mind. Leech grunted loudly as he fought for control of the gun. It went off again in the direction of the pastor. All three of them ducked and hit the floor. There was another shot, this time into the ceiling. People were scrambling and screaming.

Paraptome decided to risk damaging Leech and took over as much of his body as it could. Leech felt a surge of power swell within him while, at the same time, he sensed coldness and weakness. It was bewildering, disorienting. Paraptome muscled control of the gun as they tumbled on the floor.

Crack! Another gunshot. A life-and-death struggle was in progress. Mark was, of course, outnumbered and overpowered, as Leech was not only inhabited by a demon but also was the beneficiary of its strength.

Nonetheless, Mark was fighting the most ferocious fight of his life. In the struggle, Leech's ski mask came off. Leech, oblivious to his disclosure, was still desperately wrestling for the gun. Fear of another shot kept everyone at bay.

Mark kneed Leech in the ribs but the blow was ineffectual. Leech looked into Mark's eyes and easily forced the gun towards his stomach. Mark tried to push it away, but Paraptome squeezed the trigger. Another loud crack echoed in the sanctuary and Mark's eyes opened wide as the metal slug slammed into his body.

Paraptome threw Mark aside. It slid a few feet down the center aisle and quickly turned towards the pastor again, but Tim was right in front of him and slammed into Leech, catching him off guard. The collision forced Tim to topple over one pew and it sent Leech careening onto the corner of another, cracking a rib.

Then Sotare slammed into Paraptome. The impact didn't have much of an effect on the demonic giant, but it was felt.

Leech jerked as if slugged in the gut. He fell to his knees and grabbed his side.

Paraptome growled furiously. Leech grunted in pain and waved the gun aimlessly as he tried to get up.

Pastor Tim had regained his footing and was about to tackle Leech. But Leech raised his gun and pointed it dead center at Tim's chest and pulled the trigger. *Click, click, click.* Tim reacted by diving into the pews before he realized the gun was empty.

Paraptome realized it had failed and growled horribly as it released Leech, throwing his soul aside and violently exiting his body. It turned, faced Leech, and with all its fury it screamed at him, baring its huge fangs. Then it took its clawed hand and swung it, intersecting with Leech's body before Paraptome opened its huge wings and flew out of the church.

Leech felt a surge of vertigo and nausea. His mind seemed somehow disconnected and it was all he could do to scramble to his feet and run down the center aisle out of the almost-empty church into the crowded foyer. He thrust people aside violently as he forced his way through them.

Pastor Tim decided not to pursue Leech. Instead, he hurried to Mark's side. Kathy was already crouched next to him, as was John.

She was crying miserably, "Mark, Mark!"

Through glazed eyes, he saw her shock and misery and said, "I love you."

"Mark! Honey." She was now sobbing, "No, no, no!"

"I love you."

She kneeled over him and cried while saying his name, "Mark."

Pastor Tim pulled Mark's shirt away from the bullet wound. Blood was oozing from his stomach, forming a small puddle on the floor.

Mark winced in pain and put his hand to his stomach, then looked at the blood running down his own wrist.

Kathy had begun to cry and her tears fell on Mark's shirt. "Mark, you're going to be okay. Don't worry, baby, you're going to be fine."

Mark dropped his bloodied hand to his side. He closed his eyes and went limp.

"No!" screamed Kathy, as she fell onto his chest. "No! Mark!"

Tim was on his knees next to him. John, too, knelt down beside Mark, putting one hand on Kathy and the other on his son-in-law.

***

Paraptome propelled itself above the church sanctuary into the air where the demons were waiting. They swarmed en masse. Some were unaware of its failure. They quickly found out when it turned on them, entering their swarming mass, and, with a single blow, felled three. The rest scattered. It twisted around to find Sotare.

The angel, small by comparison, was at a safe distance, waiting to see what the principality would do, hoping to draw it away. He did not want to fight this mighty opponent, as he was no match for its power. The best he could do was flee. But the adversary's speed and strength meant he would certainly be caught.

Paraptome scanned the sky intently. Finding Sotare, it shrieked with loathing, leaned forward, and bolted towards the angel. Sotare turned and flapped his wings as rapidly as he could.

With Paraptome following him, it couldn't harm anyone else. Sotare moved through the air as fast as he could, beating his wings hard, narrowing them, and slicing through the wind with incredible speed. But, the monster was gaining quickly. It growled and narrowed its eyes as it quickly closed the distance.

Suddenly, Paraptome's rapid movements faltered and its eyes opened wide. It seemed to struggle in the air. It roared once again, but this was not a howl of anger. It was a cry of terror. As if jerked by a chain from below, Paraptome suddenly disappeared down into the earth.

***

Leech dashed through the parking lot. The chain-link fence was about forty feet away. He held his ribs and winced at every step, gritting his teeth, forcing breath through his tight lips. Saliva spattered out of his mouth. There was no stopping now. He weaved around two cars and, empowered by adrenaline, he jumped towards the top of the fence, where he tried to lunge over, but his shirt snagged on something sharp. He lost his balance, slipped, and gashed his side open on an exposed piece of thick wire. Blood spurted from the wound.

He twisted his face into a contortion of pain and then forced himself to look at his side. A piece of barbed wire was embedded between his ribs and the slightest movement sent shards of pain stabbing into his side. He knew he had no choice but to get himself free as quickly as possible so he jerked hard and ripped himself free. An explosion of pain almost caused him to pass out, as he plunged to the ground and collapsed in a heap. The bloody wound throbbed mercilessly and it was all he could do to make himself get up and hobble, hunched over, down the alley to the car. He ran, staggered, and then stumbled to the ground. He shook his head hard, then looked at the bloodied hand with which he was holding his side. He forced himself up and managed to keep his balance as he headed for the car.

He grunted in pain as he sat in the driver's seat and bent over to connect the wires. After a few seconds, the engine revved to life and he shifted the car into drive. He punched the accelerator.

Blood spilled on the seat and his wet hands spread it on the steering wheel. Nervously, he glanced in the rear view mirror, then leaned into the turn out of the alley. He wiped his nose with the back of his hand, smearing red all over himself.

The warm fluid seeped down his side and into his underpants. He clutched his side with one hand, and drove with the other, wincing and groaning repeatedly as he forced air through clenched teeth, enduring the pain that each erratic breath produced.

He was lightheaded, but something else was wrong. Something inside didn't feel right. It was as if he was somehow out of synch with his body. Everything around him seemed disconnected.

He turned a corner, shook his head, and glanced in the rearview mirror. The distance wasn't right, or was it the mirror? He looked ahead. It must be the shock from his injuries.

A fresh surge of pain helped him focus, but only momentarily. His mind began to waver, to disconnect again. He shook his head vigorously and took another nervous glance in the mirror.

He tried to concentrate. He blinked hard and groaned from the pain.

His senses—something was wrong with them. They seemed to fade in and out. Was it because of the blood loss? It had to be.

He checked his wound. Blood was oozing out through his fingers with every pounding pulse of pain.

His mind felt… he couldn't put it into words. It was odd, different. *Focus*, he thought. *Focus!* The street turned hazy and the car veered to the left. He tried to correct and over-compensated. With another correction he managed to keep the car on the road. He shook his head hard and blinked forcibly, trying to see what was ahead of him.

His arms felt heavy. They moved only with great effort. Then he noticed that his legs weren't working right. His vision blurred and he shook his head again. He looked at the speedometer. It registered forty, forty-five, then fifty miles per hour. He wanted to slow down, but he couldn't: fifty-five, sixty, sixty-five miles per hour. His mind wavered and lost its ability to recognize objects. Then to his utter surprise, the pain ceased. Everything went silent and all motion seemed to slow. Leech could see only a vague haze of light and dark shadows that moved by him as he accelerated.

A car swerved to miss him.

Puzzled, helpless, and damaged by Paraptome's violent dispossession, he was suffering a progressing disconnection from his body. He never saw the large tree he slammed into at eighty miles an hour.

The impact folded the car like an accordion. The crushing, grinding sound of bending metal reverberated through the local buildings, ricocheting down the street. Steam hissed into the air and fuel gushed onto the street. The airbag had deflated but there wasn't much left of him to matter. Then, without warning, the car erupted into flames. Barely conscious, Leech sensed the flickering light around him. In one last pathetic attempt to grasp for life, his mind forced him to experience the searing pain as his flesh turned to charred blackness. It took only a minute before his squirming and agonizing cries ended and he fell into the grip of death.

But it was not over for him.

Suddenly everything became focused. His mind was clear and alert. There was no pain. He was standing beside the burning vehicle, but he felt no heat. He could see his own body inside the inferno.

Mystified, he stepped away and looked around. Everything was crystal clear. He felt his side. The gash was gone. His ribs didn't hurt. The fear, the dread, the adrenaline, all of it vanished. In fact, he felt good, surprisingly good. What had happened? He looked back at the car then up to the clouds. He checked his side again and seeing no wound, he smiled.

Then the stark truth hit him hard. "I'm dead," he said in stunned self-realization. "I'm dead." He looked at the burning car and the people running towards it. No one noticed him. *Of course,* he thought. *They can't see me.*

He laughed and extended his hands outward as he spun around and around. "I'm dead! I'm dead!" He laughed some more as he watched the burning car. His physical body was no longer visible in the blaze.

He felt comfortable and at ease. It was wonderfully bewildering. He smiled. "Being dead ain't so bad," he said with a laugh.

He looked at the car and the street and the scrambling people. This was fantastic. There was no pain, no pain at all. "Ha ha!" he laughed again and checked his side. There was no wound. "Yes! This is great!"

A growl rumbled from behind him. Turning, his jubilation was instantly erased by the sight of the large muscular creature that sat on the ground, resting on its hind legs. It was staring at him. Leech had never seen anything like it. He stepped back, instinctively. It crept forward. Leech stepped back again. It moved forward again.

The creature had massive, powerfully muscled shoulders. Its head was flattened slightly and resembled a dog's, but without hair. It had huge jaws and fangs. Red eyes glared from deeply set sockets in its skull. Its ribcage was bony, covered with skin so tight and thin that Leech could see into its chest. Large draping sheets of what appeared to be leather fell from its back onto the ground and Leech could only conclude they were wings. Its feet had long claws that curved downward, partially disappearing into the pavement. Then Leech noticed a tail slowly sliding across the ground behind it.

It glared at him. Leech stepped back again.

The creature crouched on its huge hind legs. Leech could tell they were tense, ready to spring.

He opened his eyes wide and stopped breathing as he took another step backwards, ready to run.

The creature hunched on its rear legs and opened its jaws slightly. Leech could see a row of dagger-like fangs. It crouched a little deeper and that was when he realized that it was going to pounce. Leech turned and bolted, but the demon launched itself through the air and in an instant was upon him. It snarled as it latched onto his neck and its claws shredded his flesh. It tossed him in the air and clamped down on his chest with its powerful jaws. Fangs pierced his torso and ripped into his lungs. Leech managed a muffled scream of terrified agony.

The creature shook him violently and Leech could hear the sound of his own bones breaking. Then, the demon stopped.

Leech fell limp. He tried to scream but nothing would come out of his broken and shredded body. He couldn't move, couldn't cry, couldn't even manage a moan through his excruciating pain.

The creature remained still. Then the piercing, unbearable agony of ripped flesh and broken bones subsided for a moment and briefly disappeared before it was replaced by an equally intense misery that accompanied his body's rapid healing.

The pain revisited him with a vengeance and through it Leech somehow managed to cough up a single agonized whimper. The creature jerked him into the air slightly and bit down hard. Leech could feel its fangs in his neck, scratching against his vertebrae. He tried weakly to pull free but it was to no avail. It bit down again and Leech's body convulsed under the new pain.

The creature then growled in low rumble, bowed low, and dropped downward, dragging Leech with it into the darkness of the earth.

In the grip of this monster, and its quick descent, Leech realized that hell awaited him. He tried in vain to scream again and somehow squirm free. But it was useless. The creature and the man plummeted rapidly through the darkness, propelled by the demon's flapping wings. Their speed increased as they fell downward, further and further into the darkness.

Leech tried again to scream but his throat was pierced by a fang and nothing but a gurgle of noise emerged. He tried to free himself from the unholy grip of his captor with a feeble movement of his arm. The demon responded by taking a free hand and ripping Leech's chest open. He jerked in searing agony and then fell silent and motionless. Then, in another horrendous repetition of the agony, his chest began to heal on its own, sending shards of intense pain throughout his body.

Suddenly, the pain was gone. Leech looked into the eyes of his tormentor. The putrid breath of the demon raked across his face.

The creature slowly growled with a low rumble.

Please no, thought Leech.

The demon stared deeply into his eyes. Then, it reached with its other claw, and tore Leech's chest open once more. Rivers of agony enveloped him. A weak and muffled scream was all his mangled carcass could feebly manage. Then he began to heal once more and the throbbing agony in his body was repeated.

This went on, over and over, until finally they fell into a vast cavern, where a sudden and powerful stench forced Leech to involuntarily convulse. He tried to refuse to breathe. He tried to pass out. It was useless. The permeating filth clogged his senses. He choked and convulsed again.

Below him was the reflected light of fires bouncing off the walls. The demon swooped lower and with great speed released Leech, who fell headlong into some jagged rocks. It was a crushing impact. Racked with thudding pain, he tumbled downward, slamming against more rocks, falling limply, sliding, grinding, until he at last came to rest, but not before a there was a final, colossal blow to his stomach, which ripped open and spilled his intestines onto the ground. He was face-up, conscious, unable to move, unable to groan, completely incapacitated by the trauma and pain…and he was fully awake. That is when he realized he couldn't pass out. He would always be conscious.

All he could do was watch as a host of hideous creatures closed around him. Then his body began the healing again. His screams echoed in The Cavern.

***

Fortunately, the paramedics were close by. The call to 911 had gone out quickly, and within minutes, the police arrived. They searched the area thoroughly for Leech and after making sure he was gone and that there weren't any other gunman, they let the paramedics do their job. They hurried through the church doors to the small collection of people that were huddled around Mark. He was lying in a small pool of blood on the carpet.

They put their equipment down and kneeled over him. Kathy withdrew reluctantly, held back a little by Pastor Tim. John was praying.

One of the paramedics quickly checked Mark's pulse and breathing.

He was unconscious but alive.

"What happened?" asked the other.

"He was shot in the stomach," said Pastor Tim.

The first paramedic cut open Mark's shirt. Blood was oozing out of his stomach. The other looked at Kathy. "Are you his wife?"

She whimpered when she saw the wound and put her hands to her mouth. "Yes." The answered was muffled.

"Does he have any allergies to any medicines?"

"No," she responded.

"Has he had any recent surgeries?"

"No. No." She shook her head.

The first paramedic was kneeling in Mark's blood. The other had unpacked some saline solution and two large bore needles. He shoved them into Mark's veins.

"Ma'am," said the first. "We're using saline to keep his blood pressure up. We're going to transport him to the hospital in the ambulance.

Kathy was sobbing on the floor next to him, saying his name over and over again.

Pastor Tim gently held on to her, trying to give the paramedics room to work. She resisted and began to cry harder.

John could only watch, helpless to do anything. He held Kathy's hand in one and Mark's in another. He prayed.

She sobbed, "No. No. Please don't let..." The lights seemed to fade. Kathy grew heavy and slowly began to collapse. John gently lowered her to the floor, ignoring the pain in his side.

Within minutes the paramedics had moved Mark into the ambulance and were on their way. Pastor Tim waited for Kathy to get back on her feet so he could drive her to the hospital.

***

Mark opened his eyes. Above him the fluorescent ceiling lights glared hard. There were monitors on a wall and on the other side of a large glass window he could see a woman with a stethoscope around her neck. He was in a hospital. It looked like an emergency room. What was going on? He felt numb and confused. He looked around.

It all came back to him in a flash—the gunman, Kathy, the struggle. He had been shot. He checked his stomach and didn't find any wound.

Bewildered, he looked around and that is when he saw himself on the gurney. But he was standing up. He checked his stomach again and then looked back at his body and the people around him in white uniforms moving quickly. The woman doctor rushed into the room and a nurse began to fill her in. The commotion seemed surreal. Blood pooled in small puddles onto the floor.

Wait, it was making sense now. He was shot. Was he dead? He defied the idea. "No," he said aloud. "I'm not dead. I'm not dead."

He looked at the people. "I'm not dead!" he said loudly.

But he knew instinctively they wouldn't hear him.

Then he heard voices. He turned and had a strong urge to walk towards them. But he resisted. He turned back to his body on the gurney and noticed that they all began to fade as if the light was turned down.

Then came the voices again. This time he knew he was supposed to go. Mark walked towards it, through a door. Wait, how did he know to walk through a door without opening it?

John, Pastor Tim, and Kathy were all in a waiting room. She was bent over in a chair, crying. John had his arm around her. His eyes were closed and he was praying.

He moved towards them and noticed that his movement wasn't weighted by his body. It seemed almost effortless.

"I'm here," he said to her. "Kathy, it's me."

She kept crying, oblivious to his presence.

A bright light shone from behind. He turned around. There was no source. It just was. What was happening? The light was bright and clear and seemed to move. It was beautiful. He felt the urge to walk towards it but hesitated. He looked at Kathy. He wanted to hold her, to tell her he was okay. But he knew he couldn't.

"Hello, Mark," said Sotare.

He turned around and found that the light was gone and in its place stood Sotare in full angelic glory.

"I've been waiting for you."

"Sotare?" said Mark. "What is happening?"

"You're dead," responded Sotare solemnly. "It is time for you to come with me."

Sotare turned away and started walking. But Mark didn't move. It was all too much, too sudden. He didn't want to go, but he somehow knew he was supposed to do just that. He looked back at Kathy.

"We need to go," said Sotare.

He began to follow and noticed that as he did, a newfound peace began to envelop him. It was just like the stories he had heard from people who had died and come back. It felt good, peaceful, and serene. He stopped and looked back at Kathy again. The great love he felt for her warmed his heart.

"I love you, Kathy," he said. Then he turned to follow Sotare.

Instantly, Mark was in a huge, open field. The air was crisp and clean and smelled fresh. Beneath him the blades of grass were a bright green in the reflected light. Mark looked up into the sky, but there was no sun, only a beautiful brilliant blue. He looked everywhere and could see trees miles away on distant rolling hills. To his surprise, he could see the individual leaves on the trees. His vision was incredibly acute. It was wonderful.

"Where are we?" he asked. No answer came. Sotare was gone.

Mark took a few steps towards where Sotare had been and was surprised to find that he could hear the rustling of the blades of grass beneath his bare feet. Bare feet? As he looked down he saw that he was once again wearing filthy rags.

Confused, he examined them. They were awful. Everything around him was clean and fresh, except him. The contrast was striking.

He looked around for Sotare but he was nowhere to be found.

Then he noticed music. It was a beautiful combination of voices, a vast number of voices. Where did it come from? When did it begin? It was wonderful, the most magnificent melody and sound, seeming to set his heart at perfect peace, creating a yearning that it somehow also satisfied. The more he listened to it, the more his soul resonated in its perfection. It was breathtaking.

"This is heaven," he said as he savored the moment. "This is heaven."

He smiled. "It's all real…and I made it."

He looked into the bright sky and breathed in the air. It was a glorious experience. How could he have been so foolish as to not believe in this? But here he was. He laughed again and thought of Kathy. He missed her, but he was more drawn by the beauty of this place than by his desire to be with her. He still felt deep love for her, but it paled in comparison to the sheer joy he was now experiencing. There was no remorse, no sadness. It was amazing and natural, as though part of him knew about this place and was recognizing it. He slowly turned around with a beaming smile, breathing deeply. It was magnificent.

Something caught his attention: it was a presence, a distant presence. He focused. It was in the far distance. Something was there. No, not something. It was someone. Someone was approaching. At first he thought it was Sotare, but he somehow knew it was not. This person was walking straight towards him. Who was it?

Then an odd sensation brushed across his soul. It was simple at first but it quickly strengthened. What was it? He examined the feeling flowing upon him and in him. It was different. It was piercing. No, wait. It was enlightening.

What is that? He thought to himself. *Is it connected with this person?*

Then in a flash, he recognized it: purity. *That's weird,* he thought. He was sensing a character trait originating from whoever it was walking towards him. He did not know how he knew, but he knew that was what was happening. He was experiencing absolute purity.

Mark watched and smiled softly.

The closer the person came, the more intense the feeling of purity flowing from him grew. *Him?* thought Mark. *How do I know it is a man?* Then, Mark sensed something more. He focused and within seconds recognized it as well. It was goodness. He smiled and laughed. "Wonderful," he said. Then another sensation: faithfulness. Mark was in awe at this newly discovered ability to sense character traits.

The figure quickly grew closer.

Then another sensation touched him. But this sensation was very different from the others. He focused on the new one, experiencing it, analyzing it. He waited. It seemed both familiar and unfamiliar at the same time. It was… it was… He stopped smiling and stared straight ahead. He let out a hard breath and took a step backwards. Nothing seemed to matter for a few moments. He had to know what it was. It was important, different, and necessary that he…that…he… "Oh, no," he said aloud.

Mark averted his eyes. He had to. It was necessary somehow. He couldn't look directly at the man who was approaching.

What is this, he wondered. *What am I feeling? What is wrong with me?*

He tried to look directly at him, but he could not bring himself to do so. This puzzled him, yet at the same time he began to understand why. He could not look directly at this person because he felt the omnipotent and infinite wonder of intense holiness.

Mark had no choice but to look away. He could not bring himself to gaze directly at this Holy One. All he could do was look down. He *had* to look down. Somehow, it was the right thing for him to do and he *knew* it at the deepest level of his being.

In the midst of this barrage of new sensations, another realization forced itself into his mind as he sensed the holiness growing in intensity. He knew that he was unworthy. He knew that he was a sinner and that he was in the presence of complete, holy perfection. Mark felt bad, not because of any malevolent quality in the one approaching, but because of what he felt inside. He felt completely ashamed.

Suddenly the person was no longer at a distance. Instead, he was standing a few feet away and an unexpected intensity of glory and holiness blasted upon Mark, causing him to step backwards and drop to his knees.

He buried his face in the grass, feeling incredibly and completely unworthy to be favored with even a glimpse of this person's magnificent presence. Holiness, perfection, goodness, faithfulness—all of it permeated his soul and moved through his being as easily as light moves through empty space. It exposed every dark corner and unholy crevice of his soul.

He began to cry. He couldn't help himself. He was unworthy, completely unworthy. He was a sinner in the presence of God and all he could do was weep and keep his head down in the grass, proclaiming his utter and complete filthiness in the depths of his soul before this magnificent being. The tears fell from his face.

Then Mark heard words spoken into his mind. "Look at me." But the words were not alone. With them was total authority and Mark knew he would obey. Slowly, he raised his eyes past the blades of grass and gazed upon the feet of the one standing before him. In the feet were holes.

Mark opened his eyes wide at the realization of who it was. Mark again buried his face in the grass and squeezed his eyes shut. He could not bring himself to look above the blades of grass clenched in his hands. He wanted to disappear. He wanted to be somewhere else. He felt so inexpressibly exposed and vulnerable.

Then he heard three more words form in his mind. "Come with me."

The sound of feet moving in the grass passed him. Mark did not want to raise his eyes, but he did only enough to see which direction he was supposed to go.

Crawling would not allow him to keep pace, so he reluctantly raised himself to his feet, keeping his head as low to the ground as possible, still choking out tears, still feeling profoundly unworthy.

Waves of pure glory and majesty were emanating from Jesus, passing through Mark's body and soul and exposing every part of what he was. He felt alternating and simultaneous joy and disgust, ecstasy and agony. Each revelation of the purity and greatness of Jesus brought with it a corresponding realization of his own impurity.

Although their pace seemed slow, the distance they covered was great. It didn't make sense, but it was true. All he could do was follow as they quickly moved the great distance until finally Jesus stopped.

Mark likewise halted and dropped to his knees. He felt the eyes of Christ gaze upon him, almost burning through him. Mark kept silent, motionless, looking to the ground, waiting, not daring even to think. Then Jesus walked further and Mark once again followed, still keeping his head bowed low.

After a short time, Mark noticed that the ground began to slope slightly, as if they were walking down a hill. Then it became a little steeper and then a little more. The grass began to fade the farther down the descending path they took.

Again, they seemed to be walking leisurely, yet also covering a great distance. Then Mark noticed something else. As they went further down, the feeling of peace and joy grew weaker.

Why was that? Mark dared to wonder. Down, down, down they went. The beautiful music! He noticed that it was growing fainter until, finally, after moving what seemed like a great distance, it disappeared altogether.

As they continued their downward trek, Mark knew something was wrong and with the growing awareness came a menacing sense of dread. The sensations of wonder and peace had vanished and in their place was an escalating fear. The farther down he went, the worse it became.

No, he thought to himself. *Please, no.*

He did not want to let his mind entertain what might be happening. Then he felt a brush of warmth, followed by dry air. He clenched his eyes shut and gritted his teeth. Then he caught a whiff of a foul smell, then another. It was weak at first, but it quickly increased into a nauseating stench, the stench of burning flesh.

"No!" he said aloud. "No, no, NO, please no," he choked out the words. He wanted to stop moving but he couldn't. He continued to walk farther and farther downward. "No," he said again in a whimpering, mournful cry. "Please, I don't want to go. Please, don't take me there." But his words went unheeded. Terror pounded against his soul like a sledgehammer. He was going to hell—Jesus was taking him to hell.

He knew his pleas would make no difference, but he still cried out, imploring the Lord for mercy. "Please, no. I don't want to go hell. Please, I beg you, please." He was almost screaming the words. But they were useless. Both of them continued their downward path and with every step, anguish filled Mark's being with greater and greater intensity.

He cried hard. He cried in mournful agony, almost screaming. Why couldn't he stop following? He wanted to, but he couldn't. He knew he had to follow. He knew he had to obey.

Mark thought of stealing a glimpse of what was around him but was too terrified. He did not want to see. He did not want to look at the judgment. He forced his eyes shut. His heart was beating like a jackhammer and his throat and lungs hurt from the burning air. Intense, overwhelming terror clawed at his whole being.

"No!" he sobbed, begging, "No, oh please, no."

He stumbled over a rock and automatically opened his eyes to regain his balance. He stopped. In front of him appeared to be a shoreline of some sort. They had stopped walking.

All of Mark's five senses were stinging with fear. Dropping to his knees, he gazed out upon a mass of dark liquid. He jerked his eyes away towards the feet of Jesus, but even then he could not bring himself to look at them. Mark fell upon his hands, moaning in remorse. Waves of complete terror flushed through him and he pressed his face into a mound of rotting debris on the ground before him, trembling hard.

Through the fear, through the knowledge that condemnation was about to fall upon him, Mark also knew that it was right. This realization was one last revelation of truth that beat against him before judgment was executed. There was no explanation. There was no bargaining. He knew in that instant that he was completely and utterly unworthy to be delivered out of this verdict. He had no chance. He was absolutely aware of his own sin in the presence of the ineffable holiness of Christ and he agreed with the judgment of his condemnation. He knew it was right, even though he was terrified by it.

He forced himself to raise his eyes to see what lay before them. Through the watery blur of tears he saw a thick dark liquid filled with people in various stages of decay, writhing in agony, screaming and flailing about helplessly as they were being tormented by pockets of flame and the scalding fluid. They screamed hideously, moaning, thrashing about. He could feel their eyes on him, grasping towards him, watching him as they were trapped in an eternity of endless torment.

Mark plunged his head back into the muck, and screamed out again, "No! Please no!" He sobbed heavily and dug his fingers into the soggy ground. "Please no," he said, "I'm sorry. I'm sorry."

He moaned in absolute and complete terrified horror. His whole body shuddered violently. "Please no." It was the only thing his feeble and wretched condition would permit him to say. He cried with whimpering sobs over and over again, wailing in agony. "Please... no." Tears gushed forth as he buried his face in the ground and cried violently into the filth.

He laid there in the muck and grime, waiting for the terrifying reality of judgment to fall upon him. His whole body tensed and strained under the weight of the terror that was before him. He knew it was time to be judged.

But, then he noticed something. It was like a ray of light that had unexpectedly shined into a dark room.

Through his tears and fear he sensed a feeling coming from Jesus. It was odd. He stopped crying for a moment and listened to it, felt it, and recognized it. Keeping his head low, he opened his eyes and smelled the stench afresh. There it was, a sensation he knew well: sadness. Jesus did not enjoy the spectacle before them. It pained him.

Mark knew that Jesus cared for those who were suffering. But he also knew that their judgment was right. They had rejected Jesus and sought their own ways. Now they were living with what they had ultimately wanted, an existence without him.

Mark realized that his own refusal to seek God, his own earth bound apathy about holiness and righteousness, and his pursuit of his own desires, had blinded him from the truth. He too had chosen to live without the true God.

Then Jesus turned around. The movement snapped Mark back into place and instantly, all the terror exploded on him afresh. "No, please no," he cried out in heaving sobs. "Please, no."

Then three more words entered his mind, "Come with me."

Jesus turned around and began to walk. Mark was still terrified and sobbing, but…anything, anything at all to get away from this place. The momentum of fear and sobs pushed his strained soul towards oblivion, but he was somehow able to move in panicked obedience. He clambered frantically towards Jesus. He sobbed heavily. The Lord was not facing him. Instead, he was walking away and Mark was falling behind. He forced himself to stop crying and crawl away from the horrendous sludge of decay. Relief threw itself upon him, but he coughed out one more sob before regaining his footing and following. But now more than ever he kept his head low as he hurried to catch up.

They moved quickly. They were ascending! Could it be?

They kept moving upwards and with welcome relief, the heat and stench grew weaker. The terror was still strong, but it was being slowly replaced with the increasing hope that he might not be cast into hell, a hope he dared not embrace too strongly lest it be shattered.

Then he noticed that the air began to cool, slowly at first but then more and more. And then the music, the beautiful music returned and began to grow louder. Relief and utter liberation swept over him. Was it a reprieve? What would happen? Would Jesus take him down below again and finally cast him into the darkness? The thought terrified him. Mark kept his gaze downward in complete and total subjection, afraid even to hope that somehow he might escape that terrible judgment.

At long last, they reached the place where the grass was full and green. There was no stench, no heat—just splendor. But the terrible memory of hell had burned itself deeply upon his soul.

Jesus stopped. Mark dropped to his knees, drinking in the rich aroma of the fragrant grass and so incredibly relieved to not be in the awful place behind him. But, would he be thrown into it after all? He did not know. He allowed himself to dare think that he might be safe while he waited in total subjection to God.

Jesus turned and faced him.

Mark felt a new sensation. It stunned him. Fear left. Dread vanished. He was overshadowed, captured by something new. It was intense, totally overwhelming and absolutely pure. Mark felt, in the depth of his heart, the most wondrous and complete love he had ever experienced. It washed through him, on him, around him. He could barely move under its awesome weight. It was magnificent. It was intense, holy, and pure. He was in awe. Waves of love continued to move over him, through him, into him. He felt helpless before it, uplifted, and in complete wonder. There was no judgment, no condemnation, only a powerfully deep, loving concern from Jesus for Mark. He could feel the powerful, loving warmth and kindness as if the sun itself were inside him.

He was perplexed but in ecstasy as he experienced the awe-inspiring marvel of the love of God himself. He was completely undone, unable to move, unable to resist it.

He opened his heart. He let it fill him through and through, let it move on him and carry him away in its power.

Then, as if a sudden burst of blinding warmth had penetrated Mark, he experienced a profound urge to weep. But this was not from fear. It was not from dread. Mark knew he should be damned. He knew he should be sent to hell, but he wasn't going to be. Instead, he was loved, loved with a perfect, complete, and undeserved love.

Mark closed his eyes and began to cry. Immediately, he heard Jesus say, "I love you."

Everything went black.

Mark felt movement, then a throbbing, paralyzing pain in his stomach. He opened his eyes. Kathy was staring at him, eyes red and swollen. She gasped and shouted, "He's alive!" then she lunged to grab his hand.

Dazed and disoriented, Mark reached out for her. "I love you." he said weakly.

Kathy burst into tears, moaning loudly. Then she turned her head to one side and shouted again, "He's alive!"

Mark smiled. "I love you."

There was a commotion of movement behind him as personnel rushed into the room.

"I love you." he said again.

"I love you too." she said between sobs.

Then he passed out.

Chapter 13

MARK WAS LYING IN a hospital bed, eyes staring at the ceiling, thinking about his death experience. Machines silently recorded his heart and oxygen-saturation rates. The contents of an IV bag were slowly dripping into his arm. He moved a leg and felt his stomach muscles seize with pain. The room had the typical stale, antiseptic hospital smell.

The door opened. It was Kathy. Her hair was slightly disheveled. She moved slowly, as though she were carrying something heavy. Her eyes were not fully open. "How you feeling?" she asked tenderly.

Mark was so glad to be alive. The sight of Kathy was almost unbearably good and he was tempted to start crying. He held out his hand. She leaned against the bed as she grabbed it and bent down and kissed him, rubbing his hand on her cheek.

"I love you so much," he said. With his other hand he reached to the back of her head and mingled his fingers in her hair. He pressed her close to him.

She put both arms around him best she could, paying attention to the tubs and wires attached to him. After a bit she pulled back and looked lovingly into Mark's eyes.

"I love you," she said. "I'm so glad you're going to be okay."

With a subtle smile, Mark said, "Looks like you could use some sleep."

She leaned over, gave him a kiss and then plopped down in the chair next to his bed.

Mark had been rushed to surgery upon arriving at the hospital. They had worked on him for quite a while, but couldn't save him. After they pronounced him dead, they let Kathy and John in to see him. She was inconsolable, of course, and John was holding his daughter as she wept, when Mark unexpectedly opened his eyes. When she screamed that he was alive, the emergency room personal responded, stabilized him, and he was rushed into surgery.

The surgeons had removed his spleen, as well as the bullet. His stomach muscles were very sore. The large surgical incision burned slightly and the sutures itched.

The first two days of recovery were masked by a fog of painkillers mixed with the remnants of anesthesia. He couldn't do much more than sleep. But today was different. He finally felt clearheaded. He squeezed Kathy's hand.

"I'm so glad you're here," he said.

She looked into his eyes. She was tender, loving, and fiercely dedicated to him.

"You look exhausted," he said.

She chuckled once, automatically. "Are you saying I look bad?"

"You're the most beautiful woman in the world."

"Good answer." She yawned once. "I'm okay. I've just been worried and haven't slept much. The doctor said you're going to be fine, so I guess I will be too." She yawned again.

Mark had been awake for a couple of hours before she arrived. He'd spent the morning reviewing his journey to hell and wondered how crazy she would think he was if he told her about it and about Sotare, his visions of angels and demons. She would probably assume that the narcotics he was on were causing him to hallucinate. Although he knew he would tell her eventually, now was not the time. Besides, he didn't have the energy to convince her.

"Honey?"

"Yes?" said Mark.

"I've been meaning to ask you and I hope you don't mind, but, if you are too tired to answer, you don't have to." She gently squeezed his hand.

"What is it?"

"What were you doing at the church? I mean, why did you go there? Dad and I are completely baffled. I mean, you appeared out of nowhere and saved our lives."

Mark knew that the answer would be complicated. He looked up at the ceiling to that familiar spot on which he had been focusing while contemplating his own mortality.

"Kathy," he said, turning back to her. "I want to tell you everything, but I can't now. I have to say something first and I need you to believe me. Promise me. Promise me that you will believe what I tell you."

Kathy could tell by the tone of his voice that he was very serious. "Yes, of course. I'll believe you."

He slowly clutched a cup of water from the table next to him. Kathy intercepted him and retrieved it. She placed the straw to his lips and he took a refreshing sip. She returned the cup to the table.

Mark took a breath and winced slightly. The memory of the fire, the darkness, and the stench came back to him. The cardiac monitor beat just a little faster. He turned to Kathy.

"The doctor told me that I died in the emergency room."

Kathy nodded somberly, obviously aware of and still disturbed by that truth.

He didn't know where to begin, so he decided to just blurt it out. "I died and while I was dead I went to a green field. It was beautiful. There was wonderful music and such a sensation of peace." He looked at Kathy's face to see her reaction. She was attentive but obviously unsure. Her eyes narrowed slightly.

"You mean you had a near-death experience?" she asked.

"I wouldn't call it a *near*-death experience. I was *dead*."

She cocked her head at a slight angle, still holding his hand. "I know," she said. Tears filled her eyes as she reached for tissue paper.

He waited for her to dab her eyes.

"It was a beautiful place. It was the most wonderful thing I've ever experienced. And the best part of it was that I saw Jesus." His tone was sincere and forceful.

She froze, looked at him squarely in the eyes, furrowing her brow. Mark wasn't sure if she believed him. But he decided to continue anyway.

"I don't know how I knew it was him, I just knew. It was... it was the most humbling experience I've ever had in my entire life. Yet, at the same time it was wonderful."

His eyes were filling with tears.

"Kathy," he said as he squeezed her hand, holding it closer to him. She leaned forward on the chair just a bit. "Jesus took me to hell."

Kathy's eyes widened and she lifted her head. "What?" she said calmly.

"I know it's hard to accept. But you have to believe me. You *have* to."

Kathy was obviously taken aback. Though she had her doubts, she knew that he needed her to believe him. "I believe you," she offered through her uncertainty.

He weighed her statement.

"Kathy, I have to say something... something I learned while I was there. There is a hell, a place of fire, torment, and agony where all who have sinned against God and have not trusted in Jesus and escaped God's judgment will go for eternity."

The TV preacher flashed into her mind. Mark almost repeated his message verbatim.

She sat up. "Tell me more," she said in a serious tone.

He tried to shift his body and paid a painful price for the effort. "I went there. I went to the place of fire and torment and I saw people being tormented. It was horrible. Kathy, I actually went to hell and smelled the awful stench. I heard people screaming. I saw their bodies writhing in agony. It was awful. It was the most frightening thing I've ever experienced. Nothing I can say comes close to describing it at all." He was gently shaking her hand with each word.

His voice trembled as he continued and a tear ran down his temple. "...and I knew, I knew I was going to be thrown in. I knew that I belonged there because, because..."

Tears began to fill his eyes. "...because I am a sinner." He forced the strained words out in a trembling rhythm and closed his eyes. Tears ran down the sides of his face and over his ears. She handed him a tissue.

Kathy didn't know what to do. Mark rarely cried and he seemed so desperately sincere. She squeezed his hand and examined his face. She knew his tone, his look. He was telling the truth, at least what he believed to be the truth. She could see it. But, it was too incredible, too strange.

They both remained quiet for a couple of minutes while he regained his composure. He opened his eyes and blinked away the last of the tears. In a slightly trembling voice he continued. "When I was there, ready to be thrown in, I was so afraid." His voice trailed off again.

Kathy felt his strain and intense emotional trauma and knew to keep listening.

"I was terrified."

He stopped talking.

The only sound in the room was Mark's labored breathing. She waited, hurting for her husband.

"Kathy, I've never felt anything like it. You don't have to believe me and I wouldn't be upset with you if..."

"I believe you, Mark," she interrupted. Her tone was firm and she looked into his eyes as she squeezed his hand again and said, "I believe you."

Mark pulled her hand to his lips and firmly pressed it to them as he kissed her soft skin. More tears fell down his cheeks. He lowered her hand to his chest and pressed it close to him as if trying to press it into his heart.

"But," he said, "Jesus turned around and led me away from that horrible place. He spoke to me. He told me that he loved me." Mark was struggling to get the words out.

Tears were filling Kathy's eyes.

"After Jesus said those words, the words I didn't deserve to hear, everything went black. That's when I opened my eyes and saw you." He was still straining as he spoke. More tears streamed down his temples. She lovingly wiped them away with the back of her fingers. "I came back from hell. I saw it. I *saw* it." He squeezed his eyes shut and more tears were set free. Kathy blinked, wiping away her own.

The door to the hospital room opened and a nurse walked in. She could see that they had been crying.

"Is everything okay?" She walked over to the monitor and then checked the diodes on his chest. "Looks like you're getting a little excited."

Kathy smiled and so did Mark as he choked out, "I'm fine."

The nurse was satisfied. "Well, I'll just leave you two alone. But try not to get too excited. No jumping jacks." She dismissed herself quickly.

Mark looked at Kathy. She was feeling the cumulative weight of her own fatigue, her father's surgery, Mark's shooting, and now this. It was bearing down on her hard. She absentmindedly rubbed her forehead with her fingertips. She hadn't slept much since the shooting.

"Are you okay?" he asked.

She looked at him and in a monotone said that she was fine. But she didn't fool him. He knew that she was exhausted. He looked at her and rubbed the back of her hand with his thumb.

They remained quiet for a while. She had to absorb what he had said and he needed to recover emotionally. She gently squeezed his hand. "I'm so glad you're okay."

"Me too."

She leaned over and kissed him.

The air was thick with emotion. Mark closed his eyes and let himself relax and an unexpected wave of fatigue hit him hard. The strain was exhausting.

He exhaled loudly. Kathy wasn't faring much better.

"Looks like we're both a mess, huh?" he said with a smile, eyes still closed.

She chuckled. "Yeah."

He brought her hand to mouth and pressed it to his lips. Then fatigue hit him again, this time almost overwhelmingly. He knew he'd be falling asleep any minute.

"Honey?" he said as he looked at her, "I'm tired. I'm fading fast. I want to tell you more but I need some rest and so do you."

"I'm okay," she said. "Please finish."

Mark smiled. He wanted to close his eyes and fall into a deep sleep.

"Please. We both need rest. Go to your dad's. And when you come back later, could you please bring him here? I'd like to tell you both the rest of the story. Okay?" He squeezed her hand gently.

"All right." She exhaled audibly. "Sounds good. Now that I've talked to you and I know you're okay, I can rest."

She stood up from the chair, leaned over the bed, and gave him a kiss.

"Do you believe me? Do you really believe me?" He asked.

She looked into his eyes and asked herself if she did. She knew him to be an honest and good man who never lied to her. Besides, he had quoted exactly what the preacher had said. It was all so bizarre, but true. She believed him. "Yes I do."

"Good," he said as he closed his eyes. He sighed heavily and let the tension seep from his body. It felt good, especially before the relentless urge to sleep. "This hospital stuff isn't easy. I'm awake one minute and ready to go to sleep the next."

She studied his face and smiled. "I'll see you later."

"Sounds good. Love you."

"Love you," she said.

Mark closed his eyes, mumbled something unintelligible, and fell quickly asleep.

Kathy slowly released his hand, slipped away from the bed, and left the room. As the door closed, she looked down the hallway at the nurses clad in their colorful scrubs, busily going about their business. She headed for the elevator.

Back in Mark's room, Sotare and Nomos stood on either side

of the bed. Their wings were slightly open and they were on guard for any demons that might be in the vicinity. Mark was vulnerable but they were there and ready for battle. Through the walls, they could see Kathy. They could also see other angels in the hospital guarding other people who were completely unrelated to their charge. Sometimes the angels would see each other across the spiritual distance in the hospital and nod in recognition of one another.

Kathy approached the elevator and hit the down button. The door opened quickly and a doctor stepped out. He had a clipboard with papers. He hurried down the hallway and disappeared into a room. She stepped in and pressed the button for the bottom floor. The doors swished closed. The floor fell downward.

Something entered from below.

She did not see it, nor could she feel its evil presence. It had two backward-tilting horns sticking out of its skull. One was broken near the end. It had a large jaw with teeth protruding between its jagged lips. Green leathery skin stretched tightly across its bones and, here and there upon its body, an open wound oozed fluid. It reached a clawed hand towards Kathy's chest, holding it flat against her body. She was still one of theirs. It moved behind her and smelled her perfume. Drool was running down the corner of its mouth and onto its chin. The creature leaned close behind her neck and let it spill down through her back.

Kathy felt a fleeting wave of nausea. She grabbed the rail in the elevator with one hand and her stomach with the other. She closed her eyes and whimpered slightly. *It must have been the motion and fatigue*, she thought.

The creature leaned close to her ear and whispered, "You are going to die and go to hell."

Kathy suddenly had a mental impression of death and fire. The nausea was subsiding but it still fluttered in her stomach. Unexpectedly, she remembered the face of the creature that had appeared at her dad's place. She opened her eyes.

"It's all real," she said in sudden realization. "What Mark said was true."

The demon stepped back, leaned forward, opened its jaws and hissed.

The elevator slowed to a stop and the doors opened. Kathy stepped out. The sunlight came flooding in through the ground-floor windows of the lobby. She knew what she needed to do.

The demon followed.

Outside the hospital, a host of evil creatures were circling in the sky. As Kathy walked to her car, they would occasionally swoop low. One after another, like birds, they darted up and down, spitting at her.

***

Down in the darkness of The Cavern, the soul of Leech writhed in agony as the creatures fed upon his carcass. The seconds seemed like millennia and the sheer pulsing terror of being torn, bitten, bones breaking and healing, was unbearably brutal. Leech's cries were constant and each tormented scream brought an evil pleasure to the horde of demons that crawled on him and in him.

Nabal entered through a cave with the slave demon following at a safe distance. The creatures moved away from the mangled human form as Nabal approached. Leech lay in a heap of broken bones and torn flesh, barely able to moan through the terrifying agony, which was followed by another inevitable healing with its own searing pain. His groans gradually escalated into piercing howls.

Nabal towered over him. Leech looked up and saw the hideous creature reach down and grab him. "Judgment has not yet come to you. Until then, you belong to us." Nabal squeezed and let its talons sink into his soul, throwing the broken man into the crowd of demons that quickly converged on him.

Above The Cavern, a rift in space opened. Nabal quickly spread its wings and, with rhythmic force, raised its huge body upward. Only its slave demon dared to join it in its ascent.

***

Pastor Tim enjoyed cleaning up the church. He liked to walk through all the rooms, straightening and putting things in order, while he thought about sermons and the needs of the people.

He meandered back to his office when the door to the church opened. Kathy walked in.

"Hi, Kathy, I'm so glad to see you. How is Mark doing?"

"He's fine. In fact…." she thought about what to say. "Can we go to your office?"

Tim paused for a moment then apologetically said, "Well, the secretary isn't in today. You and I are the only ones here and, I mean no disrespect, but I don't feel comfortable being in my office alone with you. Would it be okay if we stepped outside and sat on the steps?"

Kathy understood. He was an honorable man. "Sure, that's fine."

He held the church door open for her and they both went outside. It was a beautiful day.

He smiled politely as they sat. "Okay, how can I help?"

Kathy looked at him and he noticed that she was struggling for the right words. So, trying to be helpful, he thought he'd kick-start the conversation.

"I've wanted to come by the hospital but I figured you and John would be there a lot and I did not want to intrude."

"That is what I wanted to talk to you about. Could you go see Mark tonight?"

"I'd love to." Tim waited, sensing that there was more to come. Kathy looked blankly to the street then back at Tim.

"Last week I saw a preacher on TV. He talked about God, Jesus, sin, salvation, and damnation. I've heard it all before and it never really meant anything to me until that night. I don't know why, but it just did."

She stopped talking for a moment.

"I just came from the hospital. Mark was telling me something, something strange." She thought about informing him about Mark's visit to hell, but decided not to.

"I really didn't believe him at first but the way he was talking was so convincing and then he said something that the preacher on TV also said. It was bizarre and for some reason that I can't explain, Mark said almost the exact same thing the preacher said. I mean the same thing! When he said it, it really struck me. I don't know what is going on, but I had to come here and talk to you about it." She stopped, realizing how much she had just said.

Tim didn't mind. He shifted to face her more directly. "What did Mark say that the preacher also said?"

"I don't remember exactly, but it was about there being a hell, and that people who are under the judgment of God will go there for eternity." She paused and looked away from him and out into the parking lot.

"It sounds like God is calling you," said Tim calmly.

She looked to the street at passing cars.

"Is that all the preacher said? Did he mention Jesus?"

She looked at him. "Yes, he said that Jesus was the only way to be delivered from the judgment. He said that all of us have sinned against God."

Tim said a quick and silent prayer before he spoke. "What do you think about what he said? Do you believe it's true?"

"I don't know. It's all so new and I've never been concerned about it before. But with Mark being shot, his dying and coming back to life, that horrible thing I saw, the preacher..." Her voice trailed off. Tim waited.

"I don't know. I feel something. It's almost like I hear a voice calling me. I don't know what it is. It's weird. I mean, I feel like I have to answer it soon." She exhaled forcefully. "Does that make any sense?"

"Yes it does. It makes a great deal of sense," said Tim was a smile. "The Lord is speaking into your heart and you are becoming aware of the truth."

Wearily, she buried her face in her hands and let her fingers comb through her hair. Pastor Tim prayed silently for a full minute until she spoke again.

"I have to think about this." She got up and so did Tim. "Thank you for talking to me. I feel better."

"But I hardly said anything."

"It wasn't so much what you said as what *I* needed to say. Besides, you listening means more to me than you realize."

"Kathy," he said carefully. "If there's anything at all I can do, please don't hesitate to contact me, even if it means calling me in the middle of the night. Seriously, if you feel the need to talk, I'm here." He reached into a pocket and pulled out a card as he reached to his shirt pocket and retrieved a pen. With a click he wrote on the back.

"Here is my home number."

He smiled gently and pressed the card into her hand.

"Thank you," she said. "I appreciate that." She exhaled noisily as if she had dropped a heavy load. "But for now I think I'll go to my dad's place. So much has happened and so fast that I don't know what to do. I need to think. Maybe I'll call you later." She began to walk down the steps. He followed her for a few. She turned. "Thanks, Pastor Tim."

"Sure, Kathy. I'm glad you stopped by."

He watched her until she was safely in her car and on her way, then he turned back into the church and headed into his office. He closed the door, went to the couch, and knelt by it to pray.

As Kathy drove off, demons kept hovering and twisting in the air as they catapulted themselves back and forth, down towards her, arcing broad strokes in the sky. They were getting closer. Then one demon began to descend towards the car but it unexpectedly stopped and fled.

Nabal descended from above out of the rip in space. It saw Kathy in the car and slowly glided down towards her.

***

Mark opened his eyes and shook the narcotic-induced mist from his mind. He glanced out the window and thought of Sotare. "Where are you, my friend?" He posed his question aloud.

To his right, Sotare stood guard, invisible. He solemnly and dutifully looked back and forth, scanning the spiritual horizon. Mark was still under his charge. Nomos was likewise watching.

"Where are you, Sotare?"

The angels looked at each other. "When do you speak to him again?" asked Nomos.

"My instructions are to wait." he said.

Nomos nodded.

***

Kathy was driving down the freeway, heading back to her dad's house. Above her, Nabal kept pace with the car. It was looking around, trying to find an opportunity to attack. The slave demon followed, but kept its distance.

Kathy was in the fast lane. Nabal followed. The other demons trailed far behind.

The freeway, with its speeding, unobservant drivers, was always a good place to kill. Nabal swooped down upon the top of the car, landing hard and digging its claws into the metal. The slave demon flew nearby. Nabal thrust its massive head down through the roof and let strings of viscous saliva drip from its mouth.

It raised its head and looked at the following swarm of demons. It opened both arms wide and clapped its bony hands together at once. Instantly, the demons began to draw closer. The evil creature turned its attention to the slave and pointed to a pickup two lanes over. "One of our servants. She has been brought here for this purpose. Take five demons with you and make the driver crash into this woman! Do not fail me. Do it now!"

The slave catapulted into the sky into the midst of the demon horde. It pointed to five of them. "The Master Nabal has commanded you." It looked at the pickup and pointed. "The driver is one of ours. Come! Now!"

The six of them tucked their wings and fell through the air at high speed, closing in on the pickup. Just before impact, they opened their wings like parachutes before landing on the frame of the truck, one on the hood, one on the roof, another on the trunk, one on each side. The slave entered the car. Inside, another demon sat next to her, with its hand in her mind. It said, "Command me."

"Release her!" It immediately withdrew its hand. The slave opened its mouth and extended its tongue into the brain of the woman driver. The sensation was slightly different from what she was used to, but it was familiar enough to still be pleasant. Earlier demons had convinced her that such moments were manifestations of the inner divine consciousness and that she was a goddess in embryo. She smiled.

"Let me in," whispered the slave demon. "Let me in. Let me in."

The woman opened herself and the slave demon slipped its talons deep into her mind.

Nabal opened its wings and lifted itself above Kathy's car so it could see everything better. It quickly pointed to the horde of demons above and then at the pickup truck. They began their descent.

The slave was trying to familiarize itself with the woman's mind and body so that it might take her over quickly and force the speeding truck into Kathy's car. It knew this would be difficult because, even under possession, the woman's self-preservation instinct would still be strong.

"Release," whispered the slave demon into her mind. "Release control to me," it said again and again. She was on the freeway and this required her to pay attention, something she was not easily giving up. "Release," said the demon again. It did not want to force her hands to let go of the wheel too soon lest she openly resist and the opportunity be lost.

The demons on the outside of the vehicle were joined by others from above. There wasn't enough room for all of them so they swarmed like insects, looking for any opportunity to join in the kill.

The woman's will was evaporating. She was giving in, and the slave had almost taken her over her mind completely. As soon as the car began to swerve, the demons outside would guard their charge and prevent any angels from interfering. But for now, they could only wait.

Kathy's vehicle was slightly behind. When the pickup swerved and reduced its forward momentum, it would bring their cars into a high-speed collision.

"Release!" The woman was slowing complying. "Release your mind."

Then, above them, a single ray of light pierced the sky and shot down to the ground and was followed by brightness everywhere. A group of angels descended and headed for the demons.

***

Mark was awake again. The nap had done him a world of good. He tried to lift one leg a fraction of an inch but his stomach muscles easily convinced him that that was a bad idea. He grimaced in pain. "That hurt."

It was still light outside and he knew that Kathy would be coming back shortly after dark. So, he reached for the TV remote but before he got to it, the door slowly opened. Pastor Tim's head slid in.

"Hi, Mark. It's me, Pastor Tim. Mind if I come in?"

Mark was surprised that he remembered him—and that he remembered so much of what had happened in the church.

"Not at all. I could use the company."

Tim walked over to the bed and shook his hand. "How are you feeling?"

"I'm feeling as good as can be expected…for a man who came back from the dead. The doctor said that the surgery went very well. He said I'm lucky to be alive."

"Yes, you are." responded Tim. He found a chair, pulled it towards the bed, and sat down. "I hope you don't mind me being here. Is now a good time?"

"Absolutely! I'm tired of being alone."

"I figured you would be out of it for a few days. Besides, family comes first and I didn't want to be in the way."

"Your timing is perfect. Today is the first good day I've had. The anesthesia is finally out of me enough for me to feel alert."

Tim stared straight into Mark's eyes with the kind of a look a man gives to another man when he was about to say something serious and heart-felt. "I want to thank you for saving my life."

Mark returned a half smile. "Please don't take this wrong, Pastor. But, I wasn't there to save you. I was there to save Kathy."

Tim relaxed his gaze, and was obviously bewildered.

Mark realized he had spilled the beans. "Looks like I have some explaining to do."

"I guess so. We were all wondering why you appeared out of nowhere."

Mark looked out the window as he took a deep cleansing breath, then back to the pastor. "Do you believe in hell?"

"Yes."

Mark was still sizing him up. Should he tell him what he had seen? Should he tell him that he had been talking to an angel and that he went to hell? Mark looked at Tim, who was patiently waiting for whatever he had to say. He had never met him before but there was a bond between them because of what had happened.

"Since we're doing the thank you thing, I want to thank you for risking your life to protect my wife." Mark looked deeply into the pastor's eyes without blinking.

Tim nodded, humbly.

"I really mean it." Mark's tone was deeply sincere.

Tim smiled and said, "You're welcome."

Enough said. They both knew that they didn't need to get all huggy on each other.

Mark couldn't help but realize how the pieces fit together, bringing him to this place with the pastor being right there. So, he decided to risk telling him everything.

"May I call you Tim?"

"Of course. I prefer it that way. Do you mind if I call you Mark?" Mark chuckled slightly, winced, and then said, "Well, now that we are on a first name basis, I'd like to tell you something."

"I'm all ears."

Mark looked at him, waited a few seconds, took a preparatory breath and decided to blurt it out. "While I was dead, I saw hell."

Tim had heard many things in his years in the ministry. He was experienced enough to not overreact or underreact when people made heavy statements. So his response was easy. "Alright, tell me about it."

Mark looked at Tim and felt comfortable enough to trust him. There was something about him, something kind and good. So, it made things easier.

"I'd like to tell you everything," said Mark carefully.

Tim shifted in his chair and set his Bible on a small stand nearby. "Okay, I'm listening."

***

Kathy drove down the freeway, completely unaware of the battle being fought above her. A horde of demonic forces was clashing with angels, colliding in the air, intermingled in a fierce, thrashing dissonance of attack and counterattack. The evil creatures clawed at the bodies and wings of their enemies. They spat, cursed, and tore at their adversaries. It was a fierce clash of good and evil. One demon and an angel were locked in battle, wings ineffective, plummeting downward, crashing upon the ground. Their skirmish was fought in the middle of the freeway, interlocked, wrestling, punching, each trying to gain position over the other. Cars whisked through them over and over again. They wrestled violently.

An angel fell to the earth, his wing broken. He would heal within hours, but in the meantime he was out of commission.

Another angel fell, and another. A demon with a broken wing plunged downward, disappearing into the ground. Two more demons attacked a single angel, one from the front and one from behind. They all collided with immense force. The angel fell limply towards the ground but, an instant before he hit, he recovered and opened his wings to return and fight again.

Screams pierced the air from two demons whose wings had been damaged, sending them back to The Cavern. Then an angel fell to the ground, followed by two more demons disappearing into the earth. Another angel plummeted to the ground, then another demon and another.

Screams, curses, grunts, and growls emanated from the throng of tangled beings. The mass seemed to be a single entity, moving, writhing within itself, teeming with turmoil and struggle. Occasionally, a fragment of the turbulent mass would drop downward as two beings twisted and wrestled in battle, fell to the ground intertwined, still battling.

***

Pastor Tim sat back in his chair. "That's quite a story. I've never spoken to anyone who's conversed with an angel before and gone to hell. It's amazing."

"Yes, it is." He looked carefully at the man sitting next to his bed. "Do you believe me?"

Pastor Tim chuckled ever so slightly, "Yes, I do," he said firmly. "Without a *doubt* I believe you."

"You do?"

"Yes. Mark, let's just say that the Lord has been talking to me, too. Ever since I met your father-in-law here in the hospital last week, I've had a profound urge to pray. I've known that something significant, something special, was going to happen and that you were a part of it. I don't know *how* I knew or why. I just did and I believe it was from God. Besides, it is no coincidence that all these events have led us to where we are now. So, I have no choice but to believe you."

Mark should have been surprised. But he wasn't. It all made sense. If he could see an angel, go to hell, and come back from the dead, then most certainly God could work on Tim as well.

"I'm glad," he said. "It feels good to get this off my chest. I haven't told my wife about it. I mean the part about Sotare. I told her a little bit about my experience in hell…and that is some place I never want to go to again." Mark clenched his jaw tightly and let a breath escape through his nostrils. "I don't *ever* want to go there. I don't want *anyone* to go there. Everyone has to know about this and be warned."

Pastor Tim nodded. "Do *you* want to escape the judgment of hell?"

"You have no idea how much. I'll do anything and I mean *anything* to not go there."

Tim nodded. "Well, I have the answer for you." He drew his chair closer. "Mark, the truth is, there is a God. He's pure and perfect. He can do no wrong. Although I admit that there are lots of questions about why God permits bad things to happen, the fact is, he makes no mistakes. But we do. God said do not lie, do not steal, do not bear false witness... Let me ask you, Mark. Have you ever lied, or stolen, or born false witness?"

Mark looked at Tim and was instantly reminded of being in the presence of Jesus and how his own impurity was so clearly manifested. With absolute certainty he said, "Yes, I have, and many more things much worse than those."

Pastor Tim shifted and snickered sheepishly, "Me, too." He continued.

"When God tells us not to lie or steal, we call that the Law. The Law is a reflection of God's pure character because it comes from him. God cannot lie. He cannot steal. Now, these laws are not arbitrary. They are there because of who God is, because of how pure he is. They come from him. Anyway, when we break the Laws of God, it's called sin. The consequence of breaking God's Law is his judgment. Now, the fact is, there is no law without a punishment. The punishment—that consequence, of damnation—is what you experienced." The pastor looked at Mark, who was obviously listening intently.

"I have to admit that I've never spoken to anyone before who has had a near-death experience and gone to hell. I've read about it many times, but I've never actually met anyone who's done it. So, I guess you know how fortunate you are that you were allowed to live."

"You got that right," Mark said the words with strong, clear syllables.

"Well," continued the pastor. "If God did not punish the one who sins against him, then he would be approving of sin by not dealing with it. God cannot do that." The pastor retrieved his

Bible and opened it. "I'd like to show you some verses in the book of Romans in the New Testament. It's quick and easy."

"Sure," said Mark.

Tim opened his Bible and turned it around so that Mark could read. The pastor was obviously very familiar with his well-worn Bible. He placed his finger on the page.

"The Bible tells us in Romans 3:10 that 'no one is righteous'. In Romans 3:23, it says that 'all have sinned and fallen short of the glory of God.'"

He flipped the pages, careful not to proceed too quickly. "Again, in Romans 6:23, the Bible says that 'the wages of sin is death and the free gift of God is eternal life in Jesus Christ.'" Tim stopped for a moment and gave Mark some time to absorb the words. Then he turned to another page.

"In Romans 5:8, it says 'God demonstrates his own love towards us in that, while we are yet sinners, Christ died for us.' You see Mark, Jesus is God in the flesh. We get that from verses one and fourteen in the first chapter of the Gospel of John."

"Wait," said Mark interrupting. "What do you mean God in the flesh?"

Tim responded by quoting what he had obviously memorized. "In John 1:1, it says 'In the beginning was the Word, and the Word was with God, and the Word was God.' Then in verse 14 it says, 'and the Word became flesh and dwelt among us.'"

Mark reflected on his encounter with Jesus. He stared past Tim, remembering the sensation of being with Jesus, the holiness, the intense and incredible purity that he possessed.

He looked back at Tim. "That is true," he said. "It can be no other way. When I was in His presence, He possessed a quality, a holiness that was unlike anything I've ever experienced before. It is something that only God could possess." He paused, then added, "I know what it means to see, to touch, taste, feel, and hear, but it wasn't anything like that. It was completely different, completely other. It was so real."

Tim found himself envying Mark. What so many had only read about, Mark had experienced. He wondered why he was given such a great privilege.

After catching himself thinking about this, he decided to continue. "The point is that only God can take away our sins. We can't do it because we are imperfect. We make far too many mistakes and we can never please God by our efforts. We just aren't good enough. You see, Mark, the Bible tells us that we are condemned because we have sinned against God."

He shifted slightly in his seat. "These words are serious and not popular. People like to think of themselves as somehow being good and worthy of salvation because they are sincere or nice. But the truth is different, isn't it?"

"Yes, as Sotare told me, truth doesn't care about your feelings. Truth is independent of what you want."

"He is right. By the way Mark, you probably didn't know this but your angel's name 'Sotare' is very similar to 'soterios', which is the word used in the original language of the New Testament. It means 'salvation'. Likewise, 'nomos' means 'law'. I think it is very interesting that the two angels sent to protect you are called salvation and law."

Mark stared at Tim in surprise as he realized the interesting coincidence. "It seems as though God has a sense of humor."

"Yep, and a great sense of timing."

After letting that sink in, Tim continued. "Mark, is there anything we can do to undo the sin caused by breaking this Law?"

Mark knew the answer. He had been in the presence of purity and experienced only a minute portion of the omnipotent and infinite holiness of God. Without a doubt, he knew he had absolutely nothing to offer God except his own sin. "There's nothing at all we can do," he proclaimed. "We are completely unable to help ourselves."

Pastor Tim was taken aback by Mark's accurate summation of the human predicament. But he continued. "You are right. There is nothing we can do. Therefore, the only one left to take care of our problem is God. Jesus, who is God in flesh, is the one who paid the penalty for our sins by dying on the cross in our place. He suffered death for us. He took the penalty that was ours. Therefore, all we need to do, all we are able to do, is trust in what Jesus has done because faith is all that is left for us to offer to God."

Mark nodded.

"I assume you have seen movies about Jesus, right?"

"Yes, I've seen a few over the years."

"All right, then you are quite familiar with Jesus and his crucifixion."

"Yes, I've heard that he died for our sins on the cross."

"Yes, exactly correct. The Bible says, in 1 Peter 2:24, that Jesus bore our sins in his body on the cross. Because Jesus was perfect and never sinned, God the Father transferred our sins to him so that he died on the cross with them. He paid our penalty for breaking God's Law."

"Why did he have to die to save us? Why can't God just forgive us if we try and be good and are sorry for what we've done?"

"First of all, no where does the Bible say we are forgiven if we're sorry and do good things. And second, just because a thief stops stealing doesn't mean he shouldn't go to jail for what he's done, right?"

Mark nodded. "Well, that makes sense."

"According the Bible, the punishment for breaking the Law of God is death. That's what it says in Romans 6:23. And, besides, if we could be forgiven by being good and doing good, then Jesus didn't need to die for us as it says in Galatians 2:21. But he *did* die, so our goodness isn't good enough."

Mark was listening intently to every word. It rang true.

"Our sins were put upon Jesus and he died with them. He satisfied the requirement for justice by taking our place and paying the penalty for sin."

Tim paused for a moment, "Am I going too fast?"

"Not at all. Keep going."

"Okay. Well, Jesus did not remain dead. To show that his sacrifice to God the Father was acceptable, he was raised from the dead and, as the Bible says, he then ascended into heaven many days later."

Mark was nodding. He knew the story from TV movies. But

this time, its truth was piercing his heart with power.

"Mark, if you trust in what Jesus did, and nothing in yourself, nothing in what you can do, then you can be saved from that horrible judgment that you came so close to experiencing. Mark, do you want to be saved from the righteous judgment of God?"

Mark didn't hesitate. "Yes."

The pastor turned again to the Bible. "It says right here, in Romans 10:9-10, that 'if you confess with your mouth that Jesus is Lord and believe in your heart that God raised him from the dead, you will be saved. With the heart man believes, resulting in righteousness, and with his mouth he confesses, resulting in salvation.' Do you believe that, Mark?"

Mark smiled and chuckled slightly. "Yes, I do. After seeing what I've seen, I have no doubts what you're reading me is true."

The pastor smiled and pointed to one more verse. "Romans 10:13 says that 'If you will call upon the name of the Lord, you will be saved.' This phrase, 'to call upon the name of the Lord,' is in reference to Jesus. It means that you must ask Jesus to forgive you of your sins and trust in him alone. It means to ask Jesus to be your savior. Mark, do you want to do this?"

With the memory of hell so freshly planted in his mind, he had no choice. "Yes," he said. "I want to receive Jesus as my savior."

Mark and the pastor were unaware that in the same room with them, Sotare and Nomos were listening to every word. They said nothing to each other as they scanned the spiritual horizon. Sotare looked at the two men and could not help but wonder what the Almighty saw in these frail, mortal creatures. He looked at Nomos and said, "I will never cease to be amazed at how our Lord loves these people." Nomos nodded. Then, a light shined from above them both.

The pastor smiled. "Mark, all you need to do is pray and by faith receive Christ as your savior. Ask him to deliver you from the judgment to come. Confess your sins to him. Ask him to forgive you of your sins. Turn from them and trust in what he has done on the cross for you. If you do this, God's Word says that you will be saved, saved from his judgment."

Mark was ready. "You mean I just pray out loud?"

"It doesn't have to be out loud, but it sure does help," Tim said with a smile. "Just talk to him. He is listening."

Mark felt a little awkward but at the same time he knew it was right. He closed his eyes instinctively. Pastor Tim interrupted. "There's one more thing."

Mark looked at the pastor.

"In Luke 14:28, Jesus said to count the cost. You have to realize that becoming a Christian does not mean that your life automatically gets better. It does not mean that all your problems are solved. In fact, it can mean that some things get worse. You might lose some friends over this, or even be ridiculed. It means that you must make choices that are sometimes difficult because you'll have to put God before yourself and…"

Mark interrupted, "…and even put God before your wife."

Pastor Tim's eyes widened as he raised his eyebrows, obviously surprised. "That's right, Mark. But God wants you to honor her and love her. He doesn't want to come between you and separate you. He wants to bring you closer together."

"Tim, after what I experienced, being in the presence of such utter and intense purity, it makes perfect sense. I love my wife, but I completely understand that my love for her pales in significance compared to the incredible glory and value of being in the presence of God."

Tim was taken aback once more by Mark's insight. "But," he continued, "to follow Christ and to count the cost will also mean that you are to love your wife the way he loves you."

Mark stared into Tim's eyes. "And it will also mean to love others."

Tim nodded.

"I'm ready." Mark closed his eyes.

Tim smiled and silently praised God. Then Mark began to speak. "Jesus. I know that I have sinned. I know that I deserve the judgment of hell. *Please* don't let me go there. Please save me from it. I trust completely in what you did on the cross. I accept your sacrifice and I ask you to forgive me of my sins. Please hear my words. I know that I don't have anything to offer except my faith in you. So, by faith, I trust in what you have done. Amen."

Mark opened his eyes. Pastor Tim was smiling. "Praise God," he said.

Mark smiled, too. "That's it?"

"That's it."

Mark smiled even more. "You know something? It's kind of weird, but, I feel as though a giant weight has been lifted from me. I mean, I didn't even know it was there, but I felt it when it left. I feel clean and safe now."

Pastor Tim nodded.

"This is great," continued Mark. "It is so simple and so easy. All you have to do is believe and trust in what Jesus did on the cross."

"Yep, salvation is that easy. Of course, the rest of your life won't be. God is going to work on you and slowly change you to be more like him in your actions and thoughts. It isn't always fun, but it's always good."

Mark let himself relax into the pillow, smiling hard. Pastor Tim reached over and grabbed his hand.

"This is wonderful. I feel great!" He looked at Tim as a tear rolled down his face.

"Thank you, Tim."

"Thank God."

"You know," said Mark. "If we were girls, we'd probably hug about now."

Pastor Tim chuckled again, got up, and with a huge smile he leaned over the bed. Mark reached up with his arm and the two men embraced.

"Thank you, Jesus," said Mark.

Chapter 14

KATHY WAS FAMILIAR ENOUGH with the freeway to allow her mind to wander as she drove to her father's house. Her thoughts were about Mark and his vision of hell. This again triggered the memory of the preacher on TV again and the things her father had been telling her. She glanced at her rearview mirror and back to the road. *What does this all mean? What does it all mean?*

She was driving, half paying attention to the road and half reviewing everything she had experienced lately.

The past few days had been turbulent. She was confused, yet at the same time, she felt a growing interest and an increased understanding about spiritual things. First there was seeing that creature, that horrible demonic thing. It had forced her to seek out the pastor. She reflected on Mark's confession of visiting hell, an incredible claim indeed. And why he had he so unexpectedly shown up at the church? If it hadn't been for him, she might have been dead. What was going on? She found herself wavering between two extremes: complete acceptance versus the total denial that there was a God and that spiritual forces might be at work.

She thought about how things seemed to have been arranged. Was there a God who was in control? Was he trying to tell her something? Kathy could feel a sensation, an awareness of a call, as if a voice were speaking to her without words. It was a yearning. She examined it, felt it. Each time she thought about Mark's story, she sensed a resonance deep inside. It was like she was hearing a faint, distant call. She thought about it all as she drove.

Nabal was still flying above Kathy, easily keeping up. It looked at the demons in the other car. The time was right. Everything was ready.

The distant battle of angels and demons was still ongoing, so Nabal was free to do its damage. With a fanged smile, it turned its attention to her, opened its jaws, and slowly began its descent to the car. Its wings were spread out wide, slicing through the air, casting a spiritual shadow that flittered on the passing ground. Then it hissed as it approached, just feet from the car roof.

Suddenly, from above, a light flashed. Was it sunlight? No, it was brighter than that. Nabal felt the heat upon its skin and quickly looked up.

It only had a moment to growl "No!" before the light burst open with intense purity that fell upon its flesh. The hot blaze passed through its body, instantly paralyzing it, searing its skin, and causing it to curl into a fetal position. Nabal whimpered slightly and quickly fell, disappearing into the darkness of the earth below, leaving only a faint trail of smoke behind. The slave demon whose attention had been on the woman in the pickup was unexpectedly yanked down as well, falling with its master. It screamed and clawed at the air before disappearing.

Kathy saw no light, but she was aware of its effect. It was subtle and it moved with undulating waves of softness that shined on her and through her.

It was truth. It was the glory of God and it was resting upon her and marked itself upon her.

"Yes," she said aloud. "That's it. My soul is longing to hear from God. I can see it now." The epiphany was just what she needed. Somehow God had not only orchestrated all the events around Mark but also around her, and she was being called.

"God, I hear you," she said softly. She remembered how her father had told her about Jesus so many times before, and how she'd ignored it. A pang of guilt and remorse brushed against her heart as she remembered her insensitivity.

The light grew brighter. The soft truth of God's holiness permeated her heart. Tears filled her eyes and then ran down her cheeks. She blinked them away as she focused on the road. But, they kept coming. It was like a flood of truth welling up within her.

There was an overpass just ahead. She had seen the sign: Wings Street. She decided to pull the car over under its shadow. She swallowed hard and let the tears roll down from her eyes. She wanted to cry but she forced herself to concentrate until she had safely stopped. The sound of gravel crunched under the tires and echoed inside the car. She put the car in park and turned off the engine.

As she sat there, Kathy felt the weak pulse of each car driving by as it forced air against her vehicle. People were rushing, going to and fro, oblivious to the encounter she was having with the Creator.

Her heart stirred. It was a sensation that she had never felt before. She could feel it, almost hear it, as if a voice was speaking to her. She listened.

The light grew brighter still.

Somehow it made sense that the words of the preacher were true. She *knew* they were. She could feel it down deep.

The light still shined.

Then, her mind was filled with a sense of goodness and purity and suddenly she realized her own unworthiness. She could see herself for what she really was.

Kathy felt the pain of the wrongs she had committed in her life. They were many. She could sense her immorality. She could taste her selfishness and pride. Guilt fell upon her like a crashing wave. It was so clear, so strong. She regretted her rebellion against God and said aloud, "Jesus, please forgive me. Please forgive me."

Then, there was something more, something she didn't expect, something she had never fully dealt with. The memory of her abortion from so long ago forced itself into her mind and with it she could smell the cold, sterile room, and remember the doctor and nurses as they routinely and impassively went about the medical procedure that took a life. She remembered everything: the fear, the guilt, and the regret that followed. It hurt all over again with the same, original intensity.

All the talk about the fetus being only a blob of cells had been a lie. She was guilty of destroying the life in her womb. She had betrayed life itself. She had betrayed her own child. That is why the pain never went away, no matter how much she had tried to ignore it or bury it!

Kathy groaned under the weight of the unpleasant realization. She strained and contorted her face as she tightened her facial muscles, squinting, pressing her lips together tightly, forcing back the tears.

A swell of anguish rose up from her heart. Grief and regret took form. She hated having to face what she'd done. She did not want to allow the pain to live. It would hurt too much to admit her actions and face them. She moaned again as she fought. All the years of repressing the memories had conditioned her to resist, to fight, to excuse her abortion as a necessity. But now she had to deal with it head on. Now was the time.

She resisted for only a few seconds before realizing she was holding on to a lie. It was too much. She released.

As if a dam had unexpectedly failed, she exhaled in a noisy, agonizing cry. She buried her face in her hands and hurled her groans through her fingers. She heaved out cries and sobs. She convulsed, almost yelling out. Tears poured forth as she gave birth to the inner pain and rush of guilt, of complete and utter regret.

She was no longer in control. She was totally undone.

For several minutes, all the years of denial, all the years of suppressed feelings mingled into a mess of emotions that painfully scraped over her heart as they moved through her. The guilt, the abortion, her selfishness, her pride, her rebellion against God—everything was exposed in the holy light that shone from the spiritual world.

She was a sinner in the presence of holiness. She knew it with absolute certainty.

The light kept shining and for a few more minutes she cried until, mercifully, the tears began to subside. She let the feelings move away. She released them. The relief was welcome. But, in the emotional wake was a new realization.

"God, please forgive me. Please have mercy on me. I need you. I need your forgiveness. Please have mercy on me. Please forgive me."

She cried some more.

The tears rolled down her face.

"Jesus, please forgive me. Please save me."

Above, the spiritual battle had shifted drastically. Nabal was gone and the demons were being defeated easily. Kathy was now in the presence of the divine and it was impossible to break through and harm her now. Demons fled in different directions as they realized the battle was over. Then, suddenly, it was quiet.

Kathy had stopped crying.

The light was still shining on her, opening her heart to truth, nudging her to realize her need. It was wonderful. It was painful.

Then, a strong and pure wave of love flooded into her soul and with it came the wonderful realization that God was not angry with her. He wasn't there to judge her or beat her down with guilt. He was there to forgive her.

The peace and security of God's love enveloped her. He seemed to hold her, comfort her, and embrace her with such acceptance that she felt joyous. She knew he loved her. She didn't understand how she knew, but she knew that now was the time to turn to him and be forgiven, be forgiven of everything, freely, and forever.

She laughed slightly through a sob and with closed eyes, lifted her head toward heaven.

"Lord Jesus, please forgive me. Please save me. I am a sinner. Please forgive me of all of my sins. Please forgive me of the abortion, of my lying, my pride, my selfishness. Please forgive me. Please take me. Jesus, I need you. Please Lord, save me."

Kathy sat in the front seat of her car, alone. All danger had passed. Salvation had come. She had found total and free forgiveness in the divine love and sacrifice of Christ.

***

At home, John was sitting on his couch reading the Bible. Kathy suddenly popped into his mind. That was not unusual, particularly as of late, so he kept reading. But it was strong. John laid the scriptures on his lap. He could feel that something had happened. "Lord, is she okay?" He waited.

Peace filled his heart.

He closed his eyes and let his head rest back on the couch as he began to pray. "Lord, please be with her and protect her. Please save her." It was a simple prayer, one he had prayed for her countless times in the past. But this time there was something different.

"Lord," he said again. "I don't know if this is from you or not, but as always, I pray for her protection. And Lord, please save her from her sins." With the last statement, his heart leaped. He opened his eyes. Then the urge to go to the hospital and visit Mark came over him. It was so strong that he quickly decided to go.

He got up with a single grunt of discomfort, took his Bible with him, retrieved his keys, and closed the front door behind him as he hurried to his car.

***

Kathy had stopped crying. She was wiping her eyes with tissue from the glove compartment. She felt absolutely wonderful and could not help but smile. Her eyes still held tears, but she laughed in spite of them as she wiped them away. She took deep breaths and sighed heavily. It was a wonderful sensation. She closed her eyes and laid her back against the headrest. Then, after a minute she started talking to the Lord. "I didn't expect this. This is wonderful. Thank you, God. Thank you for saving me." She smiled and the tears began to well up in her eyes again.

"Thank you for forgiving me."

In the spiritual world, the light faded and gradually disappeared.

Kathy sat in her car, slowly recovering and savoring the moment. She was so involved in relishing her salvation that she was unaware of the truck that pulled off the side of the road and parked behind her. The driver opened the door and a pair of dirty work boots planted themselves on the ground. A large man emerged. He left the door open as he began to walk slowly towards Kathy's car. Something was in his hand. He walked up to the passenger-side window and could see that she was alone. He tapped on the window.

She jumped and glanced over to the right and saw a gruff-looking man. Her heart raced. Mark always told her to never let strangers in the car since there were so many dangerous people around.

"Do you need any help?" The man asked. His voice was muffled by the glass.

Kathy reached over for the window control and lowered it a couple of inches. "No," she said. "I'm fine."

"Are you sure, ma'am?"

"Yes, really. I'm okay." She put her finger on the window control, about to close it.

"Ma'am, I hope this doesn't sound odd. But I had a dream last night where the Lord told me to drive down this freeway at this time. He told me that there would be a woman under a bridge and that I needed to give her, uh, you, this." The man lifted up a worn, obviously often-read copy of the Bible and showed it to her through the window. He smiled. A tooth was missing.

The fear instantly vanished. She lowered the window.

"Thank you, ma'am." He extended his arm through and handed her the book. "In the dream the Lord let me know that he has done a wonderful work in your life. He loves you greatly." The man smiled. "I don't know who you are ma'am, but the Lord does. God bless."

With that, he smiled again and started walking back to the truck. She watched him in the rearview mirror. He got in and quickly pulled out onto the highway. As he went by, she noticed a sign on the passenger door. It read Heaven's Tow Service.

She smiled and realized that she was entering a new world where God was real and the unexpected might very well become the norm. She glanced down at the Bible and opened it. There was a marker stuck in Matthew, chapter 5. She read the words of Jesus as he gave the Sermon on the Mount.

All she could do was smile. "I've got to tell Mark," she said. "I don't know if he's going to believe me, but I've got to tell him."

She started the car and put it in drive. Merging into traffic was easy. There was an off ramp ahead where she could turn around.

***

"I really appreciate you staying here and talking to me." said Mark.

"It's no problem. That's what I'm here for." Pastor Tim was sitting down in a chair next to Mark's bed. The two had been talking for quite a while.

"I wonder if I'm ever going to see Sotare again." he commented.

"I have a feeling you will."

"What makes you say that?"

"It's just a guess. I mean, you had so many questions for him. I bet you'll see him again. And, if you do, tell him I said hi."

Mark smiled. "I hope you're right." Then he added, "Funny thing is, those questions don't seem to matter much anymore."

"That's a good thing."

"Yeah, but what I'm worried about is how I'm going to tell Kathy that I've been talking to an angel and become a Christian. I don't know how she's going to take it. As far as she knows, I've been under a lot of stress and randomly showed up at her church. She'll probably think I'm totally whacked.

"Don't worry, the Lord is in control and he knows what he's doing. Things will work out fine."

"I suppose you're..."

There was a knock on the door.

"Come in," said Mark.

John's head appeared. "Oh, hi, Pastor. I hope I'm not disturbing you two."

"Not at all."

"How are you doing, Mark?"

"I'm doing great. I'm glad you're here. I have something to tell you." He smiled at Tim knowingly.

"Okay, I'm all ears, but first let me get to a chair. I'm still sore from the operation. This old body needs to take it easy."

"You're not old," responded Mark and with a smile added, "Well, you're not *that* old."

"Well, I'm in better shape than you are."

"He's got you there," said Tim as he got up and moved a chair into position for John.

After a nod of thanks, John said, "I sure feel old, especially lately." He slowly lowered himself into the seat, grunting lightly. "That's better."

"What brought you here?" asked the pastor.

"I was at home reading my Bible when I had the strongest urge to see you, Mark. So, here I am. Besides, it was a good excuse to get out on my own. That daughter of mine won't let me do anything." He adjusted himself in the chair. "Where is she, anyway? I thought she would be here with you."

"She left about an hour ago, dog tired. Wasn't she at your place?"

"No," said John casually. "She's probably out doing some shopping." John slowed his speech and emphasized the words as he said, "If I'm lucky, maybe she's going to fix me a nice thick, juicy steak dinner, with mashed potatoes, gravy, and hot rolls. Too bad you're stuck here in the hospital."

"Thanks," said Mark sarcastically. "I appreciate your concern. But, I'll be out of here in no time and then you and I can chow down on some serious beef."

"Sounds good. So, what's new?"

Mark smiled, "Well, I thought you'd like to know…"

There was another knock on the door. It opened and Kathy's head slipped in. "Oh, my," she said. "This looks like a town meeting."

Kathy walked into the room full of smiles and energy. Mark easily recognized that there was something different about her. He also noticed that she was carrying a Bible.

"I'm glad you're here, honey," he said, curious about the Bible.

Pastor Tim got up and offered Kathy his chair. "Oh, no, Pastor. That's okay—you sit."

Pastor Tim scratched his head. "Well, if you don't mind, I have a hard time sitting while a woman is standing in the room. Please, I'd feel more comfortable if you sat down." He offered a gentle smile and motioned towards the chair. She smiled back and quickly took it. "Thanks."

She grabbed Mark's hand and set the Bible on the bed. A glow seemed to shine from her eyes.

"What is it?" he asked.

She stared into Mark's eyes and grabbed his hand with both of hers. She scooted closer to him and leaned forward. Mark looked at her and then at John.

"Something happened," she said. His silence urged her to speak.

"I'm a Christian. I was driving home to Dad's place and the most remarkable thing happened. I can't describe it and I don't know if you're going to believe me, but the Lord spoke to me. I don't know how I knew it was him, but I could hear him in my heart. I mean, it was all so clear. I knew I was a sinner and I knew I needed forgiveness."

She was obviously excited and with each syllable, she shook his hand.

"I asked Jesus to forgive me, and he did. I'm forgiven of my sins, all of them. It was easy and simple."

Her voice was bouncy, full of energy, full of joy.

"Mark, you need him. You need to be saved."

She looked at her father. "Dad, I understand now. I understand why you love God. It's wonderful. I feel so free. Jesus forgave me."

John's mouth was open slightly, frozen. He was half in shock and half in joyous relief. He stared at Pastor Tim, and then looked back at Kathy.

She looked at Mark. "I was driving down the freeway on the way back to Dad's place, and this sensation came over me. The more I thought about it, the more I realized that I needed God. I don't know how I knew what I did, but I knew I needed him. He was so real."

"Praise God," said John with a shaky voice. He was wiping the tears from his eyes by now. "Praise God. I have been praying for this for so long." He rubbed his eyes again with his index finger and thumb and forced himself to get out of his chair. She stood up and met her father halfway. They embraced tightly.

Kathy could feel his strength and that same security she had felt in his arms when she was little. "I love you, Dad."

"I love you, too," he said with a cracking voice and a sniff.

They held each other a while longer, savoring the joyous realization of salvation in Jesus. Tears dribbled down his checks. On the table next to the bed was a box of tissues. He reached over, grabbed some, and blotted his eyes. "Thank you, Jesus."

It took a couple of minutes for John to let her go. When he did, he looked into her eyes and she returned his loving gaze with a smile.

"This is so wonderful," he said. "You have no idea how many times I've prayed for this." He chuckled and winced.

Kathy looked at Mark and then back to her dad.

"I need to sit," said John, realizing she wanted to talk to Mark so he let himself sink back into his chair. He dabbed his eyes again.

Tim blinked a few tears away and then they all looked at Mark. Kathy went back over to the chair next to the bed.

"Honey?" She said tenderly.

"Yes?" answered Mark, excited that he was about to reveal his secret as well.

"I was driving and the Lord called me in my heart. He had been preparing me and then...he called me. I stopped under a bridge and..."

She stopped as her eyes softened and began to well up with tears. Then in a tender and trembling voice, Kathy carefully said,

"… and I asked Jesus to forgive me of my sins." She looked at Mark, waiting to see what his reaction would be.

"That's wonderful," he said. "I'm so glad to hear that."

Kathy grinned with a huge smile. She did not know that Mark was also a believer, but for now, she had to tell him the rest of the story. She continued. "Then the strangest thing happened. While I was there, in the car under the bridge, this man in a tow truck pulled up behind me. I didn't see him at first until after he tapped on the window. He wanted to know if I needed some help. At first I was afraid, but I didn't have to be. Now, get this. You won't believe it."

Mark glanced at Tim, then back to Kathy.

"He said that he had a dream where God told him to go onto the freeway and he would find me there. He said he was supposed to give me this." She reached for the Bible and held it up. "Can you believe it? A complete stranger stops to help me right after I receive Jesus and he tells me that the Lord sent him to that place to give me a Bible? I mean, it's like a miracle. It *is* a miracle."

She looked at Mark to see what his reaction would be. "That's wonderful," he said tenderly. "The Lord is good, isn't he?"

Kathy clued in on his comment and tilted her head slightly. Mark gazed into her eyes and gently squeezed her hand. "Honey, I have a lot to tell you, too. But, the most important thing that to tell you is that I am also a Christian."

"What?"

"That's right. I just prayed with Pastor Tim and received Jesus as my savior."

"Praise God!" shouted John from his chair as he stamped his feet and clapped his hands. He flinched harder this time, winced, and groaned

Kathy quickly got up, leaned over the bed and hugged her husband. They embraced for a full minute as John and Tim waited silently, though John was obviously holding back his excitement. The pastor put his hand on John's shoulder. They looked at each other, smiling.

"There is so much to tell you," said Mark.

"Praise God," said John again. His voice was full of joy.

"Praise God!"

Pastor Tim walked over to Mark's bed. "God is so good."

"May I see the Bible?" asked Mark.

"Sure." She handed it to him.

"This must be what God wants us to read," he said.

"It would sure seem so," she laughed. "And there is a marker in it. It was in the book of Matthew, chapter 5. I read it. It's pretty good stuff. Jesus sure was a wise man."

"Yes, he was," said Mark, "and wondrously holy."

"Oh," said Kathy. "I just remembered. You'll like this. The name on the side of the tow truck was Heaven's Tow Service. Isn't that neat?"

Mark stared at her as the memory of Frank and his tow truck flashed back into his mind. "My car! I completely forgot about it."

Kathy interjected. "It's at the body shop. They called a few days ago on your cell. It's ready." She looked at her husband curiously. "Speaking of which, what happened to it? And, while you're at it, can you please tell me why you were at the church on Sunday?"

Every eye was on Mark. He looked at the pastor who already knew the whole story and had a broad smile on his face. "I guess now is as good a time as any. I'll tell you everything."

"Well," said Pastor Tim as he got up from his chair. "I think I'll leave you three alone. I've already heard what Mark has to say, and it's wonderful." He walked to the bed and shook his hand. "God bless, Mark." He took Kathy's hand. "God bless, Kathy. See you soon, John."

"Thanks, Pastor," said Mark. "Thanks for being here."

"Believe me. It was my pleasure."

He turned towards the door but Kathy intercepted him. She reached out her arms and gave him a hug. "Thank you," she said softly. "Thank you for being there for my husband."

Tim nodded as he smiled. "I'm the thankful one. He saved my life."

She released him and the pastor slowly walked towards the door. As he opened it, once again a sensation came over him. He began to walk out, but there was a sudden and strong impulse to speak, the same as before. He halted and turned around. All three of them were looking at him.

"Mark, Kathy, I want to tell you what I think the Lord is telling me. It may or may not be from him, and you will have to be the judge if it is or isn't." He looked at Kathy. "The future will not always be easy with Mark. But keep your eyes on Jesus and you will not fail in what God is calling you to do. Stand by him and support him. God is going to send Mark on a perilous journey. A lot of people are going to hate him. You will have to go with him. Be ready."

Tim then looked at Mark. "God has given you a great gift, and he is calling you to serve him. You have been allowed to see what you have seen for a reason. But, know that the battle is not yet over. Keep your eyes on your Savior. Do not count on visions. Do not put your trust in dreams or angels. Don't trust your feelings. Always depend on the Word of God and prayer, for they alone will guide you." He paused and smiled. "And tell Sotare I said hi."

It took a moment to absorb the words before Mark returned the smile. "I will."

The pastor disappeared out the door.

Kathy looked at Mark and then at John.

"Does he do that often?"

John just shrugged his shoulders.

She turned to Mark and asked, "Who is Sotare?"

"Well," he said with a smile. "Are you two ready to hear everything?"

"Of course," said Kathy.

"Yes," said John.

"Good, because I've been dying to tell you what's been going on."

Chapter 15

MARK AND KATHY WERE in her car on their way to Shotsky's Car Repair. Someone had called and told them the car had been repaired and was ready to be picked up. She was driving.

"There it is." she said.

Mark fingered the seatbelt release mechanism as Kathy pulled into the driveway. There were cars unevenly strewn about the place. It was rather messy.

She pulled to a stop. "This should be interesting," He opened the door and swung his legs out with a wince and a grunt.

"You okay?"

Mark nodded. He was healing well and had been out of the hospital for two days, but he wasn't a hundred percent.

"You sure you feel up to driving the car back to Dad's?"

"Yeah, I'm okay. I'll just drive slowly."

They looked around. "There it is," he said as he began to walk towards it. "Good as new."

"May I help you?" asked someone from behind. They turned around. It was Frank, the tow truck driver. He was wearing tattered, grease stained overalls that seemed a bit tight around his not so small belly.

Mark remembered him well. "What are you doing here?"

He smiled. "I work here. I'm part owner of the place."

"Okay, that makes sense," said Mark after a pause. "We're here to pick up my car."

"Why don't you follow me into the office?" Frank started walking. "I was wondering when you were going to come and get it."

"Well, to be honest, "said Mark, "we were a little preoccupied."

"I know," he said glancing back, "Someone named John, if I remember right, called in and told me you were in the hospital, that you had been shot. It weren't no big deal to just keep it here till you were ready."

"John is my father," offered Kathy. "And we appreciate your kindness."

"No problem," said Frank as he walked, but stopped abruptly and faced Mark. "Mind if I ask a personal question?"

"Sure."

"What does it feel like to get shot?"

Mark rubbed his stomach. "It burns."

"Ah, of course." Frank nodded contemplatively and started walking toward the office again.

"How much do we owe you?" Kathy asked.

"Nothing."

Mark looked at Frank quizzically and stopped in his tracts. "Excuse me?"

Frank stopped walking again and faced them. "We all know that the Lord works in mysterious ways. Let's just say that someone offered to fix your vehicle and wanted to remain anonymous."

Mark was puzzled. He let the words trickle out. "That's it? Someone fixes my car and I don't pay anything?"

"Look, just as the good Lord takes care of our sins and we don't have to pay anything, someone paid the price of your car repair. Okay?"

Frank turned around and started towards his office. Mark

and Kathy stared at each other for a moment and then started to follow.

"Was it you?" asked Mark.

"Nope."

"But who was it? I mean, who offered to pay for our car to be fixed?"

"Can't tell ya," said Frank, still walking.

"Why not?"

"The person said not to."

"It had to be your dad." said Mark to Kathy.

"I can't tell you who it was," said Frank. "But it wasn't him."

"That's it?"

"Yep."

Mark and Kathy gave up.

The office was typical. There were car calendars on the wall, two old rusty filing cabinets under a window, a water cooler, and two beat-up wooden desks. Each had stacks of paper held down by metal gears. Frank went to one of them and pulled out a piece of paper. Mark and Kathy were at the counter. Frank walked over to them and put the paper down on the counter. "If you'll sign right here, the car is all yours." He reached into a jar full of pens and handed one to Mark.

Mark fingered it, looked at Kathy, then at Frank. "Remember that day when you came to the airport rental office?"

"Yes."

"Well, this may sound weird, but was there anyone in the passenger seat with you that day?"

"No, sir."

Mark looked at Kathy. She knew the whole story and chimed in. "Do you remember that woman on the freeway a few days ago, the one you gave a Bible to? That was me. You said the Lord told you to do that."

"Oh… yes, I thought you looked familiar. Sorry for not recognizing you. I'm getting forgetful in my old age." Frank seemed rather casual about the whole thing. He smiled as he looked at them.

Kathy shifted her weight to one leg. "Do you mind if I ask

you how the Lord told you to go out there? I mean, I just trusted Jesus as my Savior and then out of nowhere, you show up with a Bible telling me that the Lord told you give it to me."

"Yep." He smiled big and a gap from missing a tooth prominently showed itself.

She looked at him expectantly.

"When the Lord calls you and you answer, it don't mean that everything will work out like you think. But the more you hear his voice in your heart, the easier it gets to do his will. Now, I've driven under that bridge where you were at a million times and every time I do I think of Psalm 36 where it says that people take refuge in the Shadow of God's Wings. It is an expression of protection and safety."

"Why do you think about that Psalm?" she asked.

"Because the name of the street you were under was Wings. You were under the shadow of Wings Street. Get it?"

Kathy cocked her head back a bit and smiled. "Yes. Yes, I get it. That is where I got saved. That is where I asked Jesus to forgive me of my sins. What a beautiful coincidence."

"Well, ma'am, I wouldn't exactly call it a coincidence. God has a way of working things out. Anyway, I also had a dream the night before about giving a Bible to a woman on the freeway. So when I saw your car there under that overpass, I figured it was you. But hey, it ain't no big deal. God does that stuff all the time."

Frank fingered the paper and nudged it towards Mark.

Kathy looked at him, smiling. "I would just like to tell you that what you did was perfect timing. In fact, I have that Bible out in the car. I want to thank you for it."

"My pleasure," said Frank. "The Lord is good. He even uses a hick like me sometimes." He grinned like the Cheshire cat revealing that gap again. "As you can see, I ain't a sophisticated man. I'm not that smart, either. I'm just a simple, hard workin' guy. But, every day I ask God to use me, however and whenever it might be. And sometimes he does."

Frank straightened up just a bit and stared at Mark without saying anything. He reached under the counter and pulled out a Bible. "Here, you need this."

Mark looked at him and the Bible. "Did God just tell you to give it to me?"

Frank smiled. "Naw, it just occurred to me that you probably need one. Am I right?"

"I guess so, but I have one at home."

"Well, then have another. It's brand new."

He slid it on the counter towards Mark. "How long have you two been Christians?"

"Just under a week," said Kathy.

"Aw, you're new in the faith. You have an exciting journey ahead of you."

Mark nodded. "If the future is anything like the recent past, then you don't know how right you are." He fanned through the pages of the Bible then laid it on the counter. "Thank you. Thank you for everything."

"My pleasure."

Mark retrieved the pen and quickly signed the paper. Frank handed him the key.

"I filled up the gas tank for you, too," said Frank. "She's ready to go."

Mark didn't want to say thank you too many times, but he didn't care. He knew not to ask why or how, but to just say thank you. "Thanks for that, too."

Frank leaned onto the counter with one elbow and with that big smile said, "She's right out there and may the Lord bless you."

Chapter 16

A COMFORTABLE MORNING BREEZE gently swept through the garden, causing the leaves on the two trees to rustle, almost as if they were applauding. Light from the sun mingled slowly with shadows on the ground and a bird, perched in a nest nearby, filled the air with its song. There were two white butterflies, one resting on a flower and the other dancing in the air nearby. The stream bathed the gazebo in a calm but constant trickle of sound as water flowed across the rocks.

Mark and Kathy sat together, holding hands. They were enjoying God's creation. Mark had his Bible. It was opened to Genesis.

"Funny. My journey began here in a garden and that's also how it started in the Bible, in a garden."

"Ours is wonderful, but I'm sure the Garden of Eden was far more beautiful."

"No doubt. And just like the Garden of Eden, ours has two trees." Mark looked at the one from which he had hung the rope a few weeks ago. He sighed quietly, eternally grateful that he was still alive and had not succeeded in his selfish and foolish act. He watched the butterflies. One was still on the flower.

"Do you think you'll ever see Sotare again?" she asked.

"Pastor Tim seemed to think so."

"What do you think?"

"I don't know," he responded. "At first I thought I would, but it's been a couple of weeks since we've been home and I haven't heard a thing." Mark watched a leaf fall from one of the trees as it swaggered back and forth before it finally landed in the stream. The water carried it a few feet until it lodged against a small rock.

He turned his attention to the butterfly. "Well, even if I never see him again, everything will be fine. Besides, the questions don't matter anymore."

"I'm glad. As long as you don't worry about Sotare, we'll be fine." She was teasing him.

He smiled appropriately. "You're not implying that I'm a little obsessive are you?"

"Me? I wasn't implying anything. It's a fact."

"If I'm so obsessive, then why do love me so much?"

She changed her tone and with the back of her hand, caressed his cheek. "I love you because you're a good man. I've always loved you. It was love at first sight."

Mark melted. He felt the pleasure of her hand on his skin and the warmth of her love. She was smiling and her eyes had that look that emanated straight from her heart. He leaned over and kissed her but his stomach muscles reminded him that he had not yet fully healed.

He sat back and stared into the garden. There was a movement. Something was there. Mark stared.

"What is it?" asked Kathy.

"I'm not sure."

"Hello." said Sotare as he appeared out of thin air.

"Sotare!" exclaimed Mark as he tried to stand up. Pain quickly eroded his intentions and he grimaced as he fell back into his seat.

Kathy looked to where Mark was staring but couldn't see or hear Sotare.

"Please, don't get up." He walked into the gazebo and sat down opposite Mark and crossed his leg. "How have you been?"

Rubbing his stomach a little, he said with a smile, "I've been fine. *Where* have you been?"

"Busy. My work is never done." He looked at Kathy. "Have you told her everything?"

Mark looked at her. "Yes. She knows everything."

Kathy wasn't sure what to do. Her eyes were wide and her eyebrows were raised a bit. She was trying to follow half a conversation.

"It's Sotare," said Mark as he looked at Kathy. He was smiling. "He's sitting right there." Mark waved his index finger towards an empty seat.

She looked to the empty seat and awkwardly said, "Hi Sotare."

The angel smiled. "Hello Kathy."

"He said hello."

Kathy nodded and darted her eyes between Mark and the empty seat. "Okay."

"Have you been helping someone else like me?" asked Mark.

"Of course, the world is full of people who need help." Sotare looked around the garden.

"Did you appear to him or her or whoever it was?"

"It sure is beautiful here."

Mark picked up on Sotare's change of topic. "Yes, it is."

"I see you're healing fine," he said as he glanced at Mark's stomach.

Mark put a hand to his abdomen again. "They took out my spleen. But the doctor said I won't have anything to worry about. I'll be as good as new in no time. He did a good job."

"I know. I was there."

"You were?"

"Of course. Did you think I left you?"

"Well, to be honest, I wasn't sure."

"I was in the hospital room with you during surgery." Sotare looked into the garden and held out his hand. One of the white butterflies Mark had seen earlier flew into the gazebo, fluttered around for a few seconds, and then landed on his open palm. It was delicate and lovely and it opened and closed its wings slowly.

"Beautiful isn't it?"

"Yes," said Mark, intrigued.

Kathy was quietly amazed. A butterfly was resting in mid air, wings still. She raised her eyebrows again and stared.

"All creatures are precious to God." Sotare stared at Mark. Then without warning, it flew away. Sotare lowered his hand. "Well?"

After a moment, "Well, what?" asked Mark a little bewildered.

"Don't we have some unfinished business to take care of?"

Mark wasn't sure what he meant. "Do you mean finish answering the questions?"

"Yes."

Mark stilled himself and looked to Kathy again. She was obviously delighted by what was happening, but also a little bewildered at only hearing one side of a conversation.

"I'm sorry honey. I hope you don't mind me talking to him."

She pressed her lips together then said, "Of course not. I'll just listen."

He put his hand on hers. "Thanks."

Did he have any questions? Not really. Most everything had been answered through his experiences. But, there was one question he wanted addressed. He adjusted himself in his seat and stared into Sotare's eyes.

"Why did Jacob have to die?"

"It was his time."

The quick and direct answer caught Mark off guard. "I don't understand. What do you mean, it was his time?"

"Why does one person live to be a hundred and another dies during birth? Why does one live here and another there? Why are you born to one set of parents and not another? It's the way it is."

Mark thought about Sotare's words for a moment and asked, "Are you saying that things just happen just because they happen, that it's all random?"

"No," said Sotare compassionately. "I don't know how to explain it all and I don't fully understand it myself. But, I know that the answer lies in the complexity of God's infinite mind where events in the world happen for reasons that only he knows. Nothing is random, but at the same time, things just happen."

Mark listened then looked at Kathy who was patiently waiting. She smiled slightly.

Sotare continued. "It wasn't a malicious act of God that your son died. It pains him to see you suffer. But it isn't that God is helpless, either. The world is complex. Yet God comprehends all of it. He knows everything and for reasons that are beyond us, reasons that only God can possibly know, he works all things after the council of his will. You can trust that things are the way they are for a reason, even if you can't understand it all."

Mark thought about it for a moment and signaled his resignation with a small exhale. "Okay, so, I guess at one level, our level, some things just happen. But, according to God, there are reasons that these things happen that only he knows." Mark nodded. "It may not be easy to accept, but I can."

"Good," said Sotare as he relaxed in his seat. "But let me add this. God uses trials and tribulations to teach you many things. These trials often show you who *God* is. And, they show you who *you* are. But the funny thing is you cannot really see how great God is until you have seen your *real* self and that often doesn't happen until you go through difficulties."

Mark nodded slowly, acknowledging the truth of Sotare's words. "I can see that, but I wish I had a more definitive answer about Jacob's death, though."

"I know, and believe me Mark when I say that I hurt for your loss—and God does, too. But, as I said, it was just his time to die. You have yours, as does Kathy, her father, and Pastor Tim."

Mark thought about it for a few seconds before finally nodding agreement. "Okay, you're right. I don't have to have every question answered perfectly. God knows it all and that's good enough."

Sotare was obviously pleased with Mark's confession. He let Mark think about it for a while, waiting until he was ready to continue.

Kathy sensed the humility with which Mark was receiving Sotare's teaching. She rubbed her hand on his thigh.

After a few seconds, Sotare asked, "How do you see yourself now, Mark?"

He thought about the answer. "A couple of months ago I would have said I was a good person, that I didn't hurt people, that I was sincere, and should naturally be allowed to go to heaven. But now, I know better. I am a man, a sinner, who has been saved by God's grace, and will be kept by his grace. I have nothing to hope for except what I can find in Christ."

"Excellent. You have learned a great deal already. And, what have you learned about God?"

Mark was surprised at how quickly his next answer came. "I've learned that God is completely other, infinitely holy, perfectly just, and that he owes us nothing at all. I've learned that he is exceedingly patient and that his love for us is so great that we cannot possibly comprehend it. This means he is trustworthy. Therefore, through my trials and my tribulations I hope to be humble before him and be thankful that no matter what happens to me, whether I am healthy or sick, wealthy or poor, that I must always trust *him* and the love he has for me, even if I cannot understand it at the time."

Sotare nodded approvingly. "I can only teach you so much. But these truths you have learned through your suffering, through your encounter with God, and through your changed heart. All of it comes together to teach you what you need to know... and to answer your questions." Sotare spoke the last five words emphatically.

Mark picked up on it. "Sometimes, answers to the tough questions aren't always that easy, are they?"

Sotare pointed at the Bible that was on Mark's lap. "You've been reading the first few chapters of Genesis, right?"

"Yes," responded Mark.

"Then you know about the lie spoken by the Evil One to Eve? The lie that you do not need to trust God and his word and that you can determine what is good and right for yourself."

"Yes," responded Mark. "I have studied the passage about the garden a lot in the past couple of weeks. There is a whole bunch of truth there."

"Yes there is, more than most people realize. Nevertheless, the death of your son was very painful, but if you had not undergone its agony, would you have been here in this garden, crying, broken, and calling out for help those few weeks ago?"

"I suppose not. Only, I wish there had been another way."

"Perhaps there is, but if God had done something different in your life, would you be who you are now?"

Mark looked down at the Bible sitting next to him. He picked it up and ran his thumb across the edge of the pages. "I suppose not."

"Would you want to be any different than who you are now?"

Mark was still thumbing across the pages. The sound was barely audible. "No."

"Then do you agree that what happened brought you to where you are now?"

Mark reflected on his own heart and how it had changed. God allowed him to suffer the loss of his son, to undergo the weight of its pain, so that it would break him, help to change him, so that God's purpose in him might be accomplished.

"Yes."

Sotare continued. "God doesn't make robots. He wants you to live, to experience, to make choices, to be responsible for those choices, and to use what he has given you for his glory."

"And what is God's purpose for me?" asked Mark as he looked up at Sotare.

"Only you can answer that. He calls people according to the kindness of his will and according to his sovereign plan. But I hope you have also learned that his calling is beyond us both."

"*That's* an understatement."

"He will communicate to you. But in the meantime, he's going to prepare you. It does not matter *what* you are called to do, big or small. It only matters *that* you do it."

Once again, Mark felt like a student listening to his teacher.

"Mark, you asked me one time which religion was true. Do you know the answer now?"

With a smile and a nod he said, "Yes. It isn't an issue of which religion is true. The issue is God, his Son, and the truth found in his Word. It is not religion that God desires, but a living and vibrant relationship with Him that can only be accomplished through fellowship with Jesus, not through ceremonies and rituals and not through a particular church."

"Very good." Sotare got up. Mark watched his movement. "Kathy is a good woman."

Surprised, Mark looked at her. She had been patiently trying to follow only one half of a conversation. He squeezed her hand. "Yes, she is a very good woman. She's better than I deserve."

"Mark, I want to bless you and Kathy."

Mark looked at Sotare quizzically. "You do?"

"Yes, and she will need to see me and hear me. Can you ask her if she'd like that?"

Mark stared at Sotare a moment, absorbing the thought of what Kathy was going to experience, and then shifted his gaze to her. He smiled big and said, "Honey, would you like to see Sotare?"

Her eyebrows shot up. "Me?"

Mark chuckled. "Yes."

"Why?"

"He said he wants to bless us."

Kathy stared into the blank space where Sotare was sitting. It didn't take long for her realize her breathing had quickened as had her pulse. She swallowed hard. "Yes. Absolutely."

"Kathy." said Sotare.

She was startled by the voice that came out of thin air.

"Yes. I'm here."

"I am speaking to you so you can get more comfortable. With your permission, in a few seconds, I would like you to close your eyes. I will then place my hand over them. When I remove my hand, you will see me."

Kathy took a deep breath and clasped Mark's hand tightly, "Okay."

"Mark, I would like to do the same with you. Is that alright?"

Without hesitation, "Of course."

"Are you ready?" asked Sotare.

"Yes," said both in unison.

"Then, both of you please close your eyes."

She looked at Mark and slowly closed her eyes as she smiled.

Sotare got up from his seat and moved close to them. He placed one hand on Kathy's eyes and the other on Mark's. After a few seconds, he withdrew.

When they opened their eyes, both had to squint because of the brightness. They were in the midst of a beautiful and brilliant radiance that seemed to shine from nowhere but was everywhere. Under their feet was green grass just like what Mark had experienced before when he had died. A perfect comfortable breeze barely moved and it seemed strangely refreshing. Kathy and Mark absorbed what they were seeing, enjoying it, savoring it.

There was a movement and both Mark and Kathy looked to see Sotare standing there in full angelic glory. He glowed slightly and the light from this place reflected on his robe, making it almost translucent.

Kathy was stunned. "You're beautiful," she said.

With a smile Sotare looked towards Kathy's body. After a few seconds, she managed to pull her eyes away from him to look down. She was wearing a white robe, a brilliant white, clean robe. She remembered how Mark had told her how in one of his visions he had been wearing filthy rags. But she was wearing pure white. The rags were gone and she knew what it meant. She was a true child of God. She smiled hugely then she looked at Mark. He too was clothed in white. His was smiling.

Sotare opened his wings. They were large, perfectly proportioned, and moved ever so slowly back and forth. Kathy was surprised at how much she enjoyed seeing him.

"You *are* beautiful," said Kathy, realizing how easily she was accepting it all. "You're just like Mark described you."

"True beauty comes from God," he said as he pointed. From the distance two figures were approaching. Her heart leapt with expectation. She looked to Mark, who was already watching them. Was she going to see Jesus as he had? She swallowed hard and waited for the sensation of holiness that he had described.

"Is this what you saw before?" she asked Mark.

"Not exactly," he said confidently.

Kathy could see the couple but they were too far away for her to make out who the man and woman were. How did she know it was a man and woman? She realized that in this place, things can be known in ways not possible on earth. On earth? She suddenly realized she didn't know where she was. It was heaven or something very close to it, but where? It didn't matter. The figures continued to come closer.

"Who are they?" she asked as she kept her eyes on them.

"I don't know," answered Mark. "But we're going to find out."

Sotare was behind them and put one hand on each of their shoulders. They both looked at him. "I will be back soon," he said and disappeared.

Kathy and Mark looked at each other momentarily, then turned their attention back to the approaching pair who were covering the distance quickly. In a short time they would be face-to-face. Kathy looked at the beautiful green grass and admired the vivid blue sky with that indescribably rich light. There was no sun, but the radiance was everywhere. It was all so beautiful.

Kathy grabbed Mark's hand. He returned her grip gently, but said nothing.

They watched the mysterious couple who were now much closer. Kathy remembered how Mark had described the approach of the Lord, how the holiness and purity grew in intensity as he came closer. He said it was an incapacitating purity. But, that wasn't what she was feeling. How did she know that? There was no majesty, no wonderment of purity. But, still, it was good. She could feel it.

The two continued to approach until she could distinguish that one was a young man and the other a young woman, both dressed in white robes. Kathy marveled at how they seemed to walk slowly but yet covered the distance quickly. It was unlike anything she'd seen before, but she realized, it was somehow natural in this place. She focused on the two. Both seemed to be in their twenties.

Mark had also been watching them carefully. He let go of Kathy's hand and took a step forward. They kept coming, framed by the distant trees and shallow rolling hills covered in shades of green. Then, suddenly, they were there a few feet away.

The young man seemed familiar.

"Hello Dad. Hello Mom."

Mark stood motionless, then after a long moment asked, "Jacob?"

"Yes Dad. It's me."

Mark felt the force of Jacob's words as if a wave had crashed against his chest. He took a half step backward, shifting under the weight of the revelation. Then, regaining his bearings, he lunged towards his son. They collided in a hard embrace. "Jacob," said Mark in a strained voice. Then, all the love, all the frustration, all the loneliness of missing him, all of it came flooding out like a torrent. Mark wept.

Kathy had put her hands over her mouth and was crying. She wanted to lunge towards Jacob but somehow she knew she was supposed to wait. She watched her son and wrestled with the reality that he was there, grown, right in front of her. Her whole body and soul seemed to be locked in yearning disbelief. But she waited and watched through tear filled eyes.

"Jacob," said Mark. "Jacob, Jacob."

Mark held his son as he sobbed, squeezing him hard. It was a beautiful embrace. His body convulsed with each rhythmic heave of tears that erupted from his soul. His moans were mingled with joy and tears. They stood there for a full minute as Mark savored the wondrous event not saying anything.

Kathy wept too, watching, waiting for her time.

Then, finally Mark broke the silence. "Jacob, my son."

Jacob patted his father on his back as they held each other. "It's okay, Dad. It's okay."

The words were calming as if they somehow brought the peace of this place into Mark's heart. He shuddered with another sob and smiled as he finally pulled back to look at Jacob. Mark knew that his time with Jacob was short and that the intense feelings he had were being shaped by the peace and love that somehow permeated this place.

His son was smiling.

"I've missed you so much. It's been hard."

"I know, Dad. I know." Jacob was looking straight into Mark's eyes.

Mark realized that somehow Jacob was aware of everything that had happened. "Have you been watching me?"

"No, but I know what you've been through."

Mark wanted to ask questions but Jacob, as if deflecting them, gently released himself from Mark, looked at Kathy, and took a step towards her. With a smile and outstretched arms he said, "Hi Mom."

Kathy lunged forward and threw her arms around him and tried to press him into her body. She cried out, "Jacob," and broke into moaning sobs.

Mark's heart broke with joy as he watched her embrace her son. It was so right, so perfect.

Kathy intertwined her fingers with the fabric of Jacob's robe. Tears rolled down her face.

"Jacob, Jacob," said Kathy as she wept. "Jacob, I love you so much."

He gently tightened his embrace.

Kathy continued to cry, her body heaving with each sob as she held him. Jacob's breath was warm on her cheek. His arms were strong and encompassing. She melted as she leaned on him.

"Jacob." Kathy savored his name each time she said it.

She was with her son, her only son whom she loved. Waves of love and gratitude cascaded out from her heart.

"Jacob," she said between softening cries. "I love you."

"I love you too, Mom."

The words caressed her soul. "Say it again. Call me Mom again."

"Mom," said Jacob as he held her. "I love you Mom. I have always loved you."

A new flood of tears erupted from her soul. She wept hard, full, groaning, heaving tears. She pressed him to her body tightly, lovingly, and savored the wondrous moment. It was heavenly to be with him and to hear the precious words he spoke. She was undone and fell willingly into the well of emotions that flooded upward and outward.

Then Jacob said softly, "It's okay, Mom. It's okay."

His words had a strong calming effect. There was a connection between them and this place. He pulled her back and looked into her eyes. "It's okay, Mom." His words brought a quick and gentle peace.

Kathy's tears began to fade until finally she was able to gently move back enough so that she could look at him again.

Jacob was smiling, wiping his wet eyes.

"I have missed you so much," she said.

"I know, Mom. I've missed you, too."

"Your father. He's been in anguish since you…since you died."

"I know Mom. I know. But it's all okay." He looked at his Dad. "It's all okay."

Mark moved close and put his arm on Jacob's shoulder. "But how? How could you know?"

Jacob smiled and said, "I just know."

Neither Mark nor Kathy needed answers. All that mattered was that they were with their son.

"Mom, Dad, there is so much I would like to talk to you about, but I can't. It isn't that I'm prohibited, it's just that, well, there is so much here that can't be explained. This place has to be experienced." He gripped his mother gently by the shoulders, looked at her, and then at his father. "But I want you to know that the wonder and joy are so good here that no malice can exist, not even in your heart. It's all because of Jesus."

Mark was smiling. He moved closer to them and all three embraced. It was perfect happiness, perfect peace. He blinked away the tears from his eyes and looked to the young woman standing nearby.

After a few seconds, Jacob said, "We don't have much time." He gently pulled away and motioned with his hand towards her. She was lovely, dark haired, with soft, pleasant, feminine features. She stepped forward.

"Mom, I want to introduce you to Beth."

Kathy nodded and reached out her hand to meet hers,

noticing a slight familiarity in her face. Her heart skipped a beat. *Could she be?*

"I am your daughter. My name is Beth," she said plainly.

Kathy stood there amazed and perplexed. Here she was, the child that Kathy had aborted back in college. Then it hit her. Beth was the name she had secretly thought of calling the child if it was a girl.

She was motionless. She stared. Her face twisted into a mass of sorrow. The accumulated guilt and regret Kathy had experienced over the years from the abortion leapt upon her like a beast and forced Kathy once again to break. But this time it was not from joy. It was from shame. She moaned out loud painfully, plunging her face into her hands, shaking as she cried, and between muffled sobs she pleaded, "I'm sorry. I'm so sorry. Please forgive me."

Beth moved close to Kathy and said, "It's okay Mom." She reached out and put her hand on Kathy's shoulder.

Kathy's knees weakened slightly. Through tear filled eyes she looked again at her daughter. Beth smiled and opened her arms.

Kathy pressed her lips together, straining to see through the tears as she stepped towards Beth. She felt hesitatant to embrace her daughter because of her shame. But, she had to. She had to touch Beth. She wanted to hold her, feel her, and love her. But Kathy hesitated and through her sobs she cried out, "I'm so sorry, Beth. Please, please forgive me. Please.."

Beth gently took Kathy's hands. "I forgive you with all my heart. I love you."

Kathy finally broke. She moaned hard as she grabbed Beth in a strong embrace and began to sob convulsively. Beth held her as her mother wept.

Mark watched, tears rolling down his face. He looked to Jacob and then back to Kathy and Beth.

Then Beth said, "The Lord has forgiven you, Mother." Her words were like medicine. They seemed to force Kathy's anguish aside.

"It's okay, Mom."

"Please forgive me," said Kathy in a strained voice.

Beth gently pulled back enough to look into her eyes. "Of course I forgive you. With all that I am, I forgive you. But, Mom, the important thing is that Jesus has forgiven you. It is all wiped away because of him. The only thing left is my love for you."

Kathy cries intensified once again as she reached out and pulled Beth to her.

Beth gently rubbed Kathy's back.

Kathy could feel the warmth and peace seep into her heart. She could sense the forgiveness and love that was so freely coming from Beth. It was wondrous.

Within a minute Kathy was able to compose herself.

"I love you, Beth," said Kathy between lessening cries. "And I am so sorry for what I did. It was wrong. I was afraid and selfish. I betrayed you."

"Mom, it doesn't matter anymore. You don't have to feel guilty. Let it go. It is all cleansed by the blood of Christ. You've received his sacrifice on the cross where he took your sorrow and bore your sin. He has forgiven you completely. There's nothing left to feel guilty about. It is gone."

Kathy squeezed her eyes tightly again and strained as she blinked out a few more tears. She knew she was forgiven. But she had to confess what she had done. She needed to say the words.

"I love you, Mom," Beth's repeated reassurance melted into Kathy's heart.

"I love you, Mom."

Kathy stuttered a cry as she inhaled and held Beth closely. They were part of each other again. It was beautiful and right.

Jacob and Mark stood nearby, watching patiently. Mark's eyes were wet with tears.

"It is all okay, Mom. I love you and I'm so glad you are my mother."

Kathy's face strained again as she tried not to cry. "I've hurt silently for so long because of this. I feel so ashamed."

Beth whispered into Kathy's ear. "I know Mom. But when Jesus forgives you, he remembers your sins no more, so why should you?"

"I know. You're right. I need to let it go. I need to let go of all the hurt."

"The only one hurting here is you. It's okay to let it go."

Kathy knew Beth was right and as she looked into her daughter's eyes, she decided to finally stop holding onto the past. If God in the flesh had taken away her sin and guilt, she had no right to hold on to it. It wasn't right for her to punish herself. She smiled and nodded.

"You're right. You're right." Kathy closed her eyes. "I'm letting it go. I give it to my Lord and receive the full forgiveness he's already given me. By faith I let it go."

A wave of peace and contentment washed over her. Her muscles relaxed and she let out one final, large sigh. Her pain was gone. She smiled as she opened her eyes to see her daughter, smiling back at her, exuding joy in her expression.

Beth looked at Mark, who was obviously waiting patiently. Kathy hugged her one more time and then relaxed her embrace. Mark came close. He was, of course, also smiling.

"Mark," said Beth. "Thank you for taking care of her."

He looked at Kathy. "It's been my privilege."

Beth approached him and held out her hands. He took them in his. He looked into her eyes and could seemingly perceive the beauty and gentleness in her. In this place love came so easily and naturally and as he gazed upon her, he realized he loved her. His heart melted and he gripped her hands more firmly.

She smiled back. "I love you, too."

Mark knew that she was aware of his love. He didn't know how and he didn't care. It was just how things were in this place.

"May I ask you something?"

"Of course," he responded.

"Would you mind if I called you Dad?"

The question was unexpected and puzzling. He was not her father. Her father was someplace else. But where? Was he a believer? Was he alive or dead? If he were dead, was he in heaven or hell? Mark looked into Beth's eyes. She knew something. She wouldn't have asked him if there wasn't a reason. Maybe her real father was a lost soul. Maybe he was…

Mark remembered a tinge of anger. It was weak and hollow,

more like a shadow. He realized that in this place negative feelings are greatly weakened. They have no life. Still, it forced Mark to examine himself. He had always resented the fact that Kathy had become pregnant by another man. He had secretly harbored anger over it, directed at her ex-lover. But, he had also resented Kathy for it, too. He knew he didn't have the right, but he had felt it nonetheless.

He looked at Kathy. She was waiting expectantly, oblivious to his inner reflection. Then he looked back at Beth. Here was a beautiful young woman who had been robbed of life, yet she was alive.

Her eyes were deeply kind and that is when Mark thought of the sacrifice of Christ and how he had been forgiven of so much. He had no right to harbor any resentment towards Beth's unknown father or for Kathy. All her sins had been forgiven.

He had no right at all. As quickly as he realized what he needed to do, he did it. Somehow he knew he needed to talk to God. The words seemed to fill his heart as he prayed silently. *Please forgive me of my sin. I had no right to be angry. It was not mine to hold. Please forgive me for hating that man and also for the resentment I've had towards Kathy. Please cleanse me yet again.*

Peace came upon him like a gentle breeze.

Was this why Beth asked to call him Dad? Was it to cause him to face this old sin? Then he realized that to accept Beth, to let her call him her father, meant that the resentment he had had for so long had to be forsaken and in its place he needed to love. It made perfect sense and as quickly as he realized it, he wanted it. He let the love flow into him as he thought of Beth's real father and realized that like himself, he was a weak man, a sinful man. He could have been that man. The resentment evaporated.

He looked to Kathy again. She smiled at him. All he could do was feel love for her.

It was a wonderful revelation of grace. Mark was awestruck at the privilege of forgiveness both received and given.

Beth was still smiling and without saying anything he gently pulled her towards him. She stepped forward and moved into his arms. He let her close in. He rested his cheek on the top of her head. He smelled her hair, felt her frame, and received her. He loved her as though she was his own precious daughter.

And that is when he understood that for him to say yes meant he had to love her as his own. The realization was perfect. It was right. It was good.

"I would love it if you called me Dad."

She looked into his eyes and Mark felt as though he would melt when she said, "I love you Dad."

He experienced what he could not understand. It was as though complete, perfect goodness was an actual thing that moved though his body and soul. It was amazingly wonderful and he knew it was from God. But, how did he know that? How did he know that when he completely forgave and forsook his resentment towards others, that it was God's grace and peace that had overshadowed him? He just knew it. He knew God was here. He looked up to the blue sky and silently prayed, *Thank you Lord for your awesome greatness.*

Then Mark felt a hand on his shoulder. It was Sotare. "It's time to go."

His heart sank. He looked to Jacob and then Kathy. She held out her arms and all of them slowly moved together and embraced. Then after a bit, Jacob motioned and stepped back to break the circle.

Reluctantly both Mark and Kathy let go, knowing they didn't have much longer. Jacob and Beth stood side by side and took a step backward.

Jacob said, "Both Beth and my concern for you is that until we meet again, and we will meet again, that your heart be not troubled. Always keep your eyes on Jesus, no matter what happens. Remember that, Mom and Dad. Through all that will come to you and against you, remember to trust him alone, no matter what."

Beth was smiling beautifully and Kathy knew deep down that everything was right between them. There was no sorrow anymore. No remorse. It was gone.

"Goodbye, Dad. Goodbye, Mom," said Jacob.

"Goodbye, Mom. Goodbye, Dad," said Beth.

In unison, Mark and Kathy said, "Goodbye."

"It is time to go." Sotare spoke gently and placed one hand on Kathy's shoulder and the other on Mark's.

"Thank you for forgiving me, Beth."

"How could I not? Jesus is so wonderful and forgiving. His love is pure and deep. Mom, I can't help but forgive and love you with all my heart. I am so glad you are my mother."

"We will see you again," said Jacob.

Mark grabbed Kathy's hand. "I love you son." He looked to Beth and smiled. "I love you my daughter."

Beth smiled beautifully yet again.

"It is time," said Sotare. "I'm going to put my hand over your eyes."

Mark and Kathy listened but did not look. Instead, they watched Jacob and Beth, memorizing every feature of their faces.

Sotare covered their eyes and then after a moment, he lowered his hands. They were both back in the gazebo.

Kathy sat down and automatically let the tears roll down her cheeks. She savored the memory of the love and fulfillment that still flowed within her from having been with her children. She let nothing else intrude while she cherished the memory.

Mark was wiping away tears. He sat down, too.

After a couple of minutes, Mark finally looked at Sotare who was still there with them. "Thank you. Thank you so much. You've given us something wonderful. Thank you. Thank you."

Sotare smiled compassionately and nodded. "I envy you for your ability to love so beautifully. It really is a reflection of God in you."

"But," said Kathy, "that is only because he has shown us how to love by dying for us."

Sotare nodded slowly. "It has been my honor to serve you both." He looked out to the garden and then back at them. "It is time for me to go."

Mark was smiling. "Will we see you again?"

Sotare didn't answer.

"When we die and go to be with the Lord, will you be there?"

Sotare put his hands on Mark shoulders and said with a gentle laugh, "Absolutely."

Mark pulled him close and gave him a strong hug. Then Sotare stood back and held out his hand.

Mark held out his.

"Remember the coin I said was buried under our feet?"

After a moment, "Yes."

"Here it is. A 1907 ten dollar gold piece. Goodbye, Mark. Goodbye, Kathy." Sotare raised his head towards the heavens, lifted his arms wide, and changed. His wings became visible and his white robe glimmered brightly. They could see rays of light radiating from him, alive, undulating, casting shadows out into the garden. The brightness forced them to squint and step back. Then with the graceful movements of his wings, Sotare slowly ascended past the trees and flew away.

They both watched him and when he was gone, Mark looked at Kathy. She closed her eyes and savored the memory of Jacob and Beth once more. Mark hugged her. "Are you okay?"

She put her arms around him. "Yes." She closed her eyes as she rested her head on his chest.

A butterfly flew into the gazebo and headed towards him. He remembered how Sotare had put out his hand. Was it the same butterfly? A butterfly! He had crushed a butterfly in his hand the morning he almost committed suicide. Mark stared at it and without thinking and extended his opened palm. It fluttered towards him, and just as it did with Sotare, it landed on his hand. The delicate creature slowly opened and closed its wings.

As he watched the fragile creature, Mark remembered that this garden was the place where he had almost died, the place where the miraculous became commonplace, and where he, and now Kathy, had spoken to an angel. It had become the place of visions, of truth, and discovery.

Mark smiled.

The butterfly flapped its wings quickly then took to flight. He realized that even something as insignificant as butterflies were important to God. He watched it as it flew out from the gazebo and up into the sky. Something large flew by. His eyes widened. What was it?

He stood up and moved out from the gazebo.

Kathy followed him. "What?" she asked.

Another quick movement from above. Mark glanced over to it, but it was gone. There! Another one. He smiled, hardly believing what he was seeing.

"What is it?" she asked again. "What do you see?"

Mark was looking into the sky, past the trees, passed the house. Above him were angels. He could see them moving, flying, going about their calling. It was beautiful, absolutely wonderful.

"What are you looking at?"

"Can you see them?" he asked.

"See what?"

Mark turned his head in another direction. More angels. He could see them clearly, flying, moving. Automatically, he looked up to the tree to see if he was being watched. There was nothing. He looked back up into the sky and smiled. The angels were shimmering, leaving small streaks of light as they went about their tasks.

He laughed, excitedly.

"What?" asked Kathy. "Are you okay? What is it?"

Mark looked at her. His smile was almost too big for his face.

"Mark?"

He looked back to the sky. "It's glorious."

"What is? Mark, are you okay?"

"Angels, I see angels."

Kathy looked into the sky. "Where?"

"Up there."

Kathy only saw sky. She looked back at him.

"It's beautiful," he said.

Kathy held onto his arm as she followed his eyes darting back and forth as he looked heavenward.

Mark smiled and watched, then he noticed that the streaks of light were getting a little faint. He saw another movement and watched it. It was a bit fainter, and then slowly, they all disappeared.

He looked down at Kathy. "That was great," he said. "For a while I was seeing them as they were moving through the sky. It was incredible."

Kathy looked at him, pondering his words.

"What do you think it means?" she asked.

He returned her gaze. "I'm not sure, but I think we're going to find out."

Last Things

WHAT JESUS DID ON the cross is the most important event in all of history. It is the place where you can receive forgiveness of sins and avoid eternal damnation. After all, eternity is a long time to be wrong.

If you are interested in becoming a Christian, then please keep reading.

First, the Law

The Bible says that we are all sinners (Rom. 3:23). This means that we have all offended God. We have all broken His Law by lying, cheating, and stealing, etc. Because of this, we are separated from God (Isaiah 59:2), are dead in our sins (Rom. 6:23; Eph. 2:3), cannot please God (Rom. 3:10-11), and will suffer damnation (2 Thess. 1:9). Think about it. Laws have punishments. To break God's Law is to incur the punishment of the Law. God says this punishment is eternal damnation.

The only way to escape this punishment, this judgment is by receiving Christ, by trusting in what Jesus did on the cross (John 14:6; Acts 4:12; 1 Pet. 2:24). Jesus took the punishment of the

Law upon himself and if you trust him, then the punishment will not fall upon you.

The Bible says we are not capable of removing the guilt of our sinfulness through our own efforts. Gal. 2:21 says, "... if righteousness comes through the Law, then Christ died needlessly." The Law is the Do's and Don't's of moral behavior. In other words, we can't become righteous by what we do because we are dead in our sins (Eph. 2:3) and all of what we do is touch by sin and is not good enough for the infinite and holy God (Isa. 64:6).

This means that since **we** cannot remove our own sins and escape God's judgment, God must do it for us. He must remove our sins.

Jesus, who is God in flesh (John 1:1,14; 8:58; Col. 2:9), bore our sins in His body on the cross (1 Pet. 2:24). He died in our place. He paid the penalty of breaking the Law of God which should have fallen upon us. He satisfied the Law of God the Father by dying on the cross and taking the punishment there.

There is no other way. Jesus said, "I am the way, and the truth, and the life; no one comes to the Father, but through Me," (John 14:6).

Do you want to be saved from the righteous judgment of God? If so, if you want to become a Christian and follow God, then you must realize that you have sinned against him, and are under his judgment. You must look to Jesus who died on the cross and trust what he did in order to be forgiven of your sins and be saved from the judgment of the Law. This can only be accomplished by faith in what Jesus has done. You cannot add your sincerity, good works, rituals, or ceremonies to what Jesus has done because all of what you do is touched by sin and cannot be accepted by God. This is why you need Jesus.

Second, count the cost

Jesus said, "For which one of you, when he wants to build a tower, does not first sit down and calculate the cost, to see if he has enough to complete it?" (Luke 14:28). Jesus tells us to count the cost. The cost of becoming a Christian can be quite high sometimes. In some parts of the world it can cost you your life. Here in America, by God's grace, it is not nearly as dangerous.

Nevertheless, if you become a Christian, God will take it very seriously. He will work in your heart and in your life to change you and make you more like Jesus. Sometimes this is an easy journey and other times it is difficult. But, this is what it means to become a Christian. It means that God will work in your life after you have been saved and change you. If you don't want this to happen, then don't become a Christian.

Third, don't become a Christian if...

Don't become a Christian if you just want to give Jesus a try, or because you want to see if your life gets better, or if you want to experiment with religion, or if you just want to see what happens. These are the wrong reasons. You come to Christ and become a Christian because you want to receive, by faith, what Jesus did on the cross as a sacrifice for sins and to remove the judgment upon you due to your sins.

Fourth, receive Christ

If you desire to receive Christ and trust in what he has done on the cross, then please consider the following prayer as an example. It is not a formula. It is a representation of what it means to trust in Christ.

"Lord Jesus, I come to you and confess that I am a sinner. I admit that I have broken your Law, that I have broken your Word, and I have sinned against you. Please forgive me of my sins. I trust in what you have done on the cross and I receive you. Please cleanse me of my sin and be the Lord of my life. Strengthen me so I might turn from sin. I trust you completely for the forgiveness of my sins and put no trust in my own efforts of righteousness. Lord Jesus, please save me."

If you have honestly asked the Lord Jesus to forgive you of your sins and trusted in him by faith alone to remove the judgment of God the Father, then you are a Christian.

Fifth, Turn from your sin

Christ will receive you as you are, but he won't leave you as you are. He will change you. He will help you turn from your old ways. This is called repentance. God will enable you to resist sin and have victory over it.

Sixth, tell others about Jesus

Tell others about your commitment to Jesus. The Bible says, "if you confess with your mouth Jesus as Lord, and believe in your heart that God raised Him from the dead, you shall be saved; for with the heart man believes, resulting in righteousness, and with the mouth he confesses, resulting in salvation," (Rom. 10:9-10). You don't have to do this every time to everyone. But, you'll find that you want to tell others. This is part of the change that God has worked in you.

Seventh, find a good church

If you are curious about what churches to attend and not attend (there are bad ones out there), then check out www.carm. org. It'll provide what you need to learn more about Christianity and to avoid the traps of false teachings.

Eighth, read your Bible.

Get a good Bible. Read it regularly. It is the word of God.

May the Lord bless you.

In Jesus,
Matt Slick

Made in the USA
Lexington, KY
12 December 2011